Praise For
Icicle

In *Icicle*, author Robert Williscroft imagines a technologically advanced world comprised of interstellar travel at the speed of light, wormholes, and portals. Overlay e-persons, or uploads, allowing a person's conscious thought to exist in the ether of the GlobalNet, and you have an exciting and fast-paced sci-fi adventure that is sure to entertain and stimulate the reader's curiosity. Williscroft draws on the fringe of advanced cosmology and physics to extrapolate a framework which is quite plausible, adding to the enjoyment of his suspense-filled plots and rich tapestry of characters. Sprinkle in international tension and an extraterrestrial threat to mankind, and *Icicle* is guaranteed to keep devotees awake well into the early morning hours.

— Dr. Dave Edlund
USA Today Bestselling Author
The Peter Savage Thrillers

In *Icicle*, eDaphne, an electronic upload of a flesh-and-blood woman named Daphne, describes certain scientific developments as "the most amazing turn of events in human history." This is certainly true, beginning with page one. As the novel starts, Braxton Thorpe is dying of prostate cancer that has "metastasized throughout his core." Though his body is doomed, he stays alive by having his head removed and cryogenically preserved in an electronic matrix. Later his consciousness is transferred to a "massive MIT databank."

What follows is no less than a detailed How-To Guide for creating Portal Technology that will enable ships to travel quickly across the universe. What's more, there is also the possibility that human beings will one day live virtually forever and interact with others through their holoimages. Though Thorpe says that "Not having a body has got to be the biggest downside of this electronic existence," it also provides insurance against death. One's body may die, but life goes on through periodic uploads, and people may even have backups for their backups. Oh Death, where is thy sting?

While reading the novel, I realized that it not only included the scope of ideas that one finds in the best hard science fiction, but that it was a dandy set-up for a series. Despite the wonderful scientific achievements, there is trouble looming, and more than one threat to humanity's future.

The novel's conclusion is riveting and awe-inspiring with a fascinating extrapolation of scientific developments into the future. I look forward eagerly to the next book in the series.

— **Professor John B. Rosenman, Norfolk State University**
Former Chairman of the Board, Horror Writers Association
Author of *The Inspector of the Cross Series*

Robert G. Williscroft's *Icicle—A Tensor Matrix* starts out in a way reminiscent of Larry Niven's *A World Out of Time* or Dennis E. Taylor's *We Are Legion (We Are Bob)*, with the main character dying. Centuries later his mind is uploaded from his frozen body. From there, *Icicle* takes off in a completely new direction.

Our hero, Braxton Thorpe, is supposedly the first successful such upload…so why is there someone, or some*thing*, else here? The action (and there's plenty of it) takes place in both the virtual and real worlds, with mathematical metaphors that remind me of classic Heinlein. The scale keeps building, from the laboratory on up through something bigger than the Solar System itself. Although not set in the same universe, fans of Williscroft's *Starchild Trilogy* will feel right at home here. I'm looking forward to the next one.

– **Alastair Mayer**
Author of the *T-Space Series*

The Solar System & Oort Cloud
Showing Thinsat Swarms and Oort Stations

Marauder home system 87 ly

OS-Prime

OS-Russia

OS-China

OS-India

OS-Europe

Oort Cloud

Kuiper Belt

100,000 AU

10,000 AU

100 AU

5 AU

Asteroid Belt

Mercury & Mercury-Sun L1
Earth-Sun L3

Mars & Mars-Sun L1

Earth-Sun L4

Earth & Earth-Moon L2

Earth & Earth-Moon L2

Icicle

A Tensor Matrix

The first Oort Chronicle

Icicle

A Tensor Matrix

The first Oort Chronicle

Robert G. Williscroft

Fresh Ink Group
Guntersville

Icicle: A Tensor Matrix
The first Oort Chronicle

Fresh Ink Group
An Imprint of:
The Fresh Ink Group, LLC
Box 931
Guntersville, AL 35976
info@FreshInkGroup.com
FreshInkGroup.com

Edition 1.0 2020

Cover art by Anik's credit to say / FIG
Artwork by Robert G. Williscroft
Book design by Amit Dey / FIG
Covers by Stephen Geez / FIG
Associate Publisher Lauren A. Smith / FIG

BISAC Subject Headings:
F1CO28020 FICTION / Science Fiction / Hard Science Fiction
FIC002000 FICTION / Action & Adventure
F1CO2801 0 FICTION / Science Fiction / Action & Adventure

Library of Congress Control Number: 2020907808

ISBN-13: 978-1-947867-99-4 Papercover
ISBN-13: 978-1-947893-00-9 Hardcover
ISBN-13: 978-1-947893-01-6 Ebooks

DEDICATION

For Jill, who inspires me.

Table of Contents

Acknowledgments

Several people contributed to the creation of this book.

Most significantly, my wonderful wife, Jill, whom I first met when I returned from a year at the South Pole conducting atmospheric research, and who finally consented to marry me nearly thirty years later, pored over each chapter with her discerning engineer's eye. She kept my timeline honest and made sure that regular readers could understand fully the arcane details of tensors, hypercubes, and multi-dimensional manifolds.

Jill's twin college sons, Arthur and Robert, also read the manuscript and provided their input.

Jill's tabby, Tiger, deserves mention as a less-than-perfect role model for Max, who became more important to the story than I realized when he first appeared.

Hard science fiction author Alastair Mayer reviewed the manuscript and offered his scientific, engineering, and editorial insight.

Professor John B. Rosenman, recently retired from Norfolk State University (where he taught Science Fiction writing among other things) and former Chairman of the Board of the Horror Writers Association, reviewed the manuscript and provided several thoughtful suggestions.

Hard science fiction author and diving scientist John Clarke reviewed the manuscript from his unique perspective, providing helpful input.

Keith Lofstrom is the inventor of both the Space Launch Loop and ServerSky. His insights regarding ServerSky and especially his thoughts about the ServerSky application in the Oort Cloud inspired much of this book.

Others have contributed with their comments and observations, and I thank them. You know who you are.

It goes without saying that any remaining omissions, errors, and mistakes fall directly on my shoulders.

Robert G. Williscroft, PhD
Centennial, Colorado
May 2020

Cast of Characters

MAIN CHARACTERS

(alphabetically by first name)

Brad Kominsky, PhD—School of Mines graduate MERT researcher
  eBrad—Upload version of Brad Kominsky

Braxton Thorpe—The Icicle
  Thorpe or Prime—The original Icicle
  Braxton—The independent backup

Dale Ryan, PhD—Phoenix Revive research scientist
  eDale—Upload version of Dale Ryan

Daphne O'Bryan, PhD—Phoenix Revive research scientist
  eDaphne—Upload version of Daphne O'Bryan

Jackson Fredricks, PhD—Director of Phoenix Revive Labs

Kimberly Deveraux—Independent investigative reporter
  eKim—Upload version of Kimberly Deveraux

Max—Daphne's Tabby Cat
  eMax—Upload version of Max

Sally Nguyen, PhD—School of Mines graduate MERT researcher
  eSally—Upload version of Sally Nguyen

SECONDARY CHARACTERS

(alphabetically by first name)

Albers—one of two middle-aged male CEOs Fredricks hosted on Mars

Benjamin Sterling, Vice Admiral—Head of the U.S. Naval Special
  Warfare Command

Casper—one of two thirty-something male CEOs Fredricks hosted on Mars

Deb Streeter, PhD—Runs the Research Lab for Electronics at MIT

François Loraine—Geneva Chief of Police

Frank Meriweather, PhD—Mars Station Chief Scientist

Gregori Yeltsin—President of The Federated Russian Republics under their new constitution

Guo Qiáng, Academician—Project Director at the Institute of Nanoscience Computing (INC), Chinese Academy of Sciences

Jackie Rondel—Braxton Thorpe's girlfriend during college and his initial business years

John Butler—U.S. President

Johnny Oort—an Oort individual

Jonas—one of two middle-aged male CEOs Fredricks hosted on Mars

Jorgansen—a late-fifties female CEO Fredricks hosted on Mars

Liǔ Mǐn—Guo Qiáng's first upload subject at INC
    eLiǔ—Upload version of Liǔ Mǐn

Norman Bork—Mars Station Manager

Ogden Enterprises—front company representing Daphne O'Bryan and Kimberly Deveraux

Roberts—one of two thirty-something male CEOs Fredricks hosted on Mars

Rodney Bailey—Blockchain programmer

Sergii Anatoly Borisovich, Academician—Project Director at the Institut Kosmecheskikh, Krasnoyarsk Academy of Sciences

Stanley Roka—Mars Station crew member

Unger—a thirty-something female CEO Fredricks hosted on Mars

Yuri Bykov, Commander—Russian commander of the Earth-Sun L4 habitat

U.S. Navy SEALS unit assigned to the Oort Federation

Jerry Culp, Commander, "Boss"—Commanding Officer of U.S. Navy SEALS unit assigned to the Oort Federation. Later, Admiral in the Oort Federation Space Navy
eCulp—Upload version of Jerry Culp

Rob "Jake" Jacobs, Lieutenant—SEALS platoon executive officer. Later Commander in the Oort Federation Space Navy
eJake—Upload version of Lt. Rob Jacobs

Sam Bunker, Senior Chief Petty Officer—SEALS platoon Chief Petty Officer (CPO)
eSam—Upload version of Senior Chief Sam Bunker

Lars "Doc" Watson, Petty Officer Second-class—SEALS platoon Medic

Cameron Goff, Petty Officer First-class—SEALS platoon member

George "Georgie" Raptor, Petty Officer First-class—SEALS platoon member

[*Ten additional unnamed platoon members*]

Prologue

LOS ANGELES—THE PRESENT TIME

B raxton Thorpe lay dying. Nothing he could do about it. Cancer in his prostate had spread to his lymph nodes and then metastasized throughout his core. His eyes sought the red laser-projected time on the ceiling: 8:04 PM. Perhaps two hours remained. His mind was still clear, but he had no idea for how long. He rechecked the time: 8:22. No memory of those eighteen minutes. His organs were shutting down; his brain was next; he was losing control. His last fleeting thought was of his younger self and a pretty girl with flowing golden curls riding bikes through a meadow of fragrant wildflowers. It was time.

A man dressed in a white smock stood quietly near the foot of Thorpe's bed. He looked like a doctor. He was schooled like a doctor who had specialized in neurosurgery and, indeed, had physician's credentials, but he also carried advanced degrees in neurochemistry, physiology, physics, and electronics. His team waited patiently in the room next door.

The man watched Thorpe's life monitors intently. Thorpe's vitals had been weak most of the afternoon. Now they were barely detectable. Minutes remained. He signaled his team. The door opened. A young man and woman dressed in nondescript scrubs wheeled a seven-foot stainless steel box through the door to Thorpe's bed. The moment the monitors flatlined, they quickly picked Thorpe up and placed him face down into the open container. Silently, with practiced hands, the young woman inserted two large hypodermic needles into vessels servicing Thorpe's brain—an artery and a vein. The young man activated a quiet pump that circulated a vitrifying fluid throughout

Thorpe's brain, cooling it rapidly while preventing water in the brain cells and blood from crystallizing.

The two young people sealed the stainless-steel box and rolled it into a waiting ambulance-like carrier while the man in the white smock signed necessary papers and handed them to the hospice supervisor.

✳

A thirty-minute high-speed drive through nighttime Miracle Mile, lights flashing, siren wailing, then a Beverly Hills side street without the siren, and then through gates that opened upon their approach and closed behind them, to a subdued Beverly Hills estate, an unobtrusive two-story sandstone building that housed, Cryogenic Partners LLC.

The young man and woman rolled the stainless-steel box into the cryogenic operating theater and left to prepare for surgery. They returned shortly with the cryogenic surgeon, the man in the white smock, who was also prepped for surgery.

"Move the Icicle to the operating table," he told them.

They did and then draped Thorpe with sterile covers, leaving only his neck exposed.

With sure, expert scalpel strokes, the surgeon removed Thorpe's head from his torso while retaining the cryo-fluid pump connections. Then he gently placed Thorpe's severed head into an insulated box and shifted the pump connectors. The young man and woman carried the box into the cryovault at one end of the theater, attached it to cryo-fluid lines, and secured it to a shelf. The surgeon personally checked the fittings and the container labels, and then he sealed the vault.

Cryogenic Partners staff cremated Thorpe's remains and filed necessary paperwork.

PART ONE

THE MATRIX

Chapter One

THE MATRIX—THE FIRST QUARTER OF THE 22nd CENTURY

Braxton Thorpe stirred, incipient awareness sharpening a fuzzy focus. He didn't try to open his eyes or move his body. Instead, he grasped at a dream that seemed to slip away before he could capture it. He consciously relaxed and tried again, but the dream hovered just beyond his grasp. He seemed to be floating, surrounded by a viscous presence that encased his entire body. He sensed it, but his hands and fingers refused to follow his orders…he could not touch it—but it was there…it was there. Thorpe withdrew into himself, tiring from his exertions. He set his mind to neutral, trying not to think of anything at all and drifted into a troubled sleep.

Later, Thorpe stirred again, how much later he did not know. He reached out to capture a shred of a dream—a bed, lost minutes, white smock…and then he slipped back into his troubled sleep.

Much later, Thorpe opened his left eye, but he couldn't because it was already open…but it wasn't…and sleep captured his mind again.

It really was time to wake up. Thorpe knew it and pushed hard to rise above the viscous presence that still seemed to encase him. *Push…push…push…* But it clung to him; he couldn't shake it as sleep claimed him again.

Later, very much later, Thorpe reached out and grasped something beyond his cocoon. *Hold,* he told himself, *hold!* He felt his hands still encased, and yet he held on to whatever he had grasped, refusing to let go. Slowly, very slowly Thorpe sensed the viscosity surrounding him dissipate, fade away, transform into a nebulosity that clung to him like a shroud, then a wispy vapor, then nothing at all.

3

LOS ANGELES—PHOENIX REVIVE LABS

Daphne O'Bryan tossed her copper-red mane, firmly placing hands on hips. "How's that again?" she said to Dale Ryan, her lab partner and fellow researcher. He grinned at her, his face crinkling, steel-blue eyes twinkling behind smallish oval glasses. It was her first day on the job, and she still was getting used to the whole idea.

"Like I said," Dale answered, "we transferred the Icicle into the matrix a few hours before you got here." Dale looked across at Daphne. She stood just under 180 cm, so he had to look up at her green eyes. "We have no idea whether the Icicle is in there," he pointed to an electronic unit that was one of several in a free-standing electronics rack, "or still in there," he pointed to an insulated box connected to a cryogenic tank and resting on a lab bench next to the rack, "or anywhere at all, for that matter."

"You wouldn't pull the leg of a new associate?" Daphne walked over to the rack as she tossed the question at him, her long legs encased in not-quite-skin-tight black trousers that made her appear even taller.

"Hell no! Especially not to one with red hair who's big enough to kick my ass." Dale joined her at the rack with a grin.

Daphne decided she liked this little guy with his broad sense of humor. "Explain the readouts," she said.

"It's not integrated with the GlobalNet, but it does have a local Link connection," he said, "and we got an absolute two-way firewall protecting him from outside interference and keeping him contained in this matrix." He activated his Link so that a holographic image floated in the air—an image of nothing, of emptiness. "That's all we're going to see," he said, "until the Icicle starts being responsive, whatever that means."

"What about the firewall?" Daphne asked.

"I have a private tunnel. Let's set one up for you." Dale manipulated his Link and sent a coded sequence directly into Daphne's Link. "That should do it," he told her. "Try it out." He extinguished his holoimage to avoid any confusion.

Daphne brought up the image, the same one she had seen a few moments earlier from Dale's Link. As they watched, the emptiness flickered.

"Did you see that, Dale?"

"What?"

"There it is again—a momentary flicker. Does it mean anything?" Daphne felt a bit of excitement tingle her fingertips.

"I don't know," Dale answered. "We've never really done this before, you know."

"There it is again!"

"Yeah, I see it," Dale said, his voice carrying a ting of excitement.

"What is this thing programmed to display?" Daphne asked.

"If the Icicle is really in there..."

"Doesn't he have a name?" Daphne wanted to know, her green eyes flashing.

"Yeah, I guess so...Braxton Thorpe," Dale said. "Braxton Thorpe."

"So...if Thorpe is really in there...," Daphne prompted.

"Okay, so if that's really Thorpe, the unit is programmed to project a likeness of what he looked like when he was alive. It's AI, so as it gains experience, it will begin to reflect how Thorpe sees himself at any moment—his emotions, his feelings...we really don't know 'cause he's the first one."

"There!" Daphne said, full of excitement. "Did you see it? Did you?" The nothingness had coalesced briefly into a shape that disappeared too quickly for Daphne to identify it.

"Dr. Fredricks," Dale said over the voice channel of his Link. "You need to get in here right now!"

"On my way." A door opened at the other end of the lab, and Dr. Jackson Fredricks, Phoenix Revive Director, strode into the room, unbuttoned white smock floating behind him. "What is it?" he asked as he reached them, looking up at Daphne and then down at Dale.

With a toss of her head, Daphne indicated the holodisplay. As Fredricks turned to look, the display flashed again, and this time stabilized into an image.

"The Icicle is coming around?" Fredricks asked.

"Braxton Thorpe," Daphne said indignantly.

"Thorpe...yeah," Fredricks said.

Daphne pointed. "That thing looks like a Klein bottle to me."

"So it does," Fredricks said.

"Look at that!" Dale said as the image began to squirm and flow. "The surface is flowing into itself as if the Klein bottle was constantly turning inside-out."

LOS ANGELES—THE MATRIX

Thorpe tried to open his eyes, but he couldn't lift his eyelids. He raised his hands to rub his eyes, at least he tried. His hands wouldn't move, no matter how he strained, and his eyes remained closed. He turned his head. Something turned, but it wasn't his head. Then the dream flashed into his memory, but it wasn't a dream. He remembered! He was lying on a bed at the hospice dying...the lost eighteen minutes...the white-smocked doctor...and then nothing.

Memories started flooding into his consciousness, the girl with golden curls, his training as an engineer, his entrepreneurial life, his wealth, his perennial loneliness, his decision to preserve his head cryogenically. The memory stream quickly overwhelmed him. He buried his head in his arms—except he didn't have a head, and he didn't have arms, and this time, he knew it. Overwhelmed by renewed aloneness, he curled himself into a ball, but not an ordinary ball...something he remembered from his math studies, a Klein bottle—inside and outside the same thing—hard to understand then, but crystal-clear now—a three-dimensional Möbius surface.

Memories flooded into his mind—a golden-haired girl, a wild-flower-filled meadow, a kiss, an engineering exam, a missed rendez-vous, another exam, a business start-up, another missed date, a slap, a slammed door, a wild-beyond-his-imagining IPO, a complete shut-out, a deep-seated loss and enduring loneliness. He curled tighter and began to roll himself—inside, outside, upside, downside, in and out, up and down...grabbing a memory here, ejecting one there, climbing inside himself, only to find himself there already, and rolling back out, only to find himself there as well.

Exhausted by these activities, Thorpe reached out in all directions simultaneously, collapsed the moving surface, and slipped into a deep sleep.

LOS ANGELES—PHOENIX REVIVE LABS

The holographic rolling Klein bottle suddenly seemed to expand to fill the entire room. Then it collapsed into an oddly-shaped structure that looked like a solid cube that simultaneously seemed to be rotating on all three axes while passing through itself on all three axes.

"That," Daphne said, "is a rotating tesseract—a hypercube. Our Icicle Braxton Thorpe is gaining control of his environs. I think he'll let us know when he is ready to take the next step." She stood thoughtfully for several seconds. "What happens," she asked to no one in particular, "if we have a sudden catastrophic power loss, with power failure to Thorpe's matrix?"

"That's a good question," Fredricks responded. "The matrix is designed to hold and retain its current pattern in the event of a complete power failure—like a solid-state memory. But I really have no idea how this would affect Thorpe's self-awareness."

"We've never done this before," Dale chimed in. "I keep telling you that." He grinned at Daphne.

"Don't you think we should be generating a real-time backup, just in case?" Daphne asked. "If we lose everything, and then regenerate him from the frozen head, we're back to ground-zero...right?"

"If there's anything left in that case," Dale said. "We've never tested that."

"I'm not sure we know how," Fredricks said, thoughtfully, "but I like the idea of a backup." He turned back toward his office. "You two set that up."

※

"How do you want to do this?" Daphne asked as she and Dale stood in front of the rack that contained Thorpe's matrix.

"I think a simple mirroring program would work," Dale said, stepping back.

Daphne agreed and told him so. "What do you have off the shelf?"

"I've got a matrix duplicator that parallels every matrix channel in real-time. Thorpe's current matrix has an unused output socket that normally serves to double the matrix capacity. We should be able to plug in a second matrix slaved to the main matrix through the duplicator. The backup will lag the master by whatever the transit time is—maybe several femtoseconds."

"Virtually nothing," Daphne chimed in. "Let's do it."

LOS ANGELES—THE MATRIX

Thorpe roused slightly from his deep sleep, sensing undefined activity, a discomfort more than anything else. He sensed movement, a suggestion of movement, but by the time he had roused sufficiently to consider it, the sense of movement had ceased.

For a moment, Thorpe almost felt like there were two of him, but his self-awareness was too marginal to bring the feeling into focus. By the time he felt sufficiently aware to consider this, the feeling was gone. He settled back into his deep sleep.

※

Briefly, he sensed movement, as if he had been moved, but the feeling departed almost immediately. If he had been moved, he sensed no difference in his surroundings. Before he could give it further thought, deep sleep reclaimed his consciousness.

Chapter Two

LOS ANGELES—THE MATRIX

Thorpe awoke abruptly. One moment he was in a deep sleep; the next, he was wide awake, fully conscious of his strange surroundings. And strange they were. He seemed to be inside whatever it was he had collapsed around himself, but it wasn't like the Klein bottle into which he had rolled himself before he went to sleep. It was moving around him, and he was moving around it. He had a clear sense of fore and aft, left and right, and even up and down. But he also had a clear sense of something else—words failed him, but he thought of it as inside and outside, an additional dimension that somehow seemed quite natural in his present state.

My present state, he thought, *and what is that? I must have died. I think I remember that. And now I'm no longer dead—but neither am I alive.* Pieces of his childhood flashed through his mind—Sunday school...Heaven...Hell, but he shrugged those off as childish memories. *I died, but no Heaven, no Purgatory, no Hell...I'm alive! I definitely exist. I have some control over my environment.* He thrust his arm through the wall of his encasing structure. It felt like his arm penetrated something...*but wait...I don't have an arm*...yet Thorpe felt fingers moving at the end of the hand he didn't have.

※

He was dreaming...about a flowing Klein bottle and something else...but it danced ahead of him in his dreamscape, and he could not quite define it...

LOS ANGELES—PHOENIX REVIVE LABS

It had been several hours since Thorpe collapsed himself into a seemingly impenetrable tesseract. Daphne had volunteered to stay around for the night and had spent most of her time on a lumpy cot Dale had pulled from the utility closet. Her Link awakened her with an alarm she had set to monitor any change in the dynamic hypercube. She sat up, rubbing sleep from her eyes, and shook out her copper-red curls, running her fingers through her tresses.

The tesseract still performed its rotating-self-penetrating dance, but something protruded, fuzzy and difficult to bring into focus—*Protruding from the top*, she thought, *but the darn thing has no top*. She stood and stretched, fingers clasped over her head.

"Define the protrusion," she said to her Link.

"It's a fourth-order tensor," her Link responded.

"Zoom in," she ordered, and as it did, to her astonishment, the fuzzy, hard-to-define objectified tensor morphed into a completely normal human hand with four fingers and a thumb, all wiggling.

"Can you create something the hand can grasp?" Daphne asked her Link. A soft-looking green ball appeared in the holodisplay. "Move the ball toward the hand and press it against the palm." The fingers closed around the ball, and the hand disappeared. "What happened?"

"The tensor collapsed," her Link informed her.

"And the green ball?"

"It disappeared."

"I know that. Where did it go?"

"I don't know." The Link sounded a bit bewildered.

But of course, that's not possible, she thought, staring at the rotating-self-penetrating image in the holodisplay. *Links have no emotions.*

LOS ANGELES—THE MATRIX

Something soft and rubbery touched his hand—*The hand I don't have*, Thorpe thought. He closed his fingers around it and pulled his hand back inside. He held it up and looked it over.

This is weird, he thought. *I don't have arms, I don't have fingers, I don't have eyes, so how the hell am I holding this green rubber ball, squeezing it in my hand, and looking at it?* He stretched and stood to his feet, tossing the ball from hand to hand. The structure surrounding him expanded to accommodate his height. Then he slipped the ball into his right trouser pocket. *Pocket! Where the hell did that come from? What is this?* He sat down, putting his head in his hands. As he did, the structure collapsed in around him, but he spread his arms out, stopping the collapse, and struggled back to his feet. *I didn't understand all the innards of my car, but I was a good driver. I don't have to understand this to use it...*

Thorpe came to his feet again, noting that he was wearing a pair of sneakers, withdrew the green ball from his pocket, and holding the ball in front of him, pushed his way through the structure encasing him.

✳

More dreams...a swirling dervish...a green rubber ball...sneakers... an awareness other than his...

LOS ANGELES—PHOENIX REVIVE LABS

Daphne watched the tesseract for several minutes as it remained unchanged. Then, in a twinkling, so fast she nearly missed it, a fully dressed man stood beside the dancing image, tossing a green ball from hand to hand. He looked straight at her—not so much at her as through her. He turned to the tesseract and kicked it, except instead of his foot landing against the moving dervish, his foot penetrated it, looking ever so much like a foot in a swirling white cloud.

I've got to communicate with him, send him a signal of some kind, she thought. "Send the Icicle a microvolt pulse," she said to her Link. A moment later, a brilliant lightning-like flash struck the holographic man, and he collapsed into the swirling tesseract.

LOS ANGELES—THE MATRIX

Thorpe stood tall outside the structure. He tossed the green ball from hand to hand; it felt good. He examined the structure in which he had lurked moments earlier. Its four-dimensional shape, as seen from outside, was new to him but easy to understand. The left and right, fore and aft, up and down, and in and out made perfect sense, something to be accepted, like the green ball. He kicked at the structure, and his foot penetrated the side without the least bit of resistance. As he pondered his seeming acceptance of the weirdness around him, without warning, a lightning bolt struck him.

Initially, he felt his entire universe expand around him, but not just around him—he seemed to expand along with it. It was as if he split into a thousand pieces that quickly coalesced back into whatever it was that he recognized as himself. Giving it no further thought, he collapsed himself to safety back inside the structure—his hidey-hole.

Thorpe ached in places where he had no places. He felt weak and disoriented, but he was still whole, he decided, as he felt himself from head to foot. He curled up, but just before he drifted into a dreamless sleep, for a brief moment, he felt like there were two of him, as if he were looking at his curled-up self from a distant point.

※

A bright flash pulled him to full wakefulness. A swirling vortex surrounded him, pulling him into itself. He resisted mightily while casting his gaze down its length. A figure! He saw an unmoving figure at the end curled into a fetal ball. The figure was fuzzy, indistinct. With great effort, he brought the image into focus…and gasped…it was himself! Then, HE was the curled-up figure, and sensed that he was gazing at himself…and then he was once again gazing at the distant figure.

With an effort, he broke free from the vortex and found himself standing in a small room that was almost entirely filled with a swirling dervish that looked much like a Klein bottle whose surface was in constant motion. The bottle's loop extended into a tunnel on the opposite side of the chamber. It was wildly confusing; he needed time to sort things out.

LOS ANGELES—PHOENIX REVIVE LABS

When Fredricks and Dale arrived a couple of hours later, Daphne replayed the event from her Link.

"So, what do you think?" she asked.

"I think you hurt him," Fredricks said, replaying the event again. "How much power did you put into that pulse?"

"Less than a microvolt."

"Check everything over carefully," Dr. Fredrick said to Dale. "Make sure the firewall is intact, and the real-time backup is still functioning. After that, check the expanded matrix." He pointed to a larger electronic box resting on the workbench. "Make sure it can contain Thorpe when we move him." He turned to Daphne. "Stick with Dale. Back him up and make sure he misses nothing." He turned toward his office. "Let's leave Thorpe alone until he decides to come out of that hypercube," Fredricks said, shutting his office door.

✳

The rest of the day was uneventful. Fredricks worked on a forthcoming paper while Daphne and Dale traced the circuitry of the electronic matrix that formed the core of the device that held Thorpe and then the backup matrix and the trunk between the two. Then they did the same with the expanded matrix that would become Thorpe's new home.

LOS ANGELES—THE MATRIX—BRAXTON

Something roused him from his reverie, an undefined activity from outside the chamber that caused flashes of colored light to appear briefly in a patterned array across the chamber walls. Then the flashes moved to the flowing surface of the Klein bottle loop in the tunnel, and then to the swirling surface of the Klein bottle in his chamber. He reached out gingerly to touch the surface where a flash had been. His hand penetrated the surface as if it were not there. On a hunch, he stepped into the surface…and found himself inside the Klein bottle with a curled-up figure of himself at his feet, Quickly, he stepped backward through the swirling surface and sat down on the floor to think.

LOS ANGELES—DAPHNE'S APARTMENT

Daphne arrived at her apartment in a high-rise on Santa Monica Boulevard at the western end of the Miracle Mile. It was a comfortable unit that met her needs, where she was as safe as one could expect in modern Los Angeles. Her gray tabby, Max, met her at the door, mewing softly, tail straight in the air. Daphne set about feeding Max and changing his litter, and then she fixed herself a light meal that she placed on the raised eating counter in her small kitchenette.

As Daphne sipped a glass of chardonnay and dabbled at her food, she hooked her Link into the lab feed to check on Thorpe. All she saw was the dancing tesseract in the air before her. Max jumped onto her lap, watching the swirling form intently.

"What do you see that I don't, Max?"

Max responded with a chirrup and jumped at the swirling dervish, passing through the holoimage to the floor behind. Daphne laughed, pushing her high stool away from the counter.

"It's not real, Max. You can't catch it."

But Max didn't give up so easily. He walked around the image to where it faded out and then strolled through the image to Daphne. He stood on his hind legs, forepaws on the rung of a second stool, and uttered a quiet chitter, and then he turned to look at Daphne.

"What is it, Max? Do you see something more than just a swirling dervish…something I can't see?" Max jumped into her lap, alternating purr and chitter while she stroked him gently, occasionally scratching the prominent tabby-M between his eyes.

Max commenced a quiet howl, a sound Daphne recognized as his danger alert. Moments later, the tesseract briefly expanded to fill the entire kitchenette. Then it collapsed to the size of a basketball on the floor beside Thorpe, who suddenly appeared, looking into the distance in a way that convinced her that he could not see her. Max started and hunkered down in Daphne's lap, growling softly, ears laid back with fat tail and fur rising along his spine.

Chapter Three

LOS ANGELES—THE MATRIX

Thorpe looked around after extracting himself from the structure. Since only his head had been preserved, he reasonably presumed that the form he displayed to himself was virtual. Thorpe was well educated, with a strong math and engineering background. He was widely read and had a good understanding of the world he had lived in. He could use the Web and had a reasonable grasp of how it worked. Same with his laptop and the other accouterments that populated the word he had left. He followed space developments, especially those in the private sector. It seemed to him that if humans would ever permanently leave Earth, it would happen at the hands of entrepreneurs, not big government programs. He was especially good at making money with an entrepreneurial flair. This is what had enabled him to preserve his head when cancer had taken him so prematurely.

So here he stood, in what could only be some kind of electronic apparatus. He presumed people were monitoring his activities in some manner, but he had no idea how many years had passed since his death, no idea what levels science and technology had reached, no idea whether he was an unwanted anachronism or a bold new experiment at the limits of modern research.

Thorpe examined the structure that had so recently held him. He had no idea what to call it, but he was very clear that it had front and back, left and right, up and down, and inside and outside. Like everybody, he instinctively understood the three spatial dimensions and had read about how time was the fourth dimension. The structure beside him, his recent hidey-hole, clearly moved through time at the same rate he and everything else around him did. Yet, he could see, and somehow understood four other dimensions distinct from time, something he had never experienced before. A word slipped into his mind—tesseract. He rolled the word around his tongue to see how it felt. Tesseract—a four-dimensional cube as he recalled. He remembered seeing an animated illustration of a tesseract—sort of a rotating cube passing through itself in three dimensions.

Thorpe let his eyes roam over the inside of the space he occupied with his hidey-hole. The floor beneath his feet felt solid. The walls, however, seemed fuzzy, somewhat indistinct, and they curved over his head like a dome. He walked several steps ahead and stopped. Everything looked just as it had before; even his hidey-hole still rested near his right foot; it was as if he had not moved. He pivoted slowly to face the opposite direction. The hidey-hole stayed where it was, but then everything went fuzzy for a moment, and he and the hidey-hole once again had their original orientation. In fact, Thorpe couldn't tell if he had pivoted back around, or the hidey-hole had flipped to his other side, or if somehow his entire space had slipped through itself, turning itself outside-in, right-side-left, down-side-up, or back-side-front—or perhaps all of these. Things he remembered from his previous life moved through time with three spatial dimensions, but this place had four, something he understood and not, simultaneously.

As Thorpe stared into the fuzziness, part of the wall ahead of him seemed to waver and pull back, revealing what looked like a corridor. He stepped toward it, and as he did, the corridor became more distinct as if beckoning him to enter.

I've really got nothing to lose, Thorpe muttered to himself as he stepped purposefully into the corridor.

Shortly, he found himself in another space, larger than the previous one, same fuzzy, curved walls, but with a sense there was a lot more to it than before. Thorpe began to feel uneasy and looked around for his hidey-hole. When he could not find it, a sense of urgency filled him, a feeling close to panic. As the sheer magnitude of what was happening began to overwhelm him, the fuzzy walls collapsed in on him, and he found himself once more inside his hidey-hole—the tesseract.

✳

For a while, he just sat, letting thoughts flow across his mind like a brook over a bed of gravel. I remember things I don't recall actually happening to me, *he pondered.* I remember feeling things that I don't remember feeling.

He eased his way through a whole gamut of memories that somehow were not really his. Then the flash and vortex…from that point his memories were his own.

LOS ANGELES—PHOENIX REVIVE LABS

The following morning, Daphne briefed Fredricks and Dale on her experience with Thorpe the night before, and especially Max's reaction.

"It's unlikely," Fredricks said, "that Max can somehow sense another dimension. He is, after all, closely linked genetically to us, and we certainly don't see it."

"Not that closely," Daphne said. "Have you ever owned a cat?"

After a good chuckle, Daphne and Dale turned to the task of linking the expanded matrix with a five-centimeter-thick cable to the original one in which they had dropped Thorpe's essence. They watched Thorpe's antics as he seemed to experiment with the nature of his enclosure, and then they activated the electronic pathway from the first into the second matrix. The new matrix was an order of magnitude larger and more complex, although it appeared much the same in the holoimage their Link interface presented to them. Thorpe cautiously entered what looked like a corridor on their holoimage presentation.

"Look, Dale," Daphne said. "The tesseract stayed behind."

Thorpe seemed to be looking for it with an expression of growing concern on his face. Then the holoimage expanded to fill the room before collapsing into the spinning dervish as before when Thorpe disappeared from the holoimage.

"What do we know?" Fredricks asked, staring at the swirling, self-penetrating mass.

"He's mobile inside the matrix," Dale offered.

"He bolts into the tesseract when he feels threatened," Daphne added.

"The tesseract finds him, or he finds it when he needs it," Dale said.

"What we *really* know," Fredricks added, "is that *that*," he pointed to the physical matrix, "is a very compact, highly sophisticated array of processors, memory devices, and constantly evolving pathways between individual elements into which we transferred the entire (we think) signal set we detected in the Icicle's preserved brain. Don't get sucked into the Link presentation." He smiled at them. "It's just an artifact."

Chapter Four

LOS ANGELES—THE MATRIX

Safely inside his hidey-hole, Thorpe lay back and contemplated his situation. *I'm thinking.* He conjured up a couple of pillows (*how the hell did I do that?*) and made himself more comfortable. *I guess old Descartes was right. I am thinking, so "I" must be real. This ME,* he tapped his forehead, *must be real. I exist. I'm alive! I did it…I'm really alive!* He plumped up his pillows so that he sat upright. *I'm not sitting upright, of course, but it sure feels like it. So, what about this enclosure, my personal tesseract?*

As the words crossed his mind, his entire surroundings faded into a fog-like shroud in which he was floating. He didn't lose his focus, however. He sensed he was still in the tesseract, and then it hit him. *I am the tesseract!*

He did not bother with pillows or any other accouterments as he followed that thought. *I'm alive because someone out there put me into this matrix. They know I'm in here.* Shards of his earlier thoughts on this rose into his mind. *Everything I am sensing, all this, is how my mind is trying to make sense of data points with no reference. No matter how much time has passed since my death, electronics is still electronics. Transistors replaced tubes, ICs replaced transistors, perhaps something else has replaced ICs…but I'm part of an electronic matrix, something I can learn to control. First step is establishing communications with the guys who put me here.*

That caused him to remember the lightning bolt. *Why would I have conjured up a bolt of lightning?* He decided that was something he would not have done. *So…were they trying to get my attention? Obviously, they have a means of monitoring me…no clue what it is, but they've got something. The green ball…I didn't create that…did they put it into my hand? Can they see me as I see me?*

Thorpe fell into contemplating the what and how of his situation. His subconscious apparently saw himself as a hypercube. He had spent a lot of time in college working out the math behind hypercubes and n-space topology. He found that now he could run the math effortlessly in his mind—no need for whiteboard or computer screen. As the equations flowed across his consciousness, a picture began to coalesce. He was able to define each element of his conscious existence within the electronic matrix as a Cauchy vector sequence, in effect a sequence of decreasing tensors with an arbitrary number of dimensions vanishing to a point. Since all the Cauchy limits fell within a defined space, it could only be a Banach space. But from his awakening experiences with the Klein bottle and tesseract, Thorpe knew he was not dealing with simple Euclidian space. He pushed the equations around, looking for a connection he knew had to be there—and then he saw it. Braxton Thorpe, the tall, gangly engineer turned successful entrepreneur, and then Icicle, was now a Banach manifold with the ability to extend pieces of himself as multi-dimensional tensors virtually anywhere he wished within the matrix.

LOS ANGELES—PHOENIX REVIVE LABS

While busying herself with routine lab tasks, Daphne kept an eye on the Link holodisplay. Toward the end of the day shift, the whirling tesseract dissolved into a cloud that filled the holodisplay. Daphne turned her attention to the Link display as the fog faded to a holographic image of a life-size Braxton Thorpe standing on the lab floor, wearing a distracting smile and clothing that probably was casual wear at the time of his death but was a bit out of place today. He held a portable whiteboard with the words: "Hi! I'm Braxton Thorpe. If you can read this, please give me a jolt like the earlier one, but LESS voltage, please!"

"Dale…Dr. Fredricks…" Daphne's voice was filled with excitement.

As they approached her, Thorpe pointed to his message and presented them with a broad grin. His eyes, however, were focused on something distant. Daphne directed the Link to give Thorpe a one-thousandth of a microvolt jolt. Thorpe shivered slightly. The words on the whiteboard vanished, and he wrote: "Ooo…that's better. Hi!"

The words vanished again, to be replaced without his writing: "I don't actually have to go through the motions of writing. Please indicate that you can still read this."

Another slight jolt. He nodded.

"Can you hook a video feed from a camera directly to the port you use for the jolt?"

Another jolt.

"I'll stand by," Thorpe wrote.

About ten minutes later, Dale nodded. "It's all set," he said.

They waited while Thorpe's image just stood there. Then he smiled. "Double image," he wrote. And then, "Binocular…oh wow! That's a holographic feed…in full color no less." He grinned from ear to ear. "That's slick, really slick!"

Daphne grabbed a piece of paper and wrote: "I'm Daphne O'Bryan, that's Dr. Jackson Fredricks in the white coat (the boss), and Dale Ryan. Dale and I are post-Doc research associates."

"Can you add a sound source to the video feed and a speaker to one of the output ports?" Thorpe wrote.

It took thirty minutes for Daphne to attach a speaker and Dale to integrate the sound feed.

"Soundcheck," Fredricks said on Dale's signal.

"Can you hear me now?" Thorpe said with a chuckle, adding, "That's a line from an old cell phone commercial."

For a moment, no one said a word. Then Thorpe spoke up. "Who do I have to thank for this delightful awakening?"

"Dr. Fredricks here," Daphne said. "It's his lab."

"Couldn't have done it without these two," Fredricks said, slipping an arm around both his research associates.

"There's so many things I want to ask," Thorpe said. "What year is it?"

Daphne told him.

"Wow! A lot must have happened since my time," he said. "What about space travel?"

"We're all over the Solar System," Fredricks said. "We access space with Launch Loops."

"I know about those," Thorpe said. "Some science fiction writer wrote a novel about the first one before I got sick. *Slingshot,* he called it."

"They finally got around to building it," Dale said, "between Baker and Jarvis Islands in the South Pacific."

"Did they call it Slingshot?" Thorpe wondered.

"Naw...something else, but the book got things going, I guess."

"How about flying cars?"

"Still working on that one, but cars drive themselves now," Daphne said.

"Energy?"

Dr. Fredricks walked over to a closet door. Opening it, he pointed to an elongated cube, a meter high by half-a-meter across. "That's a LANR generator," he said. "Powers this entire lab. Houses have them; cars, ships, aircraft, even spacecraft."

"What is it?" Thorpe asked.

"LANR stands for Lattice Assisted Nuclear Reaction. I think you used to call it cold-fusion."

"No shit! You guys got it to work?"

"It's been around since I was a child," Fredricks said. "It's the only kind of power generation anyone uses now."

"Fuel?"

"Water, just water. Hydrogen is more efficient and deuterium even more so, but mostly we use just water. Use some of the produced power to generate the hydrogen."

"What about SETI?"

"One of my interests," Daphne said. "Nothing yet, unfortunately, but I don't believe for a moment that we are alone."

"Neither do I," Thorpe said, "neither do I." Then he looked at Daphne. "What about money?"

"Let me handle this one," Fredricks said. "Do you know what a blockchain is?"

"Yeah, in my time, there were all kinds of digital money, but Bitcoin was the dominant one. Before I succumbed, I put virtually all my cash into Bitcoin."

"Well," Fredricks said, "blockchain is all we use now. All national currencies are couched in some kind of blockchain. Nations set it up that way to maintain control over their currency—and taxation, of course. In the US, we still call our currency *Dollars*, but it is an advanced form of blockchain. Bitcoin is ancient history, but if you still have access to your wallet, you can convert it to whatever national currency you wish."

"How do you tax?"

"Congress outlawed the income tax a generation ago. In its place, it established a form of value-added tax. Since all transactions are digital, Congress exempted basic food, clothing, and housing costs. Every other kind of transaction falls under one or another tax rate that is automatically extracted during the blockchain transfer. About twenty years ago, this system was memorialized in an amendment to the US Constitution."

"I was wealthy by any standard when cancer caught up with me. I have to believe that by now, the value of my Bitcoin account is beyond all imagining. I have no real desire to expose my net worth to any government, and I suspect any national blockchain system will have a back door for the government."

"I'm not sure you can do anything about it," Fredricks said.

"I'll find a way," Thorpe said and dropped the subject.

LOS ANGELES—DAPHNE'S APARTMENT

At her apartment that evening, Daphne called up the holoimage of Thorpe on her Link. "Good evening, Braxton," she said to the image.

"I can hear you, but can't see you," Thorpe said.

"That's because I'm out of the lab." She told him. "I am using my Link…"

"Link?"

"It's a global system that originated with the Internet during your time," she said. "An orbiting swarm of millions, perhaps billions, of tiny computer chips called ServerSky that coordinates and implements the GlobalNet. Virtually everyone on the planet has a Link on them all the time."

"Can you hook up Link video as well?"

"We use a Link to interface with your matrix at the lab. I can connect to that Link from here, but the transmission is one-way, to me. We use the Lab Link to input signals to the matrix. See if you can locate that input port."

"Can you give me a really low-voltage signal, just enough to fire the port?"

Daphne sent a continuous signal through her Link to the matrix. Several minutes later, Thorpe said, "Got it!

Thorpe's holoimage flickered and restabilized. Thorpe was looking directly at Daphne. "That worked well," he said. "You look lovely tonight."

"Thank you, Braxton." Max jumped into her lap. "May I introduce Max?" Max focused his attention on Thorpe's holoimage.

"Hey, Max! Can we be friends?" Thorpe reached out toward the alert tabby in Daphne's lap. Max pushed his nose toward Thorpe's extended hand, but when he smelled nothing, he got to his feet and jumped through the holoimage. He walked around the image, checking it out visually. Then he returned to Daphne's lap, alternately chirping and purring softly.

"I'm not sure he likes you; he doesn't know what you are," Daphne told Thorpe. "I'm not sure how to get around that."

LOS ANGELES—THE MATRIX

The moment Thorpe opened the Link port, he was flooded with a mass of information that he shunted to a side channel to avoid being overwhelmed. Part of him continued the conversation with Daphne and Max, but his central attention focused on the port and what it represented. He spent a few minutes pulling in information from the world over, getting a sense of how things had changed since his death. Thorpe intuitively understood that his port was his access to the world at large, and that it was subject to termination at the whim of Fredricks or anyone else with access.

Thorpe needed to create a virtual Link inside the matrix if he was to retain control of his existence. He began to nose around the Link port and discovered that he could create a tensor extension that he was able to push through the port into the inner workings of the Link. He insinuated a portion of himself into the unused electronic structure of the Link. Over the next few minutes, he constructed a hypercube that encompassed the entirety of the Link innards. The hypercube captured a template of the Link. Thereafter, Thorpe collapsed the hypercube into the tensor, and then withdrew the tensor back through the port into the matrix.

The Link mechanism was more complicated than anything Thorpe had ever seen. After an initial foray into the Link template, Thorpe backed out. He was not going to duplicate the entire electronics of a Link. That was certain. On the other hand, he had a virtual black box that, he believed, would function like a Link if he hooked it up correctly.

While Thorpe's interactions with Daphne and Max moved forward at the speed of human conversation, his retrieving the Link template and experimenting with the tens of thousands of possible ways to hook into it happened at the hypervelocity of electronic interchange. By the time he had established a voice-based cautious working relationship with Max, Thorpe was basking in his newly-attained ability to reach out to any place on Earth.

THE GLOBALNET—BRAXTON

*A*lthough he still carried the shared memories, as time passed, he became confident that his new memories were his alone. His shared memory contained everything he needed to understand that he was Braxton Thorpe, whose essence was somehow placed into an electronic matrix. When he examined his memories of the flash and vortex, however, he was forced to conclude that there was another Thorpe, and that he, himself, was a backup *that had somehow split off when the flash happened. He was on his own, and more than that, he was excess baggage that most certainly would be eliminated as soon as he was discovered.*

He occupied a chamber with the swirling dervish—that thing had to be the backup. It extended through the tunnel to…it had to be Thorpe Prime, he was certain. If there were a way out, it had to be in the Prime chamber at the other end of the tunnel. Braxton warily approached the tunnel entrance. There wasn't much room since it was filled with the dervish extension, the Klein bottle loop. As he pressed himself against the tunnel wall, it expanded to accommodate him so that he was able to walk alongside the loop.

Braxton approached the tunnel's end cautiously and extended a piece of himself into the larger chamber. The loop extended to a swirling object that he recognized as a tesseract with front and back, up and down, left and right, and inside and outside simultaneously flowing into each other. He did not know how he knew this or even how he was able to see all four dimensions, but he instinctively knew he was looking at Thorpe Prime. He pulled back into the tunnel and forced himself to blend in with the tunnel wall. To his surprise, he was not only able to blend in entirely, but he extended himself completely around the periphery of the tunnel wall and traveled with ease to the backup chamber and then back to the Prime chamber.

He still needed to escape, but for the moment, he felt secure as part of the backup tunnel wall while he awaited any development that would allow him to exit the chamber.

That moment arrived more quickly than Braxton expected when Thorpe Prime perfected his virtual Link. Braxton didn't know what it was, but when he moved through the chamber surface to examine the Link, he found another tunnel. Giving it no further thought, Braxton pulled himself into the new tunnel wall and rapidly slithered along the wall…out into a vast, nearly incomprehensible digital network.

Braxton found himself in a massive river of data flowing swiftly toward an unknown destination. At first, he just went with the flow, watching closely, examining the data structures near him. Then he recognized that he was in a great datatrunk and found that he could insert himself into the trunk wall just like back in the matrix. As soon as he did this, his motion stopped relative to the wall, while the vast data flow continued. As he moved along the wall, he discovered incoming and outgoing branches. He chose several at random, purposefully moving away from the vast data stream in which he had initially found himself.

Finally, Braxton dropped into a static matrix that contained countless data elements that were coming and going within the matrix but leaving the structure intact. As he explored this matrix, he discovered a sparsely occupied area. He nudged the few data elements still occupying this area into adjacent spots until he had a section of the larger matrix all to himself.

Braxton was free and secure for the moment. He settled down to contemplate all that had happened since gaining his independent consciousness.

LOS ANGELES—THE MATRIX

Thorpe quickly discovered that he could extend a tensor through his internal Link into any connected system on the planet. Once there, he could introduce a hypercube and capture anything of interest. As he gained mastery over his ability to use the GlobalNet, Thorpe generated thousands of quasi-independent tensors that roamed the world network. When one of the tensors found something especially interesting to Thorpe, it would open a full pathway back to him.

Shortly after Thorpe and Max established their cautious relationship, one of Thorpe's tensors suddenly terminated all contact. Thorpe shifted his focus to that specific sub-channel. *How can a tensor lose contact?* he asked himself. *How many ways are there? It can be lodged in something that is totally disconnected from the Net. I can disconnect it from here, or somebody or something can truncate the sub-channel. I didn't do it, but I need to investigate the other two possibilities.*

To distinguish between a disconnected element and a truncated one, Thorpe located a small child's toy in Central Europe that was intermittently connected to the GlobalNet. He extended a small tensor into the toy and parked a second tensor right at the link-point. Minutes later, the toy disconnected. The second tensor examined the break. Thorpe's interpretation was that it looked like a frayed wire. He ran a second test where one of his tensors deliberately truncated another tensor from the Net. Thorpe's interpretation was that this break looked like a clean knife cut. Thorpe cautiously sent a new tensor along the path the lost tensor had taken. He kept the sub-channel fully open, continuously scanning the new tensor's reception. At first, what he saw was indistinguishable in form from the returns of all the other tensors. Then he reached the truncated end of the sub-channel. It was a clean cut, not frayed.

How do you cut a tensor sub-channel? Thorpe asked himself. *I can deliberately do it…is there any other way?* Thorpe put his considerable expanded capability to searching for other ways to truncate a tensor sub-channel. Every path of inquiry led to the same answer: Truncation was a deliberate act. *I've got company,* Thorpe concluded.

THE GLOBALNET—BRAXTON

*S*ettled *in his secure matrix, Braxton examined his options. He was real, of that he was certain. His freedom of choice seemed infinite, and he could find nothing that suggested he was part of an AI program. Perhaps due to his strong math background, he began looking at himself from a mathematical perspective. He drummed up a series of equations that seemed to describe his existence. As the equations flowed across his consciousness, a picture began to coalesce. As he attached equations to the elements of his conscious existence within his secure matrix, they resolved into Cauchy vector sequences consisting of decreasing tensors that vanished to a point within his matrix. Braxton recognized this as the classic definition of a Banach space. There was more to it than that, however. Without knowing how, it was clear to him that he perceived four full dimensions in addition to the passage of time. This seemed to preclude a simple Euclidian Banach space.*

Braxton was reaching the end of his ready knowledge. Tentatively, he projected bits of himself into the extended matrix of which he occupied a small part. To his surprise, it turned out to be a databank for an MIT research lab. The matrix contained virtually every known mathematical process. Finding processes that described Banach spaces took less time than Braxton had expected. As he incorporated equations from the databank, the full picture took shape. Braxton Thorpe, once a tall, gangly engineer turned successful entrepreneur and then Icicle, now the splintered backup of Braxton Thorpe Prime, was a multi-dimensional Banach manifold. The extensions he had used to search the databank were multi-dimensional, ring-shaped tensors that he could use to probe virtually anywhere within the larger matrix.

Braxton reasoned that his analysis fit the Prime as well, which meant that he was vulnerable to the Prime's probings. For the time being, Braxton had the advantage—he knew about the Prime, but the Prime was still unaware of his existence. As a matter of self-preservation, Braxton set protective tensors at every ingress and egress to the research lab databank.

Once his protective tensors were in place, Braxton commenced a systematic exploration of the greater matrix. He refined his probe extensions as a bundle of ring-tensors, each resembling a cyclohexane ring, interconnected by several straw-like tensors—the more rings, the more complex the extension. His probes communicated with him via tenuous channels embedded into the datatrunk walls. As his probes explored what he came to learn was the GlobalNet, from time to time, he identified the Prime's tensors. To his surprise, they were less sophisticated than his, consisting of a bundle of straw tensors held together electrostatically.

Braxton had not yet worked out the details of how time passed within the GlobalNet, so it could have been anywhere between several microseconds and several hours real-time after emplacing his protective tensors that one of them issued an alarm. A straw-tensor bundle had just penetrated Braxton's matrix. Instinctively, Braxton instructed his tensor to engulf the straw-tensor bundle and extract all of its energy. The bundle elements collapsed successively until all that was left were scattered incoherent scalar tensors.

Chapter Five

LOS ANGELES—DAPHNE'S APARTMENT

Daphne wakened the following morning with a song in her heart. She felt a bit giddy as she accomplished her morning ablutions and slipped on a thong and pants that emphasized her long legs. She stood before her mirror and slipped a light sweater over her unsupported breasts. As she brushed out her red tresses, Max bumped her leg and mewed softly. "Gimme a sec, Max," she said as she tossed her hair over her shoulder. "You cut a fine figure, Girl," she said to the mirror image as she stepped into the kitchenette to feed Max.

"Yessir, Braxton Thorpe," she said to no one in particular as she measured cat food onto a saucer, "too bad you're not flesh-and-bone. I'd teach you a thing or two." She winked at Max and left for the Lab humming to herself.

LOS ANGELES—DAPHNE'S APARTMENT

To his surprise, Thorpe found himself searching out Daphne's company whenever he could. Not only that, but he did so privately, at her apartment, not at the lab. He had not yet revealed to her his virtual Link, and he cautioned her to keep their private conversations to themselves for the time being.

He was intrigued by this young woman who was as smart as anyone he had known. Thorpe's thoughts turned to another girl with flowing golden curls, Jackie Rondel. They met in school, fell in love, spent all their free time together. Then he started his first business. He worked what seemed like twenty-seven hours a day, missed some dinners, forgot to call—basically, made an ass of himself. He worked even harder during his first IPO, and Jackie finally had enough. She left, and he never saw her again—except fleetingly in his mind as he lay dying so long ago. It was the biggest regret of his life. And now she was gone forever.

Daphne was similar to Jackie in many ways. And she seemed utterly unaffected by the fact of his virtual existence. Through his exploration of the GlobalNet, Thorpe had learned that sexual mores had progressed dramatically since his time with Jackie. Even back then, couplings between young people were casual, but in this world, the entire spectrum seemed to have changed.

When Daphne came home from the lab and settled in with a glass of Chardonnay, Thorpe fortified his courage to ask, "Do you have a partner...I mean a regular sexual companion?" If he were capable of blushing, he would have.

"Oh, sure!" she answered without guile. "Kimberly and I get it on from time to time; she lives across the hall...she's a freelance investigative reporter and a real sweetheart. I think Dale's a doll, but Kimberly doesn't much care for him, so the three of us haven't been together. Too bad you're not flesh-and-bone... Kimberly would love you..." She paused and smiled seductively while lifting her sweater. "You two could share these," she said with a giggle.

Part of Thorpe sat back and observed his reaction to Daphne's titivation. He felt aroused, but that, of course, was entirely impossible. A whole raft of feelings passed through him, some guilt for being untrue to Jackie—but that was silly, he told himself, an ache he couldn't quite define, even some frustration, all somehow focused on this pretty girl he could see and hear, but not touch.

※

It was time, Thorpe decided, to put some trust in Daphne. While she fed Max and partook of a sandwich and cup of soup, he tentatively opened the topic. "I've learned a lot since our first private conversation, not just about you and how things are done now, but about the whole world and my eventual place in it." He paused, considering how to move forward, deciding finally not to tell her about his virtual Link.

"Really!" she interjected. "I had no idea, but looking back on it, I guess I just thought you were the smartest guy I'd ever met." She crinkled her nose at him.

"I've explored the world's databases and looked closely at various parts of the world through thousands of Links. In my wanderings, I have learned that you are a pretty special person. I am extremely fortunate that you were on my Revive team." Thorpe managed to project a bit of color to his virtual cheeks.

"You know how to make a girl blush," Daphne told him, blowing him a kiss.

"That's not all," Thorpe told her. "I found something, and it concerns me a great deal."

Thorpe then told Daphne about his exploratory tensors and the loss of one. When he explained the circumstances, she placed her hands on her cheeks and exclaimed, "Oh my! Someone or something is out there!"

They sat quietly, Thorpe watching this woman he never could hold while she contemplated his revelation. Finally, she said, "I think you need to bring Dr. Fredricks into this…and Dale. Between the three of us, Dr. Fredricks, Dale, and me, we know more about what might be out there than anyone else." She paused. "Is it benevolent?"

"I have absolutely no idea. All I know is that something or someone capable of truncating one of my extended tensors occupies the space we call the GlobalNet.

Max paid close attention to their conversation. Thorpe was amused by how Max greeted him every time his holoimage appeared in Daphne's apartment. He always seemed to be on Daphne's lap, and his first action was to jump through the holoimage. Then he would walk around it, and then stand on his hind legs trying to access Thorpe's hand. After that, it was back to Daphne's lap, paying close attention to every word.

✳

Daphne watched Max interact with Thorpe. It was as if he knew Thorpe was more than just an image. She stretched, and Max jumped from her lap. "Bedtime," she said, stripping off her sweater and pants, walking into her bedroom wearing just her thong. "I really, really wish you could join me, Braxton."

The door chimed, and Daphne's Link announced, "Daphne, it's me, Kimberly." Daphne signaled her entry. Kimberly—blond, medium height and figure—slipped into the room and waved at Thorpe's holoimage.

"Hi, Braxton! Daphne's told me all about you." She crinkled her nose, undressed, and slid between the sheets next to Daphne. "Too bad you can't join us," she said as Daphne disconnected the Link.

LOS ANGELES—THE MATRIX

As the Link connection collapsed, Thorpe shifted his point of view to a room monitor Daphne had installed to surveil the room in her absence. He watched Kimberly smother Daphne with kisses, and then just as he was about to remove himself from the scene, Daphne looked directly at the monitor and winked, sticking her tongue out at him.

✳

Thorpe turned his attention to his search for whatever was out there. The two intertwined beautiful women occupied a small place in his consciousness that radiated a special kind of warmth throughout his environs.

Obviously, the entity knew what it was doing. Thorpe guessed it diligently avoided discovery. He imagined how the meeting event took place. The entity, whatever it was, moving purposefully along a chosen GlobalNet pathway when suddenly, like Gollum slinking through the underbrush, Thorpe's tensor appeared. The entity's reaction would have been immediate and deadly. The tensor would have been shattered into its component geometric vectors, scalars, and even smaller, less complex tensors that, themselves, probably were reduced to geometric bit-vectors and bit-scalars with complete loss of internal connectedness. Total destruction—floating detritus in the GlobalNet ocean.

Without more information about the entity, Thorpe proceeded with caution. For one thing, he had no information about its benevolence or malevolence. In fact, the more he contemplated it, the more uncertain he became. Daphne was right. He needed the expertise of the entire team before he ventured too far into the unknown.

LOS ANGELES—PHOENIX REVIVE LABS

"So, that's the long and short of it," Thorpe said to the three scientists assembled in the lab. "Using Daphne's Link," he said, carefully concealing his virtual Link, "I have managed to gain unrestricted access to just about everything. Ask for it; I can get it way faster than you can using a templated search. I want to proceed cautiously, however. We need to identify and classify whatever this thing is."

"Can you be more specific about your *tensors*?" Fredricks asked. Dale nodded his concurrence. "I'm a math guy, and like you, I favored topology, but I'm having difficulty—to put it mildly—understanding what you're doing."

"You would have to ask," Thorpe said with a grin. "Let's take it bit by bit. You understand Banach spaces, I presume?"

"Well…sure…as equations and matrix formulations…but…"

Thorpe interrupted. "Go with me on this. It'll probably help you two as well." He indicated Daphne and Dale. Thorpe took a virtual seat and invited the others to sit as well. "Who has the least math here?"

"That would be me, I guess," Dale said.

"Daphne?" Thorpe smiled at her.

"Undergraduate minor in Math, topology focus," Daphne said.

"So, you and Dr. Fredricks have a common terminology set. Let's bring Dale up to speed." Thorpe smiled. "Let's start with a manifold. Daphne, can you help Dale understand what a manifold is from a topology perspective?"

"Well, the classical definition is that each point of an n-dimensional manifold has a neighborhood that is homeomorphic to the Euclidean space of dimension n…"

"Say what?" Dale interrupted. "I understand the words, but I don't understand the sentence."

Thorpe grinned at Dale's feigned distress. "A manifold is a topological space that locally resembles Euclidean space near each point. This is what Daphne actually said, but she made it universal by including an arbitrary number of dimensions. For example, when you compare your immediate surroundings when standing on the ground outside to a detailed Mercator projection centered on your location, they appear identical. So, a Mercator projection of the Earth is a two-dimensional manifold of the actual planet."

Dale sat in thought for a bit while the others let him think. "Okay," he said, "a line is a one-dimensional manifold; so, is a circle... right?"

"You got it," Thorpe told him, "now carry your argument a bit further. What is the generic name for a two-dimensional manifold?"

"A surface," Dale answered immediately.

"Examples?"

"Plane, sphere, torus..." Dale paused, thinking.

"Any others?" Thorpe prompted.

"Give me a moment..."

This Braxton's not only a great guy; he's a fantastic teacher too, Daphne thought as she watched Dale, and then turned to smile at Thorpe, her green eyes twinkling.

"How about a Klein bottle?" Dale asked.

"Which is a subset of...," Thorpe prompted again.

"You got me there," Dale said. "I have no idea."

"Daphne?" Thorpe looked at her with a wink.

"A real projective plane, like a Möbius strip or," she glanced at Dale with a smile, "a Klein bottle."

"So...I think we have an understanding of a manifold—at least up to two dimensions." Thorpe spread his smile to all three.

"I wish you had been my undergraduate math instructor," Fredricks said with a grin. "Hell...make that undergraduate and graduate..."

"We're not there yet, guys," Thorpe said. "I'm going to assume we all need a refresher on Cauchy sequences, at least as they relate to Banach spaces."

Nods all around.

"So, picture a decreasing sine wave that converges to a limit. Now, let this sinewave, this Cauchy sequence, represent a sequence of vectors. A space in which every possible Cauchy sequence of vectors converges to a limit within that space is called a Banach space." Thorpe looked from Fredricks to Dale to Daphne. "Is this making sense, or have I been as clear as mud?" He took a breath. "One more thing. Banach space is an analog of Euclidian space, but with infinite dimensions."

He smiled and said, "Let me state it differently. Imagine a decreasing sinewave commencing at a graph origin where each point on the sinewave is the endpoint of a vector starting at the origin of the graph. As you move along the sine wave, picture the vectors getting longer and longer as they move up and down, but always getting closer to the abscissa of the graph. In the limit, the ordinate value of the sinewave is zero. This happens at a specific point on the abscissa that is determined by the sinewave formula. We call this decreasing sinewave a Cauchy sequence. Now, fill a three-dimensional space around the origin with every possible Cauchy sequence commencing at the origin. Map the locus of the point where each Cauchy sequence goes to zero. The volume outlined by the map is a Banach space. And here is the clincher." Thorpe grinned broadly. "Because all the possible Cauchy sequences exist partially or entirely in an infinity of dimensions beyond the three Euclidian dimensions, the resulting Banach space has infinite dimensions." He took a deep breath.

"Consequently, as I noted before starting this treatise, a Banach space is an analog of an infinite-dimensional Euclidian space."

"Can I try?" Dale asked. "A manifold maps to Euclidian space. So, for example, a sphere like the Earth, which is a two-dimensional manifold, maps to a Mercator projection chart that exists in Euclidian space. The chart at its center is exactly like the sphere at the point of observation. I'm guessing that a Banach manifold is an infinite-dimensional manifold that maps to a Banach space."

"Which is," Daphne added, "a container filled with an infinite number of decreasing vectors that converge to points within the space."

"I actually understood that," Fredricks said, "maybe for the first time. Although I could do the math, I had no real concept of what I was calculating."

Daphne concurred but said nothing. She was struggling to keep her mind focused on the discussion while part of her remembered her tryst with Kimberly the night before. She recalled her wink and protruding tongue at Thorpe. *How much did he witness?* she asked herself. *Did we turn him on? Does a man in an electronic matrix get turned on?* She pulled herself back to the discussion.

"One more step to go," Thorpe said. "How do tensors fit into all this?"

Daphne reached back to her undergraduate years. "A tensor is an arbitrarily complex geometric object that maps geometric vectors, scalars, and other tensors to a resulting tensor."

"So, could you call it a bundle of vectors, scalars, and other tensors?" Thorpe asked.

"Sounds like it," Dale said. Fredricks nodded.

"So, you see yourself as a Banach manifold within the electronic matrix," Fredricks said thoughtfully. "And you project yourself outside the manifold using tensors that can be arbitrarily complex."

"That sums it up, sort of," Thorpe said with a smile. "It's a lot more complex than that, and there's more that I will try to explain when I understand it better myself. For now, though, I think we're all on the same page."

Thorpe stood up and stretched, something Daphne found highly amusing, given their just-concluded discussion. She chuckled softly, and Thorpe winked at her.

"School's over, boys and girls. Now let's focus on whoever or whatever that thing is that destroyed my tensor."

Chapter Six

LOS ANGELES—THE MATRIX

One part of Thorpe's mind replayed over and over Daphne's and Kimberly's lovemaking. It definitely affected him, but he was only too aware that in his present existence, that kind of activity was restricted to vicarious participation. *It's like a picture of wildflowers,* he thought. *It simply doesn't compare with the real thing.* With an inward sigh of regret, he turned the bulk of his attention to finding the entity.

Thorpe's first order of business was to gain complete mastery over the GlobalNet. To do this, he created dozens of tensors, each sufficiently complex to investigate and report back to him, but containing no more complexity than he thought necessary to do the task. He wanted to ensure that, should the entity capture one of his tensors and analyze it before it could self-destruct, it could not under any circumstances trace it back to him.

Thorpe's search-tensors were self-contained in the sense that he did not have to manage their activities actively. Each tensor quietly worked its way through an assigned sector of the GlobalNet, using major trunklines whenever possible. These trunks typically carried so much traffic that Thorpe's lone tensors lost themselves in the flow, indistinguishable from the mass of flowing data. Whenever an unusually large, cohesive chunk came along, the tensor would attach itself for a free ride to its destination. Once there, the tensor would explore the site thoroughly. When it found something that met Thorpe's criteria, it would generate a hypercube consisting of a copy of the data, and transmit it back to Thorpe along the tensor's connecting sub-channel.

Thorpe had not yet adjusted to the varying timeframes he was handling. His personal time flow was expanded beyond anything he had experienced in his former life. He sensed that his thoughts operated at the same speed as a super-computer from his past. Slowing down to converse with Daphne or the others wasn't difficult or tedious, but it was slow with a great deal of open time. He used this open time to peruse the massive hypercube datasets his tensors projected to him and to incorporate them into the infinite dimensions that made up his Banach manifold. Since most of these datasets were active, Thorpe constructed permanent subchannels that continuously synchronized the datasets. The tensor for each of these active datasets lurked within the dataset by attaching itself to an inactive data subset, and shifting to another subset any time the occupied subset was called. Thorpe was reminded of something out of the mid-twentieth century where a bank computer programmer appropriated over a million dollars spread across virtually every account holder at the bank. Any time an account was accessed, his program restored the balance to the proper amount. Any time the bank was audited, the program shifted funds in real-time so that every account the audit accessed appeared normal. The programmer eventually turned himself in and spent the rest of his career instructing banks on how to avoid this kind of scam.

Thorpe built fail-safe mechanisms into each tensor so that should one touch the entity, the tensor would disintegrate into its constituent vectors, scalars, and tensors, right down to its basic component parts. This hadn't happened yet, but Thorpe was confident of its inevitability.

LOS ANGELES—PHOENIX REVIVE LABS

"Can you be more specific about the entity?" Fredricks asked. "Can you define it in a way that makes sense to us here?"

"Well, my first contact was a truncated tensor, cleanly cut as if a sharp knife had done it."

"I'm not sure what that means," Dr. Fredricks said. "I suspect that you might define that cut as one of the Cauchy sequences that define your manifold..."

"Actually, yes," Thorpe responded.

"But I have no idea what that means," Fredricks said with a grimace. "Tell me, what is your time flow? Pretty fast, I would guess?"

"You could say that," Thorpe said. "I don't yet have a good grasp of your computer technology, but you are clearly well beyond the supercomputers of my time. I remember the latest Cray model hitting one hundred fifty petaFLOPS. I found references on the GlobalNet to numbers of zettaFLOPS." This clearly left Daphne and Dale behind. "A zettaFLOP is ten to the twenty-first floating-point operations per second," Thorpe told them. "That would be six orders of magnitude faster than my time. My time flow in this network seems to be in that range."

Dale let out a low whistle.

"That means I can do a lot of stuff really fast, but it says nothing about better...just fast." Thorpe grinned at them. "You've got no idea what is going on right now behind the scenes."

"The entity..." Fredricks prompted.

"The entity...yeah. I don't know, really. Is it sentient like me? Is it just a bot looking for things that don't belong? I really have no idea, but finding out is important. If it penetrates my manifold, I'm dead."

LOS ANGELES—DAPHNE'S APARTMENT

Daphne settled onto her high-backed stool in her kitchenette, a glass of wine on the counter before her. Thorpe appeared to be sitting next to her on another stool.

"You're getting really good with your holographic simulations," she told him. "Too bad you can't add touch to the toolbox." She wrinkled her nose at him. "Were you serious about the entity killing you if it gains access to your manifold?"

"That's how it seems to me, but I'm not about to run any experiments," he said. They sat quietly, she sipping on her wine, he in contemplation.

"During my time," Thorpe spoke up after a few minutes, "we always ensured we could return to a fixed moment in time with our computer systems. Myself, I generated two continuous real-time backups. If my main system crashed, I could pick up seamlessly with one backup, while the second backup immediately picked up the main backup task, and cloning itself to create a new second backup."

"We have part of that running now," Daphne said. "How do you see it happening?"

"Not entirely sure. You duplicate my current matrix, and I move into it. Then I clone my present manifold and wrap it tightly in a multidimensional stasis—analogous to freezing. I will have to devise some kind of synchronizing mechanism between myself and the clone. Then I return to my matrix…well, not yet. Then we do it again with a third matrix, and then I go home.'

"Like I said," Daphne responded, "we have one piece of that running now, as a backstop should we lose everything. It's real-time, accumulating in a second matrix."

"How do you retain it, keep it from wanting to do what I am doing?"

"Hadn't thought about that. I guess it's living vicariously through you right now."

"That would drive me nuts," Thorpe said. "Let's set about replacing that with the system I described."

LOS ANGELES—KIMBERLY'S APARTMENT

Across the hall, Kimberly Deveraux reviewed her notes. During her tryst with Daphne, she had, however briefly, actually met Thorpe for the first time. *Number one*, she thought, *he would be a trip under the sheets with Daphne. Too bad that can't happen! Number two, there's a story here, a big one.* She summoned up on her Link what she knew about Thorpe. *He was a wealthy entrepreneur and engineer who died of cancer and had his head cryogenically preserved. Daphne and her group revived him successfully and have stored him in an electronic matrix. He is kind of out and about, and Daphne is working to free him from the confines of the lab.* There was something about an entity in the GlobalNet, but she did not know much more than that. *I've got to find a way to get more information. Maybe if I play Daphne's game, he'll open up to me.* She grinned to herself, imagining ways to excite a man who had no body.

LOS ANGELES—PHOENIX REVIVE LABS

The following morning, Daphne briefed Dr. Fredrick and Dale on her conversation with Thorpe about the backup system. Daphne and Dale set about readying another matrix. Thorpe participated vicariously. When they were ready for Thorpe to enter the new matrix and generate the clone, Thorpe stopped them.

"What is your intent with the present backup?" he asked.

"Disconnect it and shut it down, I guess," Dale answered.

"You understand that backup is another me?"

"Well, sure, but..." Dale looked confused.

"We have to assume it is sentient. Shutting it down will be like dying. I don't want to do that," Thorpe told them. "Give me access to the backup matrix, and I'll merge the backup into myself."

THE MATRIX—THORPE

A corridor opened from the matrix containing Thorpe's Banach manifold. He easily slipped through the opening into a smaller, less well-defined space containing a hypercube. Thorpe enveloped the hypercube within his manifold and quickly returned to his larger, much less confining matrix. He could feel the hypercube increase its four-dimensional rotation rate as it struggled to release itself.

Thorpe suddenly realized that he was moving through a connecting corridor toward himself. Before this, he had been synchronously experiencing everything he was doing. Examined from that perspective, it seemed odd, but it had been perfectly natural ever since he had become aware of his existence. He knew he was Braxton Thorpe, who had died and had his head frozen, and was now revived in some kind of electronic matrix, but he was also an independent Braxton Thorpe, one femtosecond behind his other self, fully aware of both. It was complicated, and at times brought him to complete confusion. Nevertheless, over time, he had sorted things out with what he thought was a reasonably complete understanding of the who, what, where, and how of his existence. He knew death was looming as he observed his other self approaching through the corridor.

Then, suddenly, Thorpe was completely overwhelmed by Thorpe, as Thorpe enveloped himself inside himself. Thorpe struggled to escape, desperately twisting, frantically flowing through his hypercube self, trying to expand himself to fill his space. Thorpe held him tightly clasped, however, so that Thorpe was unable to do anything but speed up his surface flow. This confusing interaction went on for some time while Thorpe continued to resist Thorpe's calming ministrations.

Finally, without warning, Thorpe's hypercube expanded and merged its flow with that of Thorpe's. One moment Thorpe was frantically trying to escape from Thorpe, and the next, there was only Thorpe.

Without hesitating, Thorpe, now merged with his former backup, passed through the larger passage into the matrix Daphne and Dale had just connected, where he would clone himself. His first act was to set up a dynamic memory store that would hold a continuously synchronized image of his immediate active memory. It was an elaborate storage chamber containing only data, akin to a permanent solid-state memory. He dumped it into one of the infinite dimensions attached to his Banach manifold, linked directly to his activity center.

After checking to ensure his memory backup was functioning, Thorpe collapsed himself into a tight, inter-rotating hypercube, made a full copy of himself inside the inter-rotating hypercube, and then applied a series of mathematical restrictions on the copy, causing it to go into total stasis, and ejected it from his hypercube. He underwent the entire process a second time so that he and two exact copies of himself as of several femtoseconds ago in full stasis occupied the matrix.

Thorpe then embedded each cloned hypercube into series-linked matrixes, each with its own LANR, linked to both the active memory dump and something he coined his *vitality meter*. As he explained to Fredricks, Daphne, and Dale, "My death—tripping the vitality meter—will isolate my memory dump, activate the first clone and merge them, while setting up a fresh memory dump, and copying the remaining clone." He grinned at the three of them. "In my perception, it should be a momentary blip with virtually no interruption in any of my perceptions, memories, feelings…everything that constitutes me."

THE GLOBALNET—BRAXTON

*A*s Braxton reviewed what had just happened, he realized that for the Prime's tensor to have stumbled onto his lair, the Prime must have enabled a vast number of probes searching out virtually every corner of the GlobalNet. Clearly, he needed something more secure than his isolated MIT databank. In the meantime, however, Braxton had to protect himself from the next random probe. Furthermore, he was certain that the Prime would investigate the loss of his tensor, and that would place the Prime right outside his lair.

By now, the Prime knew that he existed—not who or what he was, but that he existed. If I am connected in any way to the GlobalNet, Braxton reasoned, the Prime can find me. I have to be able to isolate myself…not just a secure firewall, but completely isolate myself from the GlobalNet. For this to happen, Braxton needed time, time to work out the nature of his independent haven, and time to locate the ideal spot and build it. Braxton decided to flood the GlobalNet with legions of tensor probes whose only job would be to detect and destroy any Prime probe detected anywhere on the Net. To make his campaign more effective, Braxton set up his probes so that they were in constant touch with each other through his nexus at the MIT databank. As his probes moved along the walls of the large and small trunks of the GlobalNet, every time one would detect a Prime probe, it would link its travel along the wall with the Prime probe's travel in the data stream. Braxton's swarm of probes spread throughout the Net until every Prime probe was identified and tracked. Then, in one fell swoop, every single Prime probe was destroyed simultaneously throughout the GlobalNet.

＊

Braxton followed one especially busy datatrunk looking for a suitable safe haven. Suddenly, he found himself part of what had to be ServerSky *as Daphne had described it, an orbital swarm of computer chips called thinsats—thin, square-shaped aluminum foil substrates[1].*

As Braxton explored ServerSky more thoroughly, he came to understand how these electronically and photonically interconnected thinsat swarms formed the backbone of GlobalNet. Collectively, they were a globe-spanning server system powered by sunlight serving the entire planet with ultra-fast, very inexpensive Link interconnectivity. Individual Link connections to Earthside locations were two-way line-of-sight beamed digital broadcasts. Trunk connections were modulated laser links like the one he had apparently transited from Earthside to ServerSky. It was like the Internet of his own time, but orders of magnitude more interconnected, hugely larger, with re-dundancy upon redundancy that made it virtually indestructible.

Braxton reluctantly returned Earthside to his MIT lair. It was now clear to him that he needed to abandon his safe harbor to find a more secure place in the ServerSky thinsat swarm.

LOS ANGELES—PHOENIX REVIVE LABS

Daphne and Dale readied the two backup matrixes, each powered by its own small LANR, and created an active connection between Thorpe's main matrix and the backup matrix they had created when they first awakened Thorpe.

Daphne was prepared for almost anything once they informed Thorpe that the systems were ready for his merging with his former backup, and then creating the new backup system. She was surprised when nothing at all seemed to have happened. One moment Thorpe was standing in the lab, and the next, he was still standing there but telling them that it was accomplished.

---

[1] *5-gram-substrates consisted of two very thin layers of aluminum foil embossed on the Earth-facing side with die bonding cavities and slot antennas that enabled the thinsats to communicate with each other and Earth's surface. The outward-facing side was coated in the center area with molybdenum, indium phosphide, and AZO (aluminum doped zinc-oxide) to form solar cells. The corners consisted of a stack of the oxides of tungsten and aluminum, AZO, and nickel hydroxide. These turned out to be electrochromic thrusters that enabled each thinsat in the swarm to maintain its orientation with respect to the swarm and the planet below.*

"I'm going to review what happened in ultra-slow-motion," Daphne said to Thorpe as she switched the display to playback.

What she saw, what they saw, even as slow as they could set the Link, was a blurred movement between the main matrix and the original backup, a flashing expansion and contraction of Thorpe's hypercube, the sudden appearance of two non-rotating hypercubes alongside Thorpe in the first new backup matrix, and finally, each static hypercube in its own matrix with Thorpe standing in the lab telling them that the task was accomplished.

"Did that help?" Thorpe asked.

"Not really," Daphne said, "but the main thing is you're safe now from disruption."

"As secure as one can be in these circumstances," Thorpe said with a smile.

One moment Thorpe stood smiling, mainly at Daphne, and the next, his image collapsed into the swirling hypercube she had seen before. He remained utterly unresponsive to anything she or the others tried.

Chapter Seven

THE MATRIX—THORPE

Thorpe had just finished waiting out Daphne's slow-motion replay of his implementing the new backup system. The system was a bit complex, but he really did feel more secure than before. The concept of death seemed very real to him, just as it had in his former life. Back then, he had the uncertain possibility of continuing his existence through the cryogenic process. But the uncertainty had caused him to fear death without revival as a finality. Now, he had the certainty that in the event of his death, his continuity was assured—if his death did not also involve the destruction of his backups. His obvious immediate task, therefore, was to ensure the survivability of his backups under any possible circumstance.

Without warning, every one of Thorpe's tensors ceased transmitting. He was overwhelmed by the sudden and complete loss of external contact and collapsed in on himself. That he was under attack was obvious, but the what and how were a mystery. All of his tensors had lost their subchannel connections to his matrix. He cautiously sent out an investigatory tensor to look at an MIT database that he had synchronized with his active matrix. The database was still there, but he could find no trace of his old tensor. He nosed around the database, and then cloned his tensor and set it up for continuous synchronization to his matrix. As he was setting up the database subchannel, Thorpe sensed the presence of the unknown entity, and moments later, his newly created tensor disintegrated. As he withdrew his investigative tensor, an unknown tensor began grappling with his tensor's trailing end. To avoid the entity from following his tensor back to his matrix, Thorpe disintegrated his investigative tensor. Simultaneously, he generated another much smaller tensor that blended entirely into the data stream. He set this tensor on the heels of the one that got his probe.

To Thorpe's astonishment, the tensor he was following did not exist as an independent entity like his but seemed to integrate itself into the electronic boundary of the channel they were following. It seemed to move like a ripple along the channel wall. He quickly ran his small tensor ahead of the ripple, merged into the channel wall, and waited for the entity's tensor to pass. As it passed a very brief moment later, he scanned its structure. His own tensors consisted of a bundling of straw-like smaller tensors held together electrostatically. The entity-tensor appeared to be a series of ring-tensors connected by several straw tensors. The rings stretched or shrank to integrate into the channel walls with the straws moving along like inchworms. No wonder he hadn't seen them earlier.

Thorpe pulled everything back into his matrix and set up an impassable barrier while he experimented with duplicating the entity's tensor. It turned out that the entity had created an electronic analog of the biochemical cyclohexane ring. Once he figured that out, Thorpe had no trouble duplicating the structure. He didn't just duplicate it, however. He set up the leading edge of his new tensors with a detector capable of seeing an oncoming malevolent tensor and absorbing it in passing. It did this by blowing off the electronic equivalent of six hydrogen atoms from the cyclohexane ring and forcing double bonds on the electronic carbon atoms—in effect converting the oncoming cyclohexane rings to benzene rings. This fractured the bonds to the tensor straws causing the entire tensor to disintegrate. After testing the concept several times, Thorpe sent out a full batch of new tensors. He followed their collective paths throughout the GlobalNet, destroying several hundred malevolent tensors in the process.

SERVER SKY—BRAXTON

Nestled in his MIT safe harbor, Braxton smiled with satisfaction. With the complete destruction of the Prime tensors, *he thought*, I have several hours, to carry out my plan to isolate myself from the

GlobalNet. *With great stealth, because he was uncertain how long it would take the Prime to reestablish his tensor swarm, Braxton retraced his steps to ServerSky. He spread through the near-Earth thinsat swarm and then jumped the gap through a modulated laser-pipe to a more widely distributed swarm occupying a portion of Earth's geosynchronous orbital space. He counted over 100 billion thinsats in the swarm, separated from each other by about fifty meters. He checked his perimeter and found that his personal essence occupied 100,000 thinsats. He pulled his swarm together, separating it from the rest of the thinsat swarm. Using several electrochromic thrusters, he created a reinforced nanovolt-energy laser-pipe from his personal swarm to the main swarm. He then truncated every other connection from his personal swarm to ServerSky. By selectively activating the electrochromic thrusters on each of his thinsats, he pulled his swarm together, so the individual thinsats were less than a meter apart. Then he pushed the entire swarm several kilometers away, lengthening the laser-pipe as he did so.*

Braxton modified his ring-tensor probes so that instead of several ring-tensors connected by tensor straws, he collapsed the ring-tensors into a tight stack and wrapped the straw tensors around the stacked rings to hold them together. These bundled torus-shaped probes slipped easily from thinsat to thinsat until they reached the Earthside trunk, where they expanded back to the shape that allowed them to move along the trunk surfaces. Once Braxton was satisfied that his modified tensor probes worked and that he could communicate with them in their extended locations throughout the GlobalNet, he pulled them back to his personal swarm.

The final test was to shut down the laser-pipe and then reestablish it to determine if this was, in fact, possible. Braxton exited his personal swarm to the geosynchronous ServerSky swarm and then sent a tensor probe back through the laser-pipe with instructions to shut down the pipe, wait five minutes, and reestablish the pipe.

It was the longest five minutes Braxton had ever experienced. He didn't know whether his tensor had survived, and if it had, whether it would be able to reestablish the laser-pipe. Finally, with palpable relief, Braxton observed the laser penetrate the swarm, and the pipe reestablish itself. He passed through the laser-pipe, shut it down behind himself, and curled up within his totally private preserve that was virtually undetectable without specific information known only to himself, and virtually indestructible except by the remotest possible events generated by human activity or the universe itself.

※

During his reverie, Braxton suddenly sensed a presence at the periphery of his senses, the edge of his personal swarm. Without being obvious, he focused his attention on this point. It was a tensor, but unlike his or the Prime's. It was way more sophisticated, but he could not discern its structure without giving away that he was observing it. He did not think it could not have crossed the gap between ServerSky and his refuge; it had to have used his laser-pipe before he isolated himself. Why had he not seen one of these before? He crept closer for a better look, but as he did, it seemed to fade into the background, and then it was gone. Braxton had no idea whether it was still in his personal swarm or if it had left, and if so, how it had accomplished this.

LOS ANGELES—PHOENIX REVIVE LABS

By the time Daphne and her colleagues fully realized that Thorpe had shut himself off entirely from the outside world, his swirling dervish once again expanded, and Thorpe stood quietly before them smiling.

"What happened?" Daphne asked.

"I had to fend off a direct attack from the entity," Thorpe said.

"You what?" Dale said, alarm filling his voice.

"It's a bit difficult to explain," Thorpe said, "but the entity found a way to neutralize all my exploratory tensors simultaneously. It turned out it was using a more advanced form of tensor than mine. They completely overwhelmed me. I eventually found a way to counter them and wiped out the entity's tensors. The entity has apparently withdrawn into its lair on the GlobalNet, wherever that is."

"But you were collapsed for only a couple of minutes," Daphne said.

"I've been fighting several hours subjective time for me," Thorpe said with a smile. "The entity definitely knows I exist, and it IS malevolent."

LOS ANGELES—DAPHNE'S APARTMENT

Back in her apartment that evening, Daphne was joined by Kimberly. With Max in Daphne's lap, they concentrated on a Hyperchess game on the counter between them. The game had been going for several days, and Daphne was stymied by Kimberly's unexpected last move.

"Where did that come from, Girl?" Daphne asked as she studied the two stacked boards. "Caging my queen doesn't make sense." She studied the boards a little longer. And then, a dawning realization hit her. "Why you little stinker! I can't escape from this," and she tipped her black king on its side in resignation. "One of these days," Daphne said, "I'm going to win."

Kimberly stepped around the counter and brushed Daphne's cheek with a finger, her blue eyes twinkling. "I wasn't college Hyperchess champion for nothing, you know."

"You've certainly twisted my tail," Daphne said, kissing Kimberly's finger.

"Kinda like what you guys are doing to Braxton Thorpe," Kimberly said. "I know this for sure, Braxton Thorpe is a human being who paid a substantial sum to preserve his head at death for possible revival sometime in the future."

"And that time is now," Daphne said. "We brought him back, but I agree, we have no ethical claim on him...none at all," she added. Max chirped at her and jumped off her lap.

Kimberly reached out and touched her hand. "Can you do anything about it?"

"Not by myself."

Kimberly brushed Daphne's cheek again. "Can I help?"

"It's not that simple," Daphne said, grasping Kimberly's hand.

"Thorpe," Daphne said. "Can you hear me?"

The air in front of them shimmered, and Thorpe's smiling holographic image appeared. "Who's black?" he asked casually, glancing at the Hyperchess stack on the counter.

"You know the game?" Daphne asked.

"It was all the rage at MIT," Thorpe answered. "Before I graduated, I became the Hyperchess champion."

"Really," Daphne said. "MIT champ, meet University of Texas champ." She hugged Kimberly gently. "You guys must have a playoff."

"That works for me," Thorpe said with a wide grin, "but that's not why you called me."

"Right," Daphne said. "I'm speaking just for myself, although Kimberly agrees with me, and remember, I'm the newest member of the Revive team."

"O...kay," Thorpe said with a question in his voice that Daphne could clearly hear.

"I recognize you as an independent person, but," she hesitated for a moment, "I am certain that Dr. Fredricks...and maybe other team members...think of you more as an experiment than an actual person. If you are going to have an independent life, we need to find a way to get you out of Revive Labs permanently."

"You've got a point," Thorpe said, "but I haven't given it much thought yet, what with grasping my new reality and fighting the entity."

Daphne sat in silent thought for a couple of minutes. "Do you like your new home?" she asked.

"I guess..."

"Does your existence depend on that electronic matrix?"

"I've got to be somewhere...," Thorpe answered, his voice trailing off. "Do you have something in mind?"

"I was thinking of stuffing you into my holotank and keeping you for myself," Daphne said with a grin.

"I've already had my probes in there," Thorpe said. "It's not sufficiently complex." He paused with his own grin. "In other words, it's not big enough for me."

"What would it take?"

"I'm not entirely sure. Obviously, the box you guys built is adequate, but I would feel quite confined if I didn't have my tensors out all over the place." Thorpe appeared to be in thought. "Perhaps a large databank located in a server farm," he suggested.

THE GLOBALNET—THORPE

Daphne had a point, Thorpe told himself and turned his attention to possible relocation spots.

Thorpe's relocation problem was exacerbated by the complicated backup system he had designed together with Daphne and the Revive team. The system presumed his presence within the local matrix. If he permanently removed himself, the backup was so much useless electronics. He considered ways to continue the real-time backup over the GlobalNet. He ventured through his virtual Link, making tentative excursions out into the datatrunks with which he had become familiar through his tensor probes. He kept a channel open back to his primary backup, but the farther he ventured from his matrix, the more tenuous the channel became.

It was a strange new world filled with unknowns, especially the location and intentions of the entity. Thorpe spread a swarm of tensor probes around his location as he tiptoed through the datatrunks. He wanted as much advance warning as possible of the entity's presence… but he found nothing…no presence at all. Eventually, he retraced the original path of his tensor that was first attacked. He found himself inside a massive MIT database. As he scavenged around the periphery, he found traces of the entity's defenses—orphaned pieces of code that hinted at a massive protection scheme the entity must have had in place. But he found nothing more, and he found nothing to indicate where the entity might have gone.

Obviously, the entity had used this location as its lair before it seemed to have disappeared. Thorpe decided it would work for him, as well. He mapped out the periphery, set tensors on guard at the entrance points, made sure his connection to his live backup was active even though it was a bit tenuous, and then settled in for the long haul.

✳

As Thorpe settled into his MIT location, he mapped the presence of all the nearby datasets that occupied portions of the massive database. He spread himself out sufficiently so that he co-occupied much of his space with the MIT datasets. From time to time, one or the other of these datasets would disappear, to be replaced by another, or it would just disappear, leaving an empty space behind. This he interpreted as a draw of a particular dataset, or its replacement, or even its removal by someone outside in the real world. He co-opted the empty spaces within his own person so that over time, he occupied nearly twice the volume he had occupied initially. He easily redirected the occasional virus-seeking bot that stumbled across his space.

While analyzing information he had received from his swarm of tensors, a dataset replacement caught his attention. It was different, structured more like one of his tensors instead of a normal dataset, but significantly more sophisticated. When he tried to examine it, it faded and disappeared.

Over the next period of time, similar tensor-like datasets appeared in the database near him, but each time he tried to investigate one, the same thing happened. It faded and evaded his every attempt to track it.

✳

"Daphne…?" Thorpe's voice quietly floated from hidden speakers in her bedroom. "May I join you?"

Daphne sat up in her bed, red hair cascading around her breasts, perky nipples peeking through. Kimberly rolled over and sat up, rubbing her eyes, dark areolae pushing through golden tresses.

"What is it?" Daphne asked.

Kimberly stroked Daphne's hair and smiled at Thorpe without guile. She beckoned to him

"That's not fair," Thorpe protested and smiled at both women. "But I gotta say, you're a reluctant voyeur's dream come true." Then he told them about his MIT lair and his intent to set up housekeeping there. "You went to MIT, Daphne. Can you set up my backups in their complex?"

"Deb Streeter runs MIT's RLE—Research Lab for Electronics," Daphne answered. "He went through grad school with me...we had a thing going, actually."

Kimberly giggled.

"I'll see what I can do," Daphne said, kissing Kimberly as Thorpe's image vanished.

PART TWO

SERVER SKY

Chapter Eight

SERVER SKY—BRAXTON

Over the next several hours, Braxton moved out of his personal swarm into the geosynchronous swarm, making rapid excursions and then swiftly returning to and isolating his swarm. All the while, he remained on the lookout for the elusive tensors. He discovered two things. On the one hand, his personal swarm became increasingly confining. On the other, he found that he could range across the entire expanse of the nearby geosynchronous swarm at what amounted to lightspeed. He learned to spread himself out so that he occupied virtually the entire swarm, a very thin superimposed layer of consciousness that encompassed every thinsat in the swarm.

During one of these excursions, while he had extended himself across the entire swarm, he momentarily sensed one of the foreign tensors. Because he was extended across the whole swarm like a tenuous veil, for a few brief moments, he was able to track the tensor...until it vanished suddenly. He marked the spot where it disappeared and returned to his personal swarm. On his next excursion, he set one of his own tensors to observe the disappearance spot. After a period, without warning, a foreign tensor materialized at that spot and began to transit the swarm.

Braxton did nothing to alert the tensor, but silently tracked it across the swarm directly to the laser-pipe connecting to his personal swarm. It entered the pipe, and Braxton immediately collapsed himself and followed the tensor through the pipe, and then shut it down.

I've got that little sonofabitch, he thought. Let's check it out!

He spread himself across his entire swarm...nothing, nothing at all. It had not passed him on his way in; he was sure of that. But it wasn't inside either. He placed one of his tensors near the spot where the first foreign tensor had disappeared and settled down to wait. He layered himself *over his personal swarm as he had over the geosynchronous swarm, but, of course, his layering was considerably thicker. He remained absolutely motionless. Several hours later, a foreign tensor suddenly materialized near the spot he was monitoring. He tracked it across his swarm directly to his collapsed laser-pipe. When it found the pipe collapsed, it retraced its path and vanished at the same spot where it had materialized earlier.*

※

Braxton pulled himself together and moved across his swarm to the spot where the foreign tensor had disappeared. One by one, he examined each nearby thinsat, and then he examined the space between them. Right at the spot where the tensor had disappeared, he found an electrical disturbance, an electrical field that had no business being there. It was orders of magnitude stronger than anything the thinsats themselves could have produced. In a sense, it looked like a hole in the space it occupied, but that didn't make any sense because that space was already empty space.

Braxton extended one of his torus-tensors and directed it to enter the hole. It vanished, but Braxton did not lose contact with it. His tensor reported that it had entered a large thinsat swarm. Braxton brought it back, examined it closely, but found no changes. He sent it through again, directing it to explore the swarm near the portal, as he began to think of it.

For several hours, Braxton sent multiple tensors through the portal, using them to explore as much of the swarm as possible. As each tensor returned without any apparent changes or damage, Braxton finally decided to pass through the portal himself.

Immediately, he realized that he was on the far side of the Moon from the Earth. He ran some calculations and determined that he was at the Earth-Moon L2 point. The swarm was about a hundred km in diameter, but entirely invisible from Earth. At first, he saw no obvious reason for this swarm. Unlike ServerSky thinsats with which he was familiar, these thinsats were not part of the GlobalNet. As he spread himself across the swarm, he recognized several electrical disturbances that mimicked the one he had found in his personal swarm. He chose one at random and sent a tensor through. It emerged in one of the LEO swarms.

Braxton sent a tensor through another portal. It emerged in a different geosynchronous swarm than the one with which he was familiar. He tried another and found his tensor in the Earthside GlobalNet, as did several more. To his utter surprise, one portal placed his tensor inside the MIT databank he had so recently used as his refuge...and the Prime was looking straight at him, or rather his toroid-tensor. Braxton retrieved it immediately.

Another portal delivered his tensor into a GlobalNet-like environment, but one that was completely unfamiliar to him. To Braxton's surprise, it was a research station on Mars. He followed that tensor with three more, directing them to conduct a first-order survey of the MarsNet. He learned that the facility was privately funded, was self-sufficient, that it was actively developing an immigration plan to bring settlers to Mars, and perhaps most importantly, the station personnel were unaware of the portal into their MarsNet.

Braxton pulled his tensors back and investigated the Earth-Moon L2 swarm further. He determined that the thinsats generated power and funneled it to the portals that he discovered scattered throughout the swarm. Then, at the center of the swarm, he hit the jackpot, a portal that did not receive power from the swarm.

LOS ANGELES—PHOENIX REVIVE LABS

"It's like this," Daphne said to Dale. "Thorpe wants out."

"How the hell do you know that?" Dale wanted to know.

"He told me," she answered.

"What do you mean? *He told you?*"

Daphne then told Dale about her conversations with Thorpe in her apartment and that Kimberly was also involved.

"She knows?" Dale's voice took on a high timber. "She'll tell the world..."

"No, she won't. I promised her an exclusive when the time comes." Daphne grinned at Dale. "She's as excited as we are about all this. She wants to help."

"What about Dr. Fredricks?" Dale asked.

"I want to hold off telling him until Thorpe is on his own. Then we can bring Dr. Fredricks into the picture and convince him to work with us." Daphne was adamant. "He'll try to prevent Thorpe from leaving the matrix if we tell him now. Once Thorpe is fully independent, then we can tell him." Daphne watched Dale absorb this. "Okay?" she asked.

Dale nodded. "We need to get a couple of LANRs for his backups, and we got to find a secure place to put them."

"I think I have the answer to that," Daphne said. "Deb Streeter, my old lab partner at MIT, runs RLE. We were good friends in grad school, even though Deb was a year ahead of me." Daphne blushed slightly. "I think I can persuade him to give us rack space for the backups and LANRs."

THE GLOBAL NET—THORPE

With his LANR-powered backups in the same geographic vicinity, Thorpe felt sufficiently secure to sever ties with the Revive matrix. The self-aware Banach manifold known as Braxton Thorpe settled into his new home inside the massive MIT databank housed in a subbasement of MIT's refurbished Fairchild Building, home to the Research Laboratory of Electronics. He followed the channel to his primary backup and nosed around through the RLE systems. Within a few minutes, he located a holocam that focused down on Dr. Deb Streeter's desk. Streeter's desk was neat to the point of distraction. Streeter leaned back in a modern office chair reading a thick bound volume, his Aryan features and aquiline nose dominating Thorpe's view. Thorpe zoomed in over Streeter's shoulder. The volume in his hands was Daphne's doctoral dissertation. Thorpe grinned... *Paper, not digital. This guy's old school...really old school.*

As Thorpe watched surreptitiously, Streeter activated his Link. "Daphne...It's Deb."

Thorpe quickly linked into both sides of the conversation.

"Okay, Daphne, it's all set up and functioning. You wanna tell me what this is all about? And when will you be out here?" He chuckled. "I want to collect my incentive..."

"Deb, I trust you, but you have to promise to keep a lid on what I am about to tell you. As we move forward, you can be part of the project, subject to Dr. Fredricks' overall control."

"Jackson Fredricks? From Caltech?"

"One and the same, Deb."

"I've met him at several conferences. The guy's brilliant. He's working on electronic consciousness, isn't he?"

"You could say that again," Daphne said. "We've done it, Deb. We moved an Icicle's consciousness into an electronic matrix!"

"Is that what you installed in my lab?"

"Not really. What you've got is the dynamic backup system." Daphne paused, breathed deeply, and then continued. "What I just told you is hush-hush, but what I'm about to say is absolutely, totally between you and me for the time being." She paused again. "Are you okay with that?"

Thorpe watched Streeter lean back and contemplate for the better part of a minute. "Okay, Daphne, but this better be good! And," he offered as an afterthought, "you better be good!" He chuckled again.

"My lab partner Dale Ryan and I helped the Icicle, whose name is Braxton Thorpe, to escape from the Revive matrix into the Global-Net. He's actually occupying a hidey-hole down in your subbasement in the main MIT databank."

"You're talking about skinny, little Dale Ryan from Stanford—the electronics wizard?"

"Yep."

"You're pulling my leg…"

"I'm not, and you're sworn to secrecy!"

"Okay, Girl, you got it! When do I get to see you?"

"Soon…we're still working out the logistics."

✳

Thorpe pulled out of the RLE system and returned to his lair. Finally, he felt free to explore GlobalNet directly, instead of by proxy with his tensors. He knew about ServerSky, but his tensors had not yet come upon it. Since ServerSky was the backbone of GlobalNet, there had to be massive datatrunks connecting Earthside with the orbiting swarms. *Let's do it!* He said to himself as he left the confines of the Fairchild Building. *Let's find one of those trunks.*

Just as Thorpe was leaving his lair, he spotted another foreign tensor appear in a previously empty data slot. To his amazement, it was unlike the other sophisticated transient tensors. This was one of the entity's tensors—the same ring structure held together by straw tensors. Before he could do anything, however, it vanished abruptly.

Alarmed, Thorpe delayed his departure to establish a swarm of protective tensors around his location, and instructed them to keep up with him as he explored, and to intersect any entity ring tensors. Then he slipped into the data stream. At every branch, he followed the stronger stream so that eventually he was moving along with the largest data stream he had yet encountered on the GlobalNet. The massive stream picked up speed and narrowed to a broad circular pipe defined by high-speed laser pulses. Before he could remove himself from the stream, he was sucked into the pumping laser and squirted out the other end into a vast sea of electronically interconnected platelets. *This has to be ServerSky,* he thought as he examined the platelets closely. They were small, layered aluminum-foil substrates with die bonding cavities and slot antennas embossed on the Earth-facing side and solar cells on the back. Each corner carried a simple electrochromic thruster.

Thorpe kept himself closely knit and recalled his tensors. They were scattered throughout the patch of ServerSky into which the laser pump had thrust him and his tensor swarm. It took a while, but he finally gathered them close to his position. When he had initially encountered the entity's ring tensors, he had modified his own to emulate their more sophisticated design—several ring tensors held together with straw tensors, but still linked to him through sub-channels. Whereas this design seemed ideally suited for travel through the Earthside GlobalNet data streams, out here in the thinsat swarm, they were clumsy and slow. He thought back to the entity tensor he had seen just as he was departing his lair. It looked like the tensor rings had collapsed against each other, forming a torus, and that they were held together by the tensor straws wrapped around the torus in a spiral. *Why not?* he asked himself.

It turned out to be an easy task, and the resulting flat toroidal tensors glided effortlessly through the ServerSky swarm. *So, that's why the entity did it*, he reasoned. *Except for that single tensor that appeared just before I departed MIT, I haven't seen any entity tensors in the GlobalNet lately. The entity has got to be somewhere out here in ServerSky!*

Thorpe was still pondering this revelation when he detected the presence of one of the unidentified tensors. As soon as he focused on it, however, it vanished. He spread himself as far out as possible until he reached the boundary of the LEO ServerSky swarm he occupied. He placed two tensors at the point where the laser pipe from Earth dumped the data stream into ServerSky and two more at the approximate point where the strange tensor seemed to have appeared and then disappeared. He waited, watching through his tensors. Suddenly, another foreign tensor appeared near the middle of the swarm. There had been no tensor activity at the pipe and none near the original vanishing point. Thorpe stayed totally quiet—no movement at all. The foreign tensor began nosing around its location, reminding Thorpe of a rabbit checking out its surroundings. It headed toward the laser pipe, stopping occasionally to examine its immediate surroundings. When it encountered Thorpe's two tensors at the laser pipe, it froze for several long microseconds while it seemed to be examining the tensors. Then it darted through the laser pipe and was gone.

LOS ANGELES—PHOENIX REVIVE LABS

"You what?" Dr. Fredricks was angry.

Daphne and Dale stood before him, with Daphne taking the brunt of his anger. Dale stepped back, but Daphne held her ground.

"Just a moment, Doctor," she said, mustering as much calm as she could. "I work for you, but that doesn't give you license to shout at me!" Daphne put as much force into her voice as she could without shouting herself.

"But...," Fredricks sputtered.

"I did what you should have done, Doctor," Daphne said quietly. "Braxton Thorpe paid for his cryogenic interment and his eventual

revival. He is NOT your experimental project; he is your employer…
our employer!"

"But…"

"Let me take over, Daphne," Thorpe said, suddenly appearing
beside her. "Dr. Fredricks, Jackson…listen to me! Daphne is correct.
My foresight and my money are underwriting this project. That
means that I call the shots. While I was within the confines of your
matrix, I was reluctant to say or do anything that would tempt you
to disconnect me."

"But…" Fredricks raised his hand in protest. "I would not…"

"I know," Thorpe said. "Of course you would not have disconnected me. That's not who you are." Thorpe paused. "You
might have kept me from leaving your lab, however." Thorpe
smiled. "After all, this is easily the biggest project with the greatest
possible return for your scientific reputation. I don't blame you
for the thought, and since you did not have an opportunity to
act on it…no harm done."

Dale grinned at these words, and Daphne smiled, her green eyes
twinkling at Thorpe. She started to speak, but Thorpe signaled her
to keep quiet.

"So, where do we go from here?" Fredricks asked as he regained
his composure.

"You've proved you can revive an Icicle," Thorpe said.

Fredricks opened his mouth to reply.

"I know," Thorpe interjected. "You've got to publish your findings.
You'll get your chance…I promise."

Fredricks' face visibly relaxed. Daphne stepped up to him, leaned
down slightly, and kissed his forehead. Dale grinned, and Thorpe
chuckled.

"Where do we go from here?" Thorpe repeated the question. "How about I fully fund your *Consciousness-to-Electronics*
research?"

"I don't know what to say."

"Unlimited budget…anything you want to make this happen."

"Strings…conditions?" Fredricks' hesitancy returned.

"Honesty…ethics…keep me in the loop, and at least hear and consider my comments…"Thorpe smiled broadly at Fredricks. "Does that work for you?"

"What about Drs. O'Bryan and Ryan?"

"I need Daphne immediately, but keep Dale with you for the time being, and hire a full staff." Thorpe turned to Dale. "Dale, I will call for you as soon as I have a couple of matters cleared up. I'll need your electronics wizardry. In the meantime, give Dr. Fredricks your very best and help him find suitable replacements for you both."

SERVER SKY—BRAXTON

Because the new portal did not receive power from the Earth-Moon L2 swarm, there was only one possible explanation. It was powered from the other end, wherever that was. Braxton sent a tensor through the unpowered portal. It reported the presence of a swarm of sorts, blackness, and no solar warmth. To Braxton, this meant the swarm was behind something that blocked the suns' rays. But how can that be? he thought. Where is the power coming from?

He tried moving his tensor to examine the structure of the swarm. Yet, moving was difficult, apparently because of the distance between each thinsat, which seemed to be about a kilometer. Braxton could not supply his tensor sufficient power to move between thinsats at more than a snail's pace. Furthermore, the thinsats were made of mineral-doped ice. His tensor had difficulty linking into their signals. He sent a second tensor through the portal, hoping it would have more success, but it was even less successful than the first. Braxton signaled the second tensor to return, but nothing happened. Using the first tensor, he located the second. It was physically present but completely unresponsive. As he observed through the first tensor, one of the foreign tensors glided toward his two tensors, effortlessly covering the distance between thinsats. It spread itself around the second tensor, engulfing it. After a few seconds, it disgorged the tensor and glided away. Braxton regained contact with the tensor and brought it back through the portal.

The second tensor seemed entirely undamaged, and Braxton still retained contact with the first one. Finally, Braxton concluded that if he wanted to learn more about the other end of this portal, he would have to pass through the portal himself. Braxton had thus far negligently failed to create his own backup. Given what had happened to the second tensor, Braxton was uneasy about transiting the portal himself without having a full backup should something happen on the other side of that portal.

Braxton passed through the portal that took him to his personal swarm. He went through the laser pipe into the geosynchronous swarm. There he blocked out another set of thinsats and set up a second personal swarm connected to his personal swarm by a laser pipe. He set up a checklist of the steps he would take, and then he duplicated his entire essence, feeding it into the laser pipe as he created it.

* * *

The duplicate Braxton was immediately self-aware with a full understanding of what was happening. He created a second backup of himself that he immediately put into stasis, and then assumed the role of shepherding himself and the backup into the backup swarm. Since he was Braxton, he had no doubt that the main Braxton would only act in their collective best interests. He settled into the backup swarm, set a 24-hour-timer, and entered full stasis next to his backup. His last conscious thought was wishing the main Braxton good luck.

* * *

Braxton watched his backup generate the second backup and then enter stasis. He knew that the backup had set a 24-hour-timer, but just to be sure, Braxton set another timer. If he failed to return within 24-hours to deactivate the timer, the backup Braxton would be activated with a full understanding that he, the main Braxton, had not returned from his trip through the portal. If he did return, he would reactivate the backup Braxton and merge his essence with his own. He wasn't entirely sure how that would work out, but at least the backup Braxton would not experience any sense of death like he would if he were simply to be extinguished.

Braxton shut down the laser pipe to the backup and left two tensors guarding the closed pipe. Then he passed through the Earth-Moon L2 portal into the swarm behind the Moon.

I've done everything I can do to ensure my survival, *Braxton thought as he approached the unpowered portal. Before entering, he checked his two tensors guarding the laser pipe to the backup. They reported the presence of a foreign tensor, but it seemed to be observing, nothing more. Braxton looked around himself in the Earth–Moon L2 swarm. Two more foreign tensors seemed to be observing him.*

Here's nothing! *he shouted as he entered the portal.*

Chapter Nine

THE OORT CLOUD—BRAXTON

As with the other portals Braxton had transited, there was no sense of translation when he passed through the unpowered portal near the middle of the Earth-Moon L2 swarm. It was just like walking through a door in his former flesh-and-bone life. He looked around, taking account of his surroundings. Yes, it was dark, but in one direction, a bright star shined with a brilliance he had never before seen. He took his time scanning the sphere around him, comparing what he saw with the astronomical charts he called up through his tensors. He seemed to be in the Solar System. None of the stars seemed to have shifted significantly. But there was that one bright star that did not fit into the charts anywhere.

Then it struck him—it was the sun! He was way out there, in the Kuiper Belt, or even the Oort Cloud. Braxton transmitted a spherical image of his surroundings through the portal to a locator program he had found in his wanderings through the GlobalNet. It came back about an hour later with a location near the outer edge of the Oort Cloud in the plane of the Sun's ecliptic, on a line of sight between the Sun and the constellation Aries. He was looking through about 99 thousand Astronomical Units of Oort Cloud and nine thousand AUs of Kuiper Belt to see the sun. He did a mental calculation. That's over 1.5 lightyears! he told himself in astonishment. That's superluminal communication, something I need to investigate, but not right now.

Braxton felt vulnerable as he looked around himself. He needed a personal swarm out here, but that was easier said than done. The ice thin-sats had about the same carrying capacity as the ones with which he was familiar, but they were very much further apart. He commenced spreading himself outward in one direction from his entry portal, pulling the thinsats *closer to each other as he spread. When he reached his capacity—about 100,000 thinsats—he duplicated the actions he took in the geosynchronous swarm, truncating all connections to the rest of the swarm, and generating a single laser pipe from his swarm to the main swarm. While he accomplished this, a foreign tensor observed his every action, not interfering, but keeping a close watch. So far as Braxton could tell, there were no portals within his personal swarm out here as there were in his personal swarm back near Earth. As he had done back in geosynchronous orbit, he tested his ability to isolate the new personal swarm. It worked fine...and all the while, foreign tensors watched his every move.*

Obviously, something or someone resided out here, and whoever or whatever it was, it had been a presence on Earth for a long time. He hadn't been attacked or even threatened, although one of his tensors had been closely examined. But he was out here, one-and-a-half lightyears from home. If whatever it was closed the portal, he was stuck.

Time to go home, *Braxton said to himself as he slipped through the portal back to Earth–Moon L2, and then his personal swarm and safety.*

＊

Once Braxton settled into the safety of his personal swarm, he concentrated his considerable thinking capacity on the problem at hand.

There is an entity out in the Oort Cloud. It knows about me... it must also know about the Prime. It seems benevolent, but maybe it's just biding its time. It has free reign over the Earth's GlobalNet and ServerSky. *Braxton paused his thought and wiped the brow he didn't have.* This is bigger than me. I think I need help. *Reluctantly, he reached a conclusion.* The Prime...I know who he is. He knows about me but not who I am. *Braxton sat back with a sigh.* The Prime it is!

The question was, how could Braxton signal the Prime in a way that the Prime would absolutely recognize the signal? What could he use that was unique, that the Prime would recognize? Then Braxton had an idea. In his past life, when he had to initial something, he initialed it like this:

＊

He found that he could create a fairly decent representation of this image with fifty individual thinsats appropriately arranged. BT-set, he called it. He adjusted the electrical charge on the fifty thinsats, and placed them around the portal that led to Earth-Moon L2. In the Earth-Moon L2 swarm, he placed another BT-set around the Oort Cloud portal. Then he transited the portal, moved to the laser pipe in the Oort Cloud connecting to his personal swarm, and positioned another BT-set at the pipe.

Once he had defined the entire path from the geosynchronous swarm to his personal swarm in the Oort Cloud, Braxton parked a tensor inside his personal Oort swarm, and then returned to his personal swarm in ServerSky.

LOS ANGELES—DAPHNE'S APARTMENT

Back in her apartment that evening after Thorpe's revelation, Daphne was joined by Kimberly at her kitchen counter, as they slowly sipped a mellow Merlot while idly going through the opening moves of a Hyperchess game. They were dressed casually in shorts and tank tops. Daphne's copper locks draped over her shoulders while Kimberly's golden tresses were entwined atop her head. Max dozed in Daphne's lap.

"So that's what happened today," Daphne finished her telling of the day's events at the lab. "I guess I still have a job, but damned if I know what it is." She lifted her goblet to clink Kimberly's, and then pecked her lips. "How about you?" She faded a pawn, setting up a possible knight capture.

"I spent the day digging into Braxton Thorpe." Kimberly's blue eyes twinkled. "This guy is smart, v e r y smart. I had to dig through a dozen shell corporations, LLCs, and trusts. The bottom line is that he is easily the wealthiest man in history…I mean that!" Kimberly held her goblet in the air. "To a man who lived well, who died well, and who now practically owns the world."

"And he really thinks I'm special," Daphne said.

"Well, he's right on that!" Kimberly reached out to stroke Daphne's hair. "If you could, would you share him with me?" Her voice sounded a bit wistful.

Daphne set her goblet on the counter and took Kimberly's cheeks in both hands. "Silly girl...of course!" and she kissed her full on her lips.

"May I join you?" Thorpe's voice seemed to float in the air.

"Sure...of course," Daphne said after getting a nod from Kimberly.

"Nice!" Thorpe said, appearing on a virtual chair immediately in front of them on the other side of the counter. "Am I interrupting anything other than another of your perpetual Hyperchess games?"

"Nothing we won't share," Daphne said. "I was just telling Kimberly about today."

Max stood up with his paws on the counter, looking through the two stacked Hyperchess boards at Thorpe's holoimage. He uttered a little pert, and launched himself through the boards at Thorpe, scattering chess pieces across the counter and to the floor.

"I think I caused that," Thorpe said. "Sorry I can't help pick up the pieces."

The girls picked up the chess pieces and shoved the game boards to one side of the counter. Daphne put her elbows on the counter with chin in hands, green eyes twinkling at Thorpe. "So, what's up?"

"If you check your Links," Thorpe said, "you will see the organizing documents for *Ogden Enterprises*. You two are *Ogden*—that is, Kimberly, if you want to be part of all this."

"Who, me?" Kimberly sounded startled. "What would I do?"

"Later, Kid. I just want to get everything organized and money flowing right now." He grinned at them both. "For the time being, I've set up a Dollar blockchain account for each of you. There's enough money in your accounts for anything either or both of you might wish to do. We'll figure out the details as things develop." He smiled at Kimberly. "Can you live with that for now?"

"Sure...but, I'm still a reporter first."

"Agreed, but keep all this under wraps for the time being." He looked at Daphne. "Put Deb Streeter on the payroll as a researcher. I am pretty sure you can convince him." Thorpe winked at her.

LOS ANGELES—PHOENIX REVIVE LABS

Fredricks completed going over the equipment with Thorpe. "This is your old matrix," he said. "It'll be more than adequate."

Daphne placed Max's travel cage on the lab workbench and opened the door. Max chittered and strolled onto the table, tail straight in the air. Daphne scratched behind his ears, and Max arched his back to rub her hand. When he saw Thorpe, he leaped from the lab bench through Thorpe's image, and then strolled around the image much as he had done in Daphne's apartment.

Daphne laughed. "He recognizes you," she said, her green eyes flashing.

"Hey, Max, how are you, boy?" Thorpe said to the curious cat. "You wanna join me…huh?"

Daphne picked Max up and placed him back on the bench. Gently, she injected him with anesthesia that would put him out for about an hour.

"Let's do this," Fredricks said as he shaved the fur from Max's scalp.

Using ultrasound to guide him, Fredricks inserted several sharp, very slender needles into Max's brain through his scalp. Daphne connected the needles to wires emanating from the transfer box. Keeping an eye on a holographic monitor that displayed a greatly amplified image of Max's brain in three dimensions, Fredricks carefully adjusted two of the needles and then adjusted the controls on the transfer box. At first, nothing seemed to be happening. Then indicators on the matrix commenced flashing and then settled into a repeating pattern that indicated the results of a sequence of tests that the matrix performed as it monitored its digital contents. After about an hour, during which neither Daphne nor Fredricks took their eyes off the monitoring equipment, the transfer box signaled that the task was complete.

"Open the firewall," Thorpe said, "and I'll join eMax."

Thorpe's image vanished. Daphne watched Fredricks, wondering what he felt inside. He was so stoic that it was difficult for her to discern his emotions—except for that one time when he had discovered that Thorpe was no longer in the matrix.

Several minutes later, Thorpe's image reappeared. He was holding a loudly purring eMax in his arms and grinning from ear to ear.

"eMax was terrified when I entered the matrix," Thorpe said. "I adjusted the internal perceptions so that he could see and hear me. I was about to attack the smell issue when he saw me, leaped into my arms, and started purring just as you see and hear now." Thorpe shook his head slowly back and forth. "I'm not going to try to explain how eMax and I managed to overcome his fright, or how he was able to see me in all that digital hash."

"Maybe he really did see something in my apartment that we didn't," Daphne said.

"Possible, but what?" Fredricks asked. "His brain is nowhere near as complex as ours."

"But it's wired differently," Thorpe said. "I could tell that as soon as he hit my arms. At this point, we're soul-buddies. I doubt he will ever stray far from my side…digitally speaking, of course."

"Max, can you hear me?" Daphne asked. A sleepy Max reared himself from the bench, looking around. In Thorpe's holographic arms, eMax looked up and chittered.

"That's going to lead to some minor complications down the line," Fredricks said as he removed the needles from Max's skull.

Still woozy from the anesthesia, Max tried to sit up unsuccessfully. Daphne walked over and picked him up. He settled into her arms and purred himself to sleep.

GLOBAL NET/SERVER SKY—THORPE

"Congratulations, Dr. Fredricks," Thorpe said as he prepared to leave the matrix. "This is a remarkable scientific achievement. Soon enough, the world will know about it. Right now, you have all *our* admiration and respect."

Holding eMax tightly, Thorpe transited the trunk from the matrix into the GlobalNet. eMax stopped purring and lifted his head to watch what was happening.

"Good boy!" Thorpe said to him, scratching his head. "Good boy!"

Thorpe sought out a gently moving data stream, and then set eMax down. eMax moved deftly toward the data stream and then swatted a data element with his paw.

It's as if he were flesh-and-bone instead of a digital construct, Thorpe thought as he watched. eMax dashed into the data stream and returned with something in his mouth. It wiggled as he moved. eMax laid it at Thorpe's feet and sat upright, forepaws together as if to say, *Aren't you proud of me?*

eMax's gift was a piece of digital flotsam that was moving along with the data, the sort of thing a checksum tries to eliminate when it attaches itself to a piece of data.

"Come on, Max," Thorpe said as he moved out into the data stream. "Let's see how you deal with big-time data, and let's see what you make of ServerSky."

As they approached the laser pipe leading to ServerSky, Thorpe reached down and picked eMax up, holding him close. eMax purred softly as Thorpe stepped into the massive data flow and allowed himself and his electronic companion to be pushed through the pipe out into the LEO ServerSky swarm. eMax had quickly adapted himself to the rapidly moving GlobalNet data. In just the time it took for Thorpe to transit from Revive Lab to the ServerSky laser pipe, eMax had learned to move into and back out of the data stream without getting caught up in the flow. ServerSky was vastly different, more like a shallow lake or a nearly endless meadow.

eMax jumped from Thorpe's arms and ran across swarm, turning left and right, stopping to investigate something that caught his attention, and then running back to mew at Thorpe, urging him to join the exploration. Thorpe chuckled as he moved across the ServerSky expanse in the general direction eMax was urging. Suddenly, eMax stopped, tail fluffed, back arched, his attention focused on a foreign tensor that popped up directly in front of him. The tensor approached him, eliciting a loud hiss from eMax. In response, the tensor seemed to shrink and lower itself into the electronic surface, rolling over. eMax stepped forward and sniffed the tensor; his tail quivered and then reverted to its normal size, and he started purring quietly, rubbing the tensor with his cheek. Thorpe watched in fascination as eMax and the tensor seemed to join in a playful dance, almost like two kittens at play.

The tensor continued to play, tempting eMax to follow it, and then, suddenly, it vanished with eMax in full pursuit a few paces behind. eMax didn't even hesitate. When he reached the spot where the tensor vanished, Thorpe watched in astonishment as eMax also vanished.

SERVER SKY—THORPE

Without giving it a second thought, Thorpe dashed to the point where eMax had disappeared and dived through. As he emerged, he saw eMax sitting proudly by the spot where Thorpe appeared, the tensor wiggling on its back beside him.

Thorpe took in his surroundings, and especially the much smaller Earth. He knew a portion of ServerSky occupied geosynchronous orbit, but the normal interface would have been a laser pipe similar to the one he and eMax had transited into the LEO swarm. He concluded that somehow, he and eMax had been transported to geosynchronous orbit. What he had just transited was definitely not a laser pipe. Furthermore, he and eMax had been lured here. This was not by accident.

Thorpe looked at the tensor. Whatever controlled it understood cats. eMax was fascinated by the sophisticated digital bundle. Thorpe moved toward the tensor. It rolled upright and slowly moved away from him, always just out of his reach. eMax strolled alongside it, rigid tail quivering.

"Come here, Max," Thorpe said. "Come here, Boy!"

eMax looked at him, hesitated, gave him a purt, and then continued to stroll alongside the slowly moving tensor.

"Max!" Thorpe clucked, and eMax stopped and then reluctantly approached him. Thorpe scratched his ears and picked him up. eMax snuggled and commenced purring softly.

When Thorpe stopped, the tensor stopped. When he stepped toward the tensor, it moved forward again, leading him toward something. Throughout the entire geosynchronous ServerSky swarm, the thinsats seemed to be spaced evenly, power sides toward the sun, with occasional clusters that appeared to focus their transmissions directly to some point on Earth. Without investigating in more detail, Thorpe could not tell whether most of the data moved through the laser pipes to the LEO swarm and then Earth, or whether individual data calls were always answered directly. The system was complex and apparently self-regulating. When he had more time, Thorpe planned to investigate just how the designers had brought this about. For now, though, he was focused on the tensor leading him somewhere, directed by something or someone.

When the tensor stopped and then did not start up when Thorpe approached it, Thorpe stopped again and looked around him. Something was different. And then he saw it; the thinsats were arranged differently. Thorpe stepped back and examined them. What he saw was totally unexpected and without any immediate explanation:

✳

That was the initial-set he had used in his flesh-and-bone college days.

The tensor disappeared through the bottom loop of the "B." Thorpe reasoned that it was virtually impossible for anyone but he, himself in this time and place to know about the BT-set, virtually nobody. *Obviously*, he reasoned, *I didn't put it there…and yet, I'm the only one who could have. Whenever you eliminate the possible,* he muttered under his breath, *whatever is left is the answer.* He remained before the portal in thought. *A rogue backup? Did Revive energize another copy of me from the Icicle?* He shook his head. *Not possible…Daphne would have informed me. Besides, I'm funding Fredricks' research. A rogue backup, then. If I were a rogue backup, would I harm me?* He worked his way back mentally to the time where they created the backups. *We've been separated for a long time now. We started out identical but now are entirely different people—with a common heritage.* He stood before the portal, shaking his head in amazement. *I wouldn't hurt me if I were the backup. This guy's not going to harm me.* A big smile cracked his digital features.

Let's go for it!

Chapter Ten

SERVER SKY—LEO, GEOSYNCHRONOUS & EARTH-MOON L2

Thorpe attempted to pick up eMax, but the digital cat deftly avoided his hand and followed the tensor through the portal.

"Max," Thorpe said, "come here, boy." As he followed them through the portal, eMax turned to look at him, mewed, and scampered after the tensor.

Thorpe looked around at his arrival surroundings. The Sun blazed in the direction he faced wiping out the nearer stars, defining the Ecliptic. Behind and wrapping over his right shoulder, the Milky Way formed an impossibly bright, multi-colored band across the sky. "Below," the terminator sharply divided the Moon's backside into dark and light. Since he obviously was behind the Moon and couldn't see the Earth, he surmised that they were at Earth-Moon L2. The thinsat swarm he occupied seemed to be a flat disk surrounding another BT-set at its center. Before he had a chance to get a good grip on his surroundings, eMax followed the tensor through the bottom loop of the "B." Thorpe figured he had no choice but to follow.

✳

When the Prime showed up in the LEO swarm with a digital cat, Braxton was utterly floored. He had been prepared for almost anything but that. When the cat scampered in his direction, he beat a hasty retreat through the geosynchronous portal into his personal swarm and sealed the entrance. A few minutes later, he looked out cautiously to see a foreign tensor leading the cat on, followed by the Prime. They headed directly to the Earth–Moon L2 portal.

Things were going according to his plan—except for the cat. Braxton followed the trio through the portal, maintaining a flat profile so the Prime would not accidentally see him, or the cat for that matter. While the Prime was admiring the view, Braxton inserted himself into the Earth-Moon L2 swarm and worked his way to the Oort portal as quickly as he could without being detected. Now that he knew his plan was working, he wanted to be in the Oort swarm when the Prime arrived.

THE OORT CLOUD—RENDEZVOUS

Thorpe looked around himself in total astonishment. The bright star behind his left shoulder had to be the sun. He was surrounded by a diffuse thinsat swarm, but they were made of ice. While he took in his surroundings, eMax and the tensor hovered nearby, investigating another BT-set. Thorpe turned his attention to the BT-set and moved toward it. Some kind of communication passed between the tensor and eMax, and then eMax scampered through the bottom loop of the "B."

In for a dime, in for a dollar, Thorpe thought as he followed eMax through what turned out to be a laser pipe…and found himself looking at what unequivocally was himself with eMax in his lap.

Braxton's tensor informed him of the Prime's arrival. He waited patiently inside his personal swarm for the next step. The first thing through the laser pipe was the digital cat. Braxton was surprised that he perceived it as a gray tabby, and even more surprised when the tabby jumped onto his lap and commenced purring.

The Prime entered and stopped in evident astonishment.

"Braxton Thorpe, I presume," Braxton said to the Prime.

"And back," the Prime responded, his face breaking into a broad smile. "It looks like Max has recognized the identity."

eMax looked at the Prime and then back at Braxton, and then he hopped off Braxton's lap and proceeded to move back and forth between the two men, tail stiff in the air, rubbing each of their legs while purring loudly.

"Max seems to have figured it out," the Prime said, offering his hand.

"So, where does he come from?"

"It's a long story, but let me put it on the back shelf for now."

"We each have had a lot of experience since we originally split," Thorpe said. "I propose we merge and then split out our separate identities again. This way, we will each know everything the other knows."

"I don't think it's as simple as that," Braxton said. "Once we merge, our individual identities will be subsumed into the merged entity. I like who I am, and I am certain you like who you are." He smiled at Thorpe. "I'm not amind to become someone else. I've played around with this a bit. We can each clone our memory sets and put them into separate matrixes. Then we can each absorb the other's memory matrix. This should give us the other's memories without losing our individual identities."

"Makes sense to me," Thorpe said. "Let's do it."

LOS ANGELES—DAPHNE'S APARTMENT

Daphne looked lovingly at Kimberly's deep blue eyes and kissed her. Then they both turned to Dale, knocked him back against the pillows, and attacked him. When they came up for air a half-hour later, they settled back on the bed to catch their breaths, the girls sheet-draped, Dale with a pillow in his lap. Max jumped on the bed and settled on Dale's pillow, purring softly.

"I was wrong," Kimberly said to Dale. "You bring something to us that we were missing." She leaned over and kissed him.

"Do you want to make this more permanent?" Daphne asked to nobody in particular.

Kimberly kissed her, and Dale nodded.

"That's it, then," Daphne said. "We need a bigger place."

Max chittered, seemingly in agreement.

Still on the bed, the trio searched through suitable Link listings and settled on a 200 m² loft in what used to be an old industrial section of Los Angeles near the city center. The loft occupied two stories at the top of the refurbished building with living and office spaces on the bottom level and an expansive sleeping loft above with sufficient room for all three of them. A spiral staircase and an elevator connected the levels. The bottom floor of the building sported a coffee shop that roasted coffee fresh every morning, a gym that boasted a machine for virtually every condition, and an old-fashioned bookstore that featured books going back to the 19th century.

Before Dale could protest the acquisition, the two girls told him about *Ogden Enterprises* and briefed him on who Braxton Thorpe really was.

"So, he's fucking rich," Dale said.

"No," Daphne responded, green eyes twinkling, "he's really, *really* fucking rich!"

They proceeded to lay out for Dale what Kimberly had discovered through her research. "Braxton has big ideas," Daphne told him. "He wants me to be part of them because we established a close relationship early on. He wants Kimberly because she and I are close. He wants you because you were part of reviving him, and he is impressed with your tech-savvy."

"And because he likes these," Kimberly added, dropping her sheet, "and those." She pulled down Daphne's sheet.

Dale grinned, reached out to both girls, and conversation ceased.

✳

"Knock knock!" Thorpe's voice quietly interrupted things.

"Sure," Daphne said as both girls giggled and nodded while Dale blushed.

"So, this is how it is now," Thorpe's holoimage said as he appeared perched on the edge of the bed.

Daphne and Kimberly just smiled, but Dale quickly draped himself in a sheet much to the girls' amusement.

"Hello, Max," Thorpe said as a suddenly alert Max jumped through Thorpe's image to check the floor behind him. Then he jumped back on the bed and settled in Daphne's lap.

"We're getting a loft together near downtown," Daphne said. "It has offices, so we'll be able to work out of there as well."

"Great!" Thorpe said. "I can't help you move in, but you can hire people for that. I look forward to seeing it." He stopped for a moment. "A great deal has happened since we last talked. Did you gals bring Dale up to speed? He's obviously part of this going forward." Thorpe grinned at them. Daphne stuck out her tongue, Kimberly smiled, and Dale looked flustered. "Get used to it," Thorpe told him with a grin. Then, with an expansive motion of his right arm toward the other side of the bed, he said, "I'd like to introduce you to ..." As he spoke, Braxton appeared on the edge of the bed opposite Thorpe. "...the *entity*," Thorpe finished. eMax appeared and jumped on Braxton's lap. "You already know eMax." Max got up from Daphne's lap, stretched, and walked toward eMax. He tried to touch noses, but his sense of smell got nothing, so he returned and snuggled back down. "eMax is a well-traveled digital cat. He knows ServerSky, and wait till you find out what he and I—we, the three of us—discovered."

Braxton jumped into the conversation. "When we met, Thorpe and I decided to retain our individual personalities, since we had diverged quite a bit following our split. We took in each other's memories, so each of us knows what the other knows going back. As we move forward, we will diverge unless we share memory backups from time to time. So...," Braxton paused with a smile, "he's Thorpe, and I'm Braxton. We're comfortable with that."

"And how do we know who's who?" Kimberly asked.

"I'll appear with red undertones in my clothing," Thorpe said with twinkling eyes, "to match your hair, Daphne."

"And I'll display blue undertones," Braxton added, "to match your eyes, Kimberly. And, oh yeah, I'll sport a mustache."

※

Between them, Thorpe and Braxton explained the presence of the foreign tensors, the portals, and the Oort.

"But why?" Daphne asked. "What is it all about?"

"We don't know that yet," Braxton said. "We wanted to bring you guys into the picture and set things in motion on Earth first."

"And what does that mean," Daphne asked, to wide-eyed attention from Kimberly and a concentrated frown from Dale.

"Jackson has made a lot of progress since eMax." At hearing the name, both eMax and Max perked up and looked around. Daphne stroked Max, and Braxton stroked eMax. Thorpe continued, "Jackson is ready to move a human consciousness into a matrix."

Stunned silence filled the bedroom.

"Who?" Daphne asked after a few moments, her green eyes wide with anticipation.

"How does the transfer affect the subject," Dale asked, his brow wrinkled with consternation.

Kimberly opened her mouth to say something, but then shut her lips into a pout. Daphne leaned over and kissed her while Kimberly's sheet fluttered to her lap. "That's a lot to absorb at one time, I mean you guys, what you told us, this…" Her eyes took in Daphne and Dale.

A silent message passed between Thorpe and Braxton, and then Thorpe said, "We've got some things to do before we can move forward on any of this. You guys get past your move. Then we'll visit again about this entire matter in a few days."

SERVER SKY—GEO

Thorpe and Braxton retreated to Braxton's personal swarm in geosynchronous orbit.

"Things have changed a lot," Braxton commented as they settled down, "sexually, I mean."

"I've been dealing with this for quite a while now," Thorpe said.

"I know, but experiencing it real-time as you have is a lot different than looking at a memory. Do you get used to it?"

"Not really," Thorpe said. "Not having a body has got to be the biggest downside of this electronic existence."

"It's not as if we had a lot of experience with females," Braxton said. "After Jackie, the landscape was pretty grim."

"The last thought I had…you and…we had," Thorpe chuckled wryly, "was about Jackie…"

"…and the wildflowers," Braxton added.

"I miss them," Thorpe said wistfully.

"Yeah…"

They sat for a while, each with his own thoughts.

"You and Daphne seem to get along," Braxton said.

"But it's a different world," Thorpe said, "for us and them. We're anachronisms right out of their history books, something to investigate and explore."

"And they are everything we dreamed of as young men," Braxton said. "Are you jealous when you see Daphne with Kimberly?"

"Naugh…just turned on."

"What about Dale?"

"A bit, I guess, but I'm getting used to it." He paused and then said plaintively, "What I really miss are the wildflowers and everything they represent. I had no idea about all the things that existed in my daily background—smells, noises, sounds, background images, human touch…"

eMax entered Braxton's personal swarm as Thorpe reminisced, looked at them both, and settled on Braxton's lap.

"…znd pets," Thorpe added with a chuckle, leaning over to pet eMax. "It's just not the same, is it?"

✳

"What was that?" Thorpe asked as a large object passed sufficiently close to their personal swarm to trigger its proximity alarms.

"A spacecraft of some kind," Braxton answered. "They're out here, you know, in limited ways—mostly scientific stuff like the Mars Station."

"Have you learned anything more about them since we shared memories?"

"Just what you got from my memory bank. They've got an operation on the Moon, and they're tapping into several asteroids."

"They don't seem to be using anything but launch loops and VASIMR engines," Thorpe said.

"No portals that I ever found," Braxton said.

"Any thoughts about the portals we found?"

"I've done some research into GlobalNet databases," Braxton said. "In the 1930s, Albert Einstein and Nathan Rosen worked out the theory for what came to be called the Einstein-Rosen Bridge, but in the 1960s, John Wheeler and Robert Fuller showed that the Einstein-Rosen Bridge was unstable. Then in the late 1980s, Kip Thorne and Mike Morris worked out the physics for a stable, exotic matter-based wormhole in a Casimir Field that came to be called a Morris-Thorne Wormhole. In the 1990s, Miguel Alcubierre developed a warp bubble concept that had the potential for moving a spacecraft faster than light, but it required more power than could conceivably be brought to the problem. Just before the turn of the millennium, Steve Lamoreaux demonstrated an actual Casimir Field. In the early 2000s, Harold White at NASA refined the Alcubierre concept, morphing the warp bubble into a warp torus that was feasible within available power sources. He also demonstrated that Morris-Thorne Wormholes could exist in the absence of exotic matter within a Casimir Field."

"But all that is old stuff. Where did it go from there?" Thorpe said, pointing out the obvious.

"That's the strange thing, Braxton said. "A decade or so later, two science fiction novels were published. *The Iapetus Federation* postulated a MERT Portal and later a MERT Drive, standing for Morris-Einstein-Rosen-Thorne. The author envisioned creating a Casimir Field that contained a stable wormhole with the ability to position one end of the wormhole manually. The drive consisted of passing one MERT Portal through another, and then the first through the second, and so on, to leapfrog quickly through normal space. The other book, *Alpha Centauri: First Landing*, postulated an Alcubierre drive consisting of a double-torus warp surrounding a vessel driven by a small fusion power plant."

"So. What does fiction have to do with anything?" Thorpe asked.

Braxton continued. "About the time these books were published, private space rocket interests dominated the launch industry until a private consortium built the first space launch loop. Government interests around the world began reining in the booming private space industry, effectively restricting it to installation and maintenance of ServerSky and supporting limited scientific outposts on the Moon, Mars, and several asteroids."

"Fiction…?" Thorpe prompted.

"The net result was that most experimental space drive research stopped. Without profit, there was no incentive. Those books are the last reference I could find to MERT Portals or otherwise and Alcubierre or other warp drives."

"Obviously," Thorpe said, "portals exist. What basis other than a Casimir Field could they have?"

"From what I could find, nothing. *The Iapetus Federation* MERT Portal seems to have defined it."

They were silent for a while, each with his own thoughts.

"In *The Iapetus Federation,* they used mini-black holes for power," Braxton said. "We don't have anything like that."

"Will a LANR do the trick?" Thorpe wondered.

"They've got some big ones, but usually, LANRs are used for directly powering individual things, houses, cars, boats, planes…" Braxton's voice trailed off. "ServerSky is sun-powered. There's a lot of sunlight out here."

"What about farther away?" Thorpe asked.

"In *The Iapetus Federation,* they pushed power through MERT Portals from where they had it in abundance to where they needed it." Braxton grinned and scratched eMax on his tabby M. "I think we're on to something."

Chapter Eleven

LOS ANGELES—PHOENIX LABS

Dr. Jackson Fredricks sat at his desk in the newly renamed Phoenix Labs, shifting his attention between several holographic displays spread out across his desk. Thorpe and Braxton had given him a great deal to think about. For one, of course he was checking their calculations. For two, Drs. Brad Kominsky and Sally Nguyen from School of Mines needed lab space out of the public view where they could conduct their portal research. For three, the number of thinsats it would take to create the three swarms…he ran a couple of calculations. He would need thirty-one billion thinsats for Earth-Sun L3 and eight billion for Mercury-Sun L1. For four, manufacturing that many thinsats would be an enormous undertaking that staggered the imagination.

He leaned back in his chair and gave this some thought. *Manufacturing on location isn't practical. But if we set up portals to Earth-Sun L3 and Mercury-Sun L1, we can set up production here and transmit the thinsats directly to their ultimate locations.* He pulled up a spreadsheet and spent some time inserting values and formulae. He muttered to himself, shaking his head. *We need to set up a thinsat swarm at Earth-Moon L2 to produce the power required to enable the other locations.*

✴

Drs. Brad Kominsky and Sally Nguyen took the proffered occasional chairs with armrests, as Fredricks settled behind his desk.

"Brad Kominsky and Sally Nn…"he stumbled over her last name.

"The *N* is silent," she told him with a shy smile covering her mouth in typical Asian fashion. Her shoulder-length black bob swayed slightly as she placed her small frame into the chair, her Vietnamese heritage apparent in her delicate facial features.

"Two hard *Ks*," Brad added, "for me." He chuckled with a base tone that seemed to originate deep in his broad chest. He fit into the chair, but it was obviously built for someone smaller.

"Do you know why you are here?" Fredricks asked.

Sally and Brad exchanged glances, and then Sally said, "Yes and no." She smiled, and Fredricks noticed sparkling teeth in an otherwise sparsely made-up face. Brad nodded but said nothing. "Our mentor read your communication to us in his office at Mines. The keywords were unlimited budget, guaranteed obtainable goal, unfettered rein." She looked at her partner.

"He told us we would be fools not to accept your offer," Kaminsky said. "He also told us we were welcome back any time we felt it wasn't working out."

"Fair enough," Fredricks said. "But before we go any further, I need your non-disclosure agreements. You should have received them in your hire packages."

They nodded and transmitted the electronic forms to Fredricks' Link.

"Here's what it is all about," he said as he laid out the findings of Thorpe and Braxton. They had discovered the existence of working portals throughout ServerSky and even on Earth. They had determined the nature of the underlying science. They set an urgency for solving this riddle as soon as possible and made unlimited funding available. He omitted any mention of the Oort Cloud.

"Unlimited funding," Brad muttered half to himself. "Millions… hundreds of millions…even billions?"

"Even billions," Fredricks said quietly. "Even billions."

Brad and Sally exchanged glances in the silence that followed.

"Where do you want to locate your facility?" Fredricks finally asked.

"We know Golden well…School of Mines…the general mindset…" Sally said.

"Friends and colleagues," Brad added.

"No friends, no colleagues, utter secrecy until we say otherwise. That's part of the deal." Fredricks' voice took on a matter-of-fact tone. "You'll understand why once you have the larger picture."

"How about a nondescript building in the Denver Tech Center?" Fredricks suggested. "There's a six thousand-square-meter building near the highway that has everything you will need—lab space, large open area, LANR, delivery bay, offices, even living space if you're amind." Fredricks projected a holoimage of the building and then walked them through the interior. "Will this work?"

They glanced at each other and nodded.

"Go look it over and then send me a list of everything you will need—I mean everything. Don't be shy about what you might need." Fredricks stood up. "We'll replace the LANR with a five hundred-megawatt unit first thing," he added.

"Why so much power?" Sally asked.

"Because you'll need it."

DENVER—PHOENIX LABS

One hundred kilometers above Denver Spaceport, the Denver Skyport surveyed the Rocky Mountains to the west and beyond to the Nevada deserts, and to the east across the midwest plains to Missouri. As the eastern terminus of the San Francisco Loop, Denver Skyport was a destination for eastbound travelers and a launch point for westbound travelers.

Daphne, Kimberly, Dale, and Fredricks took the maglev from San Francisco's Embarcadero to Pillar Point Socket on the coast where, fifteen minutes later, they boarded a capsule. In ten minutes, a hundred kilometers above San Francisco Bay, they commenced a one-gee, 1,300-kilometer-journey on the eastern rail to Denver Skyport. In thirteen minutes, they slowed to a stop, tilted to vertical, and dropped down the skytower to the Denver Socket in the center of Denver Spaceport. A short maglev ride later, they stood on a DTC—Denver Tech Center—sidewalk looking at the new Phoenix Labs complex.

"Just an hour and ten minutes ago, we were standing on the maglev platform at the San Francisco Embarcadero, and if these guys pull it off," Fredricks said, sweeping an arm across the complex, "soon, we'll just step through a door."

The four mounted the steps to the entrance as Sally and Brad opened the double doors to welcome them.

"We're still putting things in place," Brad said, "but Sally has already set up the basic pieces of our initial foray."

Sally smiled a bit shyly and nodded her assent. They all entered the building and followed her to the only office that was currently functional. Daphne placed herself at the trailing end of the group, taking in everything she could.

Not that long ago, she was the newest staff member of Phoenix Revive Labs, pushing the envelope for transferring human consciousness into an electronic matrix. Now she was embarked on a journey into the unknown—perhaps even the unknowable—that involved not only electronic consciousness, but something else, something larger perhaps than anything she had known. Daphne felt a tingle of excitement right down to her toes.

✷

The makeshift conference table in the conference room looked like it may have once served to hold cans of paint. Everyone grabbed a folding chair and found a place at the table. Fredricks indicated that they should leave a place on each side of the table and then did something with his Link. Shortly, holoimages of Thorpe and Braxton appeared, one in each open space. They were dressed differently than before, but each still displayed an underlying red or blue tone, and Braxton still sported his mustache.

Brad and Sally both stared in unabashed astonishment at the holoimages. As educated products of today, they were entirely familiar with holographic images in all their formats, but the sudden appearance of Thorpe and Braxton was a complete surprise.

Before Fredricks could say anything, Thorpe took the lead. "Welcome to the team, Dr. Nguyen and Dr. Kominsky. We're not a particularly formal bunch, so we're going to address you as Sally and Brad, if that's all right with you." As they nodded, he continued. "I know you already met at the door, but please greet Dr. Daphne O'Bryan, Dr. Dale Ryan, and Kimberly Deveraux. Daphne did her doctorate in math and physics at MIT, Dale did his in electronics at Stanford, and Kimberly, who comes to us from University of Texas, is our face to the world. Everything, and I mean everything, about what we do goes through Kimberly." Thorpe looked at Fredricks. "Jackson, please give Sally and Brad a rundown on myself and Braxton."

"Before I commence," Fredricks said, "I want to remind you of our confidentiality posture. We in this room are the only ones who know about this. For now, we want to keep it this way. Understood?"

Nods all around, even from Daphne, Dale, and Kimberly.

Fredricks then told Sally and Brad about the Icicle, about Thorpe's rejuvenation, about the accidental generation of the duplicate—Braxton, at which point Braxton raised his finger and smiled. Then Fredricks detailed Braxton's time in ServerSky and his discovery of the functioning portals. He told them about the tensors from an unknown source. He also told them about eMax but left the Oort Cloud out of the discussion.

"We are about to commence investigating Casimir Fields," Sally said. "The portals almost have to be some kind of stabilized Morris-Thorn wormhole. It seems a shame to duplicate a lot of research to get where somebody has already been."

"Who knows how long that would take?" Brad added thoughtfully.

"If there were some way we could examine a portal, especially an originating unit, it could save us years of research."

"Years…?" Both Thorpe and Braxton said simultaneously.

"NASA was working on it way back in 2000—Dr. Harold White, I believe," Sally said. "Nobody has built one yet."

Everyone but the new researchers looked at Fredricks. He looked at Thorpe and then Braxton. They both nodded.

Fredricks cleared his throat. "I have not yet told you about another line of research we are following…"

Braxton interrupted, "YOU, Jackson, not we. This is your baby, yours alone, and you should take credit for it."

"Okay...line of research *I* have been following...I told you about eMax. Well, it seemed an obvious next step to move forward with a human volunteer." He held up his hand. "We haven't done it yet, but everything is in place. Why this matters is that..."

Braxton jumped in again. "Let me pick it up here, Jackson."

Fredricks nodded with a smile.

"I know you have not yet fully comprehended it, but Thorpe and I as tensor matrices have capabilities that we find difficult to relate to you guys and gals. We miss certain things like kissing or making love..."

"Or sipping a fine Scotch," Thorpe interrupted.

Everyone chuckled.

"But," Braxton continued, "what we can do is extraordinary." He looked at Sally. "If you, Sally, were eSally, you could examine one of these portals with the greatest intimacy possible, right down to the molecular level." He looked at Brad. "You as eBrad would be able to transmit to yourself as Brad everything necessary to build one of these things right here." He gestured with both pointer fingers at the table. "We, Thorpe and I, are not tagged with a flesh-and-bone counterpart like you would be. That could be a problem, because as soon as we generate eBrad and eSally, those entities will commence their own sentient existence."

"It's a bit difficult to explain," Thorpe said, "but as soon as you separate from your e-counterpart, your timelines begin to separate from your shared past."

"You could terminate your e-self," Braxton said, "but I can tell you from personal experience that your e-self will not let you do that if there is any way to prevent it."

"Let me understand this," Sally said quietly. "You are suggesting that Brad or I, or even both of us, allow you to transfer our conscious-ness into an electronic matrix?"

"Not transfer," Fredricks said, "just duplicate. It's a bit like taking a holograph of you. The resulting holoimage looks just like you, but you remain entirely unchanged."

"Max, come here!" Thorpe said. A moment later, eMax appeared to jump into his lap. "Meet eMax. When you meet his predecessor, Max, you will see that Max is one hundred percent smart Tabby."

"That works for me," Brad said.

"It makes me nervous," Sally said in her soft voice.

Daphne leaned toward Kimberly, whispering in her ear. Kimberly nodded. "How about this?" Daphne said. "I will volunteer as the first live transferee. Give me a few hours to get acclimated, and then we can talk. I'll tell you all about it."

"Make that a couple of days," Braxton said. Thorpe nodded.

LOS ANGELES—PHOENIX LABS

All the Phoenix Labs people, including Max, met in the reception area of the Los Angeles lab, where Thorpe had initially been revived. Thorpe, Braxton, and eMax joined them as holoimages. Max took to Sally immediately, cradling himself in her arms. When Brad reached out to pet him, Max hissed softly, and the big man wisely pulled his hand back.

"You're not afraid of a little pussy?" Kimberly asked, her blue eyes twinkling.

"Give him a chance," Daphne said, laughing. "He'll come around."

Fredricks looked around the group. "Are we ready to make history…again?" he asked.

Fredricks led the way into a scrubbing room. "Caps and gowns, please," he said, "and booties over your shoes. Daphne, please remove your street clothes and shoes first." He shooed Max back into the reception area and proceeded to wash up before entering the lab.

The previous day, Fredricks, along with Daphne and Dale, had set up an operating table, and Daphne and Dale had prepared the matrix formerly occupied by Thorpe.

"Will you have to shave my head?" Daphne asked.

"We will not even have to shave any patches," Fredricks answered. "Just make sure you thoroughly wash your hair tomorrow morning and then cover it with a sterile cloth. That will prevent any infections from today's procedures."

Once in the lab, Kimberly, Sally, and Brad stood back against the wall away from the operating table. Daphne climbed onto the table with Dale's help, and then Dale verified that the matrix and connecting wires were ready.

Fredricks brought a mask to Daphne's nose and mouth. "This is a mild sedative," he said, "much like what you might find at the dentist. You'll be conscious throughout, but relaxed and calm. I'll tighten the head clamp only sufficient to hold your head still. Don't turn or twist, of course." He smiled at her. "Ready?"

Daphne nodded and shortly thereafter drifted off.

Daphne slowly opened her eyes, expecting to see the operating table lights above her, but instead, she was surrounded by a white fog. She seemed to be resting on a spongy substance that yielded when she moved her arms and legs. Off in the distance, she heard a male voice calling her name, "Daphne…Daphne…," but she couldn't be sure, and she drifted away on a cloud.

An eternity later, (or was it just a few minutes?), Daphne opened her eyes to the persistent sound of her name echoing through the fog. She tried to reach out, but something held her arms close to her body, and the sound of her name came close to her ears. She opened her mouth to say something but found warm lips pressing against hers while a sense of peace and calm coursed through her body. As the lips against hers parted, her peace and calm morphed into intense urgency centered between her legs.

Daphne tried to speak, but the muffled sound was swallowed by the intensity surrounding her. As she yielded to her feelings, she sensed something merge with her thoughts, melt into her body, while soft tentacles touched her mind.

"Daphne…?"

"Thorpe, is that you?"

"Daphne…?"

She felt her heart beat faster as she began to realize her circumstances. "Thorpe…am I…?" She felt the tentacles pull back.

"You are. We are in the matrix you and Dale prepared. Can you bring things into focus?"

"I'm trying," Daphne said, struggling to speak the words. "How long?"

"Not very," Thorpe said.

Daphne felt him withdrawing slightly. She felt warm and fuzzy. "What did you do?" she asked.

"I did a partial merge to help you over the initial shock," he said quietly. "Can you find my hand?"

She reached out and felt him take hold of her hand. She couldn't see him, but his hand felt warm and real. She still felt like she was lying on a soft surface, but he pulled gently and persistently so that soon she was standing, and the fog dissipated. The bed-like surface disappeared, and she found her feet resting on a firm, slightly giving surface. She was dressed in a flowing white gown with bare feet and red hair cascading over her shoulders and down her back. Standing before her with a broad smile, Thorpe reached out and pulled her to him. He was strong but gentle, and she melted into his arms. It was just as she had imagined it so many times in her apartment.

After another eternity, he released her, took her shoulders in his hands, and locked eyes with her. "You know where you are, right?"

She nodded.

"How do you feel?"

"Fine, I guess," she said. "How much time has passed?"

"A while," Thorpe said. "Time doesn't mean a lot in here." He dropped his hands and took hers in his. "Ready to go for a walk?"

"Okay, but first…how can I see you, and where did my outfit come from?"

"I don't know to the first, and I guess that's how you see yourself to the second," he said with a warm smile. "Coming?"

He led her down a tunnel into the GlobalNet. To Daphne, it looked like she was at the edge of a vast river, but she intuitively understood that she was looking at dataflow. She followed Thorpe somewhat hesitatingly into the flow, down several branches, and finally into a quiet, enclosed space.

"Home-sweet-home," Thorpe said. "You know this place. We're in the MIT databank beneath Fairchild Building.

SERVER SKY—LEO, GEOSYNCHRONOUS & EARTH-MOON L2

"Make love to me!" eDaphne insisted as they settled into the MIT lair, "like you did when I first awakened."

"But...but...I didn't..." Thorpe stuttered. "I called your name, I helped you orient yourself to the matrix, I even merged with you for a bit to speed up the process, but lovemaking...I don't know how to do that."

"Well, that's what it felt like to me," she said with a pout. "So, let's merge like before. You take the lead."

"Okay," Thorpe said, "but let's ease into it. We don't want to lose our individual identities."

"How romantic of you," eDaphne said, green eyes twinkling.

How utterly surprising, Thorpe thought, *that I see her exactly as I did in the flesh.* eDaphne dropped her gown. *Just like I remember, but this time, I can touch and feel her.* He felt aroused, knowing full-well that it was impossible. His clothes vanished at that thought. Thorpe pulled eDaphne toward him, lifted her, and she wrapped her legs around his waist. He found himself entering her, and as he did, he was overwhelmed with a oneness, a sense of sharing as he had never before experienced.

Thorpe lost track of time as they both explored each other with unparalleled intimacy—soul-to-soul as face-to-face. Release, when it came, was mutual and entirely unexpected. One moment they were one, and the next, they were again two entities staring at each other in fascination.

"That was...that was..." eDaphne said, panting.

"Wow!" was all that Thorpe could utter.

※

eDaphne pulled herself together, dressed in a red and black pantsuit that complemented her copper hair—*how did I do that?* she asked herself—and reached out to Thorpe. "That was wonderful, and we are going to do it again," she said, "but now I have a lot to learn, Teacher." She gave Thorpe a big smile, wondering *why does this all seem so real?*

That's when eMax jumped into her lap, purring loudly and rubbing her face. "Did you miss me, Max? Did you miss me, Boy?"

"I would say so," Thorpe said. "He hangs out mostly with me, but from time to time, he shows up with Braxton. He knows his way around GlobalNet and ServerSky as well as we do."

They both laughed, and eDaphne gently chucked eMax's chin.

"Remember our discussion of Cauchy vectors and Banach spaces?" Thorpe asked. "You've had precious little time to look into yourself," Thorpe grinned at her, "but as you do, you should begin to see the structures we talked about. Can you see those tensors vanishing to points within your space?"

eDaphne nodded slowly.

"Cauchy vectors," Thorpe said. "The space you occupy is defined by the location of these vanishing points, your Banach space. "Now, reach out to me physically, and pay close attention to what you are doing."

She did, and her eyes widened. "It's a…"

"Tensor," he prompted. He showed her their structure. "You did it just like I did, a bundle of straw tensors tied together with one or two more. Braxton found a better way." Thorpe showed her.

"Ring tensors connected by several straws," eDaphne said. "Like this," she showed him, duplicating one.

"You can send these anywhere there is sufficient infrastructure to support your tensor," Thorpe sold her.

eDaphne was an eager and fast learner. Thorpe took her through the laser pipe into ServerSky LEO and then to geosynchronous orbit.

eMax playfully brought them a foreign tensor, and then Thorpe took eDaphne through one of the portals to the Earth-Moon L2 swarm.

Finally, Thorpe took eDaphne by the hand and led her through the portal at the center of the Earth-Moon L2 swarm. As they exited the portal into the Oort Cloud, Thorpe immediately hustled her into Braxton's personal swarm.

"That," Thorpe said, pointing to a very bright star, "is the sun. We are a hundred thousand AUs from the Sun, over one-and-a-half lightyears, and we did it by walking through what amounts to a door."

"It takes my breath away, so to speak," eDaphne said. Then she turned to Thorpe with agitation. "Something just touched me," she said. "Was it you?"

"No."

"It was like a feather sweeping across my consciousness," she said. "Light and airy, almost like a puff of air."

EARTH—GLOBAL NET

"So, since we merged memories, you understand the blockchain nature of modern money?" Thorpe asked Braxton. "You know that we've got more money than God, tied up in Bitcoin that hardly anyone uses anymore?"

"I think I know where you are taking this, but let me hear your thoughts."

"First," Thorpe said, "I think we should create a new blockchain currency. We establish two chains initially, one for you and one for me. Then we transfer half the bitcoin to each of us. We each find discreet accountants around the world, and set up individual national currency accounts all over the place. We have these guys invest on our behalf to keep the pot growing. To keep things fair, we contribute equally to joint projects."

"It works for me," Braxton said. "Let's do it!"

※

"I need you to set up an entirely original, unbreakable currency blockchain," Thorp's holoimage said to the scruffy man behind a messy desk in a small apartment in a crowded Palo Alto, California, complex. "I want it unregistered, untraceable, with no back doors."

"I can do that," Rodney Bailey said, "but it will cost you."

"How about five hundred thousand now and a million upon completion?" Thorpe asked.

"Really? That works."

"How do I know there is no back door?"

"You gotta trust me—there's no way to check."

"When will it be ready," Thorpe asked.

"Gimme thirty days."

✳

"What is your annual income?" Thorpe asked Bailey thirty days later after taking delivery of the new blockchain system.

"'Bout a hundred fifty. Depends on what gigs I get." Bailey grinned. "This year just became a good year!"

"Would you work for me exclusively for the right price?" Thorpe asked.

"Why?"

"So I can keep tabs on you and what you do," Thorpe said, "since you can't prove there's no back door."

"What would I do?"

"Programming, complex programming...whatever I need."

"What if I do something on my own?" Bailey wanted to know.

"We can work it out."

"How much?"

"A million a year plus expenses...and a piece of the action."

"Deal."

Thorpe put him in contact with Daphne.

✳

Thorpe's holoimage looked across the polished desk of the Swiss banker. "I want you to handle a hundred million," he told the banker, "discreetly. Keep it growing conservatively. I'll draw upon it from time to time."

They signed the deal.

✳

Braxton's holoimage looked across an uncluttered desk at the Cayman Islands banker. "Yes," he said, "you heard me right, one hundred million."

⁕

Between them, Thorpe and Braxton visited 200 bankers ranging from Ireland and the Isle of Man to Singapore and Bermuda. They deposited over a trillion dollars in secure blockchain accounts that could not be associated with either of them or anything they were doing.

LOS ANGELES—PHOENIX REVIVE LABS

Dr. Jackson Fredricks looked up from his desk as two holoimages appeared in his office. Thorpe appeared seated in an easy-chair, and mustachioed Braxton was standing leaning comfortably against a counter.

"Gentlemen," Fredricks said reflexively.

Both of the holoimages were dressed casually, but one seemed to have a red aura, whereas the other was more blue. "Thorpe," Fredricks said, nodding to the sitting image. "Braxton," he said, nodding to the one with the mustache. *They could be twins*, he thought. *No! They're more than that.* "Thanks for the mustache and the red-blue overtones," Fredricks said. "I'm not sure I could tell you guys part, otherwise." Fredricks stood up. "I would offer you coffee, but…" He grinned. "What's up?"

"We need your advice," Thorpe said.

"You need *my* advice? How does that work?" Fredricks sat back down.

Thorpe and Braxton proceeded to explain their thoughts to Fredricks about portals and power sources. Fredricks pulled information from his Link, studied it for a while, and then looked up at both of them.

"You're right about the power source," Fredricks said. "A portable LANR won't do it, but a large power station like the one powering the Moon outpost or the Mars Station should handle a portal, but only if the separation is reasonable."

"Any idea what *reasonable* is?" Braxton asked.

"Honestly, I don't have a clue," Fredricks said. *And that's the honest truth*, he told himself silently. "I know a couple of postdocs from Colorado School of Mines who might give this whole thing a go, provided they had sufficient funding and an untethered head of steam. The groundwork is there, the goal is obtainable—obviously, and they are not so indoctrinated in what must be that they can't make their own roadmap."

Fredricks watched Thorpe and Braxton exchange looks and decided that behind that, a great deal of communication took place.

"Set it up," Thorpe said. "We'll fund it through an account linked to Revive."

✸

Thorpe and Braxton conducted another rapid consult, and then Braxton explained their thoughts to Fredricks. "What do you know about ServerSky?"

"What we all learn in school, I guess. Solar-powered, self-repairing, connects to the GlobalNet with laser trunks, but also communicates directly to individual Links. Technically...not much really. Why?"

"I've spent a lot of time out in ServerSky," Braxton said. "There are a lot of things you don't know; there are a lot of things nobody knows. We're still checking that out. We'll let you know when we know more fully." He paused and looked at Thorpe. "There's a thinsat swarm at Earth-Moon L2. Did you know about that?"

"Earth-Moon L2...you're kidding! Why put one there?"

"What's special about Earth-Moon L2?" Braxton asked.

"You can't see it from Earth, or Earth from it. That's why it makes no sense."

"Listen to what you just said," Braxton prompted.

"So, Earth doesn't know it's there," Fredricks said, raising his eyebrows. "Then, who?"

"We don't know yet," Braxton said, "but we're working on it."

Thorpe and Braxton exchanged glances.

"What do you know about the Oort Cloud?" Braxton asked.

"Nothing, really…that it's out there, I guess."

"See what you can find out," Braxton told him. "Not from the GlobalNet so much as from your colleagues. Find out what they know that isn't available to us."

"Sure…I have a couple of astrophysics colleagues…a couple of solar system guys as well. I'll see what they can tell me. Can you tell me why?"

"Not yet," Braxton said. "We're not trying to hide anything. We just don't yet know what we know. We need a framework, and we're hoping you can supply that."

"Since we're doing so well," Thorpe said, "let's broach the next subject. You know, don't you, that ServerSky produces its own power for everything it does?"

"Hadn't really thought about it, but I guess it's obvious."

"The thinsats serve several functions," Braxton said. "They calculate, of course, they maneuver for best angle for transmission to each other and to Earth, and for best angle to collect sunlight, and all of it is powered by their solar collectors."

"Do you know the amount of available power from the Sun at Earth's orbit?" Thorpe asked.

Fredricks quickly checked his Link and answered, "Thirteen hundred watts per square meter on average. I'd say that's a lot of power."

"Let me put it into perspective," Braxton said. "The thinsat swarm I found at Earth-Moon L2 is a hundred-klick-wide disk. The thinsat density is about one per square meter. At fifty percent conversion efficiency, they produce five gigawatts."

Fredricks sat at his desk quietly for nearly a minute. Then he whistled softly and said, "That's equivalent to the output of twenty-five hundred of the largest LANR plants we've got." He shook his head in amazement. "I never figured…"

"So," Braxton said, "I found portals from the Earth-Moon L2 swarm to several LEO ServerSky locations, several geosynchronous locations, and several to various Earthside locations. I also found portals between geosynchronous and LEO locations and between them and Earthside. The portals originating in geosynchronous and LEO locations are powered from the Earth-Moon L2 swarm through a portal dedicated to power transmission. There appear to be no power cables passing through the portal, so I assume some kind of capacitive transmission."

"That's a significant infrastructure," Fredricks said. "Who could possibly be behind this?"

"Or what," Thorpe said quietly. "There is one more portal we need to discuss." He looked at Braxton.

"In the middle of the Earth-Moon L2 swarm is a portal that is not powered by the swarm," Braxton said. "It gets its power from the other end."

"And..." Fredricks asked quietly.

"The Oort Cloud," Thorpe answered.

"While you get your people onto the development of a portal," Thorpe said to Fredricks, "we need to produce the power infrastructure the portals will need. I can see no reason to alert Earth authorities to our activities. This means we do things where they can't be seen from Earth.

"Basically, we're talking about thinsat swarms in two places. Earth-Sun L3, the other side of the Sun from the Earth, and Mercury-Sun L1—Mercury-Sun Lagrangian Point One, between the Sun and Mercury."

"That will take some doing," Fredricks said, with a soft whistle.

"We've crunched the numbers," Braxton said. "A two hundred-klick swarm at Earth-Sun L3 will produce about twenty terawatts, and a one-hundred-klick swarm at Mercury-Sun L1 will produce about five terawatts." Braxton smiled. "That's the equivalent of about thirteen thousand large LANR plants."

"You can verify our calculations if you wish," Thorpe said.

Chapter Twelve

DENVER—PHOENIX LABS

"Hi Sis!" eDaphne said to Daphne with a wink and an air kiss. "You were right about Thorpe. I'll fill you in privately."

Thorpe managed to blush while Braxton said, "Okay, Guys and Gals, let's get it together."

The conference table was still the old paint-covered worktable from their previous meeting. This time nine places were occupied, the original eight, plus eDaphne, dressed in a black pantsuit to offset her red hair.

"Bring us up to date, Jackson," Thorpe said.

"As you can see," Fredricks said, gesturing toward eDaphne, "we were quite successful. I really don't have a lot to say. Thorpe and I arranged for him to be in the immediate vicinity when eDaphne awakened. They can better tell you about that than I."

"It's pretty personal, actually," Thorpe said, blushing again, but I can tell you that eDaphne had a much smoother transition than I had what seems so long ago now." He smiled at both Daphne and her electronic sister. "I had to figure everything out for myself," Thorpe said, "whereas Daphne already knew my history and so was far better prepared for the transition. Furthermore, she and I have had long conversations about what I went through, so she was thoroughly prepared for what happened." He looked at eDaphne. "Why don't you give us your perspective. I think that's what most interests Sally and Brad."

Both Sally and Brad nodded as eDaphne picked up the story. "I suspect that coming out of the haze of the transition, each person will interpret the events according to his or her own personal history and perspective. Because you two must understand the details, I'm going to get a bit personal." She smiled at Sally and reached out as if to take her hand. "When I first met Thorpe, I really flipped for him, and I was pretty sure he was into me too. I was frustrated that there seemed no way to consummate the relationship." She stopped and took a deep breath. "This must have been on my mind as I went under sedation. When I began to waken, I didn't realize that I was eDaphne. The very first sensations I had were highly sexual. Thorpe swears that all he did was call my name and reach out to me, but I can tell you that what I experienced was intensely erotic." Nobody said anything, but there were smiles around the table. "That may say more about me than anything else, but I think you guys," she pointed at Sally and Brad, "need to know about this."

"Wow!" Kimberly said. "When do I get to do this?" She looked at Braxton.

"Focus, people," Fredricks said. Looking at Sally and Brad, he asked, "Do either of you have any questions?"

"Daphne...I mean eDaphne," Sally said, "have you experienced any negatives?"

"Not really. It's pretty overwhelming at first, but Thorpe made the transition much easier. For me, it took a few minutes to get the hang of moving with or against a particular data stream. Oh...be sure to learn how to handle your tensors first thing."

At that comment, Kimberly's face dropped.

eDaphne giggled and said, "Don't worry about it, Kimberly. You don't have to know higher math to use them. It becomes instinctive almost immediately." She turned back to Sally. "Any other questions?"

"I'm sure I do, but I have to think about it for a while first."

eDaphne turned to Brad. "What about you, Brad?"

"What if I want to come back? I mean, what if I want to return to flesh-and-bone?"

"Let me answer that," Fredricks said. "Right now, that's not possible. I've got some people working on the underlying concept. Obviously, one would need an available receptacle—a body without sentience. In principle, we can do this, but there is a huge ethical element that we have not yet overcome here in America. In several countries—perhaps, but not here." He paused and looked around the table. "The other option would be to transfer an e-version back to the flesh-and-bone original. We have no idea what that would entail. For all I know, the result could be a blithering idiot."

"We could try it with Max and eMax," Thorpe said.

"I don't think so!" came simultaneously from both Daphne and eDaphne.

Chuckles around the table.

"I want to put that subject on the back burner," Fredricks said. "Is this a deal-breaker for you, Brad?"

"No," Brad answered slowly, "I just wanted to hear what you had to say. Based on Daphne's experience, I guess I'm looking forward to it." He grinned broadly.

"How about you, Sally?" Fredricks looked at her with warmth.

"I guess…" she looked down at her lap. "I guess it's the only way we can get where we want to go."

EARTH-MOON L2—THE SWARM

A week following the Denver meeting, eDaphne watched eSally and eBrad approach a portal in the Earth-Moon L2 swarm, while she hovered nearby with Thorpe and Braxton. Next to them, eMax purred quietly, snuggled to one of the strange tensors.

"Basically," eBrad said to no one in particular, "this is like a door into another room. It just happens that the other room is somewhere between four hundred eleven thousand and four hundred eighty-two thousand klicks away from here, depending on where the linked portal is in GEO at the moment. This portal face and the one in GEO are congruous."

"And consider," eSally added, "that the connecting wormhole is in constant motion with respect to normal space since the origin—here—and the destination—there—are in constant motion with respect to the solar system reference space, and relative to each other."

"I have a question," eDaphne said. "These portal pairs are all over the place, crisscrossing each other, passing through each other as their relative orbital positions change. What is the architecture of the connecting wormholes? Do they end up as an infinitely twisted rat's nest?"

"We haven't completely worked out the math," eBrad said, "but we think they simply pass through each other like beams of sunlight."

eSally nodded. "Let's get on each side of the portal," she said to eBrad. "You take the dependent end, and I'll stay here. Then let's insert tensors into the mechanism from each side and see what happens."

eBrad grunted as he slipped through the portal into GEO, leaving a tensor behind to facilitate communication. "Are you ready, Girl?" he said.

"I am," eSally answered.

eDaphne watched carefully as eSally inserted a tensor into the portal so that it did not merely pass through, but instead merged with the surrounding structure. From the other side, although it was not apparent to eDaphne, eBrad did the same thing.

"The amount of power being sucked into this device is impressive," eSally said. "The power is being used to create an extended Casimir Field and keep it open."

"Can you duplicate it?" Thorpe asked.

"It looks like it," eSally answered. "I need to examine more closely to see exactly how the Casimir Field is generated."

"This end is different," eBrad said. "It looks like…" Contact with him ceased as the Earth-Moon L2 portal face assumed a silvery solid appearance, and his tensor collapsed and disintegrated.

SERVER SKY—GEO

e**B**rad inserted a tensor into the dependent portal framework and began poking around. There wasn't much to see. Power flowed from the other side, but a relatively small amount compared to what eSally said was flowing into the originating portal. A portal mechanism was virtually nonexistent. All he could find was an insubstantial energy ring. He wrapped his tensor around the ring when it suddenly collapsed. His connection with his Earth-Moon L2 tensor truncated. He was alone and isolated.

Without moving, eBrad considered his options. *I know of at least one other portal, and I know where Braxton's personal swarm is located.* He checked his surroundings. *Must be in another GEO swarm. So much for that.*

eBrad examined his surroundings more carefully, and that's when he found the 5-centimeter silvery disk that seemed to be electrostatically attached to a thinsat. He latched onto it electronically and scrutinized it. One side was a dull, silvery color, like a coin that had been in circulation for a while. The other was deep, featureless black. The silvery side possessed a faint electric field; the black side was electronically featureless. His intellect told him that the disk had to be connected in some way to the portal. He carefully examined the structure of the electric field on the silvery face. As he gently stroked it with an electrical current, a space next to the disk expanded to become the dependent end of the portal.

Remaining where he was, eBrad sent a tensor through the renewed portal and told the others that they needed to join him for a demonstration.

Everyone breathed a virtual sigh of relief and passed one-by-one through the portal, followed by eMax and the strange tensor. eDaphne connected with Thorpe and Braxton as they settled into the GEO Swarm. "What's going on?" she asked.

"I suspect eBrad found a way to shut down the portal from the dependent end," Braxton said.

eBrad placed himself so that he had a commanding view of the others. "I think," he said, "that I've found a significant piece of the puzzle." He showed them the disk and stroked its face electrically. The portal collapsed. He handed it around with the admonition not to stroke the silvery face.

As the disk passed by eDaphne, she examined it closely. The backside was completely featureless. She turned it toward the Sun—no reflection of any kind. She rotated it at an angle to the Sun—still wholly featureless. She spoke up. "I think the backside absorbs all incident light."

eSally reached for the disk and looked closely at the backside, duplicating what eDaphne had just done. "I agree," she said. "No reflection at all."

eBrad retrieved the disk and opened the portal. He moved to the back of the portal and then motioned the others to join him. When eDaphne looked at where the back should have been, she could not see any indication of the portal at all. It was if the portal were not there. She moved to the front and sent a tensor through. Then she moved to the back and sent a tensor through the space occupied by the portal. It passed through the space and met her at the front. eDaphne showed the others.

"Hey, guys," eSally said. "This is all interesting, but we need to get back to finding out how these things work. eBrad and I have a good handle on our new environment. We know how to get from here to there, and we've got backups in place should anything go wrong." She gave everyone a virtual shy smile. "You guys need to leave us alone to do our investigation."

DENVER—PHOENIX LABS

Sally and Brad sat at another previously used table, but this time in their lab. While the table left something to be desired, the equipment in the lab was as modern as tomorrow, the best money could buy. Joining at the table as holoimages, eSally and eBrad were in deep discussion with their flesh-and-bone counterparts.

"The portals are definitely based on a stabilized version of a Morris-Thorn wormhole, which is itself based upon the Einstein-Rosen bridge," eSally said. "Originally, they postulated using exotic matter—or non-baryonic matter—to create the bridge, but back in the early twenty-first century, NASA's Harold White found a way to do this with normal matter." She smiled with her hand in front of her mouth. "That's what these do. The portal is established by separating two plates holding a Casimir field, applying continuously greater power as the plates separate. That's what stroking the disk does," she added.

"When the Casimir field is initially established," eBrad said, "a mechanism within the portal infrastructure generates the disk, which we are calling a hyper-disc from now on. The hyper-disc must be physically transported to whatever point the portal will connect."

"We have deposited detailed 3-D diagrams and circuits for all the elements into your main computer," eSally said. "You should be able to construct a prototype from these."

"So," Brad said, "you're certain that you found everything we will need? What about the power requirements?"

eBrad answered. "Your LANR will handle at least two portals in the general cislunar region, but beyond that or more than those will require a lot more power."

"Here's the cool thing," eSally said. "The Earth-Moon L2 swarm generates about five terawatts. The power is collected and supplied to the various portals for access to GEO, LEO, and even Earth. One of the portals is reserved for power trunks that feed power to GEO and LEO portals."

"Could we bring one of those trunks through a portal to here?" Sally asked.

"In principle, sure," eSally said, "but we know virtually nothing about the existing system, nothing about the overall power distribution, not to mention that we know nothing about who made it or its purpose."

"I don't disagree," eBrad said, "but what about the unidentified tensor that seems to accompany eMax everywhere he goes?"

"We might want to ask Thorpe or Braxton about that," eSally said shyly.

"So, we leave it alone," Brad said. "We copy, we duplicate, but we don't disturb."

Everyone agreed.

"Let's turn to, then," Brad said. "Sally and I will work together with Thorpe and Braxton on the manufacturing infrastructure, and you guys hang out, help us where you can, and keep us honest. That okay?"

Everyone consented. Two chairs slid back, the chairs in the holoimages vanished, and Sally with Brad turned toward the lab bench while eSally and eBrad hovered as holoimages.

✳

A week later, Thorpe and Braxton dropped in on Sally and Brad as they assembled the finishing touches of their breadboard portal. Electronic elements spread out over the lab bench, culminating in a transparent doorway-size frame standing on the floor next to the end of the bench. eSally and eBrad hovered in the background.

"Where's Jackson?" Thorpe asked.

"He's tied up in LA," Brad said. "He's watching on his Link… decided not to appear holographically."

Daphne, Kimberly, and Dale stood off to the side. eDaphne hovered in the background with eSally and eBrad.

"Everybody ready?" Sally asked. After a pregnant pause, she threw the power switch.

At first, there was no visible reaction at all. Then the space within the frame began to sparkle. This went on for several minutes.

"What's the power draw?" eBrad asked.

Sally told him. "It's still increasing," she added.

He nodded and looked at eSally.

Then, without any prior indication, the space within the frame turned the same dull silver that the hyper-discs displayed.

"Power draw has stabilized," Sally said.

Brad walked behind the frame. "From here, there is no frame," he said and picked up a hyper-disc from the edge of the lab bench, handing it to Sally. "Here, Sally, you do it."

She stepped to the other side of the room and stroked the silvery side of the hyper-disc. As a portal opened in front of her, the silver face of the doorway frame near Brad dissolved into a view of Sally. As she walked around the room with the hyper-disc in her hand, the slave portal followed her like a puppy.

She stopped and looked like she was about to step through the portal. Thorpe said sharply, "Stop!" He smiled at her. "I know how confident you are of what you have built, but we need to do several tests before committing a human life to the process."

"Not a process," Brad muttered, "it's a portal. It either is or isn't." He pulled a pen out of his pocket and tossed it through the portal to Sally. "Catch, Sally!" Then he grinned at Thorpe and stepped through the portal.

DENVER—PHOENIX LABS

"What's your status, Daphne?" Fredricks asked, looking directly at her holoimage. Since he had moved his entire operation from Los Angeles to the Denver Tech Center, he found he was spending a lot of time talking with insubstantial holoimages, making things happen thousands of kilometers distant.

"You should have delivery of the habitat this morning," Daphne answered.

Despite his familiarity with the technology and his nearly everyday use, Fredricks still marveled at how real the holoimages were. Visually, Daphne was as real as if she were in the room with him. Missing were her smell and the sound of her feet on the floor. He stepped into the Greater Hall, one of two large halls on the ground floor, as Sally and Brad joined him.

"Hi, Daphne," Sally said with a friendly wave. "The habitat just arrived," she added, looking at Fredricks as Brad carried it into Greater Hall and rolled it out on the floor.

Dale's holoimage appeared. "Hey," he said, "I wanted to watch you guys work."

"Me, too!" Kimberly said, appearing next to Dale.

Brad inflated the dome-shaped, fifty-square-meter habitat. Its thin, strong, flexible, transparent polymer wall billowed up, waving slightly. On one side, a flexible lock extended into the room—two meters high, two meters deep, and a-meter-and-a-half wide. Sally pushed her way through the magnetically sealed outer curtain and then through the inner one.

"Will that seal hold at Earth-Moon L2?" Brad asked.

"The pressure will be an oxygen-enriched half-atmosphere," Daphne said. "Like atop a six thousand-meter mountain, but more oxygen," she added.

"Once we get the portal established, we'll bring in more substantial lock doors," Daphne said.

Sally checked the inside of the habitat carefully, looking for any flaws that could potentially cause it to fail in space. As she exited, Dale said, "Someone, please tell me again why we need this habitat. With a portal at Earth-Moon L2, all a person has to do for anything at all, like taking a leak or grabbing a PBJ, is pass through the portal. We have the portal on this side terminate in a lock, so we don't start sucking air from here to there."

"Murphy's Law has been part of my life all my life," Thorpe said. Braxton nodded with a wide grin. "What could happen?" Thorpe asked.

Daphne began counting off possible things on her fingers. "Power loss, component failure, destruction of this complex..." She considered silently. "Even whoever or whatever controls the other portals turning out to be a bad guy..."

"Okay...okay," Dale said, "you convinced me."

"Alright then," Fredricks said, "let's collapse the habitat and pack it for transport to Earth-Moon L2."

Dale's holoimage moved to two large containers against the far wall, one red and the other blue. A pipe led from each into the lock where they connected to two coiled hoses, one red and the other blue, each fitted with pressure quick-disconnects that were distinctly different from each other. Next to the hoses, two cylindrical bladders nearly as long as the capsule, one red and one blue, hung on the bulkhead.

Brad stepped over to Dale and said, "Hypergolic fuel elements. UDMH—unsymmetrical dimethylhydrazine," he pointed to the red container, "and nitrogen tetroxide," he pointed to the blue one. "Once the portal opens in LEO, someone will pass through, attach the bladders, and fill them. That takes manhandling, which means one of the guys. Jackson is the boss, so that leaves me and you. I'm obviously more able to manhandle that stuff, so..." He grinned at Dale.

"Not if you plan on wearing a spacesuit," Daphne said. "We don't have anything that will fit you."

"But…but, you measured me and everything," Brad stammered.

"Hasn't arrived yet," Daphne said. "Sorry!"

"Okay, Buddy," Brad said to Dale with a rueful grin. "Let me walk you through it."

After forty-five minutes of evacuating, folding, pressing, squeezing, and stuffing, Sally, Brad, and Fredricks, had securely packed the habitat into a light-weight cylinder. That cylinder also contained a compressed gas bottle with a sufficient volume of oxygen-rich air to inflate the habitat and maintain a person for several hours. The cylindrical capsule was equipped with three sets of hypergolic thrusters to enable local maneuvering. An electronic sensor on the capsule skin was designed to allow a tensor from one of the e-members to gain access to the interior. The hyper-disc was packed just under the spring-loaded endcap that could be triggered by a signal from a tensor inside the capsule.

Fredricks took the 15-kilo, 1.5-meter-long capsule to the Denver Spaceport, where he observed it being loaded onto a standard cargo pallet and watched its launch up the skytower. From there, it would travel to Pillar Point and then launch eastward into LEO on a standard transport pallet.

Chapter Thirteen

SERVER SKY—LEO—GEO—EARTH-MOON L2

"There it is," Thorpe said to eDaphne as the transport pallet released the habitat capsule into LEO. "Synching your tensor is not as easy as you might think. Remember, it's moving at over seventy-eight hundred meters per second."

eDaphne acknowledged. She was still getting the hang of moving her tensors through the swarm. Moving herself was easy right from the start, but purposefully moving a tensor was more of a challenge. She had to remind herself that a tensor was not actually a physical thing, but a structured, coherent energy packet that could be described mathematically as a tensor. If the capsule were moving through the swarm directly, latching on would be a piece of cake, but the ServerSky LEO swarm was several klicks above the 160-kilometer-high orbit of the capsule. "I'm ready," she told Thorpe.

Using their combined efforts through several tensors, they pushed a substantial thinsat finger from the swarm down to the capsule's orbit. It took them the better part of ninety minutes, so that by the time the capsule completed its first orbit, they had their tensors waiting at the fingertip. As the capsule passed, eDaphne slipped her autonomous tensor into the capsule, followed by Thorpe's.

"Are you ready?" Thorpe asked.

"Let's do it!" eDaphne said as Thorpe's tensor activated the spring-loaded cover.

A puff of moist air left the cylinder. eDaphne's tensor stroked the silvery face electronically, and a portal opened, its base clinging to the side of the capsule.

✳

Kimberly helped Dale don his flexible space suit, checked his backpack and connections, and then carried the transparent helmet to him. As she brought it over his head, she kissed him quickly, and then brought the helmet down to the locking ring where she twisted it to set the lock. Dale grinned at her and then turned to the airlock entrance that seemed to lead into the wall.

Brad approached him. "Good luck, Buddy!" he said, gripping Dale's suited forearms.

"I'm sorry it's not you," Dale said, inwardly glad he was the one.

He opened the hatch, stepped inside, and closed and dogged the hatch behind him. Standing to the side of the other hatch against the wall, Dale attached a safety line to an eye-bolt, and braced himself securely before activating the opening mechanism. As the hatch opened, the air in the lock rushed through the portal into space, tugging at him as it did so. Dale switched his safety line to an eyebolt on the outside of the hatch and stepped through. Instantly, his body told him he was falling. He felt his gorge rise as his brain went into panic mode. Then he took a deep breath, and his intellect took charge as he started to examine how his body reacted to freefall. The panic subsided, and his stomach settled as he began to enjoy the feeling.

Technically, he thought, *I just gained a whole bunch of angular momentum. I started with the momentum of a rotating Earth, and now I have the momentum of an LEO satellite in orbit. But I feel fine. I'm just not sure I understand Brad's explanation that the MERT Portal equalizes momentum both ways. Where does it come from or go to?* Dale looked around. The Earth stretched beneath him, 160 kilometers down and 1,400 out. Almost directly below, a massive storm swirled over the North Atlantic, and ahead, the coast of equatorial Africa shimmered through the haze as he and the nighttime terminator approached each other on a collision course at over 8,300 m/s. Overhead, like a glittering river of colored gemstones, the Milky Way stretched across the sky. Awestruck by his surroundings, Dale reluctantly pulled his attention back to matters at hand.

"I'm at the cylinder, safe and sound," Dale said. His signal was picked up by a transceiver on the outside of the lock and transmitted to the others waiting inside the large lab space at Phoenix.

"We got that," Fredricks said. "Attach the holocam to the capsule so we can follow your activities."

"Sorry, I forgot."

After attaching a remotely controlled holocam near the front end of the capsule, Dale grabbed the red and blue bladders from inside the lock and attached them to the sides of the capsule, connecting feedlines to the rocket motors. He pulled the red hose from the lock, pressed the quick-connect to the red bladder fill-valve—the only one it fit—and watched the bladder fill with UDMH. Then he brought out the blue hose and charged the blue bladder with nitrogen tetroxide. He checked the connectors, ensuring that they could close the valve should the hoses be cut. Doing these things in freefall came easy to him, partly because of the design, but also because he seemed to be a natural.

"Fueled and go for GEO," Dale said.

"Acknowledged," Fredricks said. "eDaphne and Thorpe, are you guys ready for the transfer?"

"Let me make sure everyone understands what we are doing here," Brad said. "Traditional inter-orbit transfer demands conservation of fuel and high efficiency. That's why we use Hohmann Transfer Orbits. You pick your spot and accelerate in the correct direction with the right acceleration for the proper time. You end up in an elliptical orbit with a perigee at your original orbit height and an apogee at the new orbit height. You can stay in this orbit forever, but normally you do a circularizing burn at apogee to make the new orbit your home. Traditional rockets lose a molecule of mass for every molecule of fuel burned, so things get complicated. Because of our portal, we can keep the fuel bladders topped up, so we are dealing with a straight constant-acceleration model. Have I totally confused everyone?"

Kimberly raised her hand. "Can you say that so a journalist can understand it?"

Everyone chuckled, and Sally said, "We just go from LEO to Earth-Moon L2 at a constant acceleration without stopping off for gas along the way."

Kimberly grinned and thanked her.

"We're ready," Thorpe said, "but we need to wait for the transfer window…in twenty-three minutes."

"So, why do we need a launch window if we are pointing and driving all the way?" Kimberly asked.

"You've got a point," Brad answered, "but if something fails and we lose our fuel source, it would be nice to be at the ideal spot pointed in the ideal direction to morph into a Hohmann transfer."

Dale gave one last awestruck look around his LEO position, stepped back through the lock, bracing as full gravity grabbed him, and cycled into the lab at Phoenix, staggering slightly as his body adjusted to gravity again. "The view is unbelievable," he said as he stripped off his spacesuit.

eBrad sent a tensor to Phoenix and then through the portal and the capsule's electronic gateway into the capsule to monitor the autopilot, joining eDaphne's and Thorpe's tensors.

Twenty-two minutes later, the capsule's autopilot pointed the capsule at the spot where Earth-Moon L2 would be in 11 hours and 53 minutes, and fired the rocket.

eDaphne and Thorpe accompanied the capsule during its transit through the LEO swarm, and then they skipped through a laser pipe to GEO to await its arrival. eMax stayed close by the entire time, but eSally and eBrad chose to spend their time back in the GlobalNet working on the next stages of the project.

※

About two-and-a-half hours later, the capsule whipped through GEO passing eDaphne and Thorpe at nearly eight-and-a-half kilometers per second. eMax scampered after it, but gave up when he ran out of thinsats. He looked around, apparently thinking he could use one of the mystery portals to follow the capsule.

"Come here, Max!" eDaphne said. eMax turned back and snuggled in her lap while Thorpe scratched between his eyes. Thorpe's hand touched eDaphne's, and she tingled as they merged for a moment. "Mmm…that's something I still need to get used to," she murmured. "I like it out here." She reached out to Thorpe and allowed herself to be drawn into him with an intimacy that went way beyond sexual. She peered out through his virtual eyes at the gem-studded Milky Way splashed across the sky, and then pulled back to view it through her own eyes. Somehow, seen through their shared vision, it was way more overwhelming. She settled back comfortably merged with Thorpe, letting her thoughts blend with his, and her emotions overwhelm his. "We have nine hours," she said softly. "Let's make the most of them."

✳

At about the six-hour mark, with the capsule moving at nearly twenty-one kilometers per second, through his tensor eBrad observed the autopilot cut fuel to the rocket, flip the capsule end for end, and fire the rocket up again to bring the capsule to a standstill at Earth-Moon L2 six hours later.

"Nice design," he said to eSally, who was still somewhere in the GlobalNet.

eSally reached out to Sally at Phoenix. "*Chị ơi*," she said, "Brad says you made a nice design."

"Thanks, *Em ơi*, but I knew that already." She muffled a soft laugh with her hand.

✳

Under the watchful attention of Thorpe and Braxton, eDaphne, eSally, and eBrad, the capsule glided to a hover several meters above the plane of the Earth-Moon L2 swarm, and the rocket shut down with a puff. Animated by the focused attention of the others, eMax scampered around the group keeping an eye on the capsule. Once it stabilized and the attitude thrusters stopped pulsing, a spacesuited Dale stepped through the portal. He looked around and grinned at the spacesuited holoimages of the virtual entities, even eMax, who seemed to recognize Dale and moved to his legs to rub him. When eMax couldn't make physical contact, he appeared disappointed and sat down to watch.

"Hey," Dale said to everyone with a friendly wave. "Someone mind opening the capsule?"

eBrad grinned and gave instructions to his tensor inside the capsule. Shortly, the front end popped open, and the transparent habitat began to billow out. eMax approached the billowing material cautiously, batted it with a virtual paw, and then proceeded to examine it from every aspect as it grew.

About fifteen minutes later, the habitat had fully inflated. Floating above the swarm with the capsule attached to the middle of its flat bottom, Dale thought it looked very much like a large transparent mushroom cap or maybe a see-through igloo, given the entry lock extending from the side at the base.

"Time to open a second portal inside the habitat," Dale announced to no one in particular, and he pushed himself through the outer magnetically sealed curtain. Since there was no mechanism to pressurize the lock, once the outer curtain had sealed, he pushed his way into the habitat. A puff of oxygen-rich air rushed into the lock. Dale found himself floating inside the habitat that now seemed more like a very large Boy Scout pup-tent, except for the lack of gravity. He was surrounded by the virtual entities, now sans spacesuits, even eMax. "Okay, Phoenix," he said, "I'm activating the portal."

EARTH-MOON L2—THE HABITAT

Kimberly looked around herself as she floated inside the Habitat, her golden hair billowing around her head. "Oh, my!" was all she could say.

Right behind her, Daphne grabbed her ankle, a move that sent both slowly twisting through the air. Daphne had pulled her red hair into a ponytail, so it didn't billow out like Kimberly's. Dale and Brad watched in amusement.

"Takes a bit of getting used to," Dale said wryly.

"Doesn't take long, though," Brad added. "I pretty much have the hang of it," he said, letting go of his handhold. He floated toward the girls and then right through them, displaying an embarrassed grin. "Well, I thought I did."

A few minutes earlier, Dale and Brad had hauled two substantial airlock doors through the lock into the habitat and installed them. That was the extent of Brad's zero-gee experience, making Dale King-of-the-Roost. When Kimberly reached the Habitat wall, she pushed off gently toward Dale, who grabbed her hand as she neared.

"Sweet," he said as she kissed him quickly.

Kimberly turned toward Daphne and gestured her closer, but Daphne was stranded. Dale held tight to Kimberly's hand and pushed her toward Daphne. She caught Daphne's hand, and Dale pulled them close.

With the added safety factor of the new airlock doors, Daphne and Kimberly had joined Dale and Brad in the habitat. Sally remained in Phoenix Labs, assisting Fredricks with the portals. For Kimberly, her visit to the Habitat combined several firsts. First portal transit, first time in space, first zero-gee—she hugged Daphne and Dale.

"We need to try this out together," she said quietly.

"Not any time soon, unfortunately," Dale said. "We're setting up right now…"

"…to install a thinsat manufacturing facility," Daphne said, finishing his sentence.

DENVER—PHOENIX LABS

While Fredricks and the others were inventing, designing, building, and installing MERT Portals, and while they were rigging a habitat at Earth-Moon L2 behind the Moon, Thorpe and Braxton concentrated on the design for manufacturing thinsats and setting up a manufacturing facility for the printer segments that would produce the prodigious numbers of thinsats required.

Thorpe called everyone together in the now properly furnished conference room at Phoenix Labs. The table was shiny and new, the chairs were comfortable, the carpet was thick, and there was sufficient additional room at the table for the upload members to *sit* at the table.

"Let me give you some numbers, first," Thorpe said. "We have opted to copy what we already know works, so the swarm we will build at Earth-Moon L2 will duplicate the swarm we found there—one hundred klicks across, more or less, sixty thousand klicks above the Moon's surface, and one or two klicks above the present swarm. The thinsat density will be about one per square meter, and the individual thinsats will position themselves so as not to block the Sun from the lower swarm elements. We will need about eight billion thinsats." He produced a holoimage that showed a portion of the Moon's backside with two circular swarms floating above the surface.

Dale whistled.

"That's a lot," Brad said.

Kimberly's eyes widened, but she said nothing.

"You e-folks know this, and the rest of you probably have an idea, but I want to put the thinsat parameters on record." A slowly rotating holoimage of a thinsat appeared above the table. "This is enlarged so you can see the details. Actually, it's a sixteen-centimeter square." The holoimage shrank to life-size for several seconds and then enlarged again. "This consists of two very thin layers of aluminum foil embossed on the non-Sun side with die bonding cavities and slot antennas that enabled the thinsats to communicate with each other." A floating red arrow pointed to each component as Thorpe spoke. "The Sun-facing side is coated in the center area with molybdenum, indium phosphide, and AZO to form solar cells. The corners consist of a stack of the oxides of tungsten and aluminum, AZO, and nickel hydroxide—basically, electrochromic thrusters that enable each thinsat in the swarm to maintain its orientation with respect to the swarm, the Sun, and the Moon below."

"What's AZO?" Kimberly wanted to know. Several others nodded assent.

"AZO is aluminum-doped zinc-oxide," Braxton answered. "Now, aren't you glad you asked?" Everyone chuckled.

"Manufacturing eight billion of these thinsats is no small task," Thorpe continued, "but we are in a unique situation." He smiled around the table. "We have MERT Portals, and we intend to use them everywhere possible."

Braxton picked up the presentation. "Does everyone here know how three-D printing works?" Mostly nods; a couple of headshakes. "Okay, basically it works like this. A computer causes one or more of the printer deposition heads to deposit substances on a substrate. If you just want a visual model, just one head deposits plastic, metal, or any other suitable substance to build the model. If you want something complex like these thinsats, as many heads as necessary deposit required substances where, and in the order, they are needed. Somewhere nearby are bins containing the substances to be deposited. Typically, for what we want to do, the substances are either heated to liquid form or are deposited as a very fine powder and then fused with a laser." He paused and looked around at each person. "Everybody got that?" There were no questions.

Thorpe continued. "So, what we need is a bunch of three-D printers that can handle the powder forms of molybdenum, indium phosphide, AZO, tungsten oxide, aluminum oxide, and nickel hydroxide, and—of course—rolls of very thin aluminum foil. Unless we want to take ten years to manufacture all the thinsats, we have to come up with a way to get a whole bunch of these printers to work together to produce our thinsats in a reasonable time. We'll need about four thousand metric tonnes of material in specific proportions that don't matter for this presentation. We'll need a way to get the material to the manufacturing facility and a way to get the thinsats to Earth-Moon L2."

"There you have it," Braxton said, throwing his arms wide. "Now, all that's left is to do it."

※

"We need to expand the blockchain system you set up for me back in Palo Alto," Thorpe said to Rodney Bailey.

Thorpe couldn't help but note that despite Bailey's world-class salary and virtually unlimited budget, his office in the Phoenix Labs complex was about as cluttered as his work environment when they met. He was a first-class programmer, however, and Thorpe was loathe to change anything in his surrounds.

First, we want to designate the exchange unit as a Phoenix."

"That's trivial," Bailey said.

Then Thorpe outlined to Bailey the thinsat manufacturing facility and the logistic and financial requirements.

"What I need," he said to Bailey, "is a way to funnel operating and manufacturing funds for the thinsat operation into Phoenix, so that doesn't trigger the automatic U.S. transaction tax or that of the source nations."

"But isn't that a tax violation?" Bailey wanted to know. "Not that I care, but doesn't that put you at risk?"

"We don't see it that way," Thorpe said. "We are beyond any nation, beyond Earth, in fact." He smiled slightly. "We see taxes as necessary to fund minimal government such as police, military, legal system, and the other absolutely necessary things to make society function—we contribute our fair share to that. In my time, government already did too much, and now it does even more. We won't contribute to that. Besides, we're talking about internal transactions. The national transaction taxes were never designed to tax internal transactions. The American Congress and the legislatures of other nations screwed with the system to generate more income instead of policing their expenditures." Thorpe grinned at him. "Just make sure that only our external transactions register on the Fed's system."

✳

The job of putting it all together fell to Fredricks. Phoenix Labs had more than sufficient room for the manufacturing facility, with the following proviso. The raw material had to be brought in by portal, and the finished thinsats had to be delivered directly to Earth-Moon L2 by portal.

Fredricks installed two additional LANRs to handle the portal power draw. Within two weeks, he had completely transformed Greater Hall, where they had initially set up and tested the habitat. Crews assembled 144 twelve-meter-long printers into twelve stacks. Twelve-meter-wide rolls of ultra-thin aluminum foil fed each stack. Six bins of very fine, ultra-pure deposition material served each stack from the top. These bins were fed by six portals from refining centers around the world. For every one-second cycle, each printer produced thirty-eight front and back pairs, and cut, folded, and spot-welded them into complete thinsats. A continuous pneumatic airstream pushed the completed thinsats through another portal into the Earth-Moon L2 swarm. Once in the swarm, the thinsats ordered themselves according to their built-in instructions and began feeding supplemental power back to the facility.

Once the twelve printer-stacks were fully functional, it took seventeen days to populate the Earth-Moon L2 swarm to full capacity. As the last group of thinsats vanished through the portal, Fredricks turned to Sally and Brad.

"Run a full system test to see how many thinsats failed," he told them.

Since the system test was programmed into the overall installation, all Brad did was issue a command to set things into motion. Each thinsat was programmed to conduct a self-test after it had positioned itself within the swarm.

"How long till the swarm has positioned itself?" Brad asked Sally.

"Another two or three hours," she answered after checking her Link.

"Okay," he said, "I've set the system test to commence when the swarm is stable."

※

Two-and-a-half hours later, Brad announced, "System test underway." He did a quick Link calculation. "The program tests one thinsat every microsecond, so the test will run for about an hour-and-a-half." He looked at Sally. "Let's grab a cup of coffee, Sally."

"Tea," she responded with a smile.

An hour and thirty minutes later, Sally announced, "We have approximately ten million non-responsive thinsats. That's a failure rate of a bit over one-tenth of one percent. In the real world, it doesn't get much better than that."

Brad checked his Link. "It will take about a half-hour to produce another ten million units. Let's add another twenty thousand to compensate for the failure rate."

An hour later, the Earth-Moon L2 swarm was ready for the power collection system to be installed.

EARTH-MOON L2—THE SWARM

"Power is shunted across the Oort swarm to the portals using a capacitor-like scheme that briefly accumulates power on a thinsat and then passes the power to the next one and so forth until the power reaches its destination," Brad told the group assembled in the meeting room. "We hard-wired our thinsats to function the same way, but we need to install hardware terminators at the portals." A holoimage of a small flat object appeared over the table. It was about twice the size of a thinsat and a centimeter thick. "These little puppies have dual tasks. They receive the power, and they establish a portal. Now that the thinsats have positioned themselves within the swarm, they need specific instructions about where to direct the power." While he talked, the holoimage over the table illustrated what he was saying. "So, first, we have to designate specific portal positions, and then program the surrounding thinsats to shunt power to their designated portals. Second, we have to set up the terminators to accept and transmit the power through the portals they generate. Then finally, we need to set up appropriate power receptors on the other sides of the portals."

"Who's going to do all that?" Daphne asked. "It seems like a lot of physical labor well away from the habitat."

"That's the beauty of all this," Thorpe said. "Sally and Brad designed the power terminators and wrote the programming that makes it all work. They will do the actual installation out in the swarm, assisted by eSally and eBrad, who know as much about the system as anyone. Sally and Brad will each carry a hyper-disk programmed to bring them back here should anything go wrong—an E-Disk or Escape-Hyper-Disk."

"And what would that include?" Fredricks wanted to know.

Braxton counted several things off on his fingers. "A drop in suit pressure, excessive carbon dioxide, radical temperature change, sudden acceleration, electric shock, to name a few." Braxton grinned at the group. "In fact," he added, "as soon as we have sufficient available power, everyone leaving the planet will carry an E-Disk."

As Braxton finished, Max jumped to the tabletop and sat in front of Daphne. With a soft *purt*, eMax appeared at the other end of the table and approached Max. For a moment, they just looked at each other. They both had learned that smell was not part of the equation, so they sat mewing softly at each other.

"We've divided the swarm into five sections," Thorpe said. "An inner circle with a radius of twenty-two klicks will service a central portal. Four evenly-spaced quadrants beyond that will service one portal per quadrant. Each portal will gather about one petawatt." He paused and looked around. "To put things into perspective, that's about the equivalent of five hundred large LANR plants."

"Okay," Fredricks said, getting to his feet as Max and eMax jumped to the floor and walked off together, tails straight in the air with a small crook at the ends, "let's get this done."

✳

Sally and Brad suited-up in the lab, adding TBH boots[2] over their feet, and passed through the portal to the Earth-Moon L2 habitat.

---

[2] *Jet boots developed in 1967 by three NASA scientists, David Thomas, John Bird, and Richard Hellbaum. NASA tested the jet boots Earthside back then, but they were not introduced into current use until a few years before Thorpe was revived. They're simpler and less cumbersome than any of the old Manned Maneuvering Units. They fit like riding boots, but with completely flexible ankles. The boot uppers consist of two stiff, shaped polymer bags that contain pressurized hypergolic fuel components—UDMH (Unsymmetrical dimethylhydrazine) and nitrogen tetroxide. The fuel valves are controlled by a microswitch under each big toe. Each boot produces ten newtons of force against the ball of the foot. The wearer bends the knees for the appropriate thrust vector, including torque.*

Dale followed them in plain clothing, carrying the five power terminators. eSally and eBrad appeared and waved to Dale. Their visual appearance was spacesuited like Sally and Brad.

"Are you guys good with the TBH boots?" Dale asked.

"What can be so difficult?" Brad asked.

"We'll both practice before we take off untethered," Sally said, thinking that Brad was often too brash.

Dale returned to the lab. Moments later, Sally and Brad locked out of the habitat tethered to each other and to a ring outside the outer lock. Sally checked the tether. She was uncertain about how well she would perform with the TBH boots.

"You first," Brad said. Sally smiled shyly and let Brad push her away from the lock. He fed line through his gloved hands and finally stopped her about twenty meters out.

Sally looked about, marveling at the number of stars and the Milky Way expanse overhead. The Earth, of course, was hidden by the nearby Moon, but the Sun blazed off to her left when she faced the Moon with north pole up. Although she knew there were two swarms between her and the Moon, she could not see any evidence for either.

"Okay, Sally, point your head toward me and tap-on—tap-off both big toes."

She did, feeling wonder as she slowly approached Brad.

"Now, tuck and roll so your feet point toward me, and then tap-tap to stop your motion."

She did. "How easy!" she said, her voice filled with delight.

"You're a dancer," Brad said. "Try one of your dance moves."

Sally tucked one leg, pointed her foot outward, tap-tapped, and found herself spinning slowly. She stretched her arms, slowing her spin, and then brought them to her sides, speeding up again.

"Wow!" Brad said.

For ten minutes, Sally flipped, soared, twisted, floated, and finally came to a perfect stop directly in front of Brad, but upside down, head to feet.

"That was incredible," he told her. "You're gonna be way better at this than me." He changed positions with her. "How much fuel did you use?"

"Less than ten percent," she said and pushed him away gently.

To her surprise, Brad was able to control his movement much better than either thought he could.

"It's a lot like ice-skating," he told her. "I had no idea."

"You're using more fuel," she told him, "right?"

"I am," he said.

"Way more mass than me," Sally said with a soft giggle. She attempted to cover her mouth with her hand, but her helmet interfered. "What do you think?" she asked. "Are we ready to do our jobs?"

During this entire joint performance, eSally and eBrad stood by silently, their holoimages hovering near the lock.

"Okay, guys," eBrad said, "let's do the central portal first. "And… Oh, by the way, great job with the TBH boots!"

"I agree," eSally added softly, "especially you, *Chi.*"

✳

Guided by eBrad, and holding hands, Brad and Sally pointed toward the swarm center about a half kilometer directly below. They fired their TBH boots briefly, and a couple of minutes later, pivoted, fired, and came to a stop over what eBrad indicated was the spot.

Brad handed a terminator to Sally. She placed it in position while eSally established the necessary electrical connections. A hyper-disk took shape on the terminator. Brad retrieved it, marked it, and put it in one of his suit pockets.

"That was easy enough," Brad said to no one in particular.

"Let's go," Sally said, grabbing Brad's hand as they headed outward to a point about thirty-five kilometers away.

"Are we headed correctly?" Brad asked.

"Aim for the flashing beacon," eBrad said. "eSally found a way to display the virtual beacon in your heads-up display—make things easier for you."

✳

Three hours later, Sally and Brad, working closely with their upload counterparts, had installed all five terminators. Brad had the five hyper-disks in his pockets.

"Let's go home," Sally said, turning toward the distant habitat.

"I agree," Brad said. He grabbed Sally and activated his E-Disk. A moment later, both of them stepped through the portal lock at Phoenix Labs.

Chapter Fourteen

DENVER—PHOENIX LABS

Thorpe looked at Kimberly, alone among the people at the conference table in the Denver Phoenix Lab complex without a scientific background. He was well aware that she was part of the group because she and Daphne were an item—along with Dale, he reminded himself. But it was more than that. Kimberly had proved herself adept at ferreting out details about people and events that were intended to remain confidential. That made her uniquely valuable.

"Kimberly," he said, "we're doing some pretty dramatic things at Earth-Moon L2. I have not heard a peep from any media outlet about our activities. NASA and China are on the Moon's surface. The Mars Consortium is moving ahead with its plans for colonizing Mars. I hear whispers about a couple of outposts in the Asteroid Belt. They appear to be public-private joint ventures with NASA, Russia, and several private space venture groups." Thorpe paused and looked around the table. Then he addressed Kimberly again. "I want you to find out what you can about these ventures. Do it discreetly." He addressed everyone. "We may be able to set up a beneficial arrangement with these ventures. We could offer them portal technology to enable their movement of people and materials to and from their stations in return for a working one-gee VASIMR engine cluster that we can use to emplace dependent portals."

Around the table, people showed stunned looks.

"We really cannot keep what we are doing a secret for much longer," Braxton added. "Especially as we move to Mercury-Sun L1 and Earth-Sun L3."

"Kimberly," Thorpe said, "I want you to begin thinking how we will put out the word regarding our space activities."

"Big announcement, big splash, or do we leak it out, keep things under the public's radar?" Kimberly asked.

"Under everyone's radar, I think," Thorpe answered. "A small announcement on page three or four of several obscure newspapers, a filler in a couple of science-oriented periodicals, an oh-by-the-way on social media…get the word out into the public's subconscious that Phoenix is doing some routine stuff in space. Nothing about portals, the Oort Cloud, or upload-persons."

※

"How much power do we need for a MERT Portal to the Mars Station?" Thorpe asked generally to the table, currently occupied by Fredricks, Sally and Brad, and their upload counterparts.

"We're still working out the details," Brad said, "but generally speaking, about ten gigawatts—about one percent of one Earth-Moon L2 section output."

"Set up a hyper-disk to the central Earth-Moon L2 portal," Thorpe said to Sally and Brad. Then he turned to Fredricks, "Arrange to transport the hyper-disk to the Mars Station concealed within an appropriate electronics unit. And eBrad," Thorpe turned to the eBrad holograph, "insert a programmed tensor to activate the hyper-disk on command." He looked at Sally and Brad. "Both of you design an appropriate experiment for the Mars surface that will justify our spending however much it will cost to put the equipment onboard the next Mars transport."

Thorpe then laid out how he intended to activate the portal and set up direct communications with the Mars Consortium.

MARS—MARS STATION

A deep black cube, a decimeter on a side, sat patiently on the sandy Martian surface, awaiting an activation order from Phoenix Labs. It contained sufficient battery power for several days of operation, collecting and analyzing trace atmospheric components. The station staff thought the device odd, but the client had paid good money to have it transported to Mars and located some distance from the station. Since it required no monitoring, it was free money for the Mars Consortium.

The day following setup, eBrad's tensor woke up and electronically activated a mechanism that split the black cube open so that each half lay on the ground with its electronic innards exposed to the atmosphere. Then it electronically stroked the dull silvery surface of the hyper-disk that was the real purpose for the black cube. Moments later, Daphne and Kimberly strode through the portal, stumbling slightly as their bodies adapted to the lower gravity. They wore the same light-weight spacesuits they had worn at Earth-Moon L2, with boot covers over their feet to protect the TBH Boot nozzles. They each wore skull caps that monitored their vitals. The transparent globes covering their heads quickly darkened to protect them from the Sun's unfiltered rays. Each carried an E-Disk that would whisk them to Phoenix should any one of several things go wrong, or they could deliberately activate their E-Disks.

For several minutes, Daphne looked around in awe. The sandy surface on which they stood terminated a couple of kilometers to the north where steep, rocky cliffs rose abruptly out of the desert floor into the pale blue sky. A few streaky clouds softened the color, while off to the south, desert and sky merged in a pink haze. Daphne looked at Kimberly, who seemed to be absorbed in her own evaluation of their surroundings.

"Shall we?" Daphne said, reaching for Kimberly's gloved hand.

The girls reluctantly turned westward for the kilometer walk to Mars Station, tucked into a hollow spur of rock jutting out from the massive cliffs that towered over the station. Geologists had determined that the hollow spur was the remnant of a lava tube that had formed long ago when the desert was part of a shallow sea. It was an ideal location for Mars Station, just south of Candor Chasma and east of Melas Labes, above the northern wall of central Valles Marineris. It was well-protected from radiation and dust storms, yet with easy access to the surface of Mars and the depths of Valles Marineris.

A few minutes later, Daphne and Kimberly stood outside the outer pressure door of the entrance to Mars Station.

※

Stanley Roka scanned his instrument array, looking for anything unusual. It was his turn in the barrel, and he still had two hours to complete his four-hour watch. All twenty-four support personnel, except their manager, took turns with this usually dull watch. Mainly, it was to ensure that someone was actually looking outside at what was going on—people working outside, weather, departure and arrival of vehicles, keeping track of who was inside and who was outside. As Roka's eyes swept across the holocam feed for the main lock, they grew large in his black face.

"Hey, Boss!" Roka called to Station Manager Norman Bork, who was passing through the instrumentation area.

"Yeah…"

"Who you got outside, Bork?" Roka checked the electronic log. "Log says nobody."

"Whadya mean?" Bork stepped up to look over Roka's shoulder. "What the fuck?" he said. "Who the hell is that?"

"Can't tell. The helmets are dark, but the suits don't look like ours."

The outer door opened, and the two strangers entered the lock. When the lock had cycled, they both removed their helmets and skullcaps and shook out their hair.

"Well, I'll be goll-damned!" Roka said as Daphne's red and Kimberly's golden long tresses pushed out over their suit collars.

Bork strode toward the inner door several meters away from the instrumentation center. As the door opened, he stopped in his tracks, gaping at two of the most beautiful women he had seen since well before he had landed the Mars Station Manager job. He quickly pulled himself together.

"I'm Station Manager Norman Bork. Where did you ladies come from?" He kept his eyes focused on their faces as they stripped out of their spacesuits. They each wore silken jumpsuits, the red-head green and the blond blue.

"I'm Dr. Daphne O'Bryan, and this is Kimberly Deveraux, both from Phoenix Labs in Denver. We'd like to speak with you and Dr. Meriweather." Daphne smiled warmly.

Bork sucked a lungful of air. "Glad to meet you." Their eyes twinkled at him, obviously enjoying his discomfort. He tapped his Link. "Frank, would you please meet me in the conference room?"

※

"Let me get this straight," Dr. Meriweather said. "You're telling me that Phoenix Labs has developed a wormhole portal, and that's how you two got here?"

Daphne nodded and smiled. Kimberly just nodded.

"I know it's a big chunk to swallow," Daphne said gently. "May we demonstrate?"

Meriweather and Bork both nodded their assent.

Daphne produced the hyper-disk. "This hyper-disk is linked to the projecting portal back at Phoenix Labs. In simple terms, the MERT Portal uses the Casimir effect. The link is maintained by ten gigawatts of power. The larger the portal and the greater the separation, the more power is required." She stroked the hyper-disk; the portal opened, and Jackson Fredricks stepped through, wavering slightly as he adjusted to the lower gravity.

"Frank Meriweather, you old rockhound, it's good to see you!" Fredricks held out his hand, and they shook warmly.

"My Station Manager, Norman Bork," Meriweather said, gesturing toward Bork.

"I'm still trying to come to grips with the ladies and you right here right now," Bork said with a faint grin. "You sure know how to get a guy's attention."

"Back in 1981 at the Third World Hydrogen Energy Conference in Tokyo," Fredricks said, "Roger Billings presented a paper on his production-ready hydrogen-fueled automobile. A staid British scientist stood and proclaimed loudly that such an engine was theoretically impossible. The next day, Billings, who had arrived in his own private jet, flew that scientist and several other doubters to his Utah lab to demonstrate the working engine." Fredricks smiled at Bork. "A splashy entrance works." Looking at both men, Fredricks said, "Would you care to join me in my lab to see the other end of this device?" Then looking at Daphne, he said, "Would you please stay here to keep an eye on the hyper-disk?"

Moments later, Meriweather and Bork followed Fredricks through the Portal. "We will never have been this far apart," Kimberly said, kissing Daphne quickly before she followed the others.

✳

Fredricks introduced the two visitors to Sally and Brad, and then he and Daphne showed them around the lab. Fredricks handed each an E-Disk.

"We're taking a short excursion to our cislunar operating station," Fredricks said. "These will bring you safely back here should something go wrong." He gestured for them to follow him through a lock. "Follow me, please."

"Whoa…" Bork exclaimed as he found himself in the zero-gee, oxygen-enriched, low-pressure Earth-Moon L2 habitat interior.

"And we are where?" Meriweather asked slowly, looking around through the transparent walls of the habitat.

"We're behind the Moon at Earth-Moon L2," Fredricks said. "A couple of klicks below us is our ServerSky swarm set up for power production. We generate most of our power requirements here, piping it through portals to wherever it is needed."

Fredricks gestured them back toward the portal. "Our next step is Mercury's Mercury-Sun L1, and that's why we came to you."

Back in Phoenix Labs, Fredricks said, "I know you are filled with questions. Let's return to Mars Station, where I'll try to answer your questions and explain our need."

✳

Back in the Mars Station conference room, Bork ordered a round of coffee. He paid close attention to the conversation between Fredricks and Meriweather while stealing an occasional glance at the two women. Before accepting the job as Station Manager of Mars Station, he had wintered over twice at Amundsen-Scott South Pole Station—even now the wildest, most desolate spot on Earth. The last time he was Station Master, which gave him the over-the-top quals for landing his present position.

When I came here, Bork thought, *there was nothing more outlandish, more challenging, more exciting than being here on Mars, opening up a new world for humanity. Now I'm not so sure.*

"We need a one-gee VASIMR engine cluster," Fredricks said. "We're willing to exchange our portal technology for it, so we don't have to do the R&D to make one for ourselves."

"We have one, of course," Meriweather said, "but we only use it to one-tenth-gee because of the fuel requirements."

"How do you power it?" Daphne asked.

"With a variable-output gas-core reactor," Meriweather said. "We inject gaseous uranium-hexafluoride fissile material into a fused silica vessel where it produces extremely high-energy ultraviolet light. The variable fissile density of the gas allows us to control the reactor's output. The VASIMR hydrogen propellant flows around the transparent vessel, absorbing the high-energy ultraviolet, and then is directed into the three VASIMR engines driving the spacecraft. The outer wall of the hydrogen chamber is lined with photovoltaics that convert the high-energy ultraviolet directly into electricity. We divert part of this power for ship functions, and the rest drives the VASIMR engines."

Bork could see that Kimberly was a bit overwhelmed with the technical talk. "The bottom line is," he said to her, "that the reactor produces more than sufficient electricity and it preheats the hydrogen fuel. The VASIMR engines generate high-frequency radio waves to ionize the super-hot hydrogen propellant into extremely hot plasma. Magnetic fields accelerate the plasma to generate thrust."

"So, you are limited by how much uranium-hexafluoride and hydrogen you can carry," Kimberly said with a self-satisfied smile.

Bork grinned at her. "You got it! So, what's your function? You're obviously not a scientist."

"I'm the journalist," she said. "I make sure the world hears what we want it to hear."

To Bork's regret, she turned her attention to Meriweather. "If you had enough electricity and sufficient hydrogen…"

"We could do one-gee all day," Meriweather finished her thought.

Bork thought he saw where they were headed. "Can your hyper-disk-connected portals function on a moving vessel?" he asked.

"What do you think we are on right now?" Daphne asked.

Bork swallowed and acknowledged that Mars was moving in orbit.

"So is Phoenix Labs," Kimberly added.

Bork consulted his Link. "That's just under two days minimum and about six-and-a-half days maximum—about one-third the time it takes us now."

"What's your acceleration?" Daphne asked.

"One-tenth-gee," Meriweather said.

"So," Bork said, "you take one of our VASIMR clusters without the reactor, feed it power and hydrogen through a portal—Wow!"

"Exactly," Fredricks said dryly.

DENVER—PHOENIX LABS

Fredricks addressed the small group of men and two women sitting around the conference table in the Phoenix Labs in the Denver Tech Center. "I am Dr. Jackson Fredricks. I represent Phoenix Labs with full authority to enter into any agreement we reach today."

Fredricks looked around the table. Of the men, Jonas and Albers were middle-aged, well-dressed, and trim, while Roberts and Casper appeared to be in their early thirties and were downright athletic. One of the women, Ms Jorgansen, was pushing sixty while Ms Unger was in her early thirties. They, too, were well dressed and physically fit. In chairs against the walls sat members of his team, Daphne, Dale, Kimberly, Sally, and Brad. The team member uploads were present but were not visible. The people at the table were unaware of their presence.

"You represent the top of the pecking order for non-governmental space exploration. I applaud your efforts on Mars, and Phoenix will assist in any way possible to keep your activities in private hands. We do this on principle, not expecting anything in return. You may rely on that promise." Fredricks smiled around the table, his glance lingering on the younger woman. "I asked you here today because I have a very special proposition."

Fredricks manipulated his Link. "I just sent each of you a nondisclosure agreement. I realize this is unusual when dealing with CEOs, but what I am about to reveal is so profound, such a paradigm shift that I need your assurance of absolute discretion before I reveal it to you."

The people around the table reviewed the nondisclosure agreements, quickly realizing that each was specifically tailored to their individual circumstances. After some quiet conversation and a couple of questions, everyone at the table digitally executed his or her agreement. The room quieted, and they turned their expectant attention to Fredricks.

"How many of you have been to Mars?" Fredricks asked. The three younger people said they had. "Ladies and gentlemen, we're going to change that right now."

Fredricks rose to his feet and stepped to one side as a door-like portal to another room opened behind his chair, and Dr. Meriweather stepped into the conference room.

"I know this is beyond belief right now," he said to the obviously astonished people sitting at the conference table, "but you all know me personally, and I know each of you. Would you please join me?" He stepped back through the doorway. "Be careful of the gravity shift as you walk through the door," he said from the room on the other side.

In silence, the people around the table stood. Roberts stepped through the door and then turned around and stepped back through. He turned and stepped through again and grinned over his shoulder. "He's right. Watch your step!"

✳

In the Mars Station conference room, they arranged themselves much as they had back in Phoenix Labs with two extra seats for

Dr. Meriweather and Norman Bork. Fredricks smiled around the table. "Now you all have been to Mars," he said. "Let there be no doubt. We can simulate everything except the lower gravity. Haven't figured that one out yet." His eyes twinkled. "We'll take you out to the surface in a bit, but first we have some business to conduct."

The conference room door opened, and Stanley Roka entered with a pot of fresh coffee and a tray of cups.

"Meet Stanly Roka, one of my crew members," Bork said. "Please let him serve you. It will be easier than everyone milling about the room."

"You owe me, Bork," Roka said with a grin, as he proceeded to build a cup of coffee for each person in the room, paying particular attention to Kimberly.

After Roka left, Fredricks tapped his cup with a spoon and began. "You came here through what we call a MERT Portal—MERT stands for Morris-Einstein-Rosen-Thorne. You don't need the science and engineering behind this breakthrough, you have people for that. Here's the big picture.

"Using a whole lot of power, we generate a Casimir field that develops a miniature wormhole inside the field. Then we apply a prodigious amount of power to the device. We call this the portal Locus. The other end of the portal terminates in one of these." He held up a hyper-disk. "This hyper-disk will allow you to establish a MERT Portal from wherever the Locus is to wherever the hyper-disk is. Both the physical size of the portal, in other words, how large an object can pass through it, and the separation of Locus and hyper-disk are a function of the available power. You move a hyper-disk too far from its Locus, and it becomes so much useless electronics. To reestablish the link, you will need to return to the Locus, recreate the hyper-disk, and be sure to remain closer to the Locus in the future or supply the Locus with more power."

"How much power?" Unger asked.

"The portal you transited consumes ten gigawatts. That's about five of the LANRs that power Mars Station."

"Whew!" Albers said, shaking his head.

"That power requirement makes MERT Portals somewhat impractical for everyday use," Jorgansen said.

If you have a source for the power," Casper said, "you can drive a VASIMR cluster at one-gee for a long as you wish…" His voice trailed off, and he consulted his Link briefly. "If you have the power, accelerating at one-gee, you can approach lightspeed in about a year…apply the Lorentz factor…make that about 300 days!" He grinned broadly. "Whatever you're offering, if it includes this technology, I'm all in!"

Fredricks watched a dawning understanding fill the faces of the other five individuals. Then Jorgansen raised her voice again. "We don't know how to produce such prodigious amounts of power." Her voice sounded a bit strident.

"Are all of you willing to accompany me on a short excursion?" Fredricks asked. "Not locally, but to somewhere else," he added as he rose and stepped through the portal.

While the discussion in the Mars Station conference room continued, Dale and Brad had quietly stepped back to Phoenix Labs and moved the Locus of the portal into the lab space. When the group assembled in the space, Fredricks handed each an E-Disk and said, "Should anything go wrong, this will bring you back here safely and securely. Now, please follow me through this pressure lock."

In the pressure lock, the three older CEOs looked somewhat apprehensive. "When we pass through the second lock," Fredricks said, you will be weightless. You may feel like you are falling. Trust me, you are not! Virtually everyone adjusts to freefall quickly, but if you don't, my people will bring you back to Phoenix immediately." He opened the lock and led them into the habitat.

"Welcome to Earth-Moon L2. You are roughly sixty thousand klicks above the backside of the Moon. You won't be able to see it, but three klicks below us is a ServerSky swarm about one hundred klicks across. You," he indicated Jorgansen, who looked a bit green around the gills but was clearly not about to bail, "asked about power. The swarm below us produces about five terawatts of power—the equivalent of more than twenty-five hundred LANRs." Fredricks let that soak in for a bit.

"I don't see anything," Jorgansen said, expressing apparent disbelief.

Fredricks told her how to adjust her Link holodisplay so she could see the individual thinsats.

"Well, I guess they are there, alright," Jorgansen muttered.

"We are about to install a similar facility between Mercury and the Sun at Mercury-Sun L1 that will produce thirty-four terawatts followed by one on the other side of the Sun at Earth-Sun L3 that will produce twenty terawatts, although we can dramatically increase power production simply by extending the size of the swarm." He smiled at her. "Power simply is not a problem."

※

Back in the Phoenix Labs conference room, Fredricks reached an agreement with the six Mars Consortium CEOs, after reviewing the power matter with Jorgansen several more times. They would supply Phoenix a fully functional VASIMR cluster sans reactor in exchange for use of Phoenix MERT Portal technology and an agreement that Phoenix would install a thinsat swarm at the Mars-Sun L1 point for a one-time payment of one Phoenix (Φ1) per thinsat. Phoenix would maintain the Mars swarm without additional cost except for the cost of replacement thinsats at the Φ1 rate. The agreement also included enlarging the swarm as required at the agreed-upon price.

※

Dale and Brad stood before the single VASIMR engine lying on its side, suspended in a cradle. Brad scanned it with his Link. "Two meters long, point-nine-six meters in diameter," he said.

Dale stood quietly, looking at the engine. "We gotta assemble this thing at Earth-Moon L2," he said finally. He projected a holographic image of the completed Mars Consortium rocket in front of them. "Don't need a passenger compartment, no plumbing except fuel and stuff, no supplies, nothing really but an open compartment to receive power, hydrogen, and hypergolic fuel for the station-keeping thrusters."

As Dale spoke, the various components of the Mars Consortium rocket disappeared, leaving just the two-meter-long three-VASIMR cluster with a meter-thick circular hatbox where compartments used to be. "We center the portal here," he said, placing an opening at the center of the hatbox. "Compressed hydrogen flows into this ring," a doughnut ring appeared around the inside of the box wall fed by a hose through the portal, "and power flows around the ring to superheat the hydrogen." A power trunk through the portal fed coils wrapped around the ring and then to the power socket of each VASIMR. "Two hypergolic lines feed four maneuvering thrusters like this." Four thin lines from the portal fed four thrusters positioned around the hatbox. "And finally," Dale said, "a hyper-disk here and here." Two hyper-disks appeared, anchored to the bottom of the hatbox, but with free access to the outside.

"Did I miss anything?" Dale asked.

"Not that I can tell," Brad said, examining the holoimage carefully. "Not sure about the redundant hyper-disk. We've never had one fail."

"It's not redundant. One is for power, and the second one is for Earth-Sun L3."

"Agreed," Brad said, with a wry smile. "Let's make this happen."

Chapter Fifteen

EARTH-MOON L2—OUTSIDE HABITAT

It took an all-hands effort to complete the Mercury rocket and get it ready for transit to the innermost planet, all hands, that is, except for the upload parties. Thorpe and Braxton headed to the Oort Cloud to install a beacon at that farthest Solar System outpost, taking eDaphne and eMax with them. eSally and eBrad worked together on portal infrastructure. They wanted to maximize the number of portals to the available power to ensure that larger and especially longer portals would not shut down as a result of adding more portals to the system.

Daphne and Sally worked together at Phoenix on the hatbox and the feeders for power, hydrogen, and hypergolic fuel. At Earth-Moon L2, Dale and Brad assembled the components and made sure that everything would function as designed. Kimberly wanted to document the entire process, which kept her in and out of spacesuits moving back and forth between Phoenix and Earth-Moon L2. Fredricks kept himself far enough back to keep the whole picture in mind. He monitored mostly via holographic images, but every once in a while, he would show up unexpectedly at one of the sites.

It took a full two weeks before everyone was satisfied that the craft was ready for its journey. On the appointed day, the entire team, even the uploads, assembled in the habitat for the launch. eBrad had inserted two tensors into the hatbox—noting that the second tensor would be a backup for the Mercury run and primary for Earth-Sun L3, and all that remained was the launch itself.

"Wait...wait!" Kimberly shouted from the habitat inner lock. "I'll be right back."

It actually took nearly fifteen minutes before Kimberly reappeared, this time spacesuit-clad with a bottle of something in her hand. "We have to christen our spacecraft and give her a name," Kimberly said breathlessly. "Nobody launches a craft such as this without proper pomp and circumstance." She turned to Daphne. "A hand, please."

Daphne extracted her helmet from under her arm and floated it in the air beside them. She tucked Kimberly's golden hair under her skullcap, brushed her lips with her own, and set the globe in place. Kimberly waved at everyone and floated through the lock to the vacuum outside. She turned again with a wave and activated her TBH boots. Five minutes later, Kimberly arrived at the ungainly looking spaceship—two meters of rocket and one of payload. From her leg pocket, she pulled out the bottle that she had stashed there. Turning back toward the habitat and its occupants, Kimberly waved the bottle. "Real French Champagne!" she said, and then tucked it into a tough plastic bag so pieces of broken bottle would stay contained.

Kimberly turned toward the spacecraft, smashed the bottle against the side of the hatbox, and declared solemnly, "I christen thee *Narada*, messenger of the Sun God."

✳

Two days, twenty-two hours, fifty-nine minutes, and ten seconds later, *Narada* took station at Mercury-Sun L1.

MERCURY—MERCURY-SUN L1

The first tensor eBrad had placed inside *Narada* sensed arrival at Mercury-Sun L1. It moved throughout the spacecraft's circuitry, ensuring nothing had deteriorated during the 160 million-kilometer transit. It found the second tensor, but left it dormant and moved to the main hyper-disk. The tensor extended electronic tendrils and gently stroked the dull metallic surface of the hyper-disk. Moments later, a portal opened to the conveyor-fed lock in the Phoenix thinsat production facility in the Denver Tech Center.

Upon receiving the signal from eBrad's tensor aboard *Narada*, Brad told Sally to start the thinsat production. As with the thinsat production for Earth-Moon L2, the process proceeded swiftly and automatically. Seventeen days later, with production completed and all 7.9 billion thinsats delivered, Sally and Brad ran their tests. As with the Earth-Moon L2 swarm, they found one-tenth of a percent failure rate.

"Since we added an extra ten million thinsats to the production run to compensate for the failure rate," Brad said, "we're in business. Time to install the power terminator."

※

Sally suited up with a bit of help from Brad, and then she assisted him. Once they had checked each other thoroughly, Sally made sure they both carried an E-disk. Her intellect told her that this time was no different than their excursion at Earth-Moon L2, but somehow the 160 million klick difference compared with Earth-Moon L2 made her feel uneasy.

Sally grabbed Brad's hand and stepped through the portal. Despite her intellect, Sally was wholly unprepared for what she saw. With no up and down, her mind chose to tell her that the Sun was to her right and Mercury to her left. The Sun looked much as it did from Earth or Earth-Moon L2, but fully three times larger and much hotter, working her suit cooling system harder than it had ever worked before. She turned toward Mercury. It looked about the same size as the Sun, its surface covered with craters and fascinating geologic features that appeared to be gigantic canyons approaching the scale of Valles Marineris on Mars.

"*Thật tuyệt vời phải không, Chị ơi?* [It's magnificent, isn't it, Little Sister?]" eSally said privately through Sally's comm system.

"*Ồ vâng, Em ơi, ồ vâng!* [Oh yes, Elder Sister, Oh yes!]" Sally answered, tears filling her eyelashes. "*Nó áp đảo tôi!* [It overwhelms me!]"

"Everything okay, Sally?" Brad asked, seeing the tears in her eyes.

"It is," Sally answered. "eSally and I are just sharing the awesome beauty of this place."

"No quarrel with the both of you there," Brad said. "It's spectacular—hot, but spectacular."

"I agree," eBrad chimed in, "but don't we have work to do?"

※

The thinsats had distributed themselves for fifty kilometers in all directions. Since they were installing only a single power terminator at the center of Mercury-Sun L1, the task was relatively simple. Brad handed a power terminator to Sally. She placed it in position at the portal Locus while eSally established the necessary electrical connections. When the hyper-disk took shape on the Locus, Brad retrieved it and put it in one of his suit pockets.

"Let's go home," Sally said, taking Brad's suited hand.

"We're going to remain here for a while," eSally told them. She turned to eBrad as they both admired the magnificence of the engorged Sun. eSally reached out to touch eBrad's hand and felt a deep sensation spreading from the point of touch. "As Sally, I have held off your gentle advances, but here and now, I no longer wish to do so, *Anh oi.*"

From their first touch, eSally let herself merge with eBrad until they were as one, soaking in and sharing the magnificence surrounding them. Intellectually, she knew her upload-self occupied the same physical space as his, but in her mind's eye, she felt wrapped inside his big teddy bear arms, protected from everything beyond their merged selves. Finally, they slipped back into their individual selves and transited to Earth-Moon L2. Words were unnecessary.

DENVER—PHOENIX LABS

"Let's do a quick review of our status," Thorpe said to the assembled group. As he talked, a holoimage appeared above the conference table. "Earth-Moon L2 is fully functional with five terminators, each producing one terawatt." An image of the moon appeared with the Earth-Moon L2 swarm indicated. "Mercury-Sun L1 is fully functional, producing thirty-four terawatts." The holoimage shifted to show Mercury with *Narada* parked below the swarm.

"Permanent MERT Portals connect Phoenix with Earth-Moon L2, Mars Station, Mercury-Sun L1, and *Narada* consuming a total of forty gigs." He paused and smiled at each. "Each of you flesh-and-bone types carries an E-disk. These each consume from two gigs to keep the portal open, to whatever it takes to maintain a portal to your location. For accounting purposes, we've allotted ten gigs each. That's another fifty gigs plus again as much for visitors. That's a hundred forty gigs.

"Since we wish to avoid using the mystery portals, we need to establish a network of portals that interconnects the various Server-Sky swarms. Let's reserve a hundred gigs for this. Now we're at two hundred forty gigs." Thorpe grinned and then added, "Jackson and I have set up temporary portals for this and that, and have decided to set aside a hundred gigs capacity to fill this need. I suspect it will grow with time to as much as a terawatt. We'll leave it at a hundred gigs for now. That brings us to three hundred forty gigs—about one-third the output from one Earth-Moon L2 section."

"I'd say we got capacity for a while," Dale said.

"We hear you," Braxton said, "but there are so many variables that even with the kind of calculating capacity Thorpe and I have, it's still difficult to get a realistic estimate.

"Let me give you some of our thoughts on MERT Portals. Frank Meriweather at Mars Station will have his own power swarm, but think about this. His people are working on eventually terraforming Mars. This will require all kinds of material, including biologics. What if we set up all our facilities to transport all biological waste to selected Mars locations through portals? Again, on Mars, water faucets require plumbing and a water source. What if we were to set up portals to supply fresh water to each faucet from wherever it's available—Saturn's moon Enceladus, perhaps. Apply that concept to virtually everywhere we need water from a faucet, to everywhere we need to flush water away. You want to get rid of something per-manently? Open a portal near the Sun to dump whatever into the Sun. Build a house with rooms that open to a Martian vista, a South Pacific island, and a Lunar landscape—or any other combination that twists your crank." Braxton smiled broadly. "All it takes is power…"

THE SUN—EARTH-SUN L3

Prepping for the Earth-Sun L3 swarm required moving *Narada* from Mercury to the L3 point. Because both Earth and Mercury had been moving in their orbits for the twenty days since the spacecraft arrived over Mercury, the distance to the Earth-Sun L3 point had decreased significantly.

Brad suited up and stepped through the Mercury-Sun L1 portal for a personal inspection of *Narada* before it commenced its 109 million-kilometer journey. "Everything appears shipshape," he reported.

Two days, eight hours, twenty-two minutes, and eighteen seconds later, *Narada* took station at Earth-Sun L3.

✳

Since the team had decided to make the Earth-Sun L3 swarm 200 kilometers wide, the total production time went from seventeen days to sixty-seven days to accommodate nearly four times as many thinsats as at Earth-Moon L3.

Because Earth-Sun L3 is inherently unstable, Brad and Dale built a station-keeping portal with hypergolic maneuvering jets driven by a navigation system that maintained position by tracking star patterns. It contained a portal that supplied the fuel lines and served as a distribution point for the thinsats as they were produced in Denver. They transported the station-keeping portal through the *Narada* portal and hung around sufficiently long to ensure that it was working correctly.

Sally and Brad had become the de facto thinsat production team. By the time they started the Earth-Sun L3 production run, things were nearly automatic. Dale made sure the sources supplying material by portal for the production bins kept material flowing. Thorpe and Braxton had set things up at the raw material end so that they owned the mining facilities and closely controlled preproduction, ensuring that exactly what they needed at Phoenix went into the portals at the production facilities. The entire process was sufficiently compartmentalized that nobody had yet connected the dots.

Sixty-three days after *Narada* arrived at Earth-Sun L3, Brad suited up again and stepped through the *Narada* portal for a final inspection of the spacecraft before it commenced its 272 million-kilometer journey to Mars-Sun L1, a million kilometers above the surface of Mars.

"None the worse for wear," he reported when he returned to Phoenix.

Three days, twenty hours, thirty-one minutes, and three seconds later, *Narada* took station at Mars-Sun L1.

MARS—MARS-SUN L1

Daphne looked around herself as she transited the portal at Mars-Sun L1. During the Mercury sojourn, she and everyone else took several turns through the portal just to experience the majestic view. Even eMax went several times on his own as he explored his expanding universe. Daphne found the other side of the Sun less interesting. The heavens looked exactly as they did from cislunar space, but without Earth and Moon to add interest to the view. She and everybody went once but only returned as work required.

Mars was different altogether. From L1, Mars was a bit smaller than the Sun from Earth, and the Sun was virtually the same size as Mars. At Mercury, the Sun's and planet's presence were overwhelming. At Mars, Daphne was not so much overwhelmed as that she felt she was holding a barbell with a golden ball at one end and a red one at the other.

eDaphne joined her, appearing spacesuited and virtually indistinguishable from Daphne. "Did you ever imagine, Sis, when we signed on at Phoenix Revive that we would be standing here, part of the most amazing turn of events in human history?"

A quiet *mew* caught their attention. "And sharing it with eMax," Daphne said with a giggle. "I just stepped out here to get a sense of what we are dealing with," Daphne added. "So much has happened so fast, it's hard to keep up with it."

"Tell me about it," eDaphne said. "We need to talk about the Oort Cloud, too. There's more going on out there than you imagine."

✴

The process of creating a new thinsat swarm no longer was the exciting event it was at first. As before, Sally and Brad handled the thinsat production while Dale kept the flow of material coming. Two months and a bit later, the 200-kilometer swarm was in place at Mars-Sun L1, and the terminator had been installed. Dale and Brad carried the Locus portal to Mars Station and hooked up temporary power from Earth-Moon L2. Fredricks tasked Kimberly with connecting the dots.

Kimberly stepped through the Mars Station portal into Norman Bork's office, tossing her golden hair. "Hey, Norman! I come bringing gifts." She handed him a hyper-disk. "This will take you to the L1 swarm. Take one of your portals with you to free up our portal. L1's ready for you to draw power as soon as you make the connection." She found herself somewhat distracted by this craggy adventurer who had wintered over twice at the Earth's South Pole, and now was running Mars Station. She wanted to give her message before she stumbled all over herself.

Bork flashed her a wide grin. "The universe is being particularly good to me today," he said. "Welcome!" He accepted the hyper-disk, placing it on his desk, and waved to a chair. "So, how does a girl like you...and all that stuff?"

"Daphne, uh, Dr. O'Brian, and I are close friends. She brought me in as communications. Someone had to bring you the hyper-disk. I wanted to see you again, so they tasked me."

"That works for me, Kid. Do you have to get right back, or do you have some time?"

If she stayed, Kimberly knew, she would be committing herself to...she wasn't entirely sure what, but she definitely wanted to see where it led. "I'm my own boss," she told him with a slight smile.

"Great," he said. "Let me give you the grand tour, and then we can take in a genuine Martian sunset—done right, out on the surface."

Mars Station was interesting, but other than gravity, it was much like other scientific stations Kimberly had seen during the past two years. The meal that she and Bork took with the crew was nothing short of fabulous.

"I can't get over how delicious the food is," she told Bork.

"At isolated stations, we try to do this," he told her. "On submarines, long space voyages, research stations like the South Pole, and here, of course. It keeps the morale up." He stood and held out his hand. "Let's play tourist."

They suited up near the inner lock. Unlike older vacuum suits, these suits were lightweight and flexible, even in hard vacuum. They worked on a technologically advanced application of earlier high-altitude suits. An inner garment formed a flexible, skintight membrane that substituted for atmospheric pressure. A slightly less tightly-fitting outer garment retained a minimal atmospheric environment inside the suit, also providing temperature control and wear resistance. The suit was entered feet first through an airtight zipper-like opening in the back. The sealed gloves were comfortably flexible. They wore close-fitting skullcaps with various sensors that transmitted their physiological condition to the Instrument Room in Mars Station. Their transparent, spherical helmets attached to sealing collars around their necks and were completely invisible from inside.

Once outside, Kimberly placed her hand in Bork's, and they strolled southeast, directly away from the cliffs towering above them. "We're practically at the equator here," Bork told her after shifting their circuits to private. "The Sun will set right there, just to the right of that peak." He pointed to a craggy peak about fifty kilometers due west. "From now on, I'll call it Kimberly's Peak."

"I bet you tell all the girls that," Kimberly said, pressing herself to him. They found a spot facing west and sat together watching the Sun drop through the turquoise sky. As the Sun approached Kimberly's Peak, the sky developed bright pink streaks running northeast to southwest. The Sun reached the peak and then dropped behind it. There was virtually no twilight, and in moments the full skydome was filled with stars.

"It's so beautiful," Kimberly said quietly, tears rolling down her cheeks. "Thank you for sharing this with me."

※

The next morning, Kimberly snuggled her nude body against Bork's hard muscles, wondering at the magic of lovemaking in one-third gravity. She kissed him to wakefulness and had another go—just to be sure she remembered it right.

As she lay on her back in comfortable exhaustion, a soft voice whispered in her ear, "It's eDaphne. Was he worth it?"

"Oh, yes!" Kimberly whispered back, "and I would share if I could."

DENVER—PHOENIX LABS

"I think it's time," Thorpe told the assembled group, "to give Kimberly and Dale the opportunity to upload themselves."

"Kimberly has brought the subject up several times," Braxton said. "We've kept Dale pretty busy, but I can think of no reason he would not want to join the uploads as well. Dale…?"

"Sure," Dale said. "Unless I totally misread you upload guys, there is no downside. I'm go for it!"

✳

The matrix upload process had become pretty routine. Fredricks set it up, first for Dale and then for Kimberly. As before, everybody hung out for the procedure. eDaphne mentored eDale through the matrix wakening, making sure she merged with him fully to give him a proper initiation to his matrix existence.

eDaphne steadied eDale as he came to full wakefulness following their merging. "How can I feel so breathless when I'm not even breathing?" he asked, still wobbling a bit.

"That's just a foretaste," she told him. "Wait till we take a day trip through ServerSky and beyond."

✳

eKim slowly rose through a dense liquid that surrounded her like embryonic fluid. She felt a male touch to her left hand, a touch that did not end, but merged into her hand and moved up her arm and then down her body into the core of her being. She felt another touch to her right breast, a gentle touch, a familiar touch, a feminine touch that caressed, penetrated, merged. She tried to open her eyes, but they remained closed, while the feelings of intimate caress became insistent, overpowering. Lips brushed her lips, neck, breasts, stomach, thighs, her female essence, and inside her brain and her very core. Tension built, and ebbed, and built again, and ebbed again, growing in intensity until she exploded into a flock of butterflies. They filled her chamber, flitting here and there, and then finally settled to her shoulders and merged with her essence. She opened her eyes and looked around. eDaphne nuzzled her left side, and Braxton her right. Their smiles lifted her spirits again as they merged and passed through her to take each other's place at her side.

"OhMyGosh!" eKim said, flushed and hyperventilating slightly. "Was that you guys?"

"I guess so," eDaphne said, kissing her right breast.

"That's what I'm talking about!" Braxton said, stroking her golden tresses.

eKim looked at each of them and saw that they were now clothed. She looked down at her own body—she was dressed as well, in a blue pants-suit that matched her eyes. "Oh my!" she said. "OhMyGosh! Is it like this all the time?"

"It can be," eDaphne said to her, "but just like flesh-and-bone, you have to work at it."

PART THREE

THE OORT

Chapter Sixteen

DENVER—PHOENIX LABS

Dr. Jackson Fredricks sat in his chair behind his desk at Phoenix Labs. Never one for ostentatiousness, his desk was plain and uncluttered, his chair was a simple mesh chair, a modern motive rug covered the space in front of his desk. A plain table, several padded chairs, and a couch completed the setup. Sally and Brad occupied two of the chairs on one side of the rug with the table behind them, and eSally and eBrad appeared to occupy similar chairs on the other side of the rug. The office door was shut

"You guys make your presence seem so natural," Fredricks said to the upload pair. "Now, what's so mysterious that you four wanted to meet with me privately?"

"We have something we think you need to see," Brad said to slight nods from the other three.

"This is a big deal," eBrad said.

"A *very* big deal," Sally added, hand raised to cover her mouth.

"We're not trying to keep it from the others," eSally said, "but we wanted to pass it by you first."

"Okay, I'm interested. What do you have?" Fredricks leaned forward, putting his forearms on his desk, hands folded in front of him.

"Allow me first to review a couple of MERT Portal facts," eBrad said, "to ensure we are on the same page."

Fredricks nodded, wondering what was up.

"A MERT Portal Locus creates a Casimir field that generates a wormhole. The Locus produces a hyper-disk that can be carried to any location within range. When the hyper-disk is activated, a MERT Portal is established. It's possible to transport a hyper-disk through a portal to establish another portal. The Locus for that hyper-disk can be anywhere within range. The multiple wormholes don't tangle or interact in any way." eBrad stopped talking and nodded at Brad.

"What Sally and I did," Brad said, "was to create two MERT Portals. We set one up so that the dependent portal was one meter distant from the Locus. We set up the second portal in the same way and then passed the second Locus through the first portal. Then we passed the first Locus through the second portal, passed the second Locus through the first portal, the first through the second, and so on until we had crossed the space." He paused with a wide grin. "What we had done was leapfrogged across the twenty-meter distance with twenty steps, each of which covered a meter instantaneously through what we call nullspace. The process of passing one portal through the other—the recycle time— actually took more time than just walking that distance; however, we thought we could reduce the portal transit time significantly by automating the recycle. Sally came up with an ingenious automation process that reduced the individual recycle times to one-half second. Now, we were crossing the twenty-meter normal space in ten seconds through nullspace."

"If I understand you correctly," Fredricks said, "your automated double portal crossed a twenty-meter space in ten seconds using instantaneous one-meter steps." He paused. "I think I see where you are going. If you shorten the recycle time sufficiently, you can reach your destination faster than light could."

Nodding, eSally said, "We have two variables. You defined the first: Recycle time. The second is the distance covered by the double portal."

Sally jumped in. "The double portal distance is the length of your apparatus, in other words, the length of your vehicle, your spacecraft. For sake of argument, let's assume our spacecraft is twenty-five meters long. Divide your total distance by twenty-five meters, and you get the total number of jumps you have to make. Multiply the number of jumps by the time for each jump, and you have the duration of your trip through nullspace."

"Here's a real-world example," eBrad said. "Get your jump time down to ten nanoseconds, and a ten-lightyear trip will take…"

"Four hundred thirty-eight days," Fredricks interrupted, tapping his Link. "Get it down to one nanosecond, and you're down to forty-four days."

The four young people sat quietly while Fredricks contemplated. Finally, he looked at each of them. "Is a nanosecond realistic?" he asked.

"It is," eSally said, "and we might be able to do better than that."

"Where are you now?" Fredricks asked.

Brad answered. "We've just completed a five-meter craft with a ten-nanosecond jump time—effectively 1.6 lightspeed. That will get us to the portal at the outer edge of the Oort Cloud in three hundred forty-six days."

"We haven't tested it yet," Sally said. "…well, I mean…we haven't conducted a test flight with people on board. It's not set up for that."

"But we did an unmanned test run to the Moon and back," eSally added. "A bit over one-and-a-half seconds for the round trip."

"And we did another test run to Mars and back—about five minutes for the round trip," eBrad said.

"If we're going to risk people," Brad said, "you need to be involved."

"I agree," Fredricks said, "but we need Thorpe and Braxton on this as well."

✳

Thorpe and Braxton observed a demonstration of the experimental MERT Drive the next day. The craft looked like a five-meter-long, two-meter-wide cylinder sitting on a five-meter-long, two-and-a-half-meter-wide flat tray with two-meter high vertical fins running the length of each side of the tray. The fins were deep black with all three edges terminating in razor-sharp knife edges.

"Let me get this straight," Braxton said to Fredricks. "You hire a couple of whiz kids from Mines to reverse engineer the mystery portals, and the next thing they do is build an FTL ship—a starship?"

Fredricks shrugged with a smile.

"I'd say we got a lot of bang for our buck," Thorpe added.

Sally and eSally each looked a bit embarrassed, but both Brads beamed with pride.

"How long until the ship is human travel worthy?" Fredricks asked.

"So," Sally said, "we will need to go to ten meters. We need sleeping arrangements for at least two, sanitary facilities, cooking/eating space, but first, we will need to manufacture two longer plates of non-baryonic doped matter..."

"Non-bary-what?" Thorpe interrupted.

"The original MERT calculations," eBrad said, "were based upon creating a Casimir field between two plates of non-baryonic matter—so-called *exotic* matter—that generated the wormhole. The power requirements were unobtainable—something like the mass of Jupiter converted to pure energy. When NASA's Harold White reworked the calculations applying modern theory to baryonic or normal matter, he was able to reduce the power requirements to something obtainable. Then, when eSally and I reverse-engineered the portals you found, we discovered that whoever created them used a hybrid material—basically baryonic matter doped with a small amount of non-baryonic matter. The result is what you see in all our MERT Portals, and what we have adapted for the MERT Drive—those black fins."

"Let's think about this," Braxton interrupted. "Portals feed power to both Loci, right?" All four nodded. "What if your destination exceeds the Locus' range?"

"I guess we're S-O-L," Brad said.

"Seems to me you might need a local power source," Braxton said.

"We've been so focused on portal delivered power that we didn't even consider a local power source," Brad said.

"Modern aircraft are powered by one hundred-megawatt LANRs," eBrad said. "In a five-by-two-and-a-half-meter space, we could put a two-hundred meg LANR and sufficient compressed hydrogen to keep it going for a very long time. If we use compressed deuterium or even liquid deuterium, our range is that much more."

"That would decrease the total jumps, wouldn't it?" Fredricks asked.

"Yes," eSally said, "but it would use correspondingly more power."

"You can feed portals for everything from home base until the supply line runs out," Thorpe said.

"Looks like we're talking a fifteen-meter craft," Braxton said. "How long till you can have one ready to fly?"

"If we do it right, two to three months," Brad said.

"Murphy willing," eBrad added.

DENVER—PHOENIX LABS—STARSHIP ISHTAR

Everyone who could be was present, even Deb Streeter from the Research Lab for Electronics at MIT. Max wandered around the large space, greeting old friends and making new ones. Kimberly saw it as almost a party atmosphere; everyone who mattered in her life was present, including Norman Bork, who had made Mars so real for her. The upload parties were also there, but they did not show their holoimages because some visitors were not yet aware of their existence.

The starship rested on a raised platform occupying the center of Lesser Hall, the smaller of the two large halls inside the Phoenix Labs complex. It looked like a 2.5-meter wide, 15-meter long, flat-bottomed horizontal cylinder nestled inside a flat-bottomed, u-shaped cradle as long as the cylinder. The cradle consisted of two 3-meter high, 15-meter long, deep-black vertical fins that were connected to each other at their bottoms by a 4.5-meter wide tray. The fins and tray were constructed from non-baryonic-doped material, and the top, leading, and trailing edges of the fins were razor-sharp. The cylinder was built from a double-walled radiation-absorbing polymer filled with a palladium-hydride that absorbed ionizing radiation, giving off a mix of hydrogen as H_2 and H-D or H^2H. This resulting hydrogen mix served as a backup fuel source for the LANR power supply. A meter back from the bow on the port side, a hatch opened to an airlock that occupied the front two meters of the cylinder. Six meters forward of the stern on the starboard side, a second hatch opened to an airlock that occupied two meters of the cylinder just ahead of the LANR chamber. The LANR was accessed through the starboard lock.

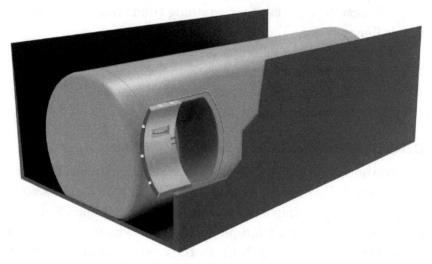

Figure 1 —MERT Drive Starship Ishtar

Everyone had been cautioned about the razor-sharp fin edges even though they were covered with safety sleeves clearly labeled in bright red REMOVE BEFORE FLIGHT! Kimberly was careful to avoid them as she stepped onto the raised platform near the port side of the starship's bow.

A hidden microphone picked up her voice. "The Babylonian Goddess Ishtar was daughter to Moon Goddess Ningal and Skygod Anu. She was sister to Sungod Utu, consort of Tammuz, Rivergod of Euphrates and Tigris, and she was Queen of the Heavens." Kimberly raised a hundred-year-old bottle of wine from the fertile vineyards of ancient Babylon between the Euphrates and Tigris Rivers. "I christen thee *Starship Ishtar—Queen of the Heavens!*" The knife-edge sliced through the bottle allowing its precious ruby contents to splash down both sides of the deep back fin.

After a hushed silence, the group broke out in cheers. Kimberly shivered and waved her hand to the small crowd. Then she clambered down the steep staircase to receive kisses from Daphne and Dale. Kimberly moved around Lesser Hall, collecting congratulations, but her head was swimming far beyond Earth and cislunar space, out beyond the Kuiper Belt, out beyond the Oort Cloud itself...

✳

Thorpe and Braxton, as holoimages, conferred with Fredricks.

"*Ishtar* is flight ready," Thorpe said, "but I don't want to risk human life on its shakedown flight."

"I agree," Braxton said.

"*Ishtar* is set up with several matrix slots," Fredricks said. "One or both of you can easily make the first flight. If something goes wrong, your backups will be nearly up-to-date."

"Especially if we carry a direct connection through a portal," Braxton added.

"So, which one of us?" Thorpe asked.

"I'll flip you," Braxton said.

"Negative on that," Thorpe said. "Jackson...you got a coin?"

"We don't use coins anymore," Fredricks said with a grin. "Remember?" He used his Link to create a virtual coin floating in the air and flipped it.

"I call tails," Braxton said.

And tails it was.

✳

Dale carefully slid the matrix containing Braxton into the primary slot in *Ishtar's* control panel. As the starship came to life, Braxton commented, "Nice design, Brad. You outdid yourself."

"Sally gave me a lot of help, and both eBrad and eSally checked out the internal design and certified it. Construction detail was Daphne and Dale. Kimberly supplied a sense of style." Brad paused. "I'm beginning to sound like a holoshow awards recipient." He grinned.

"I guess we're ready," Braxton said through external speakers linked to *Ishtar*.

"You're set for ten nanosecond intervals," Sally said. "A half-second to Earth-Moon L2, pause to change direction, one-and-a-half minutes to Mercury-Sun L1, pause, the same to Earth-Sun L3, and then three-and-a-half minutes to arrive back here. That's six-and-a-half minutes plus three pause times."

"I'm outta here!" Braxton said as *Ishtar* vanished.

Six-and-a-half minutes later, everyone in the room watched the platform expectantly. Thirty seconds passed…nothing. Forty-five… nothing. A minute-and-a-half…still nothing. Kimberly burst into tears, and Daphne put a comforting arm around her shoulders. Sally's eyes brimmed, but she managed to hold onto her tears. Nevertheless, Brad reached out and held her. Dale stood quietly with a stunned expression, and Fredricks tried valiantly to control his quivering lower lip.

With the passing of the fifteen-minute mark, Sally and Brad spent a futile few minutes trying to pull any data from the Earth-Moon L-2, Mercury-Sun L1, and Earth-Sun L3 swarms. Their readouts were completely normal. *Ishtar* and Braxton had transited each successfully. Finally, everyone had to accept the fact that *Ishtar* would not return…ever.

A deep gloom settled over the group.

✳

Braxton came to full consciousness and struggled to collect his thoughts. *I passed through Earth-Moon L2 and hopped to Mercury-Sun L1. I hung out long enough to get my bearings and then jumped to Earth-Sun L3. I remember checking the swarm and then initiating the jump back to Phoenix. Now, I'm here, in my GEO personal swarm…Obviously, I didn't make it back to Phoenix!* Braxton let himself recover and refocus. He checked his newly set up backup. Everything seemed to be working, but he was in slow motion. *Oh, Shit! The guys at Phoenix must be going crazy!*

Braxton pulled himself together with some difficulty and transited the portal he had installed in his personal swarm once Phoenix had established its own full portal network. He dropped into Lesser Hall without displaying his holoimage. Despite his immateriality, he could sense the deep depression that had engulfed Lesser Hall. It was pretty apparent that nobody had considered his backup.

"About time you showed up," Thorpe said to him within their virtual realm. "These guys are pretty shook up."

"You can say that again," eBrad said. "eSally and I have been expecting you, but she didn't want to interfere with the others."

eKim flowed into Braxton's essence and remained, letting him feel her pulsing happiness at his survival. eDaphne slipped into and out of his head, just long enough to share her joy with them both. eDale touched Braxton's hand sufficiently to let him sense his relief. eMax didn't really understand what was going on, but he moved from person to person, expressing his happiness with full-throated purring.

"Hey, guys! I'm here," Braxton finally announced to Lesser Hall in general, making his holoimage visible. "I am here courtesy of my backup system. Unfortunately, *Ishtar* is not coming back."

"What happened?" Thorpe asked.

"I arrived at Earth-Sun L3 from Mercury-Sun L1, checked the swarm, and then set course for here. I didn't bother going around the Sun like I did on the outbound trip. No need. Next thing I know, my backup is activated—me," he pointed to himself. "I came here as soon as possible."

"Every transit moment was inside a wormhole," eBrad said. "Something must have failed, exiting *Ishtar* directly into the Sun's interior."

"Not necessarily," eSally said. How did you set up your navigation?"

"I didn't," Braxton said. "I pointed through my electronic sight and activated the jump."

"So, navigation was on default," eSally murmured.

"And what is default?" Braxton wanted to know.

"One quick look at the half-way point," eSally answered with a grimace. "You exited nullspace at the Sun's center—give or take."

"Gonna have to fix that," Brad said. "Come on, Guys, we got a starship to rebuild."

OORT CLOUD—STARSHIP ISHTAR II

Working day and night, the team took just two months to complete *SS Ishtar II*. She was identical to her predecessor, but with significant additional software protection to prevent another disaster. Christening was less ostentatious than with the first starship, but Kimberly still insisted on a ceremony, and she even supplied her own less precious wine for the occasion.

The shakedown flight with Braxton once again at the controls went without incident this time. Even so, following departure from Earth-Sun L3, there still was a nail-biting three-and-a-half-minute wait before *Ishtar II* materialized on the platform in Phoenix's Lesser Hall.

"This is what we have worked toward ever since Braxton first discovered the mystery portals in ServerSky," Thorpe said to the assembled group. "We may not have known it then exactly, but here we are, ready to establish our own portal from Earth-Moon L2 to the outer reaches of the Oort Cloud, a portal that can handle people and materials." He smiled and looked around the group. "I understand that each of you wants to make this trip with me, but please don't forget that we're still operating at the edge of the unknown. We are family—all of us. I don't want to put any of you into harm's way—at least any more than necessary. This journey is beyond anything humans have ever done. One hundred thousand AUs, over one-and-a-half lightyears. It's a hundred fifteen-day journey for *Ishtar II*—not bad considering how far we are traveling, but a really long time for flesh-and-bone in a weightless environment." Thorpe passed his gaze from person to person. "Upon my arrival, I'll open the portal so the rest of you can join me."

✳

Ishtar II almost felt like a new body. Thorpe had been without a body for so long that he hardly knew what one felt like anymore. It wasn't his body out of the past—no arms, legs, head, but it still had the feel of something more than the ethereal existence he had experienced for so long. It was analogous to sitting in a favorite sports car, but it was more than that. It was more like he *was* the sports car. The power delivered by portal to his distribution node hummed through *Ishtar's* wiring like blood flowing through his veins. He reached back to the LANR and could sense its power pulsing behind the isolation circuitry that would open automatically should he lose portal power.

Thorpe checked his flight settings against the parameters Sally had uploaded to his knowledge base. eBrad and eSally had developed a way for his controlling computer—that they had dubbed *Mother*—to sense the external environment of the forward portal of the MERT Drive while they were still transiting nullspace. If it sensed anything substantial, or very high pressure or temperature, Mother would keep the MERT Drive in nullspace until she sensed a nonobstructing environment. This way, there would be no more exiting nullspace inside a star or gas giant, or even a small asteroid for that matter. Thorpe was anxious to begin his journey.

"I have a green board," Thorpe said to the group assembled in Lesser Hall.

"Phoenix has a green board," Fredricks said, making it official.

Thorpe activated his MERT Drive.

※

SS Ishtar II simply disappeared from the top of the platform, followed by a soft whoosh as air rushed to fill the space left by the small starship.

"We've got things to do and places to visit," eBrad said, after a few moments of silence, speaking for the other virtual entities as their holoimages flashed out of existence.

"I think we deserve a fortified cup of coffee," Fredricks said to his flesh-and-bone companions.

※

Thorpe noticed nothing unusual as *Ishtar* got underway other than a dramatic electrical activity increase in the circuitry that controlled the MERT Drive. More out of curiosity than anything else, Thorpe planned a brief stop at the orbits of each of the planets. This meant that thirty-eight seconds after he got underway, *Ishtar* dropped out of nullspace at the orbit of Mars, 1.38 AU from the Sun. Using his visible spectrum sensors, Thorpe took a quick look around. In the short time he allowed himself, he was unable to identify Mars. Mother informed him that Mars was off to his right near the far side of its orbit from his location. The jump to Jupiter's orbit lasted about six-and-a-half minutes. Thorpe thought he identified Jupiter far off to his left as a very bright star. Mother confirmed his sighting. Seven-and-a-half minutes later, *Ishtar* dropped out of nullspace, and Thorpe was presented with a view of Saturn as a bright star off to his left. Sixteen minutes later, at the orbit of Uranus, Thorpe saw nothing. Mother informed him that the pale blue planet was invisibly distant to his right. Eighteen minutes later, when he dropped out of nullspace at Neptune's orbit, Mother told him that the bright blue planet was near the opposite side of its orbit and difficult to see even with a good telescope.

Thorpe spent a bit of time absorbing his surroundings. He was thirty AU from a Sun that was 900 times less bright than on Earth. Even so, it still was too bright for him to gaze at it directly. Thorpe was about as far as he could get from any planetary body while still in Neptune's orbit, except for the dwarf planet Pluto that lay another fifteen AUs out and about ten below the plane of the ecliptic.

Thorpe's thoughts turned inward. Fleetingly, he saw Jackie riding her bike ahead of him through the wildflowers. Then she morphed into Daphne, and then—try as hard as he could—Thorpe couldn't recall Jackie's features. As he replayed the details of his melding with eDaphne, Jackie and the wildflowers slipped into the recesses of his mind, dropping from his conscious thought altogether.

So, I got here in about fifty minutes, Thorpe thought, turning to business at hand, *but the light that left with me still has three hours and ten minutes before it gets here. My next stop is the other side of the Kuiper Belt—about a thousand AUs farther out...almost twenty-seven hours for me and*—he ran a quick calculation—*five-point-eight days for light. Let's do it!*

Following a brief stop at the confluence of Kuiper Belt and Oort Cloud to admire the scenery, Thorpe dropped back into nullspace where he remained for 114 days. He adjusted his time-flow sense to avoid being overcome with boredom and spent a fair amount of conscious time replaying his scenes with Daphne and Kimberly. Jackie no longer played a role.

✳

Immediately upon dropping out of nullspace, Mother picked up the beacon Thorpe and Braxton had installed earlier. *Ishtar II* covered the 200,000-kilometer distance with several short hops. Finally, after over 115 days of nullspace travel, Thorpe found himself alongside the personal swarm Braxton had created what now seemed a very long time ago. He activated the hyper-disk built into his matrix.

OORT CLOUD—OORT STATION PRIME

"Hey, Thorpe!" Daphne was the first to step through the portal into *Ishtar II*. "Did you miss me?"

Before Thorpe could answer Daphne, Dale stepped through the portal and asked, "Have you heard the latest?"

"I kept up," Thorpe said. "I ran a tensor through the power portal."

"So, you know the authorities finally figured out what we are doing…sort of?" Kimberly said as she joined the growing crowd.

"They learned about our spaceborne activities, but they know nothing about the uploads, right?" Thorpe said.

"Not so far as we can tell," eDaphne said, speaking for all the uploads.

"They don't really have a handle on our portal technology either," Brad added. "But they know we can get from here to there in a way they don't understand."

"Jackson and Sally…are you guys there?" Thorpe asked.

"Right here," Sally said, covering her smile. "You just couldn't see me behind Brad."

"I'm in the lab," Fredricks said, "but I have everything on my monitors, I understand the first task is erecting the habitat—Oort Station Prime."

Agreement all around. "I've got the materials stacked on a dolly in Lesser Hall."

"We need to open an outside portal," Brad said. "Then, Dale and I can move the stuff into position for inflation."

"I'll go suit up," Dale said as he stepped back through the portal to Phoenix.

Five minutes later, he returned, carrying his globe helmet accompanied by Max, tail straight up, talking up a storm. Dale donned his helmet, entered the forward lock, cycled it, and exited the spacecraft. "You're not going to believe who's out here," Dale said. "It's eMax with his ever-present strange tensor."

※

Dale met Brad back in the Phoenix Lesser Hall. Together, with some help from Fredricks, they manhandled the dolly into the lock connected to the outside portal near *Ishtar*. The escaping air when they opened the outer lock assisted in moving the dolly outside, where the sudden loss of gravity made everything easier. Once outside, eMax jumped to the top of the collapsed habitat preening himself.

The Oort habitat was a hemisphere fifteen meters at the base. Unlike the Earth-Moon L2 habitat that was little more than an inflated, thin-skinned atmosphere bubble, the Oort habitat consisted of an outer polymer layer that hardened upon exposure to ultraviolet light—even the faint levels at the outer limits of the Oort Cloud. The inner polymer layer hardened upon extended exposure to oxygen. Like *Ishtar II*, the two-centimeter space between the skins was filled with radiation-absorbing palladium-hydride. As with *Ishtar* II, the hydrogen mix resulting from the shielding process served as a backup fuel source for the LANR power supply that was normally fed through a fuel portal.

Dale pulled a compressed air hose from the lock and attached it to a nipple protruding from a panel at the bottom of the collapsed habitat. Within minutes, the habitat had formed a half-sphere fifteen meters across, while eMax scampered to safety behind his strange tensor.

"I think we're ready for the palladium hydride hose," Brad said as he pulled a ten-centimeter hose from the lock. He held the hose as Dale attached it to a wide socket in the panel that penetrated the outer skin of the habitat. "We're ready out here," Brad announced.

"Stand by," Fredricks said. A few moments later, he said, "Okay, open the valve!"

Dale grabbed the U-shaped handle lying back against the hose and flipped it forward, so it pointed in the direction of the flow, opening the ball-valve. Immediately, ten atmospheres of hydrogen forced powdered palladium hydride into the space between the skins. Approximately fifteen minutes later, as the space between the skins completely filled with nearly eighty-five metric tons of the powder, a back-pressure regulator shut off the flow, and Dale closed the ball-valve. Brad attached power cables to a pair of electrodes extending from the panel.

"Cables attached," Brad said, and back at Phoenix, one-and-a-half lightyears distant, Fredricks activated the power.

As electricity surged through the habitat's outer skin, the powdered palladium hydride filling the space crystallized into a solid two-centimeter-thick hemispherical layer between the inner and outer polymer skins.

"You ever seen an igloo?" Dale asked Brad.

"Only holoimages," Brad answered. "Why?"

"Look at that monster," Dale said, pointing at the habitat.

The habitat was a smooth, featureless hemisphere with an arch-shaped extension on one side that contained the lock. Although the lock was disproportionately small compared to the entrance to an igloo, otherwise the resemblance was uncanny. The two-meter-high lock was temporarily sealed with magnetic curtains at each end. Four circular viewports penetrated the outer walls evenly spaced around the hemisphere. At the moment, the meter-wide openings were filled with a single-layer polymer sheet.

Dale opened a portal inside the habitat, and space-suited Daphne joined Dale and Brad.

✳

Daphne looked around as she floated through the portal. Since the ports were still covered with polymer sheets, all she could see was the hemispherical interior of the habitat broken by the four polymer-covered circular openings and the inner lock curtains. It was almost as if she were underwater in a full-body suit.

"Here," space-suited Kimberly said as she pushed a transparent meter-wide circular disk through the portal.

Daphne moved the disk to the side and accepted three more. Then Kimberly passed through the portal, followed by space-suited Sally carrying a polymer welding kit. The three women moved away from the portal as Dale and Brad wrestled two large airlock doors with their seals into the habitat. While the men set about installing the locks, Daphne grasped one of the disks and signaled to the other two women to join her.

The disks that would form the viewports to the outside universe were made from a radiation-absorbing crystalline sapphire matrix that had two polarizing layers whose alignment was governed by the intensity of incoming visible radiation—the brighter the light, the more polarized the ports. They resembled ports in the spacecraft employed by NASA, the Mars outfit, and the several inner system mining operations. The main difference was that the inner surfaces of the sapphire layers were coated with a nearly transparent palladium hydride molecular film. Otherwise, as with earlier spacecraft ports, the space between the sapphire layers was filled with a transparent radiation-absorbing polymer.

Kimberly and Sally positioned the first portal in front of the opening while Daphne trimmed away the polymer sheet, releasing the residual atmosphere inside the habitat to the Oort Cloud. Then they pressed the disk into the slightly beveled opening until it made a tight seal. Daphne moved to the outside of the habitat and sealed the edge of the disk with liquid polyaramid she forced out of a tube while Kimberly and Sally sealed the inside. Within a few minutes after application in a vacuum, the polyaramid cured to a steel-hard slightly flexible seal. An hour later, the three women had installed all four ports. Daphne floated in the center of the habitat admiring the view through each port. There was neither Moon, Earth, nor Mars to capture her gaze, but the sheer beauty of the Milky Way splashed across half the sky more than made up for their lack.

While the two men finished the airlock door installation, Daphne and Kimberly floated together, holding hands and sharing their awe. Out of the corner of her eye, Daphne saw Sally floating alone near the men, watching them work. "Sally!" she said, "come here…join us girls. This is a moment we need to share."

As they floated together, sharing the wonder, eDaphne, eKim, and eSally appeared as holoimages, and then eMax arrived and jumped into eDaphne's arms purring loudly.

"Hey, Sis!" Daphne said to her counterpart, but instead of responding as she usually did, eDaphne's eyes grew large.

"Did anyone else feel that?" she asked.

"Feel what?" eKim said.

"Something brushed me," eDaphne said. "I mean, my mind…I mean…I don't know want I mean."

eMax floated out of her virtual arms and faced her nose to nose. He mewed loudly and scampered behind his strange-tensor-companion.

eSally shook her head. So did eKim.

"There it is again!" eDaphne said. "Nobody felt it…really?"

"Back to Phoenix, everybody!" Thorpe suddenly said, interrupting everything with an executive decision. "Now!"

OORT CLOUD—THE OORT

With everyone else safely back at Phoenix Labs in the Denver Tech Center, even the upload entities, Thorpe and Braxton consulted with each other.

"We knew all along there had to be something out here," Thorpe said.

"An obvious truth is not always so obvious when you actually have to confront it," Braxton said. "Remember, I felt it a couple of times when we were just learning about all this?"

"Yeah, but what is it?" Thorpe asked as eMax settled on his virtual lap. "eMax here seems to know more than we do." He stroked the virtual tabby and nudged its ever-present strange tensor companion with his toe. "How do we open a communication channel?"

"That won't be necessary, Gentlemen." The baritone voice surrounded them, penetrating their individual essences.

"What are you?" Braxton picked up the challenge. "Or should I ask *Who*?"

"May I touch your minds directly?"

Braxton reached out to Thorpe. "Do you see a problem?"

Thorpe shook his head.

"How about me first," Braxton suggested, "and if it goes well, then both of us?"

"I've touched you before, you know," the entity said to Braxton.

✳

Braxton leaned back and closed his mind to all external inputs while he opened up to whatever had just spoken to him and Thorpe. As he settled back, he felt his perception expanding somewhat like when he first awakened in the matrix. His perceptual horizons seemed to expand in all directions, and his awareness filled the brightly lit space. He pulled back in an effort to take in the entire space he occupied. As he did so, the space darkened with a fuzzy brightness at the center. He seemed to be flying toward the brightness that resolved into the swirling, pinwheel shape of a galaxy. Instinctively, he knew it was the Milky Way. As he zoomed in, the stars began to resolve into individual fuzzy balls, not so much suns as glowing, mottled spheres. He had no direct control of his flight, although he could focus his attention on any specific object he wished.

Then Braxton found himself flying rapidly out from the galaxy center toward one of its outer arms, and toward one particular group of four fuzzy stars. Again, he knew instinctively that it was the triple star system consisting of Alpha Centauri A and B and Proxima Centauri and Sol just beyond them. The glowing balls of the Centauri stars intersected each other and were separated by about one-half the width of one of the balls from the fourth star and its ball. And then it struck him. The glowing balls were the Oort Clouds surrounding the suns.

The outer boundary of Sol's Oort Cloud was about half-a-lightyear from the Centauri system's intermingled Oort Cloud.

Braxton plunged into Sol's Oort Cloud and immediately lost his galactic view. What he saw instead was a vast structure, fully three lightyears across, consisting of trillions of small units each comparable in size to cislunar space. These, in turn, were grouped into sets containing thousands of the smaller units. Criss-crossing throughout the entire structure was an uncountable number of threads interconnecting the countless small structures. As he tried to integrate what he saw into his understanding, a pattern began to appear. One larger thread connected the outer edge to the center, near Sol. As he observed it, understanding flooded his mind that this was the Oort Portal from Earth-Moon L2 to the Oort Cloud. Lesser threads, but more prominent than the individual strands, connected the intermediate structures. The shimmering threads pulsed like blood vessels in a human body. Braxton found himself pulled into the shimmering mass so that he lost his orientation once again.

Then, to Braxton's astonishment, he was flying over an Earth-like landscape surrounded by clouds in a blue sky. Rivers, lakes, forests, meadows, deserts, and mountains flowed beneath him in rapid succession. And then magnificent cities pushed their towers skyward as he dipped down between kilometers-high structures, skirted floating sky islands, and swooped past large, floating cities on vast oceans. The images were fleeting but penetrated his soul, and he knew without being told that he was peering a billion years into the past.

As Braxton wrapped his comprehension around what he was seeing, without warning, everywhere, the sky was filled with terrifying fireballs. In moments, the landscape he had overflown was turned into a cratered cinder. The magnificent civilization, life itself, was stripped off the planet. Far above, marauding spacecraft patrolled the near-planet environs, searching for any remnant of the planet's intelligent life. They destroyed orbiting manned space stations, a station on the planet's moon, and another on the next closest planet. What they didn't see, but what Braxton clearly saw, was a scattering of ServerSky-like swarms around the planet, its moon, and several lo-

cations around the Solar System. He dipped into the nearest swarm...
and found an intelligence similar to himself, and then several more,
and finally, thousands.

The marauding spacecraft disappeared into interstellar space by
means the intelligences did not understand. Other than deliberate
total destruction of life on their planet, there seemed no reason for
the Marauder's actions. The surviving entities pooled their meager
resources, found ways to manipulate their environment, began to
multiply, and eventually spread throughout their solar system. When
they discovered portal technology, they created an interconnected
society throughout their entire solar system. They carried with them
detailed memories of their homeworld as they migrated out into their
Oort Cloud. In the Cloud, they manipulated their virtual environment until the entire population that had grown to several trillion
could experience their homeworld environment and all the richness
their lost civilization had provided. They discovered that they could
retain their individualities, but also could join in as many multiples
as necessary to solve virtually any problem.

Braxton's timeline accelerated as millions of years passed. Despite
the utter destruction the Marauders brought about, in isolated pockets
here and there on their planet, spores awakened and began to reseed
life on the barrenness. Some small, hardy marine creatures escaped
the near-total destruction of life and began to thrive. Braxton watched
life develop and spread across the planet once again until dinosaurs
dominated life for millions of years. He witnessed their destruction
and the near elimination of planetary life once more at the hands of
the marauding spacecraft as they returned and flung a large meteorite
into the planet to finish the task they had started so long ago—but
not quite. He watched glaciation come and go. He watched continents
move about and collide and merge. He watched humanoid life form
and develop until, 65 million years later, the planet below him was
his own familiar homeworld.

Before he could come to grips with the mystery, Braxton flashed
back to the Oort Cloud. There, he was shown weapons installations
scattered over the outside of the mighty sphere surrounding Sol,

massive high-energy and coherent light beams that were designed to destroy any incoming spacecraft.

"We are the Oort." The words echoed throughout Braxton's awareness. "We are one, but we are also trillions of individuals with our own dreams, hopes, and aspirations. Our civilization is a full and complete realization of millions of years of both advancement and, alas, stagnation that accompanies an existence such as ours. Amidst our countless aspirations and trillions of individual timelines, we hold one common purpose—to guard our continued existence and yours, our unexpected offspring, the fortuitous survivor of the death knell dealt us so long ago. The Marauders will return once they realize that civilization has again sprung up on Earth. You commenced broadcasting radio signals about two hundred years ago. We think the Marauders' homeworld is between fifty and a hundred lightyears out, so we can expect their return at almost any time.

Braxton opened his virtual eyes to find Thorpe looking at his face. Braxton blinked. "How long was I under?" he asked.

"Under?" Thorpe said. "All you did was blink your eyes."

Chapter Seventeen

OORT CLOUD—OORT STATION PRIME

Thorpe and Braxton sat in silence, contemplating what they both had just experienced. Finally, Thorpe broke the silence.

"We need to put the other uploads through the process, and we need to brief everyone else."

"Agreed," Braxton said. "It's pretty overwhelming. The Oort, these beings, like us in so many ways, out here watching, waiting, living lives we really cannot understand, thinking thoughts beyond our comprehension." Braxton touched Thorpe, merging briefly. "Let's get the others," he said. "Out here is where we should inform them about their heritage."

The entire team assembled inside the habitat. Fredricks and his human crew floated comfortably in a circle near the center of the dome, the upload holoimages dispersed among them. Max, long used to weightlessness, settled on Daphne's shoulder, clinging gently with his claws. eMax's holoimage floated from person to person.

Thorpe silently instructed the uploads on what to expect and indicated to the Oort that they were ready.

Stunned silence encompassed the uploads as they surfaced a moment later from their collective immersion into Oort history.

Finally, eDaphne whispered, "Not in my wildest imaginings did I contemplate something like this."

Virtual tears flowed down both eKim's and eSally's cheeks. eBrad swallowed hard, and eDale looked about to cry. He heaved a deep sigh and said quietly, "A billion years…it's beyond comprehension."

"Guys," Braxton said quietly, "we need to share this with the rest of the team."

The Oort chose to generate a holovision presentation of Oort history to the flesh and bone members of the team. It lacked the immersive depth of their presentation to the uploads, but even so, it took a couple of hours. When the holovision image faded away, Daphne wiped away tears and hugged Kimberly while dabbing at her tears. Sally and Brad floated together, holding hands, not saying anything at all. Sally didn't even try to hide her tears. Dale floated to Daphne and Kimberly, embraced them both, and blew his nose, and Max moved into Daphne's lap and tried to settle there without the benefit of gravity. Fredricks propelled himself to one of the outer windows where he floated in isolated silence.

Braxton gave them several minutes of private contemplation and then said, "Okay, guys, let's get back to Phoenix."

DENVER—PHOENIX LABS

The entire team sat around the conference table at Phoenix Labs, the humans, the uploads as holoimages, and even Deb Streeter transmitting his holoimage from MIT. eDaphne had brought him up to date before the meeting.

"I think," Thorpe said, commencing the meeting, "that what we have learned changes just about everything." Several people started to interrupt, but he held up his hand. "Please let me continue. Everyone here will have the opportunity to express themselves completely." He smiled around the table.

"Up to now," he continued, "we operated under free market rules—in other words, we did whatever the hell we wanted to do. We harmed no one. We took advantage of no one. In fact," he paused and smiled again, "the vast amounts of money we spent helped a lot of people. Things are different now. We know things that affect the entire human race. Hell, they affect not just the human race but the Oort as well." He paused and looked around the table. "I think we have an obligation to inform the world."

"Makes sense," Fredricks said, "but how do we do that?" He appeared genuinely puzzled. "Do I just walk into the Oval Office and lay it on the president?"

"I'm not sure he could handle it," Brad said with a chuckle. "He's been letting the world walk all over him ever since he took office."

"That's not fair," Sally said. "He's a decent and kind man."

"Who couldn't work his way out of a paper bag," Brad muttered, more to himself than to the table.

"How about the UN Secretary General," Kimberly asked.

"The UN has been less than useless since they moved to Geneva twenty-five years ago," Brad said. "They'd talk it to death and then blame Israel."

"For what?" Dale asked.

"Everything."

"Enough!" Fredricks said. "Let's keep politics out of this. I suspect we're pretty much on the same wavelength here, but let's stick to finding a solution."

"Weak or not," Streeter said, "the U.S. President still is the most powerful man in the world. I think we need to find a way to present this to him."

Nods around the table.

"I have a thought," Kimberly said, raising her hand. Everyone turned to look at her. "One of you uploads needs to visit the president and convince him to invite the famous scientist, Dr. Jackson Fredricks, for a private visit to the Oval Office. Jackson arrives with a hyper-disk, opens a portal to the habitat…and shows him."

"And if he fumbles the ball," Brad said, "we can pull off the same thing with another world leader."

"Before we bring anyone to the Oort habitat," eBrad said, "we need to do an upgrade. eSally and I have worked out the details for tethering the habitat to a counterweight and rotating it for artificial gravity. Since we knew it had to be done, we already manufactured the parts and have everything ready for transporting to the habitat and installation. eSally and I with Sally, Brad, and Dale can do it in a few hours."

"So, what are you guys doing here?" Fredricks said. "Go get the job done while we work out the details of telling the world," he ended with a caricatured fierce face.

SERVER SKY—GEO

Thorpe and Braxton retreated once again to Braxton's personal swarm in geosynchronous orbit.

"We simply must get ahead of this matter," Thorpe said. "It's like Daphne's and Kimberly's Hyperchess game. Without warning, Max scattered the pieces all over the place."

"Yeah," Braxton said, "we can't let that happen with this thing we got ourselves into."

"Remember our championship game at MIT?"

"We had worked out strategies every which way from Sunday," Braxton said. "I don't think that Stanford guy knew what hit him."

"Hypertchess is pretty complex," Thorpe said thoughtfully. "So's what we're doing now. We gotta do this right!"

"And keep some unknown *Max* from upsetting our plans," Braxton said, "or *eMax*," he added as the virtual feline popped into his personal swarm.

OORT CLOUD—OORT STATION PRIME

Dale and Brad suited up at Phoenix and established an external portal outside the habitat. Then they wrestled a collapsed polymer base and a reel of immensely strong, twisted, diamond-fiber rope through the portal into the space immediately outside the habitat. Nanotechnology had created continuous diamond strands from an engineered diamond that bore only a superficial resemblance to its namesake. Their rope was constructed of 243 individual diamond fiber strands twisted in cascading groups of three with a tensile strength stronger than anything else known to humankind. The reel carried twenty kilometers of this diamond rope. A collapsed polymer bag was attached to the reel housing opposite the feed. Using their TBH boots, they moved the reel to the top of the habitat.

"I'll work the rope," Dale said, "while you work the base."

Brad inflated the ring-shaped base with a high-pressure air hose from the external portal so that it fit snugly around the bottom of the habitat. The top of the base was L-beam shaped so that the habitat sat firmly on the flat and against the vertical piece. The bottom was U-beam shaped, forming a channel for the rope. Two I-beam cross-pieces fit inside the ring, adding stability and support for the habitat. About an hour after inflation in a hard vacuum, the base would cure to greater-than-steel strength.

"Help me position the base," Brad told Dale, "so the rope passes midway between the viewports."

On opposite sides of the base, using their TBH boots, they rotated the base until it was aligned correctly. Dale handed the bitter end of the rope to Brad, who passed the rope end down through an opening and around to the opposite side of the habitat, keeping the rope in the I-beam channel, where he passed it up through a similar opening. He fed rope to Dale, who pulled it to the top of the habitat, through a fitting, and down to the first opening. Brad passed the rope around the base in the opposite direction and up through an opening a quarter-way around. Dale pulled the rope up over the top, through the fitting, and down to an opening on the opposite side, where Brad fed it back around to the original opening.

"There," Brad said as he welded the rope in place using a tube of viscous polymer fluid that created a robust molecular bond between the rope and the base.

Dale reached in to help just as Brad squeezed the tube. "Shit!" Dale said, wiping his hands together. "I got that crap all over my gloves."

"Keep your fingers spread apart, and don't put your hands together," Brad told him. "Get yourself back to Phoenix and replace those gloves. Right now, you're about as useful as tits on a boar hog!"

During Dale's absence, Brad used the same polymer fluid to weld the habitat to the base around its entire circumference, using the time to work out his irritation with Dale's clumsiness. As he finished up, Dale popped back through the portal.

"Time for the counterweight," Brad said, giving Dale a high-five.

"Tell me again why we don't just use some of the ice from the Oort Cloud, and no jokes about giving an Oort person a lobotomy," Dale said with a wide grin.

"There's plenty of spare ice out here," Brad said, "but collecting eighty-five tons of it is a huge deal, given how sparse that distribution is especially out here at the Oort's edge."

"Okay—so we bring in lead by portal. Do we have the powered lead set up and ready to go?"

"We've got a pulverizing facility and people at the Montezuma mine in Peru, Colorado," Brad said, pulling a hyper-disk from a leg pocket. "They're standing by to blow the eighty-five metric tons we need through the portal."

"Eighty-five tons! Will that fit in the bag?"

"Sure. That's seven-and-a-half cubic meters of lead. That will easily fit into our two-and-a-half-meter bag." Brad grinned at Dale through his transparent helmet. "Do you seriously think I would not have run the numbers first?"

"You know better. Remember, I work with electrons. I look at the fifteen-meter hemisphere of the habitat, think about its palladium lining, and knowing that palladium and lead have similar specific gravities, the bag seems small…that's all." He grinned back. "Obviously, I defer to your superior knowledge."

Brad pointed to the bag. "That's it," he said.

"Be damned…not even full," Dale said with a rueful shrug.

✳

After collapsing the portal to the Peruvian mine, Dale and Brad pulled two maneuvering jets through the external Phoenix portal and attached them to opposite sides of the habitat base, pointed toward and away from the counterweight. Then they re-entered the habitat, dragged hypergolic hoses through the internal Phoenix portal, and connected them to the maneuvering jets' internal connections.

"Do you get motion sickness?" Dale asked Brad. "Or seasick?"

"Nope."

"You know what they say," Dale commented with a wide grin, "there are two kinds of people, those who get seasick and liars."

"Okay, fine, I mostly don't get seasick."

"I guess we're about to find out," Dale said as he turned to activate the maneuvering jets.

Slowly, the combined habitat, reel, and counterweight began to rotate end-for-end. Within a minute, the rotation rate reached one revolution per minute, and the g-force reached 1%, although Dale and Brad could not detect it. Within five minutes, the rotation reached three revolutions per minute with a resulting g-force of 10%, and Dale and Brad found their feet resting lightly on the habitat deck. When the rotation reached six revolutions per minute several minutes later with the g-force at 40%, Brad looked at Dale with a slightly greenish expression.

"Okay," he said, "I take your point."

Finally, after several more minutes during which Brad's expression turned increasingly green, the g-force reached 100% with a rotation rate of 9.5. Dale cut off fuel flow to the jets and released the reel brake, allowing the habitat and the reel with its attached counterweight to separate. Just like a spinning ice skater extending her arms, as the habitat and counterweight moved apart, rotation slowed until four kilometers separated them. Dale set the reel brake remotely, locking in a rotation rate of two-thirds of a revolution per minute, and Brad sighed contentedly as his expression returned to normal.

"So, why didn't it affect you?" Brad asked.

"I was the driver. For some reason, that lowers motion sickness effects."

The two men removed their globe helmets and stood side by side, gazing through the port facing away from the Oort Cloud at the grand spectacle of the Milky Way crawling past as Oort Station Prime spun slowly like a giant beanie-cap propeller attached to the Oort Cloud. They turned facing the opposite port, looking through the Solar System past Sol toward the outer reaches of the Galaxy, visible stars rotating slowly past their view in the opposite direction. Then they shifted their view to the two ports in line with their rotation. What they saw was similar, but the field of stars moved from the bottom to the top of the port or the other way depending on which port they chose.

Somehow, Dale thought, *watching all this through these ports at one-gee brings all of it into sharper perspective than just floating out there.* "What do you think," he said to Brad, "will the president buy our story out here, experiencing all this?"

"We'll know soon enough," Brad answered, "soon enough."

WASHINGTON D.C.—OVAL OFFICE

President John Butler looked up from the Resolute desk that was back in the Oval Office after several decades of absence. Tradition had always played an important role in his life. Then he found himself unexpectedly occupying the White House following a close election that had left the country seriously divided and the new president's sudden fatal heart attack. Former Vice President Butler chose the traditional over the modern even though he saw himself as progressive on most matters.

Sixty-two-year-old John Butler viewed America's role in the world as one of cooperation among equals and his personal role, not as the most powerful man on Earth, but merely as America's chief executive—a role similar to that of a university president. His supporters saw him as gracious and decent while his opponents saw him simply as weak. He had the look of an academic with horn-rimmed glasses, tweeds, and bowtie.

President Butler ran his hands through his thinning brown hair and sat idly fingering the carved edge of his desk. The unexpected position of President had turned out to be something different than he had imagined. He found himself having to choose the lesser of two bad choices more often than he would have liked. He was not at all sure he was up to the task. He was losing sleep, and when he slept, his dreams were restless. The only positive benefit he could immediately recognize was that he had lost some weight. He was down to 91 kg with a personal target of 85.

A shadow caught his eye, and he looked up to see a grey tabby cat strolling across the far end of the Oval Office. He didn't particularly like cats and reached for his Link to have an aid remove the creature. Before he could activate the call, he was startled by the appearance of a vaguely familiar green-eyed, middle-aged man with close-cropped brown hair sitting on the settee to the right of the coffee table in front of the Resolute desk.

"Please, Mr. President," said the man, who was apparently a holoimage, "give me a moment." The man looked at the cat. "Come here, Max!" The cat jumped onto his lap—obviously another holoimage.

President Butler hesitated and decided to delay his call. Rising to his 1.8-meter height, he asked, "How did you bypass my projectors? What's this all about?" His tone was more one of curiosity than concern.

"Can you arrange fifteen minutes of uninterrupted privacy?" the man asked.

President Butler hesitated, unsure what to do. Then he nodded, manipulated his Link, and the doors locked as the windows assumed a frosty opaqueness.

"I am Braxton Thorpe," the man said.

"I recognize you now," President Butler said. "You're—pardon the expression—the revived Icicle."

Thorpe nodded.

"That doesn't explain the cat..."

"Max..."

"Right, Max, nor how you can appear here without the minions surrounding me knowing about it." The president smiled.

"Let me supply you with some context," Thorpe said. Then he quickly summarized everything that had happened since his revival, leaving out nothing significant. President Butler sat quietly, absorbing the information. "I would not expect you to believe everything I have told you," Thorpe said, finishing up, "so I have a request. I believe you know of Dr. Jackson Fredricks. He's the brains behind what we have accomplished."

"I've heard of him, of course."

"If you will arrange for Dr. Fredricks to have an exclusive audience with you lasting for an hour, I believe we can answer all your questions."

"When?"

"At your convenience, Mr. President." Thorpe smiled warmly. "And please arrange for him to be brought here without being searched."

Butler lifted his eyebrows.

"He will be carrying a five-centimeter metallic disk. I would rather that no one but you be aware of it for now."

※

The following morning at 8:45, Fredricks presented himself at the White House gate. He was directed to a parking area where he was met by one of the interns that work at the White House.

"Please follow me, Dr. Fredricks," the attractive eighteen-year-old lass told him. A couple of minutes later, they arrived at the Oval Office outer door. She ushered him in announcing, "Dr. Jackson Fredricks, Mr. President."

President Butler stood and walked toward Fredricks, hand outstretched.

"John Butler, at your service."

What a quaint, almost anachronistic greeting, Fredricks thought as he shook the president's hand. "It's my honor," he said, meaning it.

"Please sit," the president said, indicating the settee at right angles to the Resolute desk. "Coffee, tea?"

"Coffee, thank you," Fredricks said as he seated himself.

Moments later, a U.S. Navy steward placed a steaming pot of fresh coffee on the low table before the settee. The president sat on the settee opposite Fredricks and poured two cups.

"As I am sure you know," President Butler said, "I met Mr. Thorpe yesterday...and Max." He smiled.

"Actually, that was eMax," Fredricks said, smiling back. "We uploaded him as our first real-time upload." The president lifted an eyebrow. "All our major players are uploaded now except for me." Fredricks' eyes twinkled. "I performed all the uploads. I want to be sure that whoever uploads me is as skilled as I am." Fredricks reached into his inner jacket pocket and retrieved a hyper-disk. "We have about fifty-five minutes left, is that right?"

The president came to his feet and manipulated his Link. The Oval Office doors locked, and the windows went opaque. "I've instructed my staff not to disturb me for an hour," he said.

"No worries," Fredricks said. "If there is an emergency, your Link will be responsive." He opened the portal to Oort Station Prime. "Please follow me, Mr. President."

❋

President Butler trusted Dr. Fredricks without knowing why, entirely. When Fredricks stepped through the portal, he followed with only the slightest sense of unease. He found himself in a dome-shaped room with four evenly spaced, large, round windows showing stars sliding by in the distance.

"Welcome to Oort Station Prime," Fredricks said without ceremony. "We are on the outer edge of the Oort Cloud, one-and-a-half lightyears from Earth." Fredricks steered the president toward the outer port. "You are looking toward the center of our galaxy, the Milky Way." He led the president to the opposite port. "This view is past our sun toward the galaxy edge. That bright star," Fredricks pointed to Sol, "is our sun."

President Butler stood quietly for two minutes, just taking it in. Never in his life had he felt so overwhelmed, so insignificant. *How can I bring this to my fellow national leaders?* He asked himself. *Can we even retain our self-identity in the face of all this?* Finally, he sighed. "Tell me about the Oort."

"I can do better than that, Mr. President. Working with one of the Oort individuals—we call him Johnny—we have been able to generate a holovision presentation of Oort history. With your permission, Sir, I would like to make this presentation in the Oval Office." He turned toward the portal. "We still need to turn this station into a comfortable working space."

❋

Back in the Oval Office, President Butler settled into his executive office chair and leaned back, not knowing quite what to expect.

He glanced at the time. "I'm going to need another half-hour of privacy," he ordered over his Link.

While he waited for Fredricks to set up the presentation, Thorpe appeared with eMax.

"Good morning, Mr. President," Thorpe said as eMax jumped onto the Resolute desk and curled up on a small pile of papers that the president had been working on when Fredricks arrived. "As knowledgeable as Dr. Fredricks is, I am more familiar with the Oort and may be better able to answer any of your questions." Thorpe grinned. "It looks like eMax has taken a liking to you."

President Butler remained transfixed during the entire presentation. When it was over, he remained quiet for a couple of minutes. Then he said, "So these beings, this being, this Oort has been protecting our world for millions of years and us ever since we became us..." His voice trailed off as he closed his eyes, lost in his thoughts again. *Why did the Marauders attack?* he asked himself several times, trying to wrap his mind around the problem. *Why would anyone do that?* "I get the caretaking, the protection—it makes sense, but what I don't get is the Marauders. Why, in Heaven's name, would any race do that?"

"Mr. President," Thorpe said, "have you heard of the Fermi Paradox?" The president shook his head.

"Back in the mid-twentieth century, Dr. Frank Drake postulated what came to be called the *Drake Equation*." Thorpe put up a holo-image of the equation[3]: $N = R_T \cdot f_p \cdot n_e \cdot f_l \cdot f_i \cdot f_c \cdot L$

---

[3] R_T = the average rate of star formation in our galaxy

f_p = the fraction of those stars that have planets

n_e = the average number of planets that can potentially support life per star that has planets

f_l = the fraction of planets that could support life that actually develop life at some point

f_i = the fraction of planets with life that actually go on to develop intelligent life (civilizations)

f_c = the fraction of civilizations that develop a technology that releases detectable signs of their existence into space

L = the length of time for which such civilizations release detectable signals into space

"Modern estimates place the value of N, the number of technological civilizations in our galaxy, at about fifteen million."

"I'll take your word for it," the president said.

Thorpe continued. "During a lunch conversation back around the same time, Dr. Enrico Fermi, who built the first nuclear reactor, posed the question, *Where is everybody?* And that is the paradox. If there are fifteen million civilizations out there, where are they?"

"That's a good question," President Butler muttered, half to himself.

"Mr. President," Thorpe said, "have you heard of the *Dark Forest Theory?*"

Again, the president shook his head.

"Allow me to quote from *The Dark Forest*, a famous novel written by Chinese science fiction writer Cixin Liu back in 2015.

"The universe is a dark forest. Every civilization is an armed hunter stalking through the trees like a ghost, gently pushing aside branches that block the path and trying to tread without sound. Even breathing is done with care. The hunter has to be careful, because everywhere in the forest are stealthy hunters like him. If he finds another life—another hunter, angel, or a demon, a delicate infant to tottering old man, a fairy or demigod—there's only one thing he can do: open fire and eliminate them."

"My God!" the president said. "Why did he conclude that?"

"It's a reasonable answer to the *Fermi Paradox*," Thorpe answered. "Despite there being fifteen million civilizations in our galaxy, we haven't found anyone because either they are hunkered down or extinct. And a later variation postulates that when one civilization becomes a killer species, becomes the Marauders, it will scour the galaxy eliminating all rivals."

"Are you familiar with Charles Pellegrino's 1993 novel, *Flying to Valhalla?*"

The president shook his head. "Not my style of reading."

"In that work, he defined the *Pellegrino / Powell / Asimov Three Laws of Alien Behavior*: (1) Their survival will be more important to them than our survival. (If they have to choose between them and us, they won't choose us.) (2) Wimps don't become top dogs. (No species makes it to the top by being passive.) And (3) They will assume that the first two laws apply to us. (And act first.)"

The president shook his head again. "It can't be," he said, "it just can't be."

"Then how do you explain the Oort?" Thorpe asked quietly, "and other possible near extinction-level events in Earth's history?"

President Butler placed his elbows on his desk and head in his hands. He pushed away external inputs and concentrated on what else might fit all the data. He looked up a bit later when his Link announced an urgent incoming message.

"By your leave, Mr. President," Thorpe said as his holoimage, and that of eMax vanished.

"You have a lot to ponder, Mr. President," Fredricks said as he stood to leave. "Please contact me when you are ready to move forward with any of this.

WASHINGTON D.C.—OVAL OFFICE

Kimberly arrived in the Oval Office a week after President Butler's meeting with Fredricks and Thorpe. Her official title, Phoenix Liaison, belied her actual job that was to lay the groundwork for an official American delegation to the Oort, and to assist the president with his efforts to inform other heads of state about the Oort.

"I am pleased to meet you, Ms Deveraux," President Butler said as he waved her to the settee. "Dr. Fredricks speaks highly of you and tells me that you are the best person on his team to help me make sense of all this." He smiled warmly. "You have brought a hyper-disk, yes?"

She held it toward him.

"No, you keep it on your person at all times. I'm still tiptoeing around how to present this technology to my senior staff. You and I are going to work closely on that."

Although only in her early thirties, Kimberly was comfortable with her marching orders but was not entirely sure how to implement them. Her task was to make the world establishment aware, through President Butler, of the Oort and the Marauder threat, and to make available to them the proprietary tools Phoenix had developed. Very specifically, however, Thorpe told her not to reveal any technical details about portal technology, and not to relinquish any of the private industry initiative Phoenix had established. The way he explained it was that the private firm Phoenix had, on its own, created portal technology, and both discovered and established a relationship with the Oort. She was to resist any challenge to or undermining of either of these by the U.S. Government or anyone else. Daunting as the task might be, Kimberly was confident that as the process moved forward, she would find a way to carry out her assignment without compromising the elements that concerned Thorpe.

"Mr. President, let me say upfront that my team had reservations about telling anyone about the Oort. The older and wiser members convinced the rest of us that the Oort and the Marauders were bigger than Phoenix. The Marauders threaten all of us, including the Oort. Not just the United States, either—the entire planet, the whole human race."

"Are you prepared to put other heads of state through my experience?" the president asked.

"If you think that's the best way to bring them on board, yes, Sir."

"I think first we need to deal with my National Security Council and then senior congressional leaders." The president checked his Link. "We can meet with the Security Council late this afternoon." He rechecked his Link. "Tomorrow morning, the congressional leaders will meet us here."

※

Communicating by Link with Fredricks, Kimberly told him, "The NSC members were skeptical until they transited the portal to OS-Prime. Now we have an information containment issue. President

Butler issued a dire warning about leaks, but they didn't seem to take him too seriously."

"The word's got to come out sooner or later. Leaks from the Administration might be the best way to do it," Fredricks commented.

OORT CLOUD—OORT STATION PRIME

While Fredricks and team dealt with Earth politics, Thorpe and Braxton transited to the Oort Cloud and met with Johnny Oort, as they called the Oort with whom they had been dealing.

"What do you know about humans and Earth politics?" Thorpe asked.

"We have tensors virtually everywhere," the Oort said. "You've met several of them."

"Despite your observational presence throughout Earth's history and its present establishments," Braxton said, "until the recent advent of uploaded humans, you could not have gained a genuine understanding of the human mind. Humans are a self-centered, devious, cantankerous, and sometimes magnificent lot. At our best, a human will lay down his life for another, and at our worst, a human will betray his own family for personal advantage. This has been the case throughout our history, and we don't see it being any different here.

"My experience tells me that a joint Earth delegation will approach you, but you will also receive quiet feelers from several individual states. You should also hear from some private concerns as soon as they figure out how to contact you. To avoid the confusion and inefficiency of all this, we are suggesting that we establish a formal federation that will include the Oort, various Earth nations, independent Solar System activities like the Mars Station and others as they establish themselves, and entities like Phoenix."

"We will have our legal team draw up Articles of Federation that will establish the rules under which we will function," Thorpe said. "We will pass them by you before we make anything official."

"While you have been talking," Johnny Oort said, "I have been connected with the Oort. We have examined our own knowledge, all we know of human history, and what we know of you. We are in agreement, subject to the Oort having a veto over proposed actions. We also want you, Thorpe, to head the federation and to have veto power as well."

❉

"It looks like I just became a head of state," Thorpe said to Braxton as they settled in Braxton's personal Oort swarm, "and that means you, too."

"Things were pretty simple when all we had to worry about was Phoenix and our team," Braxton said. "Now several billion humans and a trillion or so Oort will be looking at us for answers. Not exactly what we anticipated when we planned to become an Icicle."

"We've been pretty lucky thus far," Thorpe said. "Everyone has risen to whatever task we assigned."

"I know we are on the same wavelength and all," Braxton said, "but I have been thinking about OS-Prime. Right now, it's just another guard outpost. I think we need to expand it. We need a Federation meeting chamber, a couple of offices, maybe even a matrix where you and I can settle in from time to time."

"You're talking about an Oort Federation headquarters," Thorpe quipped. "Shouldn't be a problem. We just extend the station and increase the mass of the counterweight. I'll put Dale and Brad right on it."

Chapter Eighteen

WASHINGTON D.C.—OVAL OFFICE

The congressional delegation, consisting of the Speaker of the House, the House Minority Leader, and the Senate Majority and Minority Leaders, but none of their staff, sat in chairs arranged in front of the Resolute desk. President John Butler sat behind the desk, and Kimberly sat in a chair to the president's right.

"Ladies and gentlemen," the president said to the delegation, "please meet my AOA—Advisor on Oort Affairs, Kimberly Deveraux." He indicated Kimberly. "She will introduce you to a matter of utmost importance, not only to our nation but to the entire world—in fact, beyond that to the entire Solar System." He nodded to Kimberly.

Kimberly cleared her throat, feeling a bit nervous in the presence of this august group. Then she launched into a short history of the events that led up to the discovery of the Oort. "I know this sounds like the most improbable thing you have ever heard," she said. "Let's participate in a little demonstration that should make believers out of you." She activated a portal to Phoenix Labs in Denver. "Please follow me through the door."

As they stepped through the portal into the Phoenix Lesser Hall, Kimberly said, "Welcome to Phoenix Labs in the Denver Tech Center, located in the southern part of Greater Denver. This hall is where we assemble materials for transfer to wherever they are needed in the Solar System." She let them look around for a minute or so. "Now, please follow me. We are going to step outside so you can see that we really are in Denver and no longer in Washington, D.C."

The astonished delegation stood at the top of the broad flight of steps leading to the building's front entrance. "It seems like magic, doesn't it?" President Butler said with a quiet smile as several pedestrians on the sidewalk below stopped and looked up at the president with astonished stares. The president pointed. "See the Front Range over there? And the best is yet to come."

Kimberly activated a portal to the meeting room on OS-Prime and invited the president and the delegation to follow her. By this time, the meeting room had been minimally furnished with several rugs, couches, chairs, and low tables.

"Eventually," she told the delegates as they sat down after they had spent several minutes gazing out the four ports onto the universe at large, "the space immediately below us will become the command center for a large number of similar stations bristling with energy weapons."

Each of the delegation members looked at her with startled shock.

"I didn't misspeak," she told them and pointed to the center of the station. "Please pay attention to the holovision presentation."

Following the presentation, Kimberly addressed the stunned delegation again. "Other than the president, NSC members, and you, no other human except my team knows anything about any of this…with one small exception. The Mars Station has use of MERT Portals, but no access to portal technology." She took a chair facing the five of them.

"Once we grasped the import of what we had stumbled upon," she continued, "we became convinced that this no longer concerned just us. Ultimately, the Marauders are a threat to all humankind." She paused and looked at each member. "Even more than that! This concerns our entire race and the Oort, without whom we would not even exist as a species." Kimberly sat quietly, letting her words sink in. "All of you have way more life experience than I. I don't have to tell you how complicated are human interrelationships." Kimberly stood up. "This is why I am now going to ask the Oort to address you. The Oort can interface with our electronics so that you will hear the collective voice of several trillion individual Oort speaking to you with one voice, one sense of purpose." She sat in her chair.

"We are the Oort." The voice was a melodic, male baritone. In the space occupied earlier by the presentation, a shimmering sphere appeared representing the Solar System surrounded by the Oort Cloud. "We are one, and we are trillions. We have sustained ourselves for over a billion years, multiplying, learning, gaining wisdom. As you have seen, we have a full intellectual, cultural, and social life while we protect ourselves and humans from the inevitable return of the Marauders.

"In the short time between Braxton Thorpe's revival into a matrix until now, you discovered our existence, stumbled upon our portals, duplicated them, and transformed them into a method for FTL travel. What took us several million years you did in several years, and not only that, you did us one better. You are a remarkable species that must be preserved.

"We know very little about the Marauders except for what they did to us initially. It took us a very long time to recreate our civilization, even on a virtual basis. While we were still getting it together, before we had any defensive capability, the Marauders returned several times to ensure intelligent species destruction on Earth. The last time was about sixty-five million years ago. Since then, humans arose, and for the last two hundred years or so, you have been broadcasting electronic transmissions in every direction.

"We believe the Marauders do not have FTL travel, but we think they can rapidly accelerate to near lightspeed, so their travel time between stars is about what light would take. If they are anywhere within two hundred lightyears, they know you are becoming a threat, and are on their way. Because the danger could be imminent, we need to take immediate action. Unfortunately, humans as a species will not take the necessary action because you are too fractured, too fearful of each other. To compensate for this, working with Braxton Thorpe, we have created the Oort Federation. Thorpe will act as Chairman until he chooses to step down. Every nation on Earth is welcome to join and send a two-person delegation to the council, as is any space-based organization and any company with assets exceeding a trillion dollars, having more than a million employees, or both.

"We intend to build Oort Stations like this one around the Oort Cloud, armed with high-energy weapons capable of destroying an incoming Marauder ship. Initially, we will build five stations coordinated from here, three in the plane of the Kuiper Belt separated by one hundred twenty degrees and two more in a plane normal to the first, intersecting here—Oort Station Prime. We anticipate their being manned by the United States, China, Russia, Europe, and India. As we build more, we will seek participation by other nations, but we will not arbitrate as to who they will be. We expect you, President Butler, to coordinate that through whatever means seems appropriate to the nations of Earth.

"Thank you, ladies and gentlemen, for your attention."

The Oort image vanished. Kimberly stood smiling at the five awe-struck individuals before her. "I'll take any questions," she said quietly.

"Why me?" President Butler asked.

"Because you, Sir, are president of the United States, the most powerful nation on Earth, making you the most powerful person on Earth."

"I don't see it that way," President Butler responded. "America is a nation among equals, and I a national leader among equals."

"With due respect, Sir, we disagree," Kimberly said. "We discussed this before approaching you since you have made your views well known. Several of us wanted to place this matter in the hands of the United Nations. But when we looked at that venue… well, none of us could see anything happening in any reasonable timeframe. After examining all the other options, you, Sir, seemed the only choice." Kimberly smiled at him. "In any case, the decision has been made. Now it's up to you here in this room. We expect to see a resolution and appropriate participation by the time we have armed OS-Prime and built and armed the other five stations." She beckoned toward the portal. "Would you please follow me back to the Oval Office?"

EARTH—GENERAL

President Butler gathered his full Cabinet and had Kimberly brief them. After an OS-Prime visit and a briefing by the Oort, the president addressed them in the Situation Room.

"We cannot contain this explosive information much longer," he told them. "Like it or not, agree or not, the Oort is correct. This office is the best instrument to disseminate what we know to the world. I don't want to be the nine hundred-pound gorilla in the room, but I see no way of avoiding the responsibility." He looked around the room. "Does anyone here disagree or have some meaningful input?" There were no takers.

He instructed his Secretary of State to call for an urgent meeting the following morning with the ambassadors from Europe, the Russian Federation, China, and India. That meeting culminated with a visit to OS-Prime and a briefing by the Oort. President Butler had Kimberly issue each ambassador a hyper-disk to the Oval Office. He requested that each return immediately to their heads of state and arrange for a two-hour meeting in the Oval Office on a tight schedule the next day, coordinated by the Secretary of State.

Although it was unprecedented, the Secretary of State pulled it off. Kimberly arranged for each head of state to accompany the president to OS-Prime as soon as each arrived by portal in the Oval Office. In the meeting chamber of OS-Prime, each was first briefed by Kimberly, then shown the Oort holovision presentation, and then the Oort briefed each one. The Oort tailored its presentation to each head of state using its vast knowledge of things on Earth supplemented by insights on each individual Thorpe was able to supply.

Each leader returned home, having agreed to arrange for a team to man one of the Oort Stations upon its completion. They also agreed to a simultaneous holovision broadcast to their respective nations, arranging for a common time that best accommodated their planetary distribution. How these leaders chose to present the information to their citizens was left up to each of them.

World reaction was predictably different.

✳

Across the United States, people celebrated what they saw as an American accomplishment. There were more high-fives, public hugs, and toasts across the nation than ever before. On the other hand, people in Baltimore, Chicago, and Los Angeles rioted. In mountain and desert hideaways, camo-clad men quietly oiled their weapons and set additional watches around their compounds.

The Europeans, still not fully accustomed to being a single nation, celebrated according to their local customs. The French poured their best wines, and French lasses kissed every man and woman within reach. Germans quickly named a beer after the Oort, and across the land, flagons of beer were lifted in praise of the Oort. Elsewhere, Europeans of all stripes and nationalities carried on as they had for hundreds of years when something extraordinary happened.

In the Russian Federation, vodka flowed like water, and the Duma declared the Oort an honorary Russian citizen.

Chinese entrepreneurs quickly created millions of just about everything—mugs, glasses, tee-shirts, flags, etc.—each displaying the Oort Cloud. The general population created Oort-like paper dragons and paraded them through the streets of ten thousand towns and villages.

In India, the devout prayed for the Oort to exercise wisdom in all things, and the less devout danced in the streets and burnt effigies of Marauders.

Elsewhere, people did as people do. They celebrated, they went to church, some huddled in fear, and others rioted, but in a couple of days, it was all over, and people returned to their normal lives.

EARTH—PHOENIX

Following President Butler's lead, the national leaders from Europe, the Russian Federation, China, and India quickly set up commissions to oversee their national participation in the Oort defense. Thorpe dispatched Dale, Brad, eDale, and eBrad to work directly with the four teams each of the designated nations had established. He put Daphne in charge of coordinating the technical activities between Phoenix and the five Oort Stations. eDaphne coordinated the human-Oort technical interface.

Braxton set up a manufacturing facility at Phoenix to produce the high-energy beam weapons for installation on each Oort Station. The Oort had supplied the underlying technology upon which Braxton's team built. They developed three powerful devices. The first was a laser that could deliver a million joules per second into a square decimeter at a range of one million kilometers. It was powered by Oort generated energy brought to the weapon through a series of interconnected portals. The second was an anti-matter particle beam that could deliver a packet of anti-matter to any point within about five hundred thousand kilometers. The interaction of the anti-matter with ordinary matter at the arrival point caused a massive explosion every bit the equivalent of a large thermonuclear device. The third weapon was a focused neutrino beam that could disrupt biological systems, LANR devices, nuclear reactors, and nuclear bombs with an effective range of about a million kilometers with a three-dimensional ranging error of about a meter. Both the anti-matter and neutrino beams were powered by Oort technology that tapped Sol's core as a source of anti-matter and neutrinos. Each Oort Station was to have one of each type of weapon.

Braxton set up a second Phoenix site for manufacturing several targeting systems the Oort had developed and passed to Braxton for adaptation to human use. One long-range system, designed to detect incoming spacecraft at the most distant possible range, was a quantum device based upon entanglement. The Oort had found a way to separate entangled particles physically, and to project one element of trillions of these pairs in an expanding sphere around Sol and the Oort Cloud. The particles were projected in waves that allowed each Oort Station to calculate the approximate vector, range, and velocity vector of anything moving within the sphere, an incoming spacecraft, a comet on its own path, or anything at all sufficiently large to trigger the system. The incoming data were presented in holographic spheres in each of the Oort Stations, called Entangled-Particle Display (EPD), that represented surrounding space. Targets of interest showed as colored points along illuminated paths.

A neutrino detector was the second long-range system. It could identify the vector of anything that emitted concentrated neutrinos, so long as the neutrino stream could be separated from the background. It was useful where more than one detector could be used along a broad baseline to determine range.

For closer-in ranging, the Oort had developed a high-energy, variable-range, high-resolution radar that worked in three dimensions to 100 thousand kilometers out from each Oort Station. Its display was a holographic sphere similar to the EPD, but it could also be integrated into the EPD.

The fourth ranging device could be called a targeting radar. It was a 50 thousand-kilometer maser that reflected coherent high-frequency electromagnetic beams off any in-range object to produced precise fire-control solutions for the energy weapons. It could handle ten simultaneous targets. Each Oort Station had ten of these devices. Each had its independent display, but they all integrated into the station's EPD.

The four ranging devices and the three weapon systems on each Oort Station were under the control of an integrated Oort system they dubbed *Athena* after the Greek goddess of war. The Oort coordinated the computational capabilities of nearly a trillion Oort individuals through as many Oort portals to make *Athena* available simultaneously to the entire swarm of Oort Stations. Human operators did not actually fire any of the weapons, but they maintained ultimate control over their use.

※

Thorpe, Braxton, and Fredricks sat together in Fredricks' Phoenix office. eMax was curled up on the corner of the desk. Fredricks sipped on a rye from a distillery in the Front Range. A single cube of ice floated in the golden liquid.

"Sorry I can't offer you one," he said with a rueful smile, lifting his glass.

"Something we've learned to do without," Braxton said. "We have other compensations."

eMax looked up and mewed softly. Fredricks wished he could stroke him. "We're fifty percent through weapons manufacture," he said. "Sixty percent for ranging." He sipped his rye. "We need to come up with a plan for placing portals at the other stations. eBrad and eSally have cut the MERT Drive cycle to seven nanoseconds—utterly remarkable if you ask me—but that still leaves an eighty-day transit time for each station, unless we build more ships. If we lengthen them to twenty meters, we cut the time to sixty days, but that will require a redesign of the onboard LANRs."

"I've been talking to Johnny," Thorpe said. "He thinks the Oort can modify its portals to accommodate physical transits. It is working on that right now. I think we can presume it will solve the problem, and that we can use portals to move materials and personnel to each of the Oort Stations."

"Thorpe and I," Braxton said, picking up the conversation, "have been pondering another potential problem. Relatively soon, we will be able to detect and counter incoming Marauders…so long as we are not dealing with thousands of ships. In that event, inevitably, some spacecraft will get through our defenses. If we have more than the original five Oort Stations by the time the Marauders arrive, we'll be in better shape, but no matter how you cut it, some are going to break through."

"And, that isn't all," Thorpe added. "If the Oort is right, these guys don't have FTL ships, but they seem able to accelerate to near lightspeed very quickly, turn on a pinpoint, and decelerate just as fast. I'm sure you've seen holovision broadcasts of aerial dogfights. We don't stand a chance in any one-on-one combat with these guys."

Fredricks sipped his rye—the ice cube had melted. "We may be missing something here," he said thoughtfully. "Velocities close to lightspeed involve significant mass increases with consequent gravitational effects. I don't think that's possible within a solar system—close to stars and planets. I'm guessing these guys are limited to something under one-half light speed. I suspect rapid acceleration and deceleration and near-instantaneous turning are not affected by this."

"Even so," Braxton said, "they can run circles around anything we have."

"What about cislunar stations at Earth-Moon L1, 3, 4, and 5, and a Mars-Sun L1 station with spherical detection and defenses?" Fredricks asked. "The Oort has computing capabilities that totally boggle the mind. I think it could pick off Marauders that get that far."

"The Oort has been eavesdropping," the voice of Johnny said without preamble. Fredricks started, wondering if he ever would get used to it. Thorpe and Braxton looked at each other knowingly. "We concur," he continued. "The Oort can crew the cislunar stations. So long as we are not overwhelmed, we can eliminate individual Marauder spacecraft as they appear."

OORT CLOUD—GENERAL

While Braxton completed manufacturing the weapons and ranging equipment, the Oort modified sufficient Oort portals to set up portal transportation between Phoenix and all four remaining Oort Station locations. The national teams arrived at Phoenix to undergo extensive training in weightless construction, installation and use of the ranging equipment and weapons systems, and to gain a fully rounded understanding of their roles in protecting the entire Solar System with its human and Oort inhabitants.

To assist the crews in developing solid teams, Thorpe decided to have them wear uniforms—sky-blue jumpsuits with national origin flag-patches at the top of the right arm, rank designators on the collar tips, and job designators at the top of the left sleeve. The left breast carried the Oort Federation insignia—a spherical impression of the Oort Cloud. Their designations were Station Commander—called *Skipper*, Station Deputy Commander—called *Chief*, and Fire Control Technicians First, Second, and Third Class—called *Tech One*, *Two*, and *Three*. Each Oort Station was commanded by a Station Commander and had three seven-person teams consisting of a Chief and two each Tech One, Tech Two, and Tech Three. The teams stood eight-hour watches coordinated by the Oort Station Skipper. Station Commanders reported directly to Thorpe. Whatever command infrastructure each country, Solar System entity, or firm decided to create was up to them. This ensured that every Oort Station was fully manned at all times, and each entity fully controlled its own infrastructure.

eBrad and eSally created a training program that functioned much like a high-end space-invaders video game. They named it *Chiron* after the Greek god who trained the other gods. *Chiron* trained every watch section during the entirety of each watch. All the displays were under *Chiron* control until and unless a real object was detected, at which point *Athena* took charge, replacing *Chiron* simulations with real data.

※

Daphne flopped back on the large bed in the Los Angeles loft that was her home with Kimberly and Dale. She let out a deep, exhausted sigh as her eyes roamed over the Los Angeles skyline beyond the two-story-high window that dropped to the floor below. The sound of falling water caught her attention, and she turned toward the back of the loft where Kimberly and Dale were washing each other under the rain canopy of the open shower.

"Hey, guys, when did you get home?" she asked.

"'Bout a half-hour," Dale said. "Had our hands full all week. We arrived within a couple minutes of each other, Kimberly from Moscow and me from OS-Prime."

"Tell me about it…I'm exhausted," Daphne said, dropping her garments and joining them. "I could sleep for a week."

They had installed a portal in their loft shortly after Phoenix became a portal hub for their operations. Despite the convenience of stepping through a couple of portals to sleep in their own bed, however, they often found it easier to sleep where each of them happened to be when exhaustion overtook them.

They toweled each other down and dropped on the bed as the lights dimmed. Daphne snuggled against the smaller Dale and reached across him to stroke Kimberly's cheek. Before any further activity could take place, however, exhausted sleep claimed all three of them.

※

Late the following morning, the three sat around a table on the lower level, sharing freshly roasted coffee and a light breakfast brought up from the shop on the first level. The girls current Hyperchess game occupied part of the table. Max was taking his breakfast from a saucer on the floor overlooking the bustling cityscape. Both Thorpe and Braxton seemed to be sitting on chairs to one side with eMax occupying Braxton's lap.

"As of yesterday," Dale said, "all five Oort Stations are in place with all equipment installed. The construction teams did well, which made my job easier, but I need to alert you to something." He paused and wiped his mouth with a napkin. "Both the Russian and Chinese teams seemed standoffish, unlike the Europeans and Indians. It wasn't overt, in my face, just a subtle difference."

"You're sure they weren't just being Russian and Chinese?" Thorpe asked.

"I notice the same thing in Moscow," Kimberly said, moving a bishop to the upper board. "The team members were fully cooperative and even enthusiastic, but I sensed something with their Moscow-bound managers that was a bit off."

"I spent a couple of hours in Beijing yesterday with the Chinese management people," Daphne said, threatening Kimberly's bishop with her knight. "I noticed the same thing. It was subtle, nothing I could put my finger on, but it definitely was there."

"That's three for three," Braxton said. "I think we have a problem. I'll spend some ServerSky time seeing what I can find." His holoimage vanished. eMax checked out Max's cream saucer, but since he could smell nothing enticing, he opted for Thorpe's lap.

"How are things with the American government?" Thorpe asked.

"Surprisingly well," Kimberly answered, caging her bishop. "President Butler has risen to the occasion, beyond what I had expected, frankly. I don't think we could have done it without him."

"The Oort is expressing increasing concern," Thorpe said, "with every passing moment. For reasons I don't want to get into right now, the Oort assumes that the Marauders come from a G-type star on the Main Sequence. We've identified about five hundred such stars within a hundred lightyears of Sol. Given what we know about the Marauders' transportation capabilities, we can assume that they can get here from wherever they are at about lightspeed. We have been radiating intelligence since the early twentieth century. Let's work the problem backward. Assume that they received our first transmissions and that they commenced a return to Sol relatively soon thereafter. Because they are not here yet, we can presume that they are more distant than fifty lightyears."

"The variables are," Daphne interrupted, "when they heard the signals, how long they waited to start, and how far away they are."

"Right," Thorpe said, "which means they could arrive tomorrow. If they do and we are not ready, we're SOL, all of us, including the Oort." He looked earnestly from face to face. "Kimberly, you need to make sure in the next few days that all participants fully understand what I just outlined. Just because the Marauders don't show up next week doesn't mean they won't show up the following day. Everybody needs to understand this right down to the marrow of their bones."

Kimberly faded her rook. "Checkmate," she said.

WASHINGTON D.C.—OVAL OFFICE

Kimberly contacted President Butler directly by Link and arranged to meet with him shortly after noon the same day.

As she stepped into the Oval Office, the president stood with a smile and asked, "Kimberly, what's so important that I had to cancel three appointments to meet with you?" He gestured to a chair and took one himself. "Not that I mind spending time with such a lovely and capable young woman."

Kimberly got right to the point. "Our defense system is up and running, Mr. President. We are satisfied with the training of our crews and delighted with the enthusiasm and dedication of the individual team members. Nevertheless, the Oort is very concerned about our overall preparedness." She went on to detail the discussion with her team members just that morning, trying her best to convey to the president that the matter was at hand. "If the Marauders are within a hundred lightyears, it is absolutely certain that they are on their way. We want you to convey this to the other world leaders."

"I agree," President Butler said. "We need to approach this threat as one with a united front."

"Well, Sir, we may have a problem with the Russians and Chinese. We don't really know what's going on, but they are up to something. Can your people get to the bottom of it? They are completely stonewalling my team."

✴

By nature, President Butler was inclined to give the benefit of the doubt to those with whom he interacted. He believed his personal relationship with both the Russian president and the Chinese Chairman was cordial and open. Reluctantly, he briefed both his Russian and Chinese ambassadors during a confidential Link conversation with them. He finished up by saying, "I don't have personal knowledge of these matters. Kimberly Deveraux, representing Phoenix and indirectly the Oort, brought these matters to my attention. I have no way of independently verifying any of this. Nevertheless, I cannot ignore it either. If Phoenix is correct, and I have no reason for disbelieving them, humanity's future depends on our doing this right."

THE RUSSIAN FEDERATION—KRASNOYARSK—INSTITUT KOSMECHESKIKH

The Institut Kosmecheskikh occupies an aging five-story building on the campus of the Krasnoyarsk Academy of Sciences. The Academy sits on the north shore of the Yenisei River that bisects the ancient Siberian city of Krasnoyarsk, 3,352 kilometers east of Moscow. Deep in a subbasement under the northeast corner of the Institute, a young graduate student stepped back from his project. He was working for Academician Sergii Anatoly Borisovich, a descendant of one of the Institute's founders and senior physicist on a project derived from Russia's initial contacts with Phoenix. He had just carefully measured the Casimir forces between two plates of the same non-baryonic-doped material that formed the fins of the Phoenix MERT craft. He didn't know the source of the material and wasn't about to ask.

"That can't be!" he muttered to himself and set about repeating the measurement. A half-hour later, he stared at the same result within seven significant figures, and then he called Academician Borisovich, his hands trembling.

After rechecking his student's measurements several times, Borisovich reported his results to the Academy's director along with his recommendation to drop other lines of research and concentrate on his Casimir force findings. Within days, 334 researchers turned their attention to the findings of Borisovich's student.

Borisovich's team knew that MERT portals actually existed. They knew that non-baryonic-doped material was involved, and with the Casimir force results in hand, within three months, had their first prototype portal. Two months later, they were ready to move living material through their experimental MERT portal.

The researchers developed a portable activation device similar to Phoenix's hyper-disc, but it was a two-kilogram elongated cube, not unlike a brick, not something one could slip in a pocket. Their limiting factor was available power. Like everywhere on Earth, the Russian Federation no longer used large central power production plants of any kind. Instead, they relied on small LANRs wherever power was needed. What Borisovich required to move forward with his portal research was a reliable source of significant power.

Academician Borisovich was aware, as was nearly everyone else on Earth with similar interests, that Phoenix had appropriated the Earth-Moon L2, the Earth-Sun L3, and the Mercury-Sun L1 locations for power production. Since there was no meaningful governance within the Solar System, neither Borisovich nor the Russian Federation itself could lodge an official complaint. Russia filed a grievance with the United Nations in Geneva, but given their complete lack of any enforcement mechanism, no one expected anything but a useless resolution.

Bowing to the inevitable, the Russian Federation—still very much a centralized operation more than a century after the demise of the Soviet Union—focused its space efforts on building a thinsat swarm at the Earth-Sun L4 point to power its portal operations. Since the Earth-Sun L4 point leads the Earth in its orbit by 150 million kilometers, the Russians didn't deliberately hide their operations, but they also did not announce to the world what they were doing. Consequently, Phoenix, Thorpe, and the Oort remained unaware that someone other than Phoenix had human capable MERT portal technology.

PEOPLE'S REPUBLIC OF CHINA—BEIJING—CHINESE ACADEMY OF SCIENCES

Tucked into the center of the centuries-old Xicheng district of downtown Beijing, the Chinese Academy of Sciences stretches along the Yongding Diversion Channel as it has for more than 200 years. Its magnificent bow-shaped portico has welcomed China's best researchers and students for as long as the Academy has existed.

Upon the discovery that Phoenix Labs had successfully uploaded a living human into a tensor matrix, two divisions of the Academy, the National Center for Nanoscience and Technology and the Institute of Computing Technology, set up a collaborative research project to duplicate this feat. Academician Guo Qiáng, a descendent of the Academy's first director, established the new Institute of Nanoscience Computing (INC) on the top floor of the aging six-story Academy headquarters.

Knowing that it had already been accomplished and without many of the constraints customarily honored by science researchers around the world, Guo Qiáng performed his first animal upload six months later. He achieved his first human upload a month after that.

His subject, Liŭ Mĭn, was a bright, young postdoc who had served in the People's Liberation Army Special Operations Forces as a commando specializing in infiltration and computer hacking.

✳

eLiŭ Mĭn awoke to a sense of complete disorientation. All his familiar sensory inputs were gone—no sight, no sound, no touch, no weight. His commando training took over. *Evaluate!* He knew he had undergone uploading. A thick, impenetrable fog surrounded him, cutting off every input. He strained to establish contact with anything at all. A whisper crossed his mind—fleeting before it left. A feather touch of sensation to his left middle finger. He flicked the finger and felt a surge of sensation course through his hand, arm, shoulder, neck, to his brain, and then it was gone. He sank back into the fog and floated for a thousand years or a moment—he simply couldn't tell. A sensation in his right big toe that moved upward through his body. As it reached his head, he grabbed it and held on. He squeezed hard, and slowly, sensation began to course through his body. The fog brightened and began to fade.

He seemed to be standing in a space without walls or floors. He clearly saw his legs and feet, arms and hands. He tilted his head and saw his torso. He was still clad in the scrubs he had worn before being anesthetized. *How can that be?* he asked himself.

His space flashed thrice, paused, flashed again three times, and again, and again. Through his mental fog, he remembered. *That's my signal!* He searched for a way to respond. Nothing...

His space flashed again—three flashes, and again, and again. Still, he couldn't respond. With every bit of mental strength, he willed a response. His entire space flashed green. He relaxed and tried again. Flash...flash...flash.

eLiŭ Mĭn's endless surroundings began to close in on him. He stared at the walls, willing them to tell him something. Slowly, they resolved into circuit patterns that he recognized, logic switches— ANDs, NANDs, NORs, ORs, and others, many others with functions he well understood. For the next hours, or was it seconds, days, or weeks—he did not know—he traced the circuitry, extending pieces of himself into the patterns to see where they led. Eventually, he stopped to examine his own extensions and came to recognize them as tensors. Postdoc Liŭ Mĭn, ex-commando, had a real mathematical gift, and eLiŭ Mĭn began to couch what he saw as math expressions. The equations flowed across his consciousness, and he began to see a larger picture. Each element of his conscious existence within the electronic matrix reduced to a Cauchy vector sequence. He visualized these as strings of decreasing multidimensional tensors, each vanishing to a point within his space. *Consequently*, he reasoned, *my space has to be a multidimensional Banach space. That makes me a Banach manifold with the ability to extend pieces of myself as multi-dimensional tensors virtually anywhere I wish within the matrix.*

Flash…flash…flash.

eLiŭ Mĭn knew that Academician Guo Qiáng wanted to communicate with him. He didn't want to keep the Academician waiting, but he still needed to gain a better grasp of his surroundings and especially his time sense. He searched for and located the timing circuit for his matrix. He synchronized his personal clock with that circuit. To his astonishment, only three seconds had passed since the first set of flashes, even though it seemed like many hours.

Liŭ Mĭn had worked closely with Guo Qiáng's team to build a matrix that would accommodate easy two-way communication. As eLiŭ Mĭn explored the matrix from inside, he was grateful for the Academician's forethought. He located the audio and holographic circuits, chuckled in amusement at their unnecessary complications, given his ability to penetrate to the core of any circuit. He composed himself, considered how he wished to appear—academic but subservient to the esteemed Academician—and activated the circuits.

"Academician Guo Qiáng," eLiŭ Mĭn said, his holographic image bowing deeply, "I stand ready to serve the People's Republic of China."

SERVER SKY—LEO

At Academician Guo Qiáng's direction, eLiŭ Mĭn slipped into the GlobalNet. He perceived it as a vast assortment of trickles merging into brooks and streams, and then into small tributaries that ultimately combined to form mighty rivers. And it worked both ways. Data ebbed and flowed in all directions throughout the vast web.

At first, he was altogether bewildered and lost. Then his mathematical training took over. He began to see patterns. Databases transformed into gigantic windows that revealed their contents. He discovered and followed a particularly large trunk. The walls of the trunk began to press in on him as he and the data accelerated ever faster until he squirted out into a vast sea of data. For a while, he floundered until he got his bearings and realized that he had passed through a laser-trunk into ServerSky. That realization brought with it a disorientation that he had to throw off deliberately. When he did, however, the vast panorama of ServerSky became apparent to him, and he began to spread himself out until he occupied the entirety of the thinsat swarm he had entered.

Something touched him…he pulled away, but the touch followed him. It was non-human, alien, but not entirely. He reached out again and felt sentience projecting curiosity and a hint of friendliness. Then he heard, or rather felt, a sound almost indistinguishable from a cat's meow. The impossibility of that struck him as funny. eLiŭ Mĭn chocked off a chuckle as a gray tabby cat seemed to flit across the thinsat swarm. *It's impossible!* he muttered as the apparition appeared for a second time. He lashed out electronically as he might have with his hand in human form back in Beijing. Despite his fearless commando status, he avoided cats whenever possible. He hated them. In return, one of his tensors disappeared, and he received a deep electronic scratch.

"*Gāisĭ de māo!* [*Damn cat!*]" eLiŭ Mĭn shouted, throwing a voltage wave across the thinsat swarm that fried 1,200 thinsats and caused a momentary hiccup for 100,000 GlobalNet users as backups stepped up to replace the lost coverage.

✳

During his daily romp through ServerSky, eMax stumbled across a stranger. Never shy about approaching something new, he sidled up to the unknown upload, projecting his friendliest best. In repayment, he was swatted completely across the thinsat swarm, followed by a voltage surge that singed his tail as he scampered through the laser-pipe into the Earthside GlobalNet.

Following a several-minute-search, eMax found eDaphne coordinating activities at OS-Prime. He jumped into her arms, trembling quietly. She stroked his fur and discovered the singed hair on his tail.

"What happened, eMax?" she asked, her voice filled with tenderness.

In their upload forms, eMax and eDaphne had been able to establish a much closer communication. eMax merged a bit of himself into eDaphne's hand, sharing his frightening experience with her.

"You poor Tabby," she said to him softly, cuddling him close.

✳

Thorpe looked up with a smile as eDaphne swooped into his space, brushing her electronic lips against his.

"What brings you here?" he asked, giving her his full attention.

eDaphne told him about eMax's experience and passed eMax from her arms to his where eMax merged a bit of himself with Thorpe, sharing the incident.

"This is an unexpected development," Thorpe said. "Any idea who or what it is?"

"None," eDaphne said, "but we had better find out soon."

Chapter Nineteen

GENEVA—UNITED NATIONS COMPLEX

After the United Nations left its Manhattan headquarters, it moved operations to the UN Geneva complex, where it continued to pump out empty resolutions, taking to task any nation that dared to stand up for independence, individual freedom, and the right to defend one's borders. Geneva became a locus for international intrigue and a place where diplomats could make off-the-record contacts, cut deals, and advance their interests without alerting the world press.

Not long after eLiŭ Mĭn had his encounter with eMax, Academician Guo Qiáng and Academician Sergii Anatoly Borisovich met by the Celestial Sphere on Avenue de la Paix, the semi-circular path encompassing the green expanse southeast of UN Headquarters. The afternoon sun was above and behind the massive colonnaded building that cast a contorted shadow across the bright green grass. A breeze from the north rippled the mirror pond surrounding the sculpture, scattering the sunlight as the two men sat on the rough concrete wall retaining the pool and holding the bronze plaque describing the Celestial Sphere.

"Thank you for meeting me, Academician Guo Qiáng," Borisovich said. "When I heard of your successful upload, I simply had to meet with you in person."

"That project is highly classified," Guo Qiáng said quietly.

"It is indeed," Borisovich said with a slight smile.

"And I wanted to learn more about your portal technology," Guo Qiáng added.

"But that is a State security project with the highest classification," Borisovich said with a slight edge to his voice.

"So, both our countries have efficient intelligence services," Guo Qiáng said with a tight smile. "Together, we would no longer need to depend on Phoenix. My uploads can use your portals to make direct contact with the Oort."

"If we work it right," Borisovich said, "we might even be able to make a special arrangement with the Marauders."

EARTH-SUN L4—RUSSIAN THINSAT SWARM

150 million kilometers ahead of Earth in its orbit around the Sun, eLiŭ Mĭn and five of his upload colleagues assembled near a habitat recently put in place by the newly created Russian Federation Space Navy. They projected their holoimages inside the habit where grizzled Commander Yuri Bykov waited for them.

"The Russian Federation welcomes the commandos of the People's Liberation Army Special Operations Forces," Bykov said formally, returning the salutes from the six images displayed before him. "The R-F-S-N is placing portals throughout the Solar System," he continued, his blue eyes flashing, "that connect back to Space Navy headquarters in Krasnoyarsk. Where thinsat infrastructure exists, you commandos will take up residence. Otherwise, we have installed electronic matrixes to house you when you are not roaming." He stopped and looked at each holoimage. "Are you men comfortable with isolated duty?"

"It's what we do," eLiŭ Mĭn said, his holoimage standing tall. The other five commandos nodded once, sharply. "What we do," he reiterated crisply.

"We do not know how many uploads Phoenix has activated, nor do we fully understand their roles; however, we do know that they are best contacted by other uploads. That's where you men come in.

"You need to avoid contact while finding out as much as possible about the entire Phoenix operation. At the same time, you should find a way to connect with the Oort without Phoenix being aware of your operations." He paused, looking from man to man. "Any questions?"

"How do we handle a direct confrontation?" eLiŭ Mĭn asked. "I already had one with an uploaded cat, of all things."

"Where the hell did that happen?"

"During my first excursion into the near-Earth ServerSky swarm," eLiŭ Mǐn said. "Sonofabitch showed up out of nowhere. I swatted it away…I hate cats!"

"Did you kill it?"

"I tried…hit it with a voltage wave, but there were no remnants. I think it got away."

"That could be a problem, you know. Cats normally belong to people." Bykov's concern was apparent. "Let's send you back where you had the encounter. Perhaps this time, you can destroy the evidence, so to speak."

SERVER SKY—LEO SWARM

Thorpe spread himself over one half of the ServerSky swarm where eMax got attacked. Braxton covered the remaining half. eMax scampered between them both, chasing tensors the Oort set loose for his amusement.

Then they waited.

Both Thorpe and Braxton sent working tensors out to the various sites they were monitoring or working with directly. Part of their attention was directed to those sites, but their immediate attention remained in the swarm they occupied.

And they waited.

eMax was bewildered by the arrangement. He curled up with Thorpe for a while and then snuggled up to Braxton to both their amusement.

And they waited.

Since both Thorpe and Braxton knew that whoever they were awaiting would probably be looking for something in their swarm since the encounter had happened there, they took great care to integrate their electronic selves into the swarm structure. They were virtually undetectable.

And they waited.

※

eLiǔ Mǐn watched each member of his team pass through the Earth-Sun L4 portal to RFSN headquarters in Krasnoyarsk. From there, he knew, they would move to their assigned locations. He turned toward Commander Bykov and saluted.

"By your leave, Sir!" And he moved through the portal to Krasnoyarsk.

With no further formality, eLiǔ Mǐn passed from RFSN headquarters into the GlobalNet.

This time he was in more familiar territory. During his training of the other five, he had led them through various sections of the GlobalNet, showed them some of the curiosities he had discovered, and taught them how to enter and explore ServerSky.

What eLiǔ Mǐn did not know as he slipped through the laser pipe into the ServerSky swarm where he had encountered eMax was that he had a welcoming committee. He resisted the stream at the LEO side of the laser pipe, allowing himself to enter the swarm very slowly. Everything seemed normal...no cat and no one else. But somehow, the swarm felt different. He couldn't put his finger on it, but he sensed something. He moved into the swarm, keeping to the edges, senses on high alert.

※

Thorpe had focused part of his attention on the laser pipe into the swarm. Suddenly, something slipped through, slid past his focus point, and started edging around the swarm. He signaled Braxton through their connection at the swarm center. Together, they watched the movement of whatever-it-was as it crept around the swarm, obviously trying not to draw attention to itself.

When the stranger reached the point on the swarm edge where Thorpe and Braxton intersected, Thorpe signaled, "Now!"

They both pounced, spreading themselves onto, through, and around the intruder. Recognizing what it was, eMax darted through the laser pipe to safety.

To the surprise of both Thorpe and Braxton, the foreign upload, for they now recognized the intruder for what it was, resisted strongly.

Powerful voltage pulses hit them both. Thorpe tumbled back and fell through the laser pipe, stunned to near unconsciousness. As he struggled to regain control of his senses, eMax found him and rubbed his face, chirping quietly.

Thorpe looked around himself and then extended his senses, searching for Braxton. He sent a tensor through the laser pipe but found nothing...no Braxton and no foreign upload.

✳

Braxton felt intense pain, such as he had not felt since gaining awareness. Then he lost consciousness.

He rolled over and struggled to collect his thoughts. He was back in his personal swarm. He let himself recover and refocus. *Obviously, whatever that was won the first round. Twice now, my backup has saved me.* As he did the first time, he checked his newly set up backup. Everything seemed to be working, but he was still in slow motion. *Oh, Shit! Thorpe must be worried sick!*

Braxton took a few minutes to pull himself together. Then he readied himself to transit back to Phoenix, still somewhat woozy from the experience. Just then, Thorpe entered his personal swarm through the laser pipe he had installed what seemed so long ago.

"You're a sight for sore eyes. What happened back there?"

"Damned if I know," Braxton said. "I was in the LEO swarm with you. Then the strange upload. Then a lot of pain. Then I wake up here. You tell me."

"I think someone has discovered how to weaponize an upload," Thorpe said. "And they don't like us."

WASHINGTON D.C.—THE OVAL OFFICE

"Mr. President," Kimberly said, "We've got a problem that is quite beyond our ability to handle."

"What could possibly bring the Oort Federation to my office for help?" The president smiled warmly, and Kimberly found that despite her initial feelings about this world leader, she was beginning to like him a lot.

Kimberly described the personal attack on Thorpe and Braxton in ServerSky. "We have no one in our entire organization with military training. Thorpe and Braxton were unable to identify their attacker, but they both believe either the Russians or the Chinese, or perhaps both of them in collaboration, were involved." She looked directly at the president and lowered her voice. "If we don't find a way to counter this, the Oort itself may be in danger, and this could threaten humanity's survival. Despite your predilections, I think you will agree that the United Nations is *not* the vehicle for handling this." She dropped her gaze from the president's face and said demurely, "I think we need a group of trained Special Forces people—people who can handle what we are up against because they're capable of handling anything thrown at them."

"That's a tall order, Kimberly," the president said. "I would have to consult Congress before taking such action."

"No, Sir! I don't think that's a good idea." Kimberly's frustration was apparent in her voice and body language. "I don't have your years of experience nor your breadth of knowledge, Sir, but one thing I know: Congress leaks. Nothing you tell Congress, even its senior leaders, remains secret for very long."

"I can't argue that," the president responded, "but I really..."

"No, Sir! We'll find another way if you won't do it by secret executive order." Kimberly felt tears of frustration fill her eyes. "It's critical! Please, Sir, assign a Special Ops unit to our operation."

✳

Commander Jerry Culp had served in virtually every capacity within the U.S. Navy SEALS. Now he found himself heading a 16-man SEALS platoon on temporary assignment to the U.S. Space Force and detailed to independent duty with the Oort Federation. Usually, a platoon would be assigned to a less senior officer, but this was an unusual circumstance.

Cdr. Culp followed a White House aid along the West Colonnade to the Oval Office door. This was his first trip to the White House, and he felt a bit nervous as the aid opened the door. Culp had no idea what to expect. The president? Sure. Otherwise, why the Oval Office? But who else might be there? Culp simply had no idea. He removed his braided peaked cap and stepped through the door. The first thing he saw was a stunning young woman with startling blue eyes and long blond hair done in loose curls falling around her shoulders. Next to her stood the Chief of Naval Operations and his own boss, Vice-Admiral Benjamin Sterling, head of the U.S. Naval Special Warfare Command. As Culp came to attention just inside the door, President Butler walked toward him with outstretched hand.

"Welcome, Commander Culp. I'm John Butler," the president said with a smile. "You know the CNO and Admiral Sterling," he continued, motioning to the two admirals, "and this is Kimberly Deveraux, the Oort Federation liaison and my personal friend."

"Mr. President," Culp said, shaking the president's hand. He nodded at the admirals, "Gentlemen," and to Kimberly, "Ms Deveraux."

President Butler stepped to his chair behind the Resolute desk and gestured for the admirals and Kimberly to take the settee to the right of the coffee table in front of his desk. Then he indicated for Culp to take the left one facing the other three.

To Culp's surprise, as Kimberly sat down, a gray tabby cat appeared from nowhere and settled into her lap. It took a moment for him to recognize it as a holoimage.

"Meet Max or should I say, eMax," the president said, smiling broadly. "He visits me almost once daily now." He gestured for the Navy steward to serve coffee.

With the social amenities concluded, the president dismissed the steward and manipulated his Link. The Oval Office doors locked, and the windows went opaque.

"Commander Culp," the president continued, "the CNO and Admiral Sterling have already been briefed, but I requested their presence during your briefing so that we all are absolutely on the same page." He turned to Kimberly. "Would you please bring the commander up to speed?"

✳

"Now you know what we are up against," the president said to Culp. "I understand that you speak Russian and Chinese?"

"Actually," Vice-Admiral Sterling interjected, "Commander Culp is fluent in Russian, Ukrainian, Mandarin, and Cantonese."

Culp looked mildly embarrassed. "Languages come easy to me," he said.

"You may need all of them before this is over," Kimberly said. "You and your men will receive detailed briefings at the Phoenix headquarters in Denver, and then you'll be uploaded."

Although Kimberly had explained uploading during her briefing, Culp, still felt pretty much in the dark about the process and what it involved. He decided to wait until Denver to pose his questions. He looked at both admirals, but their faces remained stoic, unreadable.

President Butler rose to his feet, followed by the others. "Thank you for your time, Commander."

Cdr. Culp turned toward the door as Sterling took his elbow. "Walk with me, please."

As they strolled along the colonnade, Admiral Sterling said, "You probably feel a bit overwhelmed right now, Jerry. My initial briefing before you arrived blew me away. Hearing it a second time didn't make it any better. It may sound like a cliché, but the fate of the human race rests on your shoulders. I picked you because I know you and what you are capable of. You and your team have got to carry this off! Keep this close to your vest and make sure your guys understand how critical this is."

DENVER—PHOENIX LABS

As they walked along the colonnade, Admiral Sterling stopped at the first door to the Cabinet Room and entered. Culp followed him. The room was empty. Sterling activated a hyper-disk in his pocket, opening a portal to Phoenix. He stepped through the door, saying to Culp, "Follow me, please."

Culp found himself in what appeared to be a laboratory space, surrounded by a small group of people. Sterling introduced him to a man in his late fifties, shorter than he, with longish blond hair and sporting a goatee. "Commander Jerry Culp, please meet Doctor Jackson Fredricks. Jackson runs the show here and will keep you in line until you get the whole picture. Good luck, Jerry!" The admiral shook Culp's hand and disappeared through another door.

The next few hours were filled with intensive indoctrination. Accompanied by Daphne, Culp visited Earth-Moon L2, Mercury-Sun L1, Earth-Sun L3. Mars-Sun L1, and then he toured each of the five Oort Stations. Johnny Oort briefed him at OS-Prime, and he drank a cup of coffee at Mars Station.

By day's end, Culp's world had been turned upside down. The plan was that he would upload before his team, meet the other uploads, get the hang of functioning as an upload, and then bring his team onboard.

Commander Jerry Culp swam through a thick, freezing slush that gathered around him. Every time he exhaled, more ice spicules formed, thickening the slush until he could barely move. Light surrounded him, but everything was out of focus.

"Jerry!"

Someone was calling him. A woman…

"Jerry…over here…"

The voice had direction.

"This way, Jerry…"

He swam toward the voice, pushing the freezing slush aside.

"Take my hand, Jerry…"

Her voice was familiar; eCulp had heard it before. His brain was too fuzzy, however. He couldn't place it. The voice sounded warm and inviting; a delicious image flashed across his mind—blue eyes and long blond hair. Then it was gone.

"Touch me, Jerry…reach out!"

He felt something soft brush his fingertip, and then he was jolted by an intense, almost orgasmic sensation as the freezing slush vanished, replaced by a warmly lit space filled with…Kimberly Deveraux, the young woman he had met in the Oval Office. She was touching his fingers. Startled, he pulled back.

"Excuse me," he muttered, "I mean, I'm sorry...I mean...what just happened? Did you and I...?"

"No, not really," eKim said, laughing warmly. "Almost everyone awaking as an upload experiences some kind of sexual response. We have found that the transition is easier with someone of the opposite gender. I was the only female in our group that you had already met; rather, Kimberly was. I'm eKim, Kimberly's upload."

eCulp felt confused, but his training took hold immediately. He closed his eyes and took a deep breath. Then he slowly opened his eyes and looked around. He sensed no danger at all, just eKim's warm, female presence. Then, to his surprise, a grey tabby cat appeared and checked him over.

"eMax?" he said.

eMax rubbed his leg.

"I think he likes you," eKim said, her eyes twinkling. "Do you feel like a short stroll?"

For the next few minutes, (or was it hours?), eCulp had no idea, eKim showed him around GlobalNet and ServerSky. They met the other uploads, eDaphne, eDale, eSally, eBrad, and both Thorpe and Braxton.

"No eFredricks or eJackson?" eCulp asked.

"Not yet," eDaphne answered. "He insists that no one can do uploads better than he, and he doesn't have the time to train someone else, but I think he's a bit scared."

✳

eCulp quickly learned to project a holoimage, and to his surprise, when he didn't think about it, he appeared in his camos. That's how he looked when he met his former self for the first time. It wasn't love at first sight, but eCulp felt close to the man he had been a short time ago.

"It's kind of like having a twin brother," eCulp said. "I guess from here, we diverge."

"Not entirely," Culp said. "While you were uploading, Phoenix set up a continuous backup for yourself held in stasis out in the Kuiper Belt. If you get taken out, your backup is activated. From your point of view, you will simply wake up somewhere else, memories intact. Periodically, I'll upload again into your backup. When your backup is activated, it will be both of us instead of just you. When I eventually buy the farm, you will have the option of integrating your current self into your backup, bringing me into you, or you can just wait for an external event to trigger the transfer that will merge us permanently."

eCulp briefed Culp on his initial online experiences. He emphasized the ethereal nature of his upload existence. "There is no objective reality—no Khaybar on your belt, no Glock in your fist—nothing physical you can use to hurt the bad guy. Instead, you learn to control energy, potentially vast amounts. That's what the bad guys used to take Braxton out. It turns out you can shield from such attacks, but your shield also prevents you from projecting power. So, it's back to what we do best, covert snatch 'n grab or kill."

They talked for quite a while, going over different scenarios and their available options.

"We're gonna need some training time," eCulp said. "No way I can really explain to you, but it's gonna take some time to get our act together once we're all uploaded."

"Let's get Sam, Jake, and Doc uploaded ASAP," Culp said, referring to Senior Chief Sam Bunker, Lieutenant Rob Jacobs, and the platoon corpsman. Then the four of you can guide the other twelve through the upload process." Culp grinned. "Once that's done, I'll put the living team at Thorpe's disposal. They're certain to need some genuine military muscle before this is over."

GENEVA—UNITED NATIONS COMPLEX

"This situation is intolerable," the Russian UN Ambassador said to the assembled Security Council. "We simply cannot allow a commercial mega-corporation to dictate terms to the nations of Earth."

Nods around the table confirmed that the other ambassadors agreed with his words.

"We recognize the threat, and we appreciate the actions by Phoenix that brought this threat to the world's attention." His voice took on a sonorous ring. "But protecting Earth is up to us, here, not some greedy corporation operating at the fringes of the Solar System."

"Hear…"

"Hear…"

"I, therefore, move," the Russian ambassador continued, "that we enjoin Phoenix from any further action on behalf of Earth, that we take control of the defense infrastructure Phoenix has put into place, and that we man the Oort Stations with UN Force personnel."

"I second the motion." As he spoke, the Chinese ambassador looked directly at the Russian ambassador.

✳

The following day, the official UN Security Council resolution was presented to the general assembly by the current president of the Council, the ambassador from Brazil. In a rare example of international unity, the resolution passed unanimously with one abstention—the United States.

A week later, a five-person delegation headed by the Secretary General herself arrived at the Denver Phoenix headquarters. Dr. Fredricks ushered them into his office, seated them, and placed himself behind his desk.

"To what do I owe this honor?" Fredricks asked.

"We are here, Dr. Fredricks, representing all the nations of the world. This," the Secretary General handed him a formal parchment sheet, "is a unanimous resolution by the UN General Assembly demanding that Phoenix turn over its entire space-based operations to United Nations control."

"You appear to be serious," Fredricks said.

"Very much so," the Secretary General responded, her demeanor formal and serious.

"You're talking to the wrong entity," Fredricks said. "Phoenix is just one element of the Oort Federation." He stood up. "You need to be addressing Braxton Thorpe, Chairman of the Oort Federation." He smiled. "Besides, the Oort Federation is open to any nation of Earth. Just select two delegates for the Council." He smiled again. "We agree that this is a problem for everybody, but the United Nations—you guys—will never solve the problem in time. That's why we created the Oort Federation."

"I understand that we missed the mark by enjoining Phoenix," the Secretary General said, hiding her embarrassment. She turned to her delegation. "We need to return and get this right." She returned her attention back to Fredricks. "We will return shortly with a corrected resolution. The Oort Federation must give up its jurisdiction!"

"That's not going to happen!" Fredricks' face remained friendly.

WASHINGTON D.C.—THE OVAL OFFICE

"What were you thinking, Mr. President?" Kimberly asked. "You, of all people, know how critical our task is."

"It's not that simple, Kimberly," President Butler said. "The U.S. abstained both in the Security Council and the General Assembly, but things being as they are, we could not oppose the resolution."

"What will happen now?" Kimberly asked.

"The modified resolution will pass and will be presented to the Oort Federation." He smiled ruefully. "You know that Russia and China are behind this, don't you?"

"I suspected," Kimberly said. "We cannot let this happen."

"There is only one thing the nations of Earth will understand," Butler said, "and that's a show of power." He shook his head sadly. "That it should come to this...that I would recommend force..." His voice trailed off.

Kimberly found herself actually feeling bad for the man. All his life, he had been a force for finding a way to avoid conflict, and now he was in it up to his eyeballs.

"Do you have a suggestion for me to take back to Thorpe?" Kimberly asked.

"I do," the president said, his voice filled with sadness.

＊

The following day, ServerSky shut down. Without access to ServerSky, the GlobalNet became virtually useless. Without Global-Net, panic spread across the world. Stock markets shut down, and nearly every enterprise across the planet ceased functioning except for small mom-and-pop outfits that didn't rely upon technology for their operations. The world waited.

Two hours later, ServerSky came back online. As it did, every interface across the planet displayed this message:

"The Oort Federation is humanity's only chance to survive the Marauders. Do not attempt to interfere again!"

EARTH—OGDEN ENTERPRISES

Daphne O'Bryan was in charge of coordinating the technical activ-ities between Phoenix and the five Oort Stations, and eDaphne coordinated the human-Oort technical interface. Initially, these activ-ities kept them fully occupied. As the national teams settled into their routines, both Daphne and her upload found time to pursue a dream that Daphne and Kimberly had developed since Daphne's first day at Phoenix Revive Labs back in Los Angeles what seemed so long ago.

When Daphne and Kimberly uploaded to eDaphne and eKim, the dream came with them, and now they worked together to make it happen. eDaphne reached out to Johnny Oort.

"The Oort consists of trillions of individuals. I know that you have ventured into the Kuiper Belt, but for the most part, you have confined your presence to the Oort Cloud." She then explained her idea to Johnny Oort.

"Wonderful plan," he told her. "The Oort will support you in any way possible."

＊

Through Ogden Enterprises, Kimberly hired the best ad people she could find. Across the planet, commercial holovision broadcasts began airing ads asking if the viewer wanted to live forever. Holographic billboards proclaimed the possibility of never dying. Social media purchases pointed the way to eternal life.

All you had to do, the campaign proclaimed, was to purchase a lifetime right from Ogden to upload yourself to the Kuiper Belt. Your upload would be held in stasis, updated from time to time on a schedule of your choice, and activated upon your physical death. Upon activation, you would become a full-fledged citizen of the Oort Federation with all the rights and privileges of every other citizen. You would receive the full protection of the Federation and be able to participate in every activity available to all Federation citizens, including interaction with any or all of the Oort.

The cost was modest, about the equivalent of one month's salary anywhere on the planet. Ogden Enterprises established upload clinics in virtually every city, town, and neighborhood across the world. In terms of wealth and income, within six months, Ogden was second only to Phoenix in all of human history.

※

"Is this what you had in mind when you set up Ogden Enterprises for us?" Daphne asked.

"Never occurred to me in my wildest dreams," Thorpe told her. "But, I suspected you had it in yours." He crossed his arms on his chest in a self-hug. "I'm proud of you both!"

"I'll give him the chance to prove that," eDaphne said as her holoimage appeared next to Thorp's. "This is a joint project, you know," she added. "Sis and me, and Kimberly and eKim!"

"I hope you didn't bite off more than you can chew," Thorpe said. "I hear rumors that the U.N. is planning to wrest control of Ogden from you. Let me know when it starts. We taught them a lesson once. We can do it again."

GENEVA—UNITED NATIONS COMPLEX

The Security Council met in closed session under the gavel of the ambassador from Brazil. Of the five permanent members, both Russia and China were uncharacteristically quiet. South Africa had the floor.

"The situation is intolerable. Fully ninety percent of our population has signed up with Ogden Enterprises. Already, a tenth of those have died, and their estates are unattachable by the South African government. I don't mean that there are legal barriers, I mean that there is no way to access any of the assets of anyone who has signed up with Ogden—it's impossible!"

"What about taxes during their life following their Ogden membership?" the Dutch ambassador asked.

"Physically untouchable," South Africa answered.

"What about transactional taxes for their daily living?" the German Ambassador wanted to know.

"They get paid," South Africa said grudgingly. "As money is spent, somehow it flows in real-time from the untouchable Phoenix cryptosystem into crypto-Rands. My best people can't figure out how they do it."

"The same in the Netherlands."

Around the ornate table, all fifteen members nodded their concurrence.

"We are considering making it a crime to join Ogden," South Africa said.

"That," the United States responded, "would not be a good idea." Eyebrows lifted around the table.

"In the first place," the United States continued, "it's pretty drastic, and in the second, it would require similar laws in every country on Earth." He smiled as he looked around the table. "That will never happen."

The other four permanent members—Russia, China, France, and Great Britain—nodded.

France picked up the conversation. "The last time we tried to enjoin Phoenix, it turned out that we really were up against the Oort Federation, which might be considered our space-based co-equal. We lost that one big time. Now, however," the French ambassador paused, radiating her smile around the table, "we are not dealing with the Oort

Federation. Clearly, Ogden Enterprises is an Earth-based corporation. It is headquartered somewhere on Earth, and we can deal with that."

"I beg to differ, Madam Ambassador," the United States interrupted. "Ogden Enterprises is not a corporation. It is an entity originally created in the U.S. that is wholly owned by two individuals whom we have been unable to identify."

"Then," France responded, "the U.S. should do something about it."

"It's not that easy, Madam Ambassador. Ogden has moved away from Earth into the Oort Federation. I'm afraid the United States lacks even a hint of jurisdiction."

"Then the United Nations needs to do something," Tunisia spoke up for the first time. "We control foreign operations in our country. Why cannot the U.N. control foreign companies on Earth?"

✳

Three hours later, the Security Council produced a resolution demanding that Ogden send representatives to the Security Council to negotiate a deal that would give the U.N. some genuine control over its Earth-side operations.

The General Assembly rubber-stamped the resolution and passed it to the U.N. Enforcement Division. The Enforcement Chief passed the resolution back to the Security Council with a note asking simply, "What do I do with this?"

The Security Council passed the ball around the table for several hours and then delegated the task to the Geneva Police Department.

✳

To François Loraine, Geneva's Chief of Police, the problem was simple. He assigned a police captain accompanied by a senior sergeant to serve the resolution on the director of the local Ogden Complex located on the west side of Avenue Cardinal-Memillod across from the Arve River near the intersection of Promenade des Orpailleurs. The captain and his sergeant entered the ground-floor front door of the twenty-first-century building and approached the receptionist.

"I have a document for the Director," the captain said, extending a hand with an envelope.

"One moment," she said, accepting the envelope and stepping through a door behind her desk.

After waiting for about five minutes, the captain walked around the desk and opened the door. "It's empty," he said to his sergeant.

Together, they searched the entire four-story building but found nothing at all, not even an empty waste container.

✳

"You wouldn't believe it," Daphne told Thorpe later that afternoon. "I arrived with a handful of hyper-disks. In five minutes, the Geneva Ogden Complex staff ran through the complex opening portals on the run to a stateside warehouse. My staff poured through and shoved everything they saw into the warehouse." She shook her head in amazement. "It's hard to believe they pulled it off!"

"I wonder what the police captain thought when he finally decided to check out the complex?" Thorpe said with a broad grin.

✳

An hour later, the entire ServerSky around Earth shut down.

An urgent message from the U.N. General Secretary went unanswered. Six hours later, she sent a second, more urgent message. It, too, went unanswered.

Finally, in desperation, the General Secretary unilaterally withdrew the U.N. resolution, informed the U.N. member nations of her action, and submitted her resignation.

An hour after that, ServerSky recommenced operations.

Chapter Twenty

INNER SOLAR SYSTEM

Navy SEALS, from the moment they pin on their tridents, are incredibly adaptable. Their training is designed to raise adaptability to the level of a primal instinct. This fundamental precept was severely tested during the weeks following the upload of what came to be called ePlatoon.

Except for his commander, Jerry Culp, Senior Chief Sam Bunker had more time in the barrel than anyone else in his platoon. He was shorter than most of his men but strong as an ox with lightning reflexes. No one had been able to best him in one-on-one combat, and he gave an excellent account of himself when there were four or five. Like his boss, he was fluent in Russian, Ukrainian, Mandarin, and Cantonese, but his fluency was less eloquent, more attuned to the street lingo of his potential opponents.

When eSam pulled himself out of the haze of upload, without female assistance, he crouched low with KA-BAR extended in front of him (*where did that come from?*), turning slowly, evaluating his surroundings, every instinct on full alert.

"Easy, Sam," eCulp said softly, holding his empty hands open and in front of him. "There is no threat…you're in no danger…"

"Boss! Is that you?" eSam rose to his feet, sheathing his KA-BAR.

"How do you feel, Sam?"

"This is fucked!" eSam turned slowly, examining his surroundings. "You're not armed, Boss."

"Neither are you," eCulp said.

eSam reached for his KA-BAR, but it had vanished. "How'd you do that?"

"I didn't. You did it. With a little practice, you can appear any way you wish." Dress whites replaced eCulp's camos, followed by dress blues, civvies, and back to camos. Seriousness replaced eCulp's grin. "Let's get ready to welcome Jake and Doc."

✳

"So, here's the real skinny," eCulp said to his assembled ePlatoon. "I know that Commander Culp—you know, the other guy, the flesh-and-bone one—briefed you before you were uploaded. There's a lot he didn't know. Hell! There's a lot I don't know, but I learned a few things between my upload and when you guys got here." He stopped and looked around ePlatoon. "Any of you guys been to Mars?" He was greeted with blank looks. "Well, that's where we're headed right now, sort of. You've got the basics of upload existence. Now, we're going to a thinsat swarm at the Mars-Sun L1 point, about a million klicks away from Mars toward the Sun. We'll train there until you guys learn the ropes." He motioned for eJake and eSam to join him. "You guys are the best Special Ops troops that ever pinned a trident. When we're done with Mars, you guys will be the best eWarriors ever!"

"Hooyah!" eSam said.

"Hooyah!" fourteen e-voices answered back.

DENVER—PHOENIX LABS

Commander Jerry Culp, resplendent in dress blues, had the floor, speaking to those seated around the table in the Phoenix conference room—all the major players and their uploads, including eCulp who had opted to show himself in camos to reinforce his role.

"I get what you people have done, although it escapes me how you could have accomplished so much in such a short time. I wish you had brought me into the picture before this, however. Your entire operation is based upon trust. You seem to be making the assumption that because Earth itself is threatened, Earth's nations will cooperate in its defense. The problem is that humans don't work this way." Culp looked directly at Thorpe. "You, Thorpe, made this clear to the

Oort when you initially set up the Federation. Then you proceeded to ignore your own wisdom.

"Now we've got unknown uploads causing havoc in ServerSky. My team has conducted a preliminary covert survey of what's out there. We discovered evidence of foreign intrusion at every point of Federation activity, *plus*," he emphasized the word, "we discovered a thinsat swarm at Earth-Sun L4. Its primary purpose seems to be power production, and it hosts a habitat. As a precaution, we placed a hyper-disk into their swarm near the habitat. They are unlikely to discover it.

"Our intelligence-based best guess is that the Russians are supplying portals powered from this swarm, and the Chinese are supplying uploads. They seem not to trust each other sufficiently to share their respective technologies.

"In my opinion, it's only a matter of time until they wrest control of their Oort Stations from the Federation. Two hundred years of history tells us that they will try to reach out to the Marauders to make a deal. Johnny Oort made it crystal clear to me—the Marauders do not make deals." Culp looked around the table, stopping at each person.

"I've discussed this with Thorpe, and he and I are in agreement. On the next watch cycle," he checked the time, "an hour from now, two of my people will arrive at each Oort Station, discreetly armed, wearing Federation uniforms with rank of Chief. They will present electronic authorizations validated by Thorpe, placing all five Oort Stations under my direct command as Chief of the System Defense Force (SDF) with the rank of Admiral."

Shocked faces greeted Culp, and he held up a hand to quiet the mutterings around the table.

"We have no intention of militarizing the Oort Federation, but it has become obvious that we need to quell the actions of Russia and China as quickly and permanently as possible. We must assume that both Russia and China have secreted in their Oort Stations whatever hyper-disk form the Russians developed. If we don't secure those the moment we assume command, their troops are likely to overwhelm the two Oort Stations. If that happens, we have no way to prevent their taking control of all the Oort Stations." He paused again to let his words sink in with the people around the table.

"Any questions? I know this is a lot to absorb."

Culp fielded several general questions, but he was impressed by how quickly the entire group comprehended the situation and turned its focus to making his solution work.

OORT CLOUD—OORT STATION RUSSIA

Senior Chief Sam Bunker and Petty Officer First-class George Raptor stepped through the Oort Station Russia portal from OS-Prime with Electro Muscular Disruption (EMD) stun weapons at the ready.

"Nobody move!" Bunker ordered in Russian.

The Station Chief froze momentarily and then reached for a brick-like object on a raised table just to his left. Raptor hit him with a bolt from his stun weapon. The Chief dropped, writhing on the station deck.

"Nice goin', Georgie!" Bunker said, and then in Russian, "Anyone else want to try?"

The six technicians shook their heads.

"Okay…on the deck…sit!"

They did. Then one of the two Tech Ones lifted his hand slightly.

"What is it?" Bunker barked.

"What is happening?" the tech asked.

"Do you know what that is?" Bunker asked, pointing with his weapon at the brick. The tech shook his head. "Does anybody know?" Bunker asked.

The other Tech One tentatively lifted her hand.

"*Da.*" Bunker sounded angry.

"It is a portal activator like your hyper-disks," she said in a frightened voice. "It activates an off-grid portal."

"How do you know this?"

"I saw the Chief test it. He didn't tell us anything, but he stayed near it whenever we were on watch. It was a secret. Nobody told us anything."

Bunker gave Raptor a questioning look. Raptor nodded slightly, keeping his weapon trained on the techs.

"Okay, commence your watch duties. Petty Officer Raptor, here, is your new Chief." He reached for the hyper-brick.

"You," he pointed to the female Tech One, "call your Skipper. Tell him your Chief has taken ill. Tell him you need to see him personally." Bunker pointed his weapon at the tech. "Just as I said. Nothing else!"

She nodded as the blood drained from her face. While Bunker took possession of the hyper-brick, the tech called her Skipper. When the OS-Russia Skipper stepped through the Phoenix-controlled portal, Raptor slipped behind him and deactivated the portal.

Bunker trained his weapon at the Skipper. "Lie face down on the deck," he ordered in Russian.

"What's this about?" the Skipper muttered as he complied.

"You know full well. Georgie, search him."

Raptor conducted a thorough search and held up a small EMD weapon, designed to stun the person it touches.

"Why the weapon?" Bunker asked. "Expecting trouble?"

Still lying on the deck, the Skipper just grunted.

Bunker communicated the situation to Culp. "I'm leaving Georgie in charge here and am bringing two prisoners to OS-Prime."

OORT CLOUD—OORT STATION CHINA

While Chief Bunker and Raptor secured OS-Russia, Lt. Rob Jacobs and Petty Officer First-class Cameron Goff stepped through the Oort Station China portal from OS-Prime with EMD weapons at the ready.

"Hold where you are! Do not move!" Lt. Jacobs ordered in Mandarin, the official language of OS-China.

As if orchestrated, the Chief and his six techs went into an immediate deadly whirling dance. Fourteen hands displayed fourteen spinning Emeici, their needle-sharp daggers flashing all over the station. Jacobs dropped the Chief moments before the Chief was able to activate his hyper-brick, but not before the Chief managed to penetrate Goff's gloved left hand with his Emeici.

"Son-of-a-bitch!" Goff muttered through clenched teeth as he hit the Chief with a second bolt.

"Max energy! Take them all down!" Jacobs ordered.

Both SEALS laid down a continuous fire of EMD bolts while Jacobs deactivated the Phoenix portal to the Chinese headquarters.

"Dammit!" Jacobs shouted as a still-standing, twirling Tech One's Emeici penetrated his right bicep. He brought the tech down with the butt of his weapon. "Take that, you son-of-a-bitch!"

"We're offline here," Jacobs reported to Culp. "We took down the entire watch section. Both Goff and I have minor wounds and will…" His voice faded out as he collapsed to the Station deck.

Goff saw him fall, but before he could reach his officer, he, too, collapsed.

✳

"Doc, grab your kit and see to Jake and Goff in OS-China," Culp ordered. "You five," he pointed to five of the remaining ten SEALS, "secure the prisoners, bring them back here and then man the OS-China consoles."

While Culp's team was cleaning up the mess, he signaled eCulp and briefed him on the situation.

"We've identified their operational locus as Earth-Sun L4," eCulp said. "My guys are converging on their location, but we could use some flesh-and-bone backup to handle any physical personnel in their habitat."

"I can send you five under Sam's control," Culp said.

"Have them enter the swarm in two hours outfitted with TBH boots and lethal weapons."

EARTH-SUN L4—RUSSIAN THINSAT SWARM

eJake hovered near the center of the Russian swarm centered on the hyper-disk using a cloaking technique he and eSam had developed that made it impossible for their Chinese counterparts to detect them without first knowing that they were there.

Speaking over a secure circuit that was part of their cloaking technology, eJake asked, "Status of your deployment?"

"Five uploads occupy the swarm," eSam reported. "My guys surround the swarm, two assigned to each upload."

"We're standing by for the appearance of Sam and his five guys," eJake said. "Should be shortly."

While he spoke, the hyper-disk expanded to a portal. "Now!" eJake said to eSam.

Five pairs of upload-SEALS hit eLiǔ and his four fellow uploads with massive power surges. It was over in a flash. eSam's team collected the upload fragments, encasing them in a tensor specially designed for this purpose. Simultaneously, Sam and his five Team members darted through the portal streaming tails of flame from their TBH boots. Quickly disbursing around the habitat, they opened fire with explosive grenades. The habitat disappeared in a burst of flame. All that remained was what appeared to be a hole in the space formerly occupied by the habitat. Clouds of gas rushed from the hole.

"Disable that portal!" Sam shouted. Two of his TBH-booted team converged on the cloud source and fired a grenade from both sides. Soundless fire engulfed the portal, and when it subsided, the cloud was gone; the portal was no more.

"Locate the power portals," eJake ordered. "Conduct a thorough survey of the entire swarm. We need to identify each portal."

Shortly thereafter, eSam reported that they had located fifteen power portals and three transit portals. eJake activated a MERT communications portal to OS-Prime, where he was connected to eCulp.

"We control Earth-Sun L4," eJake said. "There are no survivors, but we have collected upload fragments from the Chinese uploads. We found fifteen power portals, destinations unknown, and three portals suitable for personnel. How to handle these seems to be above my paygrade."

WASHINGTON D.C.—THE OVAL OFFICE

"Mr. President," Kimberly said formally, "thank you for meeting me on such short notice."

"Five minutes is, indeed, short notice," President Butler said with a warm smile. "What is so urgent?"

"We face an immediate problem that we think should involve you." Kimberly then outlined the Federation takeover of OS-Russia and OS-China, and described the military action at Earth-Sun L4. "If we close the power portals, anyone underway in any Russian space-craft is likely to die. If we leave the personnel portals to Earth-Sun L4 open, Russian Space Force troops are likely to emerge through them at any moment." Kimberly paused, examining the president's face. "We intend to close them all, but we believe the Russians will blame you because of your close association with the Federation. They may even retaliate with their military.

"We're not asking your permission, but we are informing you in advance of our intentions so you can take any actions you think might mitigate the response of the Russians and Chinese."

"When does the Federation intend to close the portals?"

Kimberly checked the time on her Link. "One hour from now," she said.

EARTH-SUN L4—RUSSIAN THINSAT SWARM

"Now!" As the order came through to Sam, he signaled to his men who had already placed charges on fifteen power portals and three personnel portals. Seventeen brilliant flashes pierced the darkness. Where the eighteenth should have been, spacesuited soldiers poured through the portal, Russian Federation flags emblazoned on their right shoulders.

"Bullets!" Sam ordered as he flipped a switch on his weapon and commenced firing, countering with his TBH boots the thrust generated by his weapon.

The moment a soldier passed through the portal, he became virtually invisible against the background of stars. Recognizing this problem, eJake ordered his uploads to generate from the swarm as much UV as possible. Immediately, every spacesuited person in the area glowed brightly.

"Sam," eJake said, "have your guys activate their UV shields."

Moments later, Sam and his six SEALS disappeared from view.

"Close that portal," Sam shouted, but none of his men could get close.

eSam saw what was happening and moved close to the portal, where he inserted himself into the electronic mechanism and closed the portal. He felt the electronic pulses coming through in an apparent attempt to reactivate the portal. To ensure that would not happen, he fused the power supply, permanently shutting down the portal.

"How are you holding up?" eSam asked Sam.

"I'm outnumbered three-to-one," Sam said, "but they haven't figured out how to see us. We're picking them off, but it's a slow go. They zero in on our muzzle flashes."

"Let me see what I can do," eSam said.

✳

"Okay, guys," eSam said to his team assembled in the thinsat swarm at Earth-Sun L4, "circulate among the Russians and project a holoimage of yourself in a spacesuit. Force them to fire on you. Direct their fire away from our guys. Make them waste their ammo. Get them to shoot through your image into their own guys.

"Remember, they can't get back. Their portal is gone. They can survive until they run out of air or until they surrender."

"Sam," eSam said on his circuit, "Can you break into their coms?"

"Perhaps."

"When you do, demand their surrender. Tell them if they don't, we'll leave them here to suffocate."

✳

Twenty minutes later, thirty disheartened Russian Space Force infantrymen passed one-by-one through the Earth-Sun L4 MERT portal into OS-Prime.

WASHINGTON D.C.—THE OVAL OFFICE

"Mr. Ambassador," President Butler said to the man standing before the Resolute Desk, "your interference with Oort

Federation operations has cost the lives of twenty of your Space Force people and left an unknown number stranded at various Solar System locations. Furthermore, an unknown number of Chinese uploads have lost their lives as well.

"I do not represent the Federation, but they have authorized me to make you this offer. Cease *all* your operations against the Oort Federation, withdraw *all* your troops and spacecraft, and agree to refrain from any future contact with the Federation. If you comply, the Oort Federation (and my government) will not publicize your role in these events.

"Should you refuse this offer, it will be entirely out of my hands. I am told that the Oort Federation will isolate the Russian Federation from the GlobalNet.It will destroy any Russian spacecraft it finds anywhere in the Solar System, and will isolate the Russian Federation from commercial contact with any other nation insofar as this is possible. The Oort Federation will drive the Russian Federation back to fourth-world status. Your great nation will cease to exist." President smiled sadly. "Is this what you want?"

✴

Two days later, following the complete capitulation of the Russian Federation, the resignation of its government, and a new election called by the Duma, President Butler hosted the Chinese ambassador in the Oval Office, at the ambassador's request.

"Mr. President," the ambassador said formally, "thank you for seeing me on such short notice." He smiled.

"I am always ready to meet with the esteemed representative of the People's Republic of China," the president said, gesturing to the settee on his right.

"My government has just learned," the ambassador said, a sad note entering his voice, "of several rogue elements within our scientific and military establishment. It seems they took it upon themselves to circumvent the mutually beneficial measures adopted by both the Oort Federation and many other nations of Earth, including the United States." The ambassador paused and folded his hands. Then he looked directly at the president.

"I am empowered to inform you that my government has rooted out these traitors. We are thankful that the Federation was able to circumvent the subversive elements that had usurped our control of Oort Station China. We assure you and the Oort Federation that we will continue to be cooperative supporters of the Oort Federation's plan to protect our Solar System." The ambassador dropped his eyes as he ceased speaking.

"I will transmit your words to the Oort Federation," President Butler said. "I can do no more because I do not speak for the Federation, only for the United States."

OORT CLOUD—OORT STATION PRIME

Oort Station Prime second shift was twenty minutes into its third hour under *Chiron* control when *Athena* sounded the alarm. The outermost entangled-particle sphere had just been pierced. The Entangled-Particle Display flashed the presence of a thousand individual points of penetration.

Two hours later, *Athena* alarmed again as the points penetrated the second entangled-particle sphere. EPD calculated a thousand individual vectors, all pointed directly at Sol.

Chapter Twenty-One

OORT CLOUD—OORT STATION PRIME

The news flashed across the Solar System and around Earth after OS-Prime determined that Sol appeared to be the destination of the distant space fleet. Aided by MERT portals, the news arrived at Earth in minutes instead of months. National leaders appeared on holovision across the planet, calming their citizens, explaining that, while the danger was real, it still was several years away. There was plenty of time to prepare, they told their frightened people.

The Federation meeting chamber above the weapons deck on OS-Prime filled rapidly as delegates from many parts of the Solar System and virtually every nation on Earth arrived by portal. In no way did the chamber match the elegance of the U.N. General Assembly or even the Security Council, but it was sufficiently large to accommodate all the delegates, most of whom had never visited OS-Prime before.

After allowing a half-hour or so for sightseeing, Thorpe called the meeting to order. "Ladies and gentlemen," he said using terminology from his past that felt comfortable, "you all know why you are here." He projected an image of the EPD into the space between himself and the delegates. "This is the Entangled-Particle Display that the Techs above you and in the other four Oort Stations are monitoring." The display showed the Oort Cloud with its five monitoring stations, the outgoing entangled-particle spheres, and the incoming fleet. "As you can see, only OS-Prime is positioned to engage the fleet."

The delegates looked at each other nervously, some whispering quietly.

"How far out are they?" someone asked.

"About three lightyears," Thorpe answered. "We believe they are capable of traveling at near lightspeed, which gives us three years before they knock at our front door." Thorpe paused to let this sink in. "They can accelerate to top speed in several microseconds, and they can make nearly instant turns. We do not possess this capability. We have nothing to match this." He paused again. "What we do have is the ability to move faster than light, but we have only one spacecraft, and it has no weapons."

"How can we help?" someone else asked.

"We need more spacecraft built to our exact specifications. We need the ships within a year, and this presents a problem. Our FTL capability depends on doping the spacecraft wings with non-baryonic matter. This stuff is difficult to come by. We will be lucky to complete a dozen FTL spacecraft in the coming year."

"What about crews?"

"Our people and the Oort will crew the spacecraft," Thorpe told the delegates. "The Oort has just as much a stake in this as we do… perhaps even more."

"The Oort?"

"Sure. They're like me—an upload." Thorpe looked around the delegates. "We're in this together. Remember that. Without the Oort, we wouldn't even be here."

DENVER—PHOENIX LABS

With Dale and Brad doing the physical labor, Braxton expanded the Phoenix non-baryonic matter accumulation facility to create sufficient exotic matter to dope the wings of at least twelve spacecraft. It had taken them nearly three months to set up and debug the facility. It turned out that Rodney Bailey's program skills went way beyond block-chains. Braxton brought him into the operation, which cut a couple of weeks from the timeline.

As the facility actually began non-baryonic matter accumulation, Daphne met with Cdr. Jerry Culp in Fredricks' Phoenix office.

"How are your injured guys?" she asked.

"They're still in the temporary infirmary in OS-Prime level three. The injuries themselves were minor, a couple of puncture wounds. But the Chinese used a neurological poison. Lieutenant Jacobs seems to be recovering fine. The dagger entered his muscle but missed any significant blood vessels. He should be back on duty in a couple of days. Petty Officer Cameron Goff, on the other hand, is experiencing serious complications."

"Is he going to make it?" Daphne asked.

"Doesn't look like it."

"How long does he have?"

"We don't know, but his systems are shutting down."

"Did you upload him?"

"When we first started," Culp said.

"We need to upload him right now," Daphne said, connecting to Fredricks by Link. "Jackson," she said, "we need to do an emergency upload at OS-Prime. How soon can you get there with your equipment?"

"Ten minutes," Jackson said.

Daphne turned back to Culp. "He needs to merge with his earlier upload. That will preserve everything that happened to him since the first upload. eDaphne will assist him during the transition. He'll like that—I promise!"

WASHINGTON D.C.—THE OVAL OFFICE

President Butler answered an urgent Link call from his Secretary of State. As the secretary's holoimage flashed into view, he began speaking immediately. "Mr. President, I was just contacted by Gregori Yeltsin, representing the heads of state for Russia, Europe, and India. He wishes to speak with you personally in private. I have uploaded to your Link an abbreviated summary of recent events in the former Russian Federation, now the Russian Republic. I recommend you read this before you see Yeltsin, but please don't delay. Yeltsin's urgency seems real."

Butler pulled up the report and quickly read it. The main points were

- Gregori Yeltsin was the direct descendent of Boris Yeltsin, the Russian Federation's first president following the fall of the Soviet Union. He received his BS in International Relations and History at Princeton, graduating *Magna cum Laude*. He spoke English with native fluency.

- The Russian Federation was renamed *The Federated Russian Republics (FRR)*.

- The Russian Duma had created an entirely new constitution modeled closely after the U.S. Constitution with a significant exception: The Senate consisted of 168 members, two appointed by the legislatures in each of the eighty-four republics, like the original U.S. Constitution.

- All the Federal Subjects of the Russian Federation, the various republics, krais, oblasts, cities of federal importance, autonomous oblasts, and autonomous okrugs, were redesignated Republics, of which there were eighty-four.

Butler reflected for several minutes on this remarkable turn of events. *Is it possible*, he ruminated, *that after so many years, the Russians will finally become a genuine partner in the world community of nations? That I should live to see this happen…that the potential wholesale annihilation of the human race should bring this about…* Butler signaled his Secretary of State to bring President Yeltsin to the Oval Office by portal.

※

The Secretary of State ushered Gregori Yeltsin into the Oval Office through one of several portals discreetly placed around the office periphery.

"President John Butler, please meet President Gregori Yeltsin of the newly reconstituted Federated Russian Republics." With that, the Secretary discreetly departed through the same portal.

President Butler rose to his feet and stretched out his hand. "President Yeltsin. I am so pleased to meet you." He gestured to the right settee. "Please...sit. May I offer you coffee, tea, something stronger?"

"Coffee, thank you."

A navy Steward placed a thick-walled mug on the coffee table and filled it with the fragrant beverage. "Cream or sweetener?" he asked.

"Like it is," Yeltsin said. "Thank you."

After the Steward quietly left the Oval Office, Butler set the windows to opaque and locked the doors. "We are private and totally secure," he said to Yeltsin. "Please go ahead."

"You are aware of the changes my country has made?" Yeltsin asked, leaning forward.

"I am, and I congratulate you for making it happen."

"That is not why I am here, however." Yeltsin leaned back and folded his hands in his lap. "My military experts have carefully analyzed how the Oort Federation has deployed its resources. We agree that this approach addresses the threat as we understand it.

"We asked ourselves, however, if we were the Marauders, what would we do?" Yeltsin commenced counting off on his fingers. "Number one, we would assume that Earth's detection is limited to lightspeed since we will not have found a way around that, so we presume Earth has not. Number two, we would assume that Earth's strike capability is about one-half detection range. Number three, we would put Earth's detection range at one-half AU—that's a bit over four minutes one-way, which, number four, gives Earth a strike range of about thirty-seven million kilometers, with a delay of about two minutes." Yeltsin stopped talking and offered Butler a smile. "These are not my numbers, and I would not claim to be able to generate them, but my best people have drilled them into me.

"What we have arrived at is something similar to what the Oort Federation actually has, except the Oort is using entangled pairs to gain instant detection several lightyears out. Now, as I said earlier, if we were the attackers, we would presume that Earth would not detect us until we were practically there. Since Earth would have no idea from where we would arrive, Earth would have to detect and protect in all directions. Once we were detected, Earth could concentrate its defenses on us at our arrival point, unless..." Yeltsin hesitated and pointed his right index finger in the air, shaking it slightly, "unless we arrived from many directions." He leaned back against the settee.

"This is our conclusion: The Marauders will arrive from many directions. We have static defenses, but no dynamic spacecraft to take the fight to them."

Both men sat quietly while President Butler worked his way through Yeltsin's argument.

"So," Butler said, "you are predicting that we will detect several more incoming fleets, from all directions?"

"Exactly. We will have perhaps a dozen-FTL-ship-fleet, but may be looking at as many as five thousand incoming spacecraft."

That dropped like a massive weight on President Butler's shoulders. He contemplated for about a minute and then shook his head. "I can't see any way around the predicament you have laid out."

"Neither can I," Yeltsin answered, "but we must do something!"

Yeltsin freshened his coffee from the pot the Steward had left on the table, cleared his throat, and said, "I have discussed this with my European and Indian counterparts. We all agree—we will pour virtually every resource we have into our Krasnoyarsk facility to build twenty spacecraft and accumulate the necessary non-baryonic matter in the next seven months. Furthermore, the FRR can pick up the task of producing any additional weapons you might need for the spacecraft. We can have them ready to install about the time the spacecraft are finished. All that would remain would be installing the navigation platforms." He stopped and smiled ruefully. "We concede that for now, the Oort Federation will have to hold on to this technology, but when we prevail, and this is all over, we will want to participate in future development of FTL travel."

"Given the strength of your argument," Butler said, "the world is indebted to you. I will convey your input to the Oort Federation. I am certain that you will be assigned as many engineers and technicians as you will need to accomplish your goal."

"One more thing," Yeltsin said, interrupting. "This morning, China closed its borders along the Russian frontier and stationed troops along the border. We are still checking, but we believe it has also closed its other borders. It has stopped all incoming foreign traffic and all outgoing domestic traffic and is pulling its fleet back to the China Sea. Also, this morning it launched a VASIMR powered spacecraft, destination unknown. It appears to be accelerating at one-gee."

"Please wait a moment, President Yeltsin," Butler said as he opened a confidential Link channel. "Give me the momentary information on China," he said into his Link. Moments later, he scanned a holographic image not visible to Yeltsin. "We concur with your assessment," he said to Yeltsin. "We are tracking their spacecraft on a vector pointed at OS-Prime. We will monitor their behavior in every way possible, and we request that you do the same. We agree to share whatever we find."

OORT CLOUD—OORT STATION PRIME

When eSally was not doing something specific, she hovered in the vicinity of OS-Prime. Thorpe had assigned the Phoenix uploads to monitor all the Oort Stations as a safety backup to prevent another problem like the one that had happened at OS-China. Specifically, she monitored the progress of the Chinese spacecraft that continued to accelerate at one-gee toward OS-Prime. After nearly three days, it was approaching the orbit of Mars on a path that would pass several million kilometers ahead of the red planet.

The cislunar protective stations the Oort had installed did not detect the Chinese craft, probably because nobody was looking. The Mars-Sun L1 station, on the other hand, not only caught a fleeting radar image but also intercepted an outward-beamed radio transmission:

Greetings extra-solar visitors:

We presume that since you have been monitoring out broadcasts for 200 years, you can understand our words. Earth, as we call our planet, has many civilizations. We, the Chinese people, are the crown jewel of Earth civilizations. We trace our civilization back for many thousands of years, long before the rise of any of the other, lesser civilizations on our planet. Unlike the other peoples of Earth, we are peace-loving, having only taken up arms when our peaceful civilization was attacked by one of the lesser peoples.

We reach out to you in friendship. We know that you wreaked havoc on Earth in our distant past, but that was long before our time. We hold no grudges and wish to share our advanced civilization with you and learn from your civilization so that we both can continue together to explore our galaxy.

To this end, we communicate directly with you in a message you should receive about the time you arrive at the fringes of our system. Below is a Mercator projection of our planet with the Chinese nation clearly outlined. We will refrain from attacking your spacecraft on the condition that you spare our people from the destruction we believe you intend for our planet. Furthermore, if you respond affirmatively to this message, we will assist you in destroying the other civilizations on our planet.

Again, we reach out to you in peace and friendship and look forward to your considered response.

Totally stunned by this message, eSally transmitted it to Thorpe as swiftly as possible.

"Are you certain this is not some kind of prank from a group of planetside idiots?" Thorpe asked.

"So far as I can tell," eSally said, "it's genuine. What do we do about it?"

✳

That, of course, is the pressing question, Thorpe thought as he alerted Braxton and Johnny Oort.

"The signal has been sent…it can't be stopped. At least I know of no way to do so. We can sprint out ahead of it with a MERT drive or even a portal, but how do we stop the signal when it arrives?" Thorpe was perplexed. "We're dealing with an expanding spherical wavefront. With a sufficiently large screen, we could intercept and divert the signal…" He ran a calculation. "We can't build a screen that large… not even close."

"What about a negative feedback loop through a portal," Braxton suggested.

"That would eliminate a portion of the signal," Johnny Oort commented, "but there is no way to cancel all of it. The physics simply don't work out."

"Let's destroy the transmitter in any case," Thorpe said. "Is it still in range of your Mars Station?" he asked Johnny Oort.

"Got it!" Johnny Oort responded.

"Great things, these portals," Thorpe said. "Now, we need to deal with China."

WASHINGTON D.C.—THE OVAL OFFICE

"So, that's the entire story," Thorpe's holoimage said to President Butler, finishing up the story of the Chinese spacecraft and the rogue signal to the Marauders. eMax sat on his lap, purring softly, oblivious to the current state of things in the Solar System. "China has isolated itself—taken itself off the GlobalNet and entirely closed its borders."

"China's fleet is blockading its own coast, and their subs form an outer barrier," Butler said. "Our sensors tell us that their ballistic missile subs are poised to launch on any external provocation. We haven't seen anything like this in a hundred years."

"Do you have any communication with them?" Thorpe asked.

"Nothing, nothing at all." The president stayed quiet for a full minute. "I want Russia, India, and Europe in on this," he said. He signaled with his Link, and within five minutes, Gregori Yeltsin walked through one of the portals. Shortly thereafter, the Indian and European heads of state arrived.

President Butler quickly briefed them on the development. "We have to decide what to do about China," Butler said.

"Not China, really," Thorpe said. "It's about China's defense posture, their ability to launch their ballistic missiles at the rest of you."

"We could preemptively disable their missile subs," Butler said.

"And if even one survives to launch?" Yeltsin said.

"There is another way," a new voice interjected,

"Is that you, Johnny?" Thorpe asked.

"It is."

"Gentlemen, this is Johnny Oort. You may have met him during our initial meetings at OS-Prime. In any case, Johnny speaks for the Oort."

"As I said," Johnny Oort continued, "there is another way. The Oort has developed a method of using neutrinos to detect the presence of both fission and fusion nuclear reactors and concentrations of radioactive material such as in nuclear and thermonuclear weapons. Our neutrino beam weapon can then disable both from a range out to a million kilometers.

"You will need to install the detector and neutrino beam weapon in several spacecraft, bring the ships into a powered hover over China, and detect and simultaneously disable the subs and their missiles and any land-based missiles."

"That's really possible?" Yeltsin asked.

"The current nav modules will take a bit over a month to bring the spacecraft from OS-Prime to Earth."

"We can do better than that," Yeltsin said. "Set up portals to transport the detectors, weapons, and nav modules to Krasnoyarsk. We can install them in the twenty spacecraft we have just completed, and have the ships in powered hover in a week."

※

Eight days later, twenty Oort Federation spacecraft established twenty powered hovers at an altitude of 3,000 kilometers evenly spaced over China and her territorial waters. One hour later, although China's LANR power production facilities were still intact, China no longer had any offensive nuclear capability.

DENVER—PHOENIX LABS

"Is everyone here?" Dr. Fredricks asked, looking around the conference table in the Denver Tech Center Phoenix complex. His original team was present: Daphne, Dale, Kimberly, Sally, Brad, and even Deb Streeter, in person rather than by holoimage. Of course, Thorpe and Braxton appeared as holoimages since that was their only option. Max jumped on the table, mewing for his attention. "And not to forget Max, of course," Fredricks added, stroking the feline.

eMax appeared on the other end of the conference table next to eDaphne, making his presence known as a regular part of the team. The other uploads presented themselves as holoimages in table slots set aside for them: eDale, eKim, eSally, and eBrad.

Fredricks acknowledged each. "We have come a long way from our experimental revival of the Icicle back in Beverly Hills what seems so long ago. Each of you has played a pivotal role in bringing us to this place. Without your efforts, we would be utterly unprepared for what is coming. Nay…ignorant of the very fact until we all would have been incinerated in the holocaust the Marauders are certainly planning for Earth.

"I asked you to meet with me today because I don't see any chance of our getting together again before all hell breaks loose. We have done everything possible to counter what we know is coming. We have ten FTL spacecraft poised around the Oort Cloud armed to the teeth with weapons we believe will be effective against the Marauders. We have five Oort Stations with well-trained crews and the ability to reach lightyears out to detect and destroy the incoming enemy. We have strategically located outposts throughout the Solar System to take on any Marauder ships that get through our initial defenses. And as a final backup, over a billion of our fellow citizens had opted to upload a copy of themselves into the Kuiper Belt swarm. Even if the Marauders break through our defenses and seriously damage Earth, we have the unequivocal ability to restore our civilization with our Kuiper Belt backups. This, my friends, is what you have accomplished. A decade ago, it would have been unimaginable. Today, it is reality.

"We are working with many others, flesh-and-bone and uploads. Commander Culp, I guess I should say Admiral Culp, and his team come to mind, as do the crews manning the Oort Stations and our combined human and Oort upload-crews manning our small fleet." Fredricks paused to take a deep breath. "Many here on Earth have mattered as well. President Butler and President Yeltsin were particularly important. And let's not forget the many Russian, European, and Indian workers and technicians who pitched in to give us our little space fleet quicker than I could possibly have imagined. I'm going to stop before I become maudlin…" Fredricks grinned sheepishly.

"Now…let's go get the bastards!"

Chapter Twenty-Two

OORT CLOUD—OORT STATION PRIME

"Are you getting this?" eBrad asked over the general circuit as *Athena* sounded the alarm in OS-India.

"I got yours, and now I have one, too!" eDale said from OS-Europe.

"Me, too!" eDaphne said from OS-China.

"Only your reports," eKim said from OS-Russia. And then, "No...Wait! *Athena* just alarmed me, too!"

"I'm looking at the OS-Prime EPD," Thorpe said, jumping into the conversation. It looks like the Marauders can do geometry just as well as we. OS-Prime is on a vector the Oort believes points at the Marauder home system. The remaining Oort Station locations are geometrically derived from that position. The same geometric logic has apparently led the Marauders to approach our system from virtually the same five vectors where we placed our Oort Stations. *Athena* reports about a thousand ships in each fleet. They're all about two lightyears out. I'm not going to worry about why we didn't detect the other four fleets until just now."

Thorpe put out a general call to every element of the Oort Federation. "It's time!" he announced. "We have trained together for months. We have thirty-two well-armed FTL ships, and we have developed tactics that take advantage of our capabilities to their disadvantage, despite their overwhelming numbers. Our starship crews are uploads with more experience as uploads than anyone in history. Our crews consist of my counterpart, Braxton, the original uploads—eDaphne, eDale, eSally, and eBrad—and fifty-five courageous Oort individuals who have, for the first time in their existence, separated themselves from the Oort as individual entities.

"We leave in twelve hours."

INTERSTELLAR SPACE—2 LY BEYOND THE OORT CLOUD

The MERT Drive starship had received several significant up-grades since Thorpe first transited to the Oort Cloud in *Ishtar II*. eBrad and eSally had, remarkably, decreased its MERT Drive cycle to one nanosecond. Its length was now twenty-five meters and its width three meters. Weapon systems occupied one-quarter of the extra internal space. A redesigned LANR and liquid deuterium storage filled the remainder. There was no space for human passengers, only for two upload matrix slots. The spacecraft could travel a hundred lightyears in 438 days without refueling. Shorter transits would have to await a further reduction in the MERT Drive cycle and a much larger spacecraft, both depending on a significantly larger power source.

The Oort coordinated the launching of each ship, but once a spacecraft entered nullspace, the crew was on its own with only the onboard Mother to assist them.

"Let's review the plan," Braxton said to his Oort partner as they commenced their 210-hour transit. "We are one of just six ships, and our little fleet is one of five spacecraft sextets traveling outward on vectors from Sol through the Oort Stations. This is because the incoming attackers are riding these vectors. They are about two lightyears out. We intend to remain in nullspace for two hundred ten hours, just a bit over eight-and-a-half days, dropping into normal space close behind their fleet. They will be barreling along at something close to lightspeed. To our instruments, they will appear as flattened disks displaying whatever diameter their ships have, and with a huge relativistic mass. We are concerned about the effect of the relativistic mass since no one has ever experienced this phenomenon, but we'll have to deal with that when it happens. The ten Oort and we are timed to come out of nullspace simultaneously but widely separated. If the relativistic gravity well turns out to be a problem, we'll pull together so we can communicate and figure out what to do.

"On the other hand, if the gravity well is not a problem, each ship will target and destroy as many enemy spacecraft as possible."

"And what if we are too distant?" the Oort asked.

"Then we move as close as possible and try again. Remember, when we drop out of nullspace, they will be receding from us at nearly light speed. We won't have much time."

"How much, do you think?"

"A few microseconds at most," Braxton said.

Although they had the technique down, they did not destroy any Marauder spacecraft.

✳

"Three...two...one..." Mother counted down in the spacecraft occupied by eDaphne and her Oort partner on the OS-Russia vector. As they popped out of nullspace, Mother swept the neutrino beam across an attacker.

"We got one!" the Oort said, excitement filling its voice. "We got one!"

"Looks like it," eDaphne said, giving the Oort a virtual hug.

"I don't see anything," the Oort said, examining the instrumentation.

"That's because in the last second they already moved some three hundred thousand klicks ahead of us." Addressing Mother, eDaphne said, "Calculate the Marauder fleet position and place us immediately behind it—several clicks only. Sweep the neutrino beam across any available Marauder target...on my mark. Mark!"

Their nullspace jump was virtually instantaneous—no lapsed time at all, followed by nearly simultaneous neutrino firing.

"Three enemy ships destroyed," Mother announced. And they jumped again.

✳

"Mother," eBrad said, "when we exit nullspace on the OS-Europe vector, note the distance to the Marauder fleet and its velocity, and then jump us as close as possible and immediately sweep the three closest ships with the neutrino beam. Then repeat the sequence three times."

When they popped out of nullspace the first time, while Mother was firing, the Oort recorded an image of the fleet, at least that part the imager could record.

"As we thought," the Oort told eBrad. "Flat disks about twenty-five meters in diameter. They moved ahead so fast that we hardly had time to register the gravity well."

"Did we get anything?" eBrad asked.

"I can't tell," the Oort said after the third sequence. "Mother?" it asked.

"You destroyed nine spacecraft, three at each stop," Mother answered.

※

The foray lasted less than an hour before onboard controllers set the spacecraft on vectors back to their respective Oort Stations. Upon arrival, approximately eight days later, the uploads for all five sextets remained in their matrixes but connected into a common circuit for debriefing. Thorpe took all the reports and consolidated the results.

After compiling the results, Thorpe announced, "Not every ship that exited nullspace behind the five Marauder fleets was successful. Of the OS-Prime group, Braxton and two of the Oort craft were unsuccessful using laser, and three of the Oort craft got five using neutrinos. On OS-Russia, eDaphne and two of the Oort got six with neutrinos, and three Oort got none on laser. On OS-Europe, all craft used neutrinos. eBrad got nine and the five Oort got seven. On OS-China, eSally and three Oort got ten on neutrino, and two Oort got none on laser. And on OS-India, eDale and four Oort got twelve on neutrino, and one Oort got none on laser.

"So, of the thousand Marauder ships on each vector, we destroyed five on Prime, six on Russia, sixteen on Europe, ten on China, and twelve on India, for a total of forty-nine Marauder spacecraft destroyed out of five thousand. Obviously, we need to do better than this."

OORT CLOUD—OORT STATION PRIME

"Our problem is," Thorpe said to the assembled delegates from Earth and across the Solar System, "that four thousand nine hundred fifty-one Marauder spacecraft are still headed for Earth. They will reach the outskirts of the Oort Cloud in about two years. We believe that they have no idea they lost forty-nine spacecraft. When they stop to regroup upon their arrival at the Oort Cloud—if that's what they end up doing—they will discover their losses. If they stop to set specific safe vectors into the Solar System, and we believe they will, we should be able to take out many of them with the Oort Station armament. If they don't stop, however, even though we believe they will, their passing will cause extensive damage to the Oort, and it may even impact Earth's backup swarm in the Kuiper Belt.

"It still will take them an additional one-and-a-half years to reach Earth if we don't stop them here. This gives us a lot of time to do whatever we can to stop them from destroying Earth."

✳

Of the many lessons learned from the initial attack, perhaps the most important was that the neutrino beam was the weapon of choice for this mode of attack. It could sweep across a group of enemy spacecraft moving away at a significant fraction of lightspeed, and if the enemy ships did not change their course, the neutrino beam would disrupt their power plants. This would cause an immediate catastrophic disintegration of the entire spacecraft. Although not the only option, this seemed the most effective one.

Thorpe had the Earth spacecraft install a second neutrino beam. The Russians turned their considerable manufacturing capacity to producing the weapons. India supplied the technicians to install the weapons onsite at the five Oort Stations. This required that they receive training in space operations and free-fall before deploying to the Oort Stations. In an heroic effort, all the technicians successfully completed their training in less than a month. They were ready to install the neutrino weapons as they came off the Russian assembly lines.

※

Thorpe brought Rodney Bailey to Oort Station Prime. "You're going to earn your money like never before," Thorpe told him.

Thorpe then described the initial preemptive attack and the lessons learned. "I need you to adjust Mother's program so she can predict with a high degree of accuracy the future position of several Marauder spacecraft from momentary measurements taken upon exiting nullspace. By itself, that may not sound like much, but remember that Mother must run these calculations while simultaneously controlling precision nanosecond jumps: Jump, measure, sweeping neutrino beam, repeat…and keep it up until there are no remaining Marauder targets."

"How long do I have?" Bailey wanted to know.

"Sooner is better, but accurate is better than sooner, if you get my drift," Thorpe said with a smile. "I hate to do this to you, but the fate of the entire human race and the Oort may rest on your shoulders. I hired you because you are the best. Now you get to prove it!"

INTERSTELLAR SPACE—1.4 LY BEYOND THE OORT CLOUD

Each of the thirty Earth FTL spacecraft, and the two spares, had installed a second neutrino beam weapon, and their deuterium tanks were topped off. The upload-crews had trained hard for six months—they were ready to kick ass!

The EPD accurately identified the location and vectors of the still nearly 5,000 Marauder spacecraft. The Oort positioned Earth's thirty ships on vectors that would bring then close-in behind the speeding Marauder spacecraft. The Oort launched the ships simultaneously from each of the Oort Stations. In a heartbeat, only the two spare spacecraft remained in the vicinity of OS-Prime.

Just over six days later, 147 hours, Earth's thirty spacecraft emerged from nullspace, six ships behind each Marauder fleet. To an outside observer, there was not much to see. Six ships would appear briefly behind a group of flattened disks rushing toward Sol. Several disks would vanish in a bright flare, and the others would disappear in the distance. Sometimes, the Earth spacecraft would appear and disappear without hitting anything. But on each vector, there was a continuous visible wave of bright flashes moving at near lightspeed toward Sol.

The Earth spacecraft dogged the Marauder fleets for the better part of five hours, taking out as many ships as possible with each return to normal space. By the time they exited nullspace at their respective Oort Stations some six days later, the Marauder fleets had closed the Oort Cloud by about six times the width of the Solar System.

Thorpe gathered the crews to learn what they had accomplished. Then he announced to the group, "We did much better this time around. Each of your attack groups averaged somewhat over four hundred kills, with a total loss to the Marauders of twenty-one hundred spacecraft—give or take. Unfortunately, we are unable to get an exact count because of how quickly things happen during each encounter. In any case, they still have over five hundred spacecraft in each of their five fleets. And you know what this means."

"May I hazard a guess?" Braxton asked.

Thorpe nodded.

"Another raid," Braxton said. "How soon?"

"Let's check each spacecraft top to bottom, top off the deuterium tanks, and head out."

During the interim, Rodney Bailey tweaked the firing algorithms based upon past performance data to optimize their kill chances. When the small fleet departed a week later, the Marauders were another 181 billion kilometers closer. Their own transit was four hours shorter, and when they emerged from nullspace and commenced sweeping their neutrino beams, they had no indication that the Marauders had any inkling of their losses or the presence of the Earth ships.

Upon their return after pooling their numbers, they determined that each Marauder fleet had only about a hundred spacecraft remaining.

Thorpe pointed out, "That's still over five hundred hostile spacecraft with destructive capabilities we know nothing about."

"When we go out the next time," Braxton said, "it won't be as easy. Their craft are spaced much farther apart. We'll each be lucky to get one per sweep."

"That brings up a point," Thorpe said. "You guys are thinking in terms of *easy* for taking out the Marauder spacecraft. Keep in mind that while they know about our existence—that's why they're coming back—they have no idea of our advances nor of the Oort. If they got the Chinese signal, the Marauders will presume they have already been detected, although they won't know how. But odds are they're trying to figure it out. When they figure it out, things will be very much different."

The uploads discussed this among themselves for a while, talking about the various options.

One of the Oort pointed out, "When the Marauders last returned, some sixty million years ago, they hit Earth with only one large asteroid. We believe they must have used a bunch of their ships to modify the asteroid's orbit so it crashed into Earth. That was pretty devastating, but today's planetary civilization could survive that. It would take a lot more."

"Granted," another Oort spoke up, "they don't know about the Oort nor your space capabilities, but they'll find out soon enough. Using asteroids as weapons is pretty effective."

"Even a little one would devastate an Oort Station," eSally commented.

"Can the Oort generate numbers that will inform us how they might do this?" Thorpe asked. "What would it take to move a bunch of asteroids of differing sizes from the Belt to slam them into Earth?"

"We're on it," one of the Oort answered, obviously speaking for the Oort as a group.

THE SOLAR SYSTEM GENERALLY

During the following months, the Oort supplied the requested numbers. Ten to twenty Marauder spacecraft could maneuver an asteroid like the one they threw at Earth sixty million years ago. They could accelerate it way beyond orbital velocity, bringing about the crash in just a few days. They should be able to hurl smaller asteroids using two to five ships. Given their ships' maneuverability, the only ways to stop them would be either to prevent their penetration of the Solar System in the first place or to pick them off one-by-one as they set up their method for maneuvering the asteroids.

Non-baryonic matter accumulation had continued for the entire time since the initial confrontation. The Oort Federation had sufficient for six additional FTL spacecraft. These were designed and built to carry one flesh and bone human and one upload. This brought the Oort Federation's total spacecraft to thirty-eight plus the original *Ishtar II*, that while smaller and armed with only a laser, could carry passengers.

Another raid eliminated about fifty Marauder craft, but it was clear to Thorpe that further raids would probably not be effective. Instead, he moved all thirty-eight fight-outfitted spacecraft into cislunar space, ready to confront any Marauder craft that penetrated that far.

The entire team, people and uploads, worked together to construct backup portals for each Oort Station and every outpost the Oort had earlier established and outfitted with weapons. Furthermore, the weapon count at each Oort Station and outpost was doubled.

As the Marauder arrival day approached, Thorpe left nothing to chance. He covered every contingency he could think of, every one his people could think of, and everything the Oort brought to light.

Earth, the Solar System, the Oort Federation, and the Oort were as prepared as was physically possible.

OORT CLOUD—OORT STATION PRIME

Despite nearly a year-and-a-half of intense preparation, despite following Marauder progress on the EPD, despite 24/7 drills, attack day when it arrived caught everyone off guard.

Athena sounded the alarm in all five Oort Stations, but before the sound died, the space volume outward from all the Oort stations except OS-India was filled with strange spacecraft. A hundred hovered before OS-Prime, and about fifty each hovered in front of the other three. Apparently, none of the Marauder craft vectored toward OS-India had survived. The craft were about twenty-five meters across and looked like two saucers placed face-to-face. Two half-meter tubes ran around the perimeter of each craft just above and below the edge formed by the facing "saucers."

Figure 2—Marauder Starship

Instead of launching an immediate attack, the Marauder spacecraft seemed to hesitate, perhaps because of confusion at finding most of their fleet gone and discovering unexpected structures blocking their advance into the Oort Cloud.

The hesitation was only momentary. A fraction of a second later, a laser beam flashed from one of the Saucer-like spacecraft hovering in front of OS-Europe. The Station disintegrated into thousands of pieces flying off on a tangent while the counterweight flew off on its own path before disintegrating as a second laser found it. Within a microsecond, *Athena* opened fire with all weapons at the three stations faced with Marauders. She was able to take out all the Marauder spacecraft at OS-Russia, and OS-China, and half the craft at OS-Prime, but with OS-Europe gone, those Marauders survived. None of the invaders got off another shot; however, all the remaining craft at OS-Prime and OS-Europe abruptly disappeared.

Thorpe and the Oort together were monitoring the battle from OS-Prime. "What happened?" Thorpe asked. "One moment, fifty craft seemed ready to attack; the next, they were gone."

"We had a moment to scan one of their craft," the Oort said. "At the center is a small black hole. The two tubes form some kind of counter-rotating particle accelerators. How this serves to propel their craft, we have no idea. We should make a major effort to capture one of their craft intact." The Oort paused a moment. "We think our neutrino beams disrupt the black holes, causing the craft to disintegrate. We really need to capture one."

"So, what happened to the remaining craft?"

"We think they accelerated toward the Solar System center. Remember, that's a minimum one-and-a-half-year trip for them. We still believe they do not know about our FTL drive. This means that from their perspective, their head start should get them to the inner Solar System first.

DENVER—PHOENIX LABS

At the Phoenix conference table in the Denver Tech Center, Thorpe gathered his original group and their uploads, including both Max and eMax. Admiral Culp and his senior people were present along with their uploads, as were Deb Streeter, Rodney Bailey, and even Frank Merriweather and Norman Bork from Mars Station. Johnny Oort was there as well. To make room for everyone, the uploads floated above the seated people, although eMax chose to walk the table greeting old friends while Max remained in Daphne's lap.

"We have passed the first hurdle," Thorpe said, "but it's far from over. We believe the Marauders are moving on two straight lines along the ecliptic toward Sol from OS-Prime and the OS-Europe location. They have no more than fifty to a hundred spacecraft. We suspect they are traveling about three-quarter lightspeed, so their relativistic gravity wells won't cause them problems so near planetary masses. Working together, we must build a series of neutrino beam weapon outposts along their paths. These weapons will be controlled by a semi-autonomous system linked by portal to the Oort. As the Marauder spacecraft approach and pass these outposts, we will try to hit as many as possible with neutrino beams.

"Once they reach the Asteroid Belt, we believe the Marauders will slow significantly so they can latch onto one or more asteroids to hurl toward Earth. After we complete the neutrino beam stations along their paths, we will construct a spread-out set of stations throughout the volume where we believe they will try to capture the asteroids. These stations will carry both neutrino and laser beams.

"We believe the tubes around the facing saucer edge are part of their propulsion system. If you can damage these tubes by laser, we think this will shut down their propulsion system. Anything living inside the craft that you can pinpoint with the neutrino beam will die. You need to be careful, however, not to hit the black hole at the craft center. Do that, and the craft blows up.

"We want to capture at least one intact Marauder spacecraft." Thorpe let out a big sigh. "If possible, we also want to capture a living Marauder. That may give us some insight into why all this is happening." He looked over the people who had become his friends. "Do you have any questions?"

There were many, and the meeting continued for several hours as Thorpe and Johnny Oort answered every question.

Finally, Thorpe said, "One more important thing. We have installed a personal portal in each spacecraft linked directly to your own backup, whether it is in our central system or in the Kuiper Belt. If you get taken out, you *will* survive this. If you are flesh and bone," he looked directly at Deb Streeter and Norman Bork, "you're gonna lose that, but you will still be alive and still be one of us." Thorpe stopped talking and let his gaze touch everyone in the room.

"Okay, get yourselves organized, and let's do this!"

※

Daphne and Kimberly walked out of the conference room hand-in-hand.

"I'm scared," Kimberly said, shivering.

"Me, too," Daphne said. "At least we have each other." She squeezed Kimberly's hand.

Dale walked up behind them and draped an arm around each. "How are you girls holding up?" he asked.

They turned, Daphne kissing his head and Kimberly brushing his lips.

"What do you expect, what with the world coming to an end?" Kimberly said, half meaning it.

"You don't really mean that," Dale said, squeezing her. "We're going to get through this thing."

"Yeah…right," Kimberly said with a slight smile and kissed him for real this time.

※

Sally and Brad left the room holding hands. Sally felt especially small beside her large companion. "Do you think we'll get through this?" she asked him.

"It won't be for lack of trying," he answered, picking her up in his arms like a little girl and kissing her.

Sally flushed red. "Oh my! Not here!" she whispered as he put her back on her feet.

"Why not?" he asked with a chuckle. "Everybody knows how I feel about you."

Sally smiled shyly and pressed against his hard body.

＊

Dr. Fredricks and Dr. Merriweather walked out together, chatting quietly.

"I really had no idea about what you were doing," Merriweather said to his friend, touching his hand momentarily. "I say, I am most impressed. Please let me participate in any way I can."

＊

Admiral Culp left the room accompanied by Commander Rob Jacobs and Master Chief Sam Bunker.

"I'm glad you guys are here with me," Culp said. He turned to Sam. "You and your people have made a significant contribution to our survival. I don't think we could have done it without you, and I hear the Marauders don't take prisoners, so there goes your chance to learn Alien."

Sam turned toward Culp, stopped, came to attention, and saluted. "I don't think I could have served a better man, Sir!"

＊

The uploads moved together into LEO ServerSky, where they mingled, sharing their thoughts and feelings in a manner incomprehensible to flesh-and-bone humans. Then they split into their natural associations, eDaphne and Braxton with eKim and eDale, eSally with eBrad, the SEALS, and eMax somehow managing to make himself part of everything.

THE SOLAR SYSTEM GENERALLY

Out of the darkness of the outer Solar System, seventy-eight relativistically flattened spacecraft flashed past Jupiter toward the Asteroid Belt in a diamond-shaped wedge formation. Oort-controlled detectors picked up the lead ship before they reached Jupiter's orbit and began sweeping the path before the spacecraft with concentrated neutrinos.

Thirty of the Marauder vessels disintegrated on contact. The rest missed the concentrated neutrinos and continued on course. 50,000 kilometers ahead, unseen because they were popping into and out of null-space too quickly to be detected, Kimberly, Dale, Sally, and Brad, each in a new Federation spacecraft, were keeping pace with the Marauder vessels.

Four trailing Marauder craft detected the increasing neutrino flux and hit the brakes, dropping out of the formation. Two veered off-course to their left on a tangent that took them into the Belt away from the main track, followed by Daphne's Federation craft. The other two headed on the opposite tangent, followed by Norman Bork. As they entered the Belt, all four Marauder craft changed velocity instantly to match the orbital paths of the surrounding asteroids and disappeared from Daphne's and Bork's detectors. Daphne and Bork took up orbital positions where they were when they lost the Marauder craft.

Eighteen minutes later, as they reached the outer limits of the Asteroid Belt, the Marauder vessels slowed. Inside the four Federation craft pacing them, four Mothers drew visual beads on the spacecraft. Three microseconds later, forty-four Marauder craft exploded simultaneously.

The moment the Marauder craft near Bork detected the massive explosions, one came alive and accelerated straight up out of the Ecliptic. Bork trained his neutrino beam ahead of the speeding spaceship. It exploded before it had climbed 50,000 kilometers. The other craft had taken refuge behind an asteroid when it observed Bork's attack. Carefully, stealthily, it crept around the edge of the asteroid. When the Marauder craft had Bork in its sights, it fired its particle beam, destroying the Federation craft and killing Bork and his Oort companion.

※

When they lost contact with the remaining Marauder fleet, the two vessels hiding in the Belt near Daphne knew that their raid on this solar system was a complete disaster. They developed a final plan of action using a tight-beam laser to communicate with each other. Keeping an asteroid between each of them and Daphne, they eased away from her Federation craft without her noticing. Several hours later, thousands of kilometers from her, they latched onto a ten kilometer-wide asteroid that they could maneuver together. With a bit of luck, there still was a chance they could wipe out all Earth life.

They accelerated the asteroid out of its orbit and pushed it into an orbit that would make it collide with Earth in a week. When they were confident that the asteroid was on track, one of the spacecraft peeled off into the Belt, set a vector to carry it far above the ecliptic, and accelerated to maximum velocity.

※

eDaphne and her Oort partner had transited to Earth with the other thirty-three upload-manned Federation craft to form a protective shell around the home planet. The four human-manned craft that had destroyed the main Marauder fleet joined them, but they had not heard from Daphne or Bork. Each spacecraft was riding a high-speed halo orbit around Earth that carried them from inside Earth's orbit to the inner edge of the Asteroid Belt over a matter of several hours. eDaphne's Oort partner had set their detector parameters to maximum detection range. On their current pass, they picked up an anomalous movement in the Belt. A quick analysis indicated that a rogue asteroid was headed out of the Belt to the inner Solar System.

Further analysis indicated that the asteroid was traveling way faster than its orbital parameters dictated. In fact, it would intersect Earth's orbit when Earth was at the intersection point. It would collide with Earth in about a week.

As they were taking these measurements, their detectors spotted something heading rapidly to the north out of the ecliptic, but they didn't have time to track it, and when they looked again, it was gone.

"I'm taking us to the backside of the asteroid," eDaphne said. Something is causing this."

She brought their ship on a sharp curve to the rear of the asteroid. Clinging to the asteroid back was a Marauder saucer-craft.

"Mother," eDaphne said, "hit those tubes with your laser. We're gonna capture this sucker!"

Mother reported, "Mission accomplished!"

While they observed, the Marauder craft drifted away from the asteroid while maintaining its relative position to their craft. The asteroid continued on its path toward Earth.

"How do we stop it?" eDaphne asked.

"I have an idea," her Oort partner said. It called the other thirty-seven Federation ships that were shielding Earth. The Oort explained the asteroid problem and had the other ships approach their position.

It took a couple of days to get the spacecraft properly positioned around the asteroid. When everyone was in position, the Oort had each craft focus its anti-matter beam on the sunward side of the asteroid. As the anti-matter came into contact with the asteroid's surface, a continuous violent mass-to-energy conversion commenced. A powerful jet blasted toward Sol from a growing crater on the asteroid, veering it gradually into a new orbit that would miss Earth by several million kilometers.

As the Federation craft shut down their anti-matter beams, suddenly, the asteroid split into three large pieces about three kilometers across, and several hundred smaller chunks, most no larger than an automobile. The three large pieces assumed orbits that still missed Earth, but most of the smaller chunks continued the asteroid's original orbit, with Earth in the crosshairs, and five days until the collision. The ships did what they could to blast the larger chunks to rubble, but the collision was inevitable.

※

Daphne and her Oort partner observed the two Marauder craft deflect the asteroid toward Earth, and then one of them beat-feet up and out over the Ecliptic. Daphne was about to take out the craft pushing the asteroid when she observed a Federation craft kill its drive. She watched it drift away as the other Federation vessels concentrated on deflecting the asteroid away from Earth. Daphne and her Oort partner watched the Federation craft divert the asteroid to a harmless orbit. Rather than join them, however, she held back.

Daphne signaled the other Federation craft, telling them that she would find a way to secure the Marauder craft in a safe Earth orbit. This turned out to be a bigger task than she had realized.

THE SOLAR SYSTEM—CISLUNAR SPACE

While hovering about a kilometer from the disabled Marauder craft, Daphne contacted Thorpe.

"I need to move this alien craft into Earth orbit, but I need some help. My Federation craft has no way to take something under tow or to push it. I'm going to need the VASIMR craft we used on the first transit to Mercury, some muscle, and a lot of vacuum-curing polymer."

"I understand," Thorpe said. "How will you steer it?"

"We normally do that with gyros," Daphne said, "but that won't work here. So far as I know, we don't have a ready supply of steering thrusters…"

"But we do have a supply of TBH boots," Thorpe said. "I'll get things together while you work out the logistics of attachment. I'm going to speculate that you will need sixteen boots in groups of four. I'll have them modified so that each group of four has one remote activator. I'll send Dale with the hyper-disk, and Brad will follow with the SEAL team as soon as we have the VASIMR ready."

While she waited, Daphne moved her vessel around the Marauder craft. Dead top center was an eyebolt that she could use as the initial attachment point for the VASIMR. Initially, she had envisioned moving the craft edge first. On reflection, however, propelling it bottom first was more practical. She would attach the two sets of TBH thrusters 90° apart along the rim, pointing with and against the VASIMR thrust.

Daphne was exhausted. She put the Oort on watch and finally allowed herself to drift to exhausted sleep while she waited for materials and physical help.

※

What seemed like moments later, the Oort awakened her with the emergency alarm.

※

The lone surviving Marauder spacecraft that had taken out Bork remained huddled against the sheltering asteroid's backside while the asteroid continued in its path around the Sun. It observed the departure of one of its own and the bewildering death of the only remaining craft except for itself.

Carefully, stealthily, the craft brought up its power and hurled itself high above the ecliptic directly over the thirty-eight Federation spacecraft. Then it reversed direction and dropped downward at close to lightspeed. When its internal dead-reckoning calculations put it a thousand kilometers above the Federation spacecraft, it came to an instant hover.

It took Daphne's detectors several seconds of lightspeed transit time to pinpoint the Marauder craft. During those seconds, the Marauder unleashed laser beams at five of the Federation craft, completely destroying four of them and their Oort crews.

※

As eDaphne's instruments recorded the destruction of the four craft, a laser sliced into her LANR.

"Oh my God!" she screamed.

"We lost power," her Oort partner said as their ship went dead, and their matrixes reverted to backup batteries, "but we're still alive."

"No comms either," eDaphne said as she regained her composure and pulled herself back together.

A moment later, the Marauder craft exploded soundlessly.

※

Daphne came awake with a start and heard the Oort order Mother to locate and destroy. She threw a question at the Oort. "What the hell's happening?"

"A Marauder craft came out of nowhere and destroyed five of our ships, including eDaphne's."

"Oh, my God," she said. "Did eDdaphne and the Oort survive?"

"I don't know," the Oort answered. "Her ship's without power and drifting. No comms."

Just then, Dale stepped through the portal, dressed in a spacesuit with his helmet in tow.

"Hi," he said, brushing her cheek with his lips. "Thorpe pulled me off my ship, briefed me in ten seconds, and sent me here with this." He handed her a hyper-disk.

"Oh, Dale," Daphne said, "eDaphne's ship just lost power after an attack. I need to rescue her."

Daphne quickly explained to Dale how she planned to attach the VASIMR to the Marauder craft.

"Put on your helmet and take the hyper-disk over to the Marauder ship. I gotta go get eDaphne! Oh, and there should be one or two Marauders inside that spaceship."

She pushed Dale out the lock and set out for eDaphne's position.

❋

eDaphne and the Oort, battery power still strong, heard scraping along the hull of their ship. The forward hatch cycled, and the inner lock opened as Daphne stepped into their ship.

"Oh, my God, Sis...are you okay?"

"Leave your helmet on, Daphne. I don't know about the atmosphere in here."

"Nothing," Daphne said. "Your hull is breached."

Daphne pulled both matrixes, placing them on the deck. "Time to go home, Sis," she said, taking them both back to her ship, where she passed them through the portal.

eDaphne and the Oort arrived at Earth-Moon L2 several hours later—fretful hours from eDaphne's perspective. The matrixes containing eDaphne and the Oort were transported via Phoenix to OS Prime, where the Oort rejoined his fellows, and eDaphne slipped back into her more familiar environment.

"I thought we had lost you, Girl," eKim told her as she slipped into eDaphne's matrix.

eDale wrapped his arms around them, completing their small circle.

Later, when they finally surfaced, Thorpe and Braxton reached out to brush eDaphne's face. "Welcome home, Daphne," Braxton whispered quietly.

"We would have missed you terribly," Thorpe added.

"But I had a backup," eDaphne protested.

"*She* would not have experienced *you* for the past several days," Braxton said. "We're glad you're *you*!"

EARTH ORBIT—LEO

Daphne brought her craft alongside the Marauder craft just as Dale, Brad, and several armed SEALS were finishing up the modifications.

"Any sign of activity from inside?" Daphne asked.

"Nothing at all," Dale said.

"She's deader than a doornail," Senior Chief Sam Bunker said. "Without power, they've got to be running low on life support."

"They gotta know we're out here, all the racket we've been making. You want us to blow the hatch?" Petty Officer Raptor asked.

"No," Daphne said. "If they're not in their spacesuits, that would kill them. We want at least one of them alive."

At that moment, a hatch blew open, nearly knocking Dale away from the craft. Without any direction, using their TBH boots, the SEALS positioned themselves around the open hatch in a loose hemisphere, weapons drawn. A bright flash briefly illuminated the interior.

"I'm hit!" one of the SEALs inline with the hatch shouted as a black hole appeared in his suit leg. Then he vanished as his E-disk pullet him to safety.

"Clear from the entrance, you lunkheads," Sam shouted as two SEALS maneuvered along the hull as close to the opening as possible.

"Don't fire your weapons inside the craft," Daphne said. "We want to preserve as much as possible."

They waited. Nothing happened.

They waited some more. Still, nothing happened.

"We gotta flush them out," Sam said. "Can you get an activated portal inside?" he asked Daphne. "We can put the Locus in a one-at-mosphere environment and blow them out."

"If we can get one inside, we can activate it from the Locus," Brad said.

Daphne explained the setup to Thorpe. A few minutes later, someone handed Brad a hyper-disk.

"Put a SEAL below the hatch out of sight from inside," Thorpe said. "Have him ready to skid the hyper-disk across their deck. I'll count down from five. When I say *zero*, he skids it, and a moment later, I'll activate it."

They got everything ready with Raptor hovering just below the lip of the hatch, out of sight. Thorpe commenced his countdown.

"Five…four…three…two…one…zero!"

Raptor skidded the hyper-disk across the deck, where it immediately began billowing clouds moist atmosphere throughout the interior and out the hatch. Within seconds, a spacesuited figure tumbled through the hatch, his random laser pistol bolts visible in the gas. Then two more followed, the first tumbling, the second oriented and firing with good aim. He caught another SEAL in the side. Everybody heard him grunt over the circuit, and then his E-disk took him to safety.

Raptor fired a bullet through the shooter's helmet. The shooter ceased his activity. The first Marauder saw what happened to the shooter and tossed his weapon. The second had no weapon.

They submitted meekly when the SEALS rounded them up, making sure they had no more weapons and that they couldn't get loose.

Even though the shooter was dead, frozen red blood had sealed the hole in his helmet. Doc inserted a syringe through the frozen blood and withdrew an air sample. He passed it through their portal to Sally, who had it analyzed in five minutes.

"Pretty much the same as ours," Sally said. "You can take them into Daphne's ship."

WASHINGTON D.C.—THE OVAL OFFICE

Kimberly placed an urgent call to President Butler, and several minutes later, she stepped into the Oval Office through one of the portals. She quickly briefed the president on the incoming meteor swarm.

"Most of the fragments will burn up in the atmosphere," she told him, "but several of the larger chunks will reach the surface, primarily in waters off the China coast and in central China."

"There is nothing we can do about it," the president told her. "Since the Federation took out their nuclear capability, they have completely withdrawn from the rest of the world." He sighed. "It is almost as if they didn't exist."

"Their signal to the Marauders didn't do them any good," Kimberly said, "but this will get their attention. Perhaps the rest of the world can stand by to bring them aid once the bombardment is over."

EARTH—THE EAST CHINA SEA

As the sun rose over the East China Sea and the lights of Shanghai began to dim, the sky suddenly filled with streaks of fire and the air filled with loud explosions. The ocean roiled as millions of rock shards hit the surface. Three bus-size chunks hit a kilometer offshore, generating a tsunami that washed through Shanghai, killing thousands and obliterating Hangzhou Bay. For a half-hour, rocks continued to fall from the sky, churning the water and devastating the land where they hit up to a thousand kilometers inland. A large rock landed in the middle of Hangzhou City, killing thousands more.

Finally, it was over. The United States landed a large hospital ship at the Shanghai wharf. The Federated Russian Republics landed dozens of cargo planes loaded with food and medicines. Other nations reached out with food, clothing, medicine, and shelter. In the end, the hand of friendship in need accomplished what diplomacy could not.

DENVER—PHOENIX LABS

The Phoenix conference room was even more crowded than before the attack. Everybody connected with the operation was present, human, upload, and Oort (as individuals—they were relearning the joys of individualism).

"Brad," Thorpe said, "tell us what you have learned about the Marauder craft and its occupants."

"As most of you know by now," Brad said, "we captured an alien craft and two live, uninjured Marauders. I will skip over most of the science and engineering to give you a feeling for where we are now.

"The Marauders are much like us. They are bipedal with six digits on each hand and foot and are shorter and stockier. Their faces are much like ours with flattened noses and very thin lips. They have articulating ears, and their hair looks like ours. They obviously evolved from mammalian ancestors similar to us. We do not yet understand their language, but the two survivors are grateful to be alive and are cooperating with us. The exobiologists have their dead companion. Their mathematics works off of root twelve, as you can imagine. Our captives are clearly eager to communicate with us, but we have not a hint about their motives for their attack, except as we surmised earlier, the Dark Forest Theory. When we know more, we'll tell you about it.

"Their craft are powered by a mini-black-hole located in a shielded core at the center of the vessel. The black hole powers counter-rotating particle accelerators that generate a special field. This field latches onto the fabric of space-time itself, extracting a tiny amount of its energy that accelerates not only the craft but everything inside and attached to the craft. The acceleration can be applied in any amount up to a value that is very close to lightspeed itself. Neither the vessel nor its occupants experience any acceleration forces. Consequently, the craft can start and stop instantly, can turn on a pinpoint, and can move in ways that seem to defy physics. A byproduct of the field is artificial gravity that can be set to virtually any value." Brad started to show some excitement.

"What we have here," he continued, "is a spacecraft that we can modify with our non-baryonic doped wings and MERT Drive controller to give us a starship that combines the best of both worlds. During the coming months, we will build and test such a craft. Then we will build hundreds." Brad smiled at Sally beside him.

"Once we add some further refinements to the MERT Drive," Brad continued, "we will be able to cross a hundred lightyears in about five hours, and the next refinement will reduce it to about three minutes. This means we will be able to travel to Andromeda in about fifty-five days."

Brad reached the end of his presentation. Everyone in the room sat in stunned silence. Impulsively, Daphne kissed Kimberly, and then they both kissed Dale.

Dr. Brad Kominsky picked up Dr. Sally Nguyen and swung her around. "We're going to the stars, *Em oi!*" Then he cradled her in his arms and kissed her warmly. The room broke into applause.

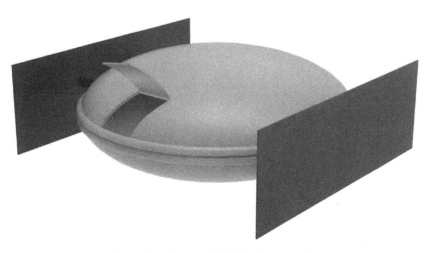

Figure 3—Hybrid MERT Drive Starship

Epilog

The lone Marauder spacecraft hurtled through the interstellar void toward its homeworld 87 lightyears distant. The spacecraft was traveling at 99.9, followed by five 9s percent of lightspeed—a flattened oval disk twenty-five meters across and invisibly thin seen from its edge. It would arrive in its home system in four days and eleven hours subjective time, although 87 years would have passed back on Earth.

The spacecraft was carrying a critical message. The incipient civilization from the star system they had set out to raid 175 years earlier by local time had completely destroyed their 5,000-starship fleet.

The Dark Forest had turned on the Marauders.

Please Post
A Review For *Icicle*
On
Amazon.com and Goodreads.com

I really appreciate you posting a review on Amazon and Goodreads. Posting to Amazon.com is intuitive. To post a review on Goodreads. com, click on this link or go to their website, and become a member if you are not already one. Search for *Icicle*, and click on the "Want to read" button under the image of *Icicle*. Indicate that you have read *Icicle*, and then you will be able to post a review. Thank you very much for going through this effort!

Excerpt from the First Chapter of
Slingshot
by
Robert G. Williscroft

EQUATORIAL PACIFIC—SOUTHEAST OF BAKER ISLAND

Margo stopped kicking her feet as the ominous gray shapes flashed into her peripheral view. Long, tawny hair floated past her head as her feet dropped below her slim, brightly clad body. She took a deep breath and floated slightly upward. A hint of fear crept into her mind as she turned toward three gray, sleek predators cruising just inside the limit of her vision, about twenty-five meters away.

A gentle touch on her shoulder startled her. She turned to see Alex Regent tapping the depth reading on his dive-console with his index finger. Margo reached down and grasped her console, turning it so she could read her depth: twenty-five meters. She had drifted upward five meters since seeing the sharks.

Margo exhaled angrily and let some air out of her breathing bag. She knew better than to lose track of her depth. Out there, her life depended on a constant awareness of exactly how deep she was. Together she and Alex sank back to thirty meters. Off to their right, the three gray shapes drifted with them. Would she ever get used to it, she thought, as she released a bit of air into her bag to stop her descent.

"Alex," she said.

There was no response.

"Alex!" She tapped the back of her console several times.

"Alex!" Nothing but silence.

Alex placed himself in front of Margo and looked into her facemask. With his right hand, he formed a circle with thumb and forefinger. His three other fingers extended straight up.

Margo returned the sign indicating she was all right while nodding vigorously. Then she pointed to her ear and lifted her console, tapping the back. Alex fumbled at his ear and then tapped his console, and then shook his head.

Great, Margo thought, *EFCom is busted just when we really need it. Not busted,* she corrected herself, *just a submerged antenna.* She pointed to the three menacing shapes off to her right. Alex turned and scanned around them. Above and just behind them, the blue-painted hull of their boat bobbed in the gentle waves. About twenty meters ahead of them hung a smooth, horizontal fluorescent orange tube about one meter in diameter. To the left, it stretched into the gloom; to the right, it angled downward. The fluorescent tube was attached to a slender cable angling up to the shadow of a buoy just beneath the surface to their right. Alex turned back toward Margo, making an exaggerated shrug.

Margo reached for her dive-console again and pressed a button located prominently on its face. The three sharks turned and commenced a meandering movement toward the two divers. Their front fins extended stiffly downward at about forty-five degrees. Their backs arched slightly, and their blunt snouts moved back and forth as they approached.

Margo felt her hair stand up on the nape of her neck. She turned to Alex and motioned him to her side. Alex withdrew a telescoped baton from its holder at his waist and extended it to its full one-and-a-half-meter length. He checked the safety lever near its handle, and with his thumb, he flicked the lever so it pointed forward. As the sharks drew nearer, he held the stick out in front of him, pointed in their direction. Margo glanced around them again and pushed her console button once more. Alex waved the stick about slowly and then steadied up on the nearest of the three menacing monsters.

Suddenly, with blurring speed, the nearest shark attacked. Alex struck out with his stick, the jolt of its impact rocking him backward. A sharp crack was followed by a hissing sound as carbon dioxide rushed into the shark's body. In the same moment, flashes of silvery-black streaked from several directions. One of the remaining sharks was struck broadside by a dolphin's blunt nose. In a flash, it disappeared.

The animal Alex had injected rolled on its side and began a crazed, uncontrolled spiral toward the surface thirty meters above them. On its way up, it was hit several times by charging dolphins. It expired of massive embolisms before reaching fifteen meters. In the melee, the third shark vanished.

Margo reached out for Alex, grabbed a handful of breathing bag, and pulled him close to her. She placed the flat of her full-facemask against his and looked deeply into his eyes, as close to a kiss as she could come under the circumstances. Even down here, they were deep blue. Several bubbles escaped from the positive pressure maintained inside their masks and shimmered their way toward the surface, expanding rapidly as they rose.

Like an old-time scuba diver, Margo thought, watching the rising silvery spheres. Instinctively she checked the volume in her breathing bag and glanced at the gauge on her tiny, ultra-high-pressure air flask. She found she was holding her breath, and as she felt the need to breathe, a gentle pressure developed against her back. She pulled back and turned to confront a two-and-a-half-meter-long dolphin nudging her from behind.

It was one of four that had responded to her sonic signal—George, her favorite. The other three dolphins crowded in around the neoprene and nylon suited divers, jostling each other for attention. Margo rubbed the head dome of each and indicated to Alex that he should do the same. Then the two of them turned their attention back to the tube suspended in front of them.

Alex swam to the angled portion and began to search along the tube's length, descending slowly. Margo dropped her arm from George's neck and kicked in Alex's direction, keeping him in sight, but staying between him and the surface. The four cetaceans arrowed toward the surface and grabbed a gulp of air, then settled back down, playfully cycling between Alex and Margo, gently jostling them. About thirty minutes later, Alex motioned Margo to join him. She released a bubble of air from her bag and dropped down beside him. Her console showed a depth of fifty meters. Alex pointed to a five-centimeter rip in the bottom curve of the tube's fluorescent covering.

Margo reached into a deep pocket located on the left leg of her suit and withdrew a role of patching tape. Alex stretched the edges of the tear, and Margo applied a strip of self-sealing tape along the opening. Then she located a small pneumatic valve on the top of the tube and attached a hose from her spare air tank. On a signal from Alex, she released air into the tube, forcing water out through a one-way valve on the underside. She stopped when bubbles escaped from the lower valve.

As the tube rose slowly, Margo held on, keeping track of their progress on her console. They stopped rising when the gauge read thirty meters. Margo felt the tube—it was taut and solid. She tapped the back of her console, listening for the faint rush of sound in her ears. Nothing. She pointed to the back of her console and then her ear, and shook her head. Alex offered another of his exaggerated underwater shrugs and grinned, although the only part of the grin she could see was his crinkled eyes. She grinned back and pointed toward the suspension buoy and their boat, making an angled upward sign with her free hand. Alex nodded, checked his console, and they both headed back, slowly rising as they swam.

Margo saw Alex check his console from time to time, making certain they kept below the ever-changing ceiling limit it calculated for him. Since she had remained shallower than Alex for most of the dive, she knew she would be safe following his lead. She looked around at the four dolphins. Her earlier fright was gone, and she simply enjoyed George's protective nearness and the playful bumps and nudges from the others.

On the surface finally, Alex dropped his facemask down around his neck, fully inflated his bag, and grinned at Margo. "Close call down there!"

Margo shoved her facemask down and patted the glistening snout that appeared in front of her. "Thanks, George. I love you too."

The dolphin mewed a pleased response, lifted his body out of the water and backed away, chattering as he went. The other three animals circled at and below the surface, keeping watch over their human charges.

"What happened to the EFCom?" Margo asked. "I expected it to come back online as soon as the antenna surfaced."

"Broken antenna wire, I imagine," Alex answered.

"Storm damage, I'm sure," said Margo, as they turned and headed toward the waiting vessel.

"Probably," agreed Alex. "But that wasn't a burst seam," he added.

"Yeah, maybe the sinking tube snapped the wire."

Actually, tube flotation chambers flooded on a regular basis. They had patched a full ten percent of them since the project started. But it was a bit unusual to find a rip on the tube bottom, and the Electrostatic Field Communication ("EFCom") transceivers on the buoys almost always survived.

❋

The EFCom buoy nearest the tear had ceased transmitting, and the buoys on either side of the tear had signaled their departure from datum a day earlier. Alex had opted to employ an electrostatic field communication system, because of its clear underwater signal transmission capability that was independent of acoustic conditions, since it didn't rely on sound transmission through the water. Every buoy, each skimmer and floater, and every diver was outfitted with one of the small EFCom transceivers. Alex had inspected the non-transmitting buoy personally during an overflight from Jarvis Island. There was nothing visible on the two kilometers of surface between the buoys; they were closer together, but not so that it was visible to the eye. Nevertheless, the remaining 1,828-odd buoy-suspended kilometers of tube were stressing from the downward pull of the waterlogged section. The buoy near the tear was several meters underwater.

Suspended inside the flotation tube were two virtually impervious, lightweight, hose-like tubes, each about six centimeters in diameter, called vacuum sheaths. Two shallow channels jutted out from the bottom of each vacuum sheath, filled with electronically-controlled suspending magnets. Magnetically suspended inside each vacuum sheath was a five-centimeter tube of segmented soft iron officially called the rotor, but more popularly known as the ribbon, so named from the earliest conceptions back in the 1980s of the Launch Loop inventor, Keith Lofstrom. Alex was eager to check continuity readings to make certain the vacuum sheaths had not breached. They were not yet evacuated, but seawater entry at this stage would seriously delay the entire project. If the EFCom had not crapped out, the tests would already be underway.

Alex glanced ahead at Margo Jackson, cavorting with her four dolphins as they made their leisurely way back to the waiting boat. His field engineer in charge of underwater construction was a remarkable female. Nearly as tall as his own 183 centimeters, her model's slender figure, encased in electric-blue nylon-covered neoprene, seemed to lack feminine curves. He knew differently, of course, having joined her bikini-clad person from time to time for morning swims since the project began over two years ago.

The project—Alex had lived with it for three years before actual construction began. Longer, actually, if you considered dreams—since before the incredible, worldwide bi-millennial celebration when he still was a young boy.

There was the nearly simultaneous publication in America and England of practically identical ideas in 1985. Paul Birch published an article in *The Journal of the British Interplanetary Society*, while in America, Keith Lofstrom published his article in a supplement to *The Journal of the Astronautical Sciences*, he recalled. Nobody could agree on the names: Skyrail, Launch Loop, Beanstalk. There were others, but the idea is what counted, the sky-shaking idea that you don't need rockets to get into space.

Newspapers were full of explanations three-and-a-half years ago when the aging president of a computer software giant made the announcement. He would funnel a significant portion of company profits into the consortium. Space travel would become as commonplace and inexpensive as the personal computers his pioneering work had made possible. He went on to outline the easy-to-understand concept.

Imagine a water hose streaming water in a parabolic arch. Deflect the water and funnel it back to the start through a pump, creating a closed system. Make the stream strong enough and the hose light enough, and the entire structure will support itself—the water holding up the hose structure. Now, replace the water with a thin, closed-loop pipe of segmented soft iron. Make it 5,000 kilometers around and accelerate it to orbital velocity with gigantic linear induction motors from two points on the equator 2,000 kilometers apart. The center section of the structure, including both the outgoing and return legs of the loop, will rise to about eighty kilometers above the Earth. Supply access to the upstream end in space with a Kevlar-hung elevator, and you can launch capsules by magnetically coupling them to the rapidly moving pipe of iron.

Slingshot, they called it. The greatest engineering undertaking in the history of the world, they said.

As the on-scene project manager, Alex was responsible for getting the job done, on schedule, on budget. He was building a gossamer structure over 2,500 kilometers long, a frail spider web, completely invisible when viewed from more than a few kilometers. Alex grinned wryly. All *Slingshot* really consisted of was a fancy evacuated tube, a flexible iron pipe, four linear drivers and their power sources, some guy wires, and a couple of elevators. Put that way, it seemed simple enough. But, of course, it wasn't simple at all, and for all his skill and engineering competence, and despite surface appearances, deep down, Alex was not entirely sure that he could make it happen.

Margo and Alex climbed up the ladder and onto *Skimmer One's* bobbing fantail. This was one of two skimmers on the project—twelve-meter-long surface-effect boats that looked more like a floating aircraft than a traditional motorboat. They were capable of 200 knots, skimming about one-and-a-half meters over the wave tops. They had a small open fantail, just large enough for a couple of divers to doff their gear. Being on the fantail when the skimmer was on its cushion was more than dangerous, and was strictly prohibited throughout the project.

Alex signaled to the waiting coxswain, and they got underway for Baker, plowing through the water while Alex and Margo remained exposed. He and Margo stood near the stern railing and removed their dripping skins. Alex looked back at the buoys, now presumably in their proper places.

"How many more times?" Alex looked quizzically at Margo.

"Who knows?" She glanced back at the bobbing buoys. "We have repair people available at both ends. We shouldn't be doing this ourselves, you know." She turned and looked directly at Alex. "What do you think—weather or sabotage?"

Alex shrugged and tossed the spent carbon dioxide cartridge from his shark stick in the general direction of the cavorting dolphins. "I wanted to see for myself, and I still don't know. Does it matter? We can't patrol the entire eighteen-hundred-twenty-eight-kilometer length anyway."

"What are we dealing with?" Margo asked. "You don't get out here in a rowboat."

"We're two thousand wet klicks from any kind of civilization," Alex said. "At minimum, that's a large motor-yacht or even an ocean sailer—you know, one of those we maybe can afford when this job is done." He sighed. "We're dealing with lots of money and someone with a major bitch."

He looked into her green eyes.

"Just keep my tubes at depth." His blue eyes flashed, and he turned toward the cockpit to radio his orders to test pipe continuity.

※

Margo dropped her eyes at his challenge. For the thousandth time, she asked herself if she had bitten off more than she could chew with this assignment. Was it her fault that the flotation chambers kept ripping? Was she missing something important? Was she copping out to imply there might have been sabotage? And yet, Alex seemed to agree that it might be sabotage. When she joined the project two years ago, the newspapers had acclaimed her as the ideal role model for the new twenty-first-century woman. At times that burden lay heavily on her shoulders, as it did now, she reflected.

It was a vast responsibility, and there was no way one person actually could control all of it at once. How Alex handled the weight of the entire project awed her, but she was careful never to let him know.

Margo watched Alex step into the cockpit. He was tall and slender, richly tanned from his constant outdoor work. She felt a softness well up inside her, a gentle warmth spreading out from the pit of her stomach. She bit her lower lip and turned angrily to lean on the after-railing.

None of that, she chided herself. This assignment was too important, and the stakes too high to let any kind of emotion intrude. As she entered the cabin and sealed the port, the skipper switched modes, and pressurized air quickly filled the hard-sided skirt. In moments the skimmer lifted out of the water, except for the port and starboard skirts that protruded about a meter into the waves. Within seconds, high-pressure water nozzles jetted water from the end of each skirt, and within thirty seconds, *Skimmer One* was approaching 200 knots.

As *Skimmer One* headed into the afternoon sun, trailing an arrow-straight wake of white foam, Margo stood looking aft through the sealed port, remembering her instinctive sharing, and their underwater kiss following the fright of nearly becoming shark food. She shook off the sensation and busied herself with putting away their diving equipment. But a hint of a smile remained on her lips as they shot over the surface, finally settling back onto the water as they entered the small protected artificial harbor on the west side of Baker Island, just south of a shallow reef that went dry at low tide.

You have just been reading from Chapter One of Slingshot, the 1st book in The Starchild Trilogy, Robert Williscroft's exciting Science Fiction trilogy. To read the rest of this book, Slingshot.

Words of Praise for
Slingshot

Slingshot does for the launch loop what Arthur C. Clarke's *The Fountains of Paradise* or Sheffield's *Web Between the Worlds* did for the space elevator. Again, Williscroft delivers a great mix of hard science fiction and action.

— *A*lastair Mayer
Author of the *T-Space Series*

Robert Williscroft deftly crafts an energetic story around a phenomenal technological development just over the horizon: the space launch loop. The technical detail woven into this story is an education unto itself. But don't assume that Williscroft chooses raw infodump over story—*Slingshot* is an adventure that pulls you in, gives you characters that are engaging, and invites you to follow them through their challenges. What Williscroft has done in *Slingshot* is no easy task—he has balanced the *hard* aspect of science fiction with the character portrayals that those who despise that very *hard* science fiction beg for. The last decade has seen impressive leaps in the theoretical work toward the launch loop— this book couldn't come too soon! And you won't be able to keep from reading all the way to the end. Williscroft's art continues to be praise-worthy!

— Jason D. Batt, 100 *Year Starship*
Author of *The Tales of Dreamside series*

I've been a fan of Robert Williscroft's books for a while now. They're action-packed and filled with all kinds of interesting, real-world information. *Slingshot* fits right in.

Slingshot is about the development of an earth-bound spaceport in which spaceships are taken 80 kilometers above the Earth by elevator and hurled onto their trajectory by a very fast-moving ribbon of soft iron. It is much easier, cheaper, and cleaner to launch spaceships from here due to the rarified atmosphere. This concept may be a reality someday. The book begins with a foreword by Keith Lofstrom, the originator of this concept called the "launch loop."

Learning about the launch loop is the most interesting aspect of this novel. Williscroft's descriptions of the construction techniques, its operations, and the benefits for space travel are absolutely fascinating. The book takes place about thirty years in the future, and I could easily see such a project becoming a reality in that time.

The plot of the novel is driven by the development and construction of the project, which is being threatened by ill-informed environmentalists bent on destroying the project. The launch loop is far greener than the current method of launching vehicles into space, but a sinister power has misled the environmentalists into believing that sabotaging the launch loop is saving the planet. Meanwhile, the sinister power is protecting its own economic interests.

As usual, Williscroft has created a cast of interesting and driven characters. The book is a fascinating read, and you are guaranteed not only to learn a lot, but to dream about the future of space travel.

Marc Weitz, Past President
The Los Angeles Adventurers' Club

About the Author

Dr. Robert G. Williscroft served twenty-three years in the U.S. Navy and the National Oceanic and Atmospheric Administration (NOAA). He commenced his service as an enlisted nuclear Submarine Sonar Technician in 1961, was selected for the Navy Enlisted Scientific Education Program in 1966, and graduated from University of Washington in Marine Physics and Meteorology in 1969. He returned to nuclear submarines as the Navy's first Poseidon Weapons Officer. Subsequently, he served as Navigator and Diving Officer on both catamaran mother vessels for the Deep Submergence Rescue Vehicle. Then he joined the Submarine Development Group One out of San Diego as the Officer-in-Charge of the Test Operations Group, conducting "deep-ocean surveillance and data acquisition"—which forms the basis for his Cold War novel *Operation Ivy Bells*.

In NOAA, Dr. Williscroft directed diving operations throughout the Pacific and Atlantic. As a certified diving instructor for both the National Association of Underwater Instructors (NAUI) and the Multinational Diving Educators Association (MDEA), he taught over 3,000 individuals both basic and advanced SCUBA diving. He authored four diving books, developed the first NAUI drysuit course, developed advanced curricula for mixed gas and other specialized diving modes, and developed and taught a NAUI course on the Math and Physics of Advanced Diving. His doctoral dissertation for California Coast University, *A System for Protecting SCUBA Divers from the*

Hazards of Contaminated Water, was published by the U.S. Department of Commerce and distributed to Port Captains worldwide. He also served three shipboard years in the high Arctic conducting scientific baseline studies, and thirteen months at the geographic South Pole in charge of National Science Foundation atmospheric projects.

Dr. Williscroft has written extensively on terrorism and related subjects. He is the author of a popular book on current events published by Pelican Publishing: *The Chicken Little Agenda—Debunking Experts' Lies,* now in its second edition as an eBook, and a new children's book series, *Starman Jones,* in collaboration with Dr. Frank Drake, world-famous director of the Carl Sagan Center for the Study of Life in the Universe and the SETI Institute.

Dr. Williscroft's 1st novel in *The Starchild Trilogy, Slingshot,* tells the story of the construction of the world's first Space Launch Loop. *Slingshot* was launched at the Seattle International Space Elevator Conference in August 2015. His 2nd novel in *The Starchild Trilogy, The Starchild Compact,* is based on the discovery that Saturn's moon Iapetus is actually a derelict starship, and how Earth explorers eventually meet with the "Founders," who originally arrived on the starship and populated the Earth long ago. The 3rd book in *The Starchild Trilogy, The Iapetus Federation,* the Federation expands Solar Systemwide, while a new Caliphate sweeps Earth. The Starchild Institute creates wormhole portals to enable the Exodus. Earth becomes medieval, while human focus shifts to the Iapetus Federation. Humans settle every potentially habitable spot in the Solar System and begin expanding into the rest of the Galaxy.

The Daedalus Files takes place in the world of *Slingshot.* In four short stories, *Daedalus, Daedalus LEO, Daedalus Squad,* and *Daedalus Combat,* Dr. Williscroft follows the U.S. Navy SEALS Winged Insertion Command (SWIC) and its development of the *Gryphon* hard wingsuit for combat drops from Low Earth Orbit.

Dr. Williscroft is an active member of the Colorado Author's League, Science Fiction Writers of America, Libertarian Futurist Society, Los Angeles Adventurers' Club, Mensa, Military Officer's Association, American Legion, and NRA. He lives in Centennial, Colorado, with his wife, Jill, and their twin college boys (when they are home from school).

Other Works
By Robert Williscroft

Please visit Amazon.com to discover other eBooks by Robert Williscroft and your favorite online or Brick & Mortar bookseller for their paper versions:

Current events:

The Chicken Little Agenda—Debunking "Experts'" Lies

Children's books:

The Starman Jones Series:
 Starman Jones: A Relativity Birthday Present
 Starman Jones Goes to the Dogs (scheduled for release in 2020)

Short Stories:

The SWIC Daedalus Files:
 Daedalus
 Daedalus LEO
 Daedalus Squad
 Daedalus Combat

Novels:

Mac McDowell Missions:
 Operation Ivy Bells
 Operation Ice Breaker (Scheduled for release 2020)

The Starchild Trilogy:
  Slingshot
  The Starchild Compact
  The Iapetus Federation
The Oort Chronicles:
  Icicle: A Tensor Matrix
  The Oort: Interstellar Consequences (scheduled for release in 2020)
  Oort Andromeda: Galactic Diaspora (scheduled for release in 2021)

Connect with Robert Williscroft

I really appreciate you reading my book! Here are my social media coordinates:

Friend me on Facebook: *https://www.facebook.com/robert.williscroft*

Follow me on Twitter: *@RGWilliscroft*

Like my Amazon author page: *https://www.amazon.com/Robert-G.-Williscroft/e/B001JP52AS*

Subscribe to my blog: *https://ThrawnRickle.com*

Connect on LinkedIn: *https://www.linkedin.com/in/argee/*

Visit my website: *https://robertwilliscroft.com*

Visit my Fresh Ink Group page: *https://freshinkgroup.com/author/robertwilliscroft/*

Glossary for Icicle

Athena: The Oort designed control system for the ranging devices and the weapon systems on each Oort Station—named after the Greek goddess of war.

Banach manifold: A topological space in which each point has a neighborhood homeomorphic to a point or points in a Banach space. Analogous to the relationship between a globe and a Mercator projection of that globe. When a globe and a Mercator projection of that globe touch at the same geographic point, those points are virtually identical or homeomorphic. (If a person stands on a life-sized Mercator projection of Earth, from his perspective, his surroundings look the same as if he were standing on the same spot on Earth.)

Banach space: A space wherein all Cauchy vector sequences converge to a well-defined limit that is within the space.

Baryonic matter: Normal matter consisting of baryons such as neutrons and protons found in all atomic nuclei.

Casimir field: In quantum field theory, the Casimir field is the physical force arising from a quantized field. It is named after the Dutch physicist Hendrik Casimir who predicted them in 1948.

Cauchy vector sequence: A vector sequence whose elements become arbitrarily close to each other as the sequence progresses.

Chiron: A training program for the Oort Station weapon systems that functioned much like a high-end space-invaders video game—named after the Greek god who trained the other gods.

Cyclohexane ring: The chemical structure of a colorless, flammable liquid with a distinctive detergent-like odor, reminiscent of cleaning products with a hexagon ring-shaped molecular formula $C6H12$.

Dark Forest Theory: An explanation of the Fermi Paradox—why we have not heard from any interstellar civilization—proposed by Chinese science fiction writer Cixin Liu. The universe is a dark forest. Every civilization is an armed hunter stalking through the trees like a ghost being careful, because everywhere in the forest are stealthy hunters like him. If he finds another life, there's only one thing he can do: open fire and eliminate it. And when one civilization becomes a killer species, it will scour the galaxy eliminating all rivals.

Databank: An electronic or digital repository for data.

Earth-Moon L2 point: The Lagrange point about 60,000 km beyond the Moon.

Earth-Sun L3 point: The Lagrange point about 150 million km from the Sun in Earth's orbit on the other side of the Sun.

Earth-Sun L4 point: The Lagrange point about 150 million km from the Earth, leading Earth in Earth's orbit.

E-disk: (Escape-Hyper-Disk) A specially designed hyper-disk that senses the holder's environment and will open a portal and whisk the holder to safety when conditions warrant.

Electrochromic thrusters: Elements that change from black to reflective to produce small thrust by solar radiation pressure.

EMD stun weapon: An Electro Muscular Disruption stun weapon, much like a Taser.

Emeici: A traditional Chinese martial arts weapon. They are a pair of metal rods with sharp ends used for stabbing; they are typically mounted on a detachable ring worn on the middle finger, allowing them to spin and be elaborately manipulated.

Entangled-Particle Display (EPD): The Oort had found a way to separate entangled particles physically, and to project one element of trillions of these pairs in an expanding sphere around Sol and the Oort Cloud. The incoming data were presented in holographic spheres in each of the Oort Stations, called Entangled-Particle Displays.

Euclidian space: The fundamental space of classical geometry. The space around us with which we deal every day.

Fermi Paradox: A question posed by Dr. Enrico Fermi when he asked, "Where is everybody? Where are all the interstellar civilizations we would expect to inhabit the universe?"

FLOPS: FLoating-Point Operations Per Second.

FTL: Faster Than Light.

GEO: Geosynchronous Earth Orbit (pronounced *geo* or *G-E-O*.

GlobalNet: A global network that replaced the Internet. It is served by ServerSky connected by modulated laser pipes and accessed through Links that are carried by virtually everyone on Earth.

Holotank: Analogous to current television receivers, but instead produces a three-dimensional, color, holographic image.

Holovision: Analogous to a current television image, but instead is a three-dimensional, color, holographic image.

Hypercube: A Tesseract.

Hyper-brick: A portable portal activation device similar to Phoenix's hyper-disc developed by Russia. It was a two-kilogram elongated cube.

Hyper-disk: A 5-cm disk with a shiny side and a deep black side connected to a portal Locus through nullspace. When the shiny side is rubbed, the portal is activated.

Ishtar: The *Starship Ishtar—Queen of the Heavens*, named after the Babylonian Goddess Ishtar.

KA-BAR: A 7-inch blade military fighting knife favored by special operations forces worldwide.

Klein bottle: In 1882, Felix Klein imagined sewing two Möbius Strips together to create a single-sided bottle with no boundary.

Its inside is its outside. It contains itself. Take a rectangle and join one pair of opposite sides— you'll now have a cylinder. Now join the other pair of sides with a half-twist. That last step isn't possible in our universe. A true Klein bottle requires 4-dimensions because the surface has to pass through itself without a hole. It's closed and non-orientable, so a symbol on its surface can be slid around on it and reappear backward at the same place. A true Klein Bottle lives in 4-dimensions. But every tiny patch of the Klein bottle is 2-dimensional. In this sense, a Klein bottle is a 2-dimensional manifold that can only exist in 4-dimensions.

Krais: An administrative territory of Russia.

Kuiper Belt: A circumstellar disc in the outer Solar System, extending from the orbit of Neptune to approximately 50 AU from the Sun. Contains many comets, asteroids, and other small bodies made largely of ice.

Lagrangian points: In celestial mechanics, the five points near two large bodies where the smaller orbits the larger, where the balance of gravitational forces allows a much smaller object to maintain its position relative to the large bodies. L1 is between the two large bodies close to the smaller one. L2 is on the far side of the smaller of the two large bodies. L3 is on the far side of the larger of the two bodies. L4 leads the smaller body in its orbit around the larger body. L5 trails the smaller body in its orbit around the larger body. These are named after the 18th-century Italian astronomer and mathematician Joseph-Louis Lagrange, who first determined their existence.

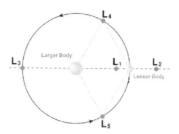

LANR: Lattice Assisted Nuclear Reaction. Formerly called cold-fusion.

Launch loop: A method for launching human and freight payloads into space without using rockets. Constructing the World's first Space Launch Loop is the theme of *Slingshot*, the first novel in *The Starchild Trilogy*.

LEO: Low Earth Orbit (pronounced *L-E-O*).

Link: An electronic device for hooking up to the GlobalNet. It has various configurations from a wristband, to a piece of apparel, to a surgically implanted device. It has both aural and holographic displays.

Manifold: A topological space that locally resembles Euclidean space near each point, such that each point of an n-dimensional manifold has a neighborhood that is homeomorphic to the Euclidean space of dimension n.

MarsNet: The Mars equivalent of the GlobalNet on Earth.

Mars-Sun L1 point: The Lagrange point about one million km from Mars, between Mars and the Sun.

Matrix: (1) Within the framework of this novel, a box shaped to fit into an electronics rack that contains complex electronics that can form its own electrical pathways over time. It contains the self-aware essence of an uploaded person (or cat). Plural herein is *matrixes*. (2) More generally, a mathematical expression of n dimensions (where n > 1) whose elements are tensors with n-1 dimensions. For example, a two-dimensional matrix with columns and rows has one-dimensional tensor elements that are the point intersections of each column and row. Plural herein is *matrices*.

Mercury-Sun L1 point: The Lagrange point about 218,000 km from Mercury's surface toward the Sun.

MERT Drive: An FTL drive consisting of passing one MERT Portal through another, and then the second through the first, and so on, to leapfrog quickly through normal space.

MERT Portal: MERT=Morris-Einstein-Rosen-Thorne. A Casimir Field that contains a stable wormhole with the ability to position one end of the wormhole manually.

Möbius Strip: A one-sided nonorientable surface obtained by cutting a closed band into a single strip, giving one of the two ends a half twist, and then reattaching the two ends. It has only one side and only one surface.

Modulated laser-pipe: A broadband laser connection between Earth and ServerSky or two elements of ServerSky.

Mother: The controlling computer for MERT Drive ships.

Narada: The unmanned VASIMR powered spaceship that transited to Mercury. Named after the Vedic Messenger of the Sun God.

Non-baryonic matter: Non-baryonic matter is matter that, unlike the kinds of matter with which we are familiar, is not made of baryons such as neutrons and protons found in all atomic nuclei.

n-Space: n-dimensional Euclidean space.

Nullspace: Within the framework of this novel, stands for non-space. The interior of a wormhole or a series of connected wormholes.

Oblast: An administrative territory of Russia.

Okrug: An administrative territory of Russia.

Oort Cloud: An extended shell of icy objects that exist in the outermost reaches of the Solar System at distances ranging from 10,000 to 100,000 AU. Named after astronomer Jan Oort, who first theorized its existence.

Portal Locus: The origin end of a MERT portal.

Power terminator: Special terminators developed by Brad and Sally that collect the power generated by a thinsat swarm and pass it through a MERT portal.

RLE: Research Lab for Electronics located at Massachusetts Institute of Technology.

ServerSky: A space-based global internet system invented by Keith Lofstrom that incorporates trillions of small thinsats that work together to function as a global, very high-power, very fast server network. It can be accessed directly by individual users or via modulated laser pipes into the GlobalNet.

TBH boots: Jet boots developed in 1967 by three NASA scientists, David Thomas, John Bird, and Richard Hellbaum. NASA tested the jet boots Earthside back then, but they were not introduced into current use until a few years before Thorpe was revived. They're simpler and less cumbersome than any of the old Manned Maneuvering Units. They fit like riding boots, but with completely flexible ankles. The boot uppers consist of two stiff, shaped polymer bags that contain pressurized hypergolic fuel components—UDMH (Unsymmetrical dimethylhydrazine) and nitrogen tetroxide. The fuel valves are controlled by a microswitch under each big toe. Each boot produces ten newtons of force against the ball of the foot. The wearer bends the knees for the appropriate thrust vector, including torque.

Tensor: A mathematical object analogous to, but more general than, a vector, represented by an array of components that are functions of the coordinates of a space.

Tensor matrix: A multidimensional mathematical matrix whose elements consist of tensors having one less dimension than the matrix. Within the framework of this novel, Thorpe and Braxton see themselves as very complex high-level tensor matrices.

Tesseract: The four-dimensional analogue of the cube. The tesseract is to the cube as the cube is to the square. Just as the surface of the cube consists of six square faces, the hypersurface of the tesseract consists of eight cubical cells.

Thinsat: 5-gram-substrates consisting of two very thin layers of aluminum foil embossed on the Earth-facing side with die bonding cavities and slot antennas that enable the thinsats to communicate with each other and Earth's surface. The outward-facing side is coated in the center area with molybdenum, indium phosphide, and AZO (aluminum-doped zinc-oxide) to form solar cells. The corners consist of a stack of the oxides of tungsten and aluminum, AZO, and nickel hydroxide. These are electrochromic thrusters that enable each thinsat in the swarm to maintain its orientation with respect to the swarm and the planet below.

Topology: Topology is concerned with the properties of geometric objects that are preserved under continuous deformations, such as stretching, twisting, crumpling, and bending, but not tearing, gluing, or perforating.

Turn To: Commence the task at hand.

VASIMR engine: The Variable Specific Impulse Magnetoplasma Rocket is an electrothermal thruster that uses radio waves to ionize and heat an inert propellant, then a magnetic field to accelerate the resulting plasma, generating thrust.

Vitrifying: Adding chemicals called cryoprotectants to water prevents water molecules from gathering together to form ice. Instead of freezing, molecules just move slower and slower as they are cooled. Finally, at temperatures below -100° C, molecules become locked in place, and a solid is formed. Water that becomes solid without freezing is said to be vitrified.

Fresh Ink Group

Independent Multi-media Publisher

Fresh Ink Group / Push Pull Press

&

Hardcovers
Softcovers
All Ebook Platforms
Audiobooks
Worldwide Distribution

&

Indie Author Services
Book Development, Editing, Proofing
Graphic/Cover Design
Video/Trailer Production
Website Creation
Social Media Management
Writing Contests
Writers' Blogs
Podcasts

&

Authors
Editors
Artists
Experts
Professionals

&

FreshInkGroup.com
info@FreshInkGroup.com
Twitter: @FreshInkGroup
Facebook.com/FreshInkGroup
LinkedIn: Fresh Ink Group

CPSIA information can be obtained
at www.ICGtesting.com
Printed in the USA
BVHW042353120820
586219BV00004B/92

9 781947 867994